DANGER SIGNALS

"Dammit, you're in danger," Caleb O'Brien told Sophia. "If a Yankee soldier comes into this house, you won't be able to stop him from doing what he wants."

"Of course I can. I can get Papa's rifle. Major O'Brien, I don't want to hear another thing about what I can and cannot do," Sophia retorted.

She started to pass him to leave the room. But he caught her arm and jerked her around. He slid his arms around her, hauling her hard against him.

"I've wanted to do this," he said, and bent his head, his mouth pressing over hers as he held her firm against him.

She melted, hot, breathless. She was shocked at her own desire. She moaned softly, letting her hips shift against him. She shouldn't kiss him and allow him to kiss her. It wasn't proper, and he soon would be out of her life forever. Then thoughts stopped as she ran her hands along his strong shoulders. She was lost with longing.

Sophia knew the danger that came from the North. But this was a different kind of danger. . . . a different kind of a war . . . a war she fought with herself. . . . unsure which side she wanted to win. . . .

MEMPHIS

MEMPHIS

by

Sara Orwig

AN ONYX BOOK

ONYX
Published by the Penguin Group
Penguin Books USA Inc., 375 Hudson Street,
New York, New York 10014, U.S.A.
Penguin Books Ltd, 27 Wrights Lane,
London W8 5TZ, England
Penguin Books Australia Ltd, Ringwood,
Victoria, Australia
Penguin Books Canada Ltd, 10 Alcorn Avenue,
Toronto, Ontario, Canada M4V 3B2
Penguin Books (N.Z.) Ltd, 182–190 Wairau Road,
Auckland 10, New Zealand

Penguin Books Ltd, Registered Offices:
Harmondsworth, Middlesex, England

First published by Onyx, an imprint of Dutton Signet,
a division of Penguin Books USA Inc.

First Printing, April, 1994
10 9 8 7 6 5 4 3 2 1

With thanks to: John Nelson, Tom Drum, Kim Thomas, Susan Jennings, *The Commercial Appeal,* Mrs. Patricia La Pointe, the Memphis Public Library, Jane Roberts, Germantown Branch Library, Fayette County Chamber of Commerce, and Jennifer Enderlin.

Chapter 1

April 6, 1862
Union Army Encampment, Tennessee

"Aren't you up early, Private?" Private Elwin Crossley asked in a raspy voice.

Alarmed, Sophia Virginia Merrick spun around, dropping the bedding in her hands to the ground. Mist swirled as Crossley moved closer. Her heart thudded against her ribs. She cursed her luck. Had she left a few minutes earlier, she would have been headed back home to safety.

"It's cold," she replied, picking up the blanket, and grateful that she had her cap on her head and her hair tucked beneath it. She should have started home to Memphis last night, she thought. All evening by the campfire Crossley kept watching her as he moved around, trying to talk to her. The way Crossley looked at her, she felt certain he knew she was no eighteen-year-old boy who had joined the Union army. If he learned she was a Confederate spy, she could go to prison.

"You sleep out here alone? You don't like people?" he asked, spitting a stream of tobacco juice near her feet.

"I haven't been away from home before. I feel better off by myself."

"I'd think it would be the other way around. A bunch of us are going to the river to bathe. Come join us."

"Thanks, but I'll pass," she said, hoping her voice was calm. "It's too chilly to bathe, and I don't mind dirt." She edged toward her rifle. The last time she had ridden to the Union camp to get war news for the paper, no one had paid any attention to her, but she hadn't stayed overnight.

"Charlie, you're going to have that bath," he said in a flat voice, his eyes gleaming while he licked his thick lips. His blue eyes raked over her boldly, and she felt a chill of apprehension.

"All right, I'll be there in a minute."

"No, you're coming now. You're not a very friendly soldier, Charlie. Some of us think it's time that changed, so I'm taking you with me."

"I said I'll be there in a minute," she said, glaring at him, hoping he couldn't tell she was terrified. Why hadn't she gone home yesterday? Waiting for reinforcements, the Federals had been camped here for almost a month, and she could have come back again, instead of staying and running such risks. Frightened, she glanced at her father's rifle. It was yards away propped against a tree.

"You're coming with me," Crossley said, moving closer.

"No!" When she turned to run, his footsteps thudded behind her. Feeling desperate, she ran for the rifle. Her hands flailed the air as Crossley grabbed her around the waist and yanked her back, spinning her around, running his hands over her breasts.

"Just what I thought! A little patriot who wants to fight for her country!" He pinned her arms to her sides.

"Let me go! I'm from a newspaper in Memphis!" She struggled uselessly.

"The hell you say! Missy, my general hates news people. He won't care what we do with you. He won't know either. 'Sides, you're lying. No newspaper would allow a young girl to go to a battlefield."

"My family owns the paper," she said, feeling hot tears of frustration and fright. "It was just for a few hours. Let me go!"

He ran his hand over her buttocks and then caught her chin to tilt her face up. She stomped on his instep and he yelped.

"Dammit—"

She yanked her knee up, striking him forcefully. When he groaned and doubled over, he released his grip. Snatching up the rifle, she ran, her feet skimming over the damp ground. She slid down an embankment and lay still.

"Come back here, dammit! You can't get away," he

shouted. He thrashed through the woods, his steps growing louder, and her heart pounded. She brought up the rifle. She couldn't kill him. She was surrounded by Federals and if she shot one of their own, they would catch her and hang her. Twigs cracked and grass swished as he came closer. A dark shape loomed up yards away.

She shrank against the ground, holding her breath, hearing his ragged breathing.

"I'll find you and when I do, we're going to have fun. Come out. I got twenty dollars that's yours. You can't get away." He strode forward and was swallowed in the fog.

"You're surrounded by soldiers," he continued, his footsteps and voice fading. "In a minute I'll alert the others, and then hundreds of men will be hunting you. You keep hiding and you'll regret it."

She shook with fright and felt weak. How could she get away? Forty thousand soldiers were camped around her and to the south was the Confederate army. Wearing a Union uniform, a Confederate might shoot without asking questions. She had to get away before Private Crossley started a searching party. If the Federals learned she had ridden out from Memphis to gather war news for the family newspaper, they would know she was a Confederate sympathizer. She listened to silence. Standing, she moved, trying to make as little noise as possible.

In minutes she felt hopelessly lost and stopped to listen again. If she could just get away from the soldiers and head west, she could take the La Grange road and return to Memphis. Her horse was tethered five miles away from the Federal encampment. She was afraid to wait, afraid to go. Every tree looked the same; in the mist she could walk in circles and blunder back into camp, yet staying close to where she left Crossley was dangerous. *Move! Don't just stand there until they find you.*

Hoping she headed west away from the Federal camp, she edged forward with caution. Mist was thinning, burning off and giving yards of visibility. In minutes she would have the sun to follow. She ran, pausing every few minutes to listen for footsteps.

Winded, she slowed to walk through thick woods. A man's voice and the jingle of harness carried through the mist. Her heart felt as if it jumped to her throat, and she stopped.

Deep voices came, and she reversed her steps. Then she heard hoofbeats. Men's voices were behind her, the sound of horses in front of her. She shifted directions again. Men's voices grew louder, and she turned. She felt desperate and terrified, because every direction seemed to bring a circle of men closing in on her.

Horses whinnied, voices and hoofbeats unmistakable. She ran and encountered more voices and hoofbeats.

Pausing, her heart pounding and her palms damp, she stood still, trying to decide which way to turn. Shapes appeared. Emerging from the mist, an unending line of soldiers on horseback rode toward her. Her breathing stopped; her fists clenched. Feeling immobilized by terror, she stared at hundreds of soldiers only yards away. Behind her men's voices grew louder. Which way should she run?

"Quiet, dammit!" Major Caleb O'Brien snapped to a group of his Louisiana Cavalry whose voices were rising as they moved through tall oak trees. Hardee's men edged forward. To Caleb's right more Confederates advanced, led by Major Aaron Hardcastle, Third Mississippi Infantry Battalion. Behind him were the Tennessee Regulars with Captain Will Stanton.

Mist swirled around the horses. Wild grass was high and green, and spring was in the air. Caleb felt the tingling in his middle that meant they were on the edge of battle. After a month of waiting with both armies camped within miles of each other, they would finally see action. Most of the men on the field were fresh recruits who hadn't seen a battle. Their trial by fire was coming this morning.

"We get a chance at them today. No more waiting and no more running," came a loud whisper as Will Stanton reined beside him.

"Our army has been camped in Corinth for almost a month now. In all that time why the hell haven't the Federals attacked or prepared for battle?"

"Maybe after Fort Donelson, they think all Johnston's men can do is run."

"This will be Manassas again," Caleb said, feeling an eagerness to meet the enemy. "We'll send them running." Federal voices carried on the morning air; they weren't far away through the trees. Why were the damned Bluebellies so certain they wouldn't be attacked? Caleb wondered. Because of Johnston's retreats through Tennessee? It wasn't known what had kept Johnston from attacking long before now, but delays fanned his rage until there was no turning back.

"There must be a million tents along the Tennessee River and around that church."

"According to reconnaissance, Sherman has forty thousand men," Caleb replied dryly. "But Johnston said he would fight them if they were a million." As the mist thinned, Caleb glimpsed tents and shebangs, the makeshift shelters of poles with thatched tops. "Johnston expects us to cut them off from the river and push them west to Owl Creek."

"While Beauregard wants to drive them east farther into Tennessee. Our commanders better get in agreement."

"I'd ride through hell with Johnston," Caleb declared.

"You'd ride through hell with *anybody*, because you crave adventure."

Caleb grinned while he listened to the steady movement of horses through the woods, glancing over his shoulder at the long line of his deployed men and men from other regiments. Thousands of Confederates clad in various color uniforms moved forward toward the enemy camp.

"We may ride through hell today unless the damn Yankees turn tail and run like they did at Manassas," Will said.

"They're probably saying that about us and Fort Donelson."

"I like a general who wants to stay out of battle." Will glanced at him. "You still won't wear a saber?"

"My Colt can out perform a saber any day. A saber is good for roasting meat, not fighting."

"Sometimes I think you got your promotions because of your damned Colt and your Sharps Carbine and your never-miss shooting while the rest of us carry sabers and Enfield muskets and often miss a target."

With a grin Caleb glanced into Will's friendly brown eyes. Caleb looked around at the greening earth. "I like Tennessee, Will."

"Of course, you do—with its emerald hills and tall trees and magnificent horses, it's Eden."

"Not Eden. It's like Ireland," Caleb answered, thinking of his birthplace.

"Why did you leave there, Caleb? Or is that none of my affair?"

"My father gambled away all we had. The family came here to start again. And now I'm in a war."

A shot rang out, followed by silence.

"Dammit, who fired a shot?" Caleb wheeled his horse away and rode down the line, his green eyes searching for anyone reloading. He heard horses and men's voices.

To his right a Yankee reconnaissance patrol of several hundred men advanced, laughing and talking. Were they blind? Caleb's spine tingled as he watched them march without caution through the trees. Riding in front of the line of his men, he drew his pistol.

His men raised muskets as Yankees advanced. And still they hadn't spotted the Confederates. Only yards apart now. Caleb felt his muscles tighten. They would send the Yankees running as they had at Manassas. Any second—

"Rebs!" a Union soldier yelled and raised his rifle.

Caleb swung his pistol high overhead and fired. "Charge!" As his horse leaped forward, Caleb's cry was joined by others while his men surged to meet the enemy. Rebel yells carried, and musket blasts added to the noise.

In minutes Caleb was engaged in fighting, other Federals running back through the woods, shouting alarm to the men in camp, soldiers riding out to join the fight. A Yankee rode toward him, saber raised; Caleb aimed his pistol and fired, and the man tumbled from his saddle.

Feeling a wild surge of exhilaration, Caleb fought. The battlefield was chaos, men yelling and running. They had caught the Bluebellies by surprise this spring morning!

Gaining ground, they drove the Yankees back. As Caleb fought, shots nicked a tree beside him; his horse lurched and fell, killed by a minié ball. Caleb jumped from the saddle and hit the ground running. A soldier appeared, his eyes going wide with fear. He swung up a rifle to aim, the black eye of the muzzle focused on Caleb's heart.

Caleb lunged against the slight Yankee. As Caleb tackled him, the shot went wild. The Yankees were using boys for soldiers; the body he grappled with felt like the slender frame of his twelve-year-old brother Darcy.

Caleb and the Yankee fell to the ground, rolling down an embankment. The body beneath his was soft and round and as they rolled to a stop, Caleb straddled the soldier, looking into blue eyes. *A woman!* Slender fingers were still locked around the rifle. Her cap had fallen off and her blond braids spilled from pins.

The damn Yankees would allow a woman to fight! He had heard of Yankee women dressed in trousers, but he hadn't heard of them fighting alongside their men. He should kill her. If he didn't, she would get up and kill him. She met his gaze with a wide-eyed, steady stare.

He couldn't kill a woman. Not even if she would get up and shoot him. "Dammit!" he shouted. "You don't belong on a bloody battlefield!"

Yanking the rifle from her hands, he stood up and flung it away, watching it fly through the air and strike a tree, falling into weeds. He looked down at her sprawled on the muddy ground. "Get the hell home before you're killed, Yankee!"

A shot clipped his shoulder and part of his uniform ripped away. He ran before the next shot, taking a riderless horse and swinging into the saddle to raise his pistol and fire.

In minutes he was in the thick of fighting, reaching Yankee tents, pursuing them across the field toward high ground.

"Regroup!" Caleb shouted, circling and allowing his men to gather. They were in the shelter of trees and ahead stretched a wide meadow.

"They've dug in behind the fence," Will shouted, riding close. "There's a sunken wagon road on the other side of that fence."

"Ready to attack, Major," General Joseph E. Johnston ordered. "Wait for the word."

"Yes, sir." Caleb looked at the field they would have to cross, the thick woods where the Federals could hide. Was there any other way to attack? A direct march would be deadly.

"Gibson!" General Braxton Bragg shouted.

The colonel wheeled his horse around and rode toward the general. A deep boom resounded from the trees and the earth exploded yards away. Now that the Federals had cannon behind the fence, any charge against them would be even more deadly.

General Bragg rode to Caleb's right. "Colonel Gibson, take your men and attack. We have to drive the enemy off that road," Bragg commanded.

"Yes, sir." Colonel Gibson's face was pale, a scowl creasing his forehead as he called the order to his men.

Caleb drew a deep breath, anger surging. The men would walk across an open field into cannons. Damn the Bluebellies! He fired while soldiers stretched in a long line to march toward the scrub oak at the edge of the field near the rail fence.

"Hold your fire!" Caleb yelled the command, afraid his regiment would hit Gibson's men who were now deployed ahead. Caleb felt another flash of rage. It was Gibson's first battle, and his men marched against the Federals's defensive position that was a natural protection. Where was the Confederate artillery? Where was support?

The sun rose higher, glinting on bayonets and brass buttons. Gibson's men charged again, racing across the open field, shouting, the first wave almost to the rail fence.

Cannon roared sending canister through the Confederate line, cutting men down like a sickle through grass. Caleb's stomach churned at the sight. Amid screams and destruction, it was Caleb's turn. The charge would mean certain death for his men.

"Major O'Brien!" He heard the deep voice of his commanding officer. In a rush, Caleb urged his horse forward and brandished his pistol.

"Charge!" Caleb yelled, leading his men across the smoke-filled ground.

He felt a hot bite in his thigh, another in his calf as he kept firing, riding toward the fence that soon vanished from sight amid smoke from the cannon. Like one continual roar of thunder, the blast of cannon was all he could hear. They had to be twelve-pounders. The bitter smell of blood mingled with the odor of gunpowder. In minutes Caleb's thigh was soaked with blood. He glanced over and saw Will's horse fall, Will running.

Canister hit ahead, sending a shower of dirt flying, sharp bites stinging Caleb's hands and arms. The guidon fell, and another soldier snatched it up to continue running. Too many men were going down, and they couldn't reach the fence. The deadly black snouts of the cannon faced him, a solid defense for the Federals.

"Retreat! Regroup!" he yelled, wheeling his horse around. As he raced back, he spotted a soldier writhing on the ground, his leg crimson from a wound.

"Will!"

Moaning, Will struggled to rise. Caleb jumped off his horse, snatching Will up over his shoulder, flinging him across his horse as he mounted to ride behind their lines and leave Will in safety.

Again he was in a charge that was repulsed, watching Gibson charge again and again and lose more men. Feeling a growing dismay at the carnage, Caleb fought doggedly, his enthusiasm turning to a stomach-wrenching sickness. No one expected Yankees to dig in and fight like this—as if their homes and families were at stake. Manassas had been a rout. This was a slaughter, and the killing and loss of good men shocked and sickened him. As the sun shifted across the sky, his despair over the slaughter changed to anger at the uselessness of the attacks.

In late afternoon Caleb spotted the rumpled uniform, dark hair, and craggy profile of General Bragg. To hell with insubordination, he told himself. Good men were dropping all around him. Trying to curb the anger he felt, he rode to the general.

"Sir, 'tis support we need to attack," Caleb said, lapsing into a thick Irish brogue. "There have been a dozen bloody charges; we're losing hundreds of men."

"General Ruggles is getting his cannon in line."

Bragg's voice was impassive, the words clipped. "Hold your men until I give the order."

"Thank God. Yes, sir." Relief made him weak. Caleb saluted and rode down the line. Beyond him near a creek, a doctor was tending the wounded, both Union and Confederate. Will was stretched on the ground, a man tying a bandage around his leg.

Caleb spotted the first cannon and then others as General Ruggles massed a line facing the road. Wheels creaking, cannon were rolled into place. ". . . twenty-three, twenty-four, twenty-five," he counted aloud, amazed by the massive artillery being lined up.

It was the most cannon Caleb had seen in a battle, the line stretching out of sight over a rise. Feeling relief tempered by a grim knowledge of how much death the cannon would bring, he turned to find what was left of his men. Then the roar of cannon and screaming canister shut out all other sounds, hurling two rounds a minute into the Federal line.

Captain Dickinson rode up. "I'm to commence attacking again. We'll take that damned hornet's nest," he called as he passed Caleb.

Caleb moved to the front while his remaining men lined up to charge. He gazed across the ground at the woods. He might not survive the next clash. Why had he ever thought war an adventure? Taking a deep breath he flicked the reins.

"Charge!" Caleb galloped forward, and in minutes he was across the fence. A shot hit Caleb in the shoulder. He pitched off his horse, striking a tree and falling to the ground. When he regained his feet, pain shot up his arm. Caleb reached for his rifle and gasped. He couldn't straighten out his arm. White flags appeared while Yankees threw up their hands and dropped their weapons. As Caleb's head swam, he collapsed.

He stirred and looked up at green leaves. Cannon and shot were in the distance; moans were loud and close beside him. Rows of wounded men surrounded him on the ground. He sat up, pain making him dizzy. His arm throbbed and ached; wounds in his shoulder and thigh burned unmercifully.

"Cal—"

Will was stretched on the ground with two men between them. Before he could answer Will, a scream from a soldier sent a chill down Caleb's spine. Feeling his stomach twist, he turned to see a doctor working on the wounded man. Beneath interlocking branches of oaks, a surgical table had been set up with planks across two tables.

"Caleb." Will's voice was feeble.

Caleb struggled to get to Will. Every movement sent pain shooting through his arm and leg. A bloody bandage swathed Will's leg.

"He'll take off my leg," Will said. "Get me out of here, Caleb, and back to my family in Memphis. I know Doctor Perkins there. Please, get me home."

Caleb looked at the doctor bending over the man on the makeshift table. He felt gorge rise and fought it down. "Can you travel as far as Memphis?"

"Can you get us horses?"

"I'll try."

It took half an hour before Caleb found a horse. Pain from his arm was consuming him like flames, but he didn't want to lose his arm and he didn't want Will to lose his leg. He knelt beside Will.

"I've hurt my arm. I'll help you up, but I can't carry you."

"Let's go," Will whispered.

As they struggled, Caleb gasped with pain. Will's face turned ashen as they hobbled away from the wounded. When they were out of sight of the men, Caleb leaned Will against a tree.

"Hang on. I'll bring the horse. I could only get one."

When he returned, Will was slumped unconscious on the ground. At twenty-three, Will was two years older than Caleb, but he looked like a boy now. His cheeks were flushed, his sandy hair full of grass and leaves.

"Will!" Caleb shook him until Will's lashes fluttered and raised. "You have to climb on the horse. I can't move my arm." Together, the two mounted and Caleb rode behind, turning the horse east along Lick Creek as he heard the first rumble of thunder.

"We're almost to the Tennessee River," Will mumbled. "Drop south, Caleb, we'll head west. We'll go through La Grange and Germantown."

"We have to go through our men and theirs," Caleb said, feeling doubts assail him. Both men were on the verge of losing consciousness, yet they could lose limbs if they didn't get to Memphis.

What had happened to the woman soldier? Caleb wondered. Had she survived the carnage?

In minutes Caleb turned east to avoid Confederates. Will slumped against him, his weight sagging. Thunder rumbled, and in the growing darkness Caleb strained to see. Alongside a creek he topped a small rise and finally headed west to follow a path through the trees.

Hours later he was drifting in and out of awareness. Pain consumed him. Cold driving rain poured over them; Will felt as if he were burning with fever and every time he stirred, he wanted water. They had to find some kind of shelter. Another hour passed before a silvery flash of lightning illuminated a weathered barn. Caleb tugged the reins and headed for the dark interior.

As he dismounted, Will slid from the saddle. When Caleb tried to catch him, they both toppled down and pain made Caleb's head spin.

"Dammit!" He moved out from under the dead weight of Will and rolled him over. It was awkward and tedious to spread a blanket and get Will bedded down. Caleb could use only one arm. He sank down exhausted, enveloped in pain, hungry, leaning back against a stall. Closing his eyes, he wished he could lose consciousness briefly as a respite from hurting.

Caleb heard a whicker, then horses moving about in the barn. Close by, straw rustled, and a soft hiss of breath was barely audible.

Caleb felt a tingle across the back of his neck. His hand slid to the butt of his Colt to ease it from his gun belt. He and Will weren't the only people in the barn.

Chapter 2

Straining to hear, Caleb listened. He was fully alert now, sensing danger.

Straw rustled. Someone was in the empty, hay-strewn stall behind him. As quietly as possible, Caleb shifted and stood up, biting back a gasp from pain in his leg.

Caleb's eyes adjusted to the darkness until a flash of lightning brought the brilliance of noonday, and then he was blind again for seconds afterward.

Keeping his eyes closed to avoid momentary blindness during the next lightning flash, he waited with his finger on the trigger. After the flash, he slipped into the stall and pressed against the wall, counting on lightning blinding the other man.

He saw the muzzle of the rifle first, and then golden hair that was a dull sheen in the darkness. The man faced the front of the stall, unaware that Caleb was almost beside him.

Caleb stepped forward and thrust the muzzle of the Colt against the man's temple. "Drop the gun," he ordered.

Lightning crackled, a snapping pop that sounded as if it hit the barn. Dazzling white light bathed them. Caleb looked at the female in a Yankee uniform; her eyes were enormous and strands of yellow hair curled around her face.

Startled blue eyes met his. He saw the flare of rage and recognition before the barn plunged into darkness.

"Drop the damn rifle!" he snapped, prodding her.

With a thud it hit the hay-strewn dirt floor. "I thought all our men were gentlemen, but I was wrong," said a voice that had a soft drawl, the "our" coming out in two syllables.

"Our men?" he repeated, lowering his pistol and scooping up her rifle. "Get your hands on top of your head."

"You were a beast on the battlefield!" she flung at him.

"You've a Southern accent, yet you wear a Yankee uniform and you came out of the Yankee line, so you must be a Union soldier."

His eyes adjusted, and he saw her chin tilt up in a haughty air. "I'm not a soldier. This uniform enables me to be with the men. You startled me today. I wouldn't have shot you."

She was Southern—no mistaking the accent. But if she wasn't a soldier, what the hell was she? He clamped his jaw shut and stared at her. There was only one other reason for a woman to want to follow an army of men. The chit was a camp follower, plying her trade during the long days when the Union army had camped by the Tennessee River. Lightning flashed, and his gaze raked over her.

"You said, 'our men,' yet you're in a Federal uniform."

"All my loyalty is with the South, sir!"

Her Confederate loyalties weren't as hopeful to him as her profession. She should be willing to do most anything for a dollar. Was she a Bluecoat or a camp follower? He felt dizzy and hot as fire and had to make a decision. Her accent was Southern and she was miles from the battlefield now, on the road to Memphis. He didn't have a choice; he had to trust her. He and Will needed help desperately. He prayed she was a camp follower and loyal to the South.

"I can make it worth your while to get me and my friend to Memphis. I'll pay you fifty dollars in gold," he said.

"You're both Confederates?"

"Yes, we are," he said. "My friend is hurt badly."

"Why Memphis?" she asked.

"He's from there," he said, growing weaker and more impatient.

"Who is he?"

"What does that matter?" Caleb snapped, feeling his knees shake. "Will you or won't you?"

"What choice do I have?"

"You have a hell of a choice, because I'm going to pass out any minute now," he said, hearing his words slur, feeling the earth shift beneath his feet. "Fifty in gold. I'm Major Caleb O'Brien and I have an older brother, Rafferty O'Brien, in New Orleans," he added. Why didn't she answer him? What was she debating? Had he guessed wrong and she was really a Federal? Or did she want more money?

"I'll take you without pay, because of your Memphis friend. I'm from Memphis, too." She drew herself up. "Otherwise, sir, I wouldn't take you to the devil."

His head spun and he needed to sit down. He had to trust her. Wondering if he was being a gullible fool, yet knowing he had little choice other than to kill her, Caleb lowered the pistol. "We have a deal. I'll pay you fifty," he said. Whatever she was, sooner or later she would want money. "Now I want the truth—are you a Bluecoat sympathizer? You were ready to shoot me."

"I told you, you startled me. I was trying to get away from the battle and behind Confederate lines when I encountered you." Again he watched her draw herself up. "I'm as loyal to the Confederacy as General Robert E. Lee or President Jeff—"

"Spare me the speech. We're on the same side."

"Sir, you and I will never be on the same side. I was on the battlefield because I was spying."

"You're a spy!" Spy, soldier, frustrated spinster, whatever she was, she was too touchy to be a camp follower. The loose women he had known were always ready for a good time. Particularly when money was involved.

"You'll get us to Memphis. Both of us?" he asked, emphasizing both. He didn't believe she was a spy. From what he had seen of Southern families, women were sheltered and protected and they didn't traipse around on battlefields in enemy uniforms.

"I'll consider it my patriotic duty since you're dressed in gray."

His head spun and spots danced before his eyes. He moved away from her. "I'll help you with Will, but we have to wait until the rain lets up or he'll get pneumonia."

"Will? What's his name?"

"He's Captain Will Stanton."

"Oh, my heaven!" she gasped and moved forward. "Where is he?"

"You know Will?" he asked, feeling another jolt of surprise. Who was she? How did she know Will? Caleb didn't hear her answer as he followed her out of the stall and sank down. Dizziness came as he watched her kneel beside Will's still form. "We may both be unconscious by morning. Remember, fifty in gold." Caleb leaned back, yielding to blackness that swept over him.

Sophia Merrick smoothed Will's hair off his forehead and turned to look over her shoulder. Major Caleb O'Brien was the name the soldier had given. She crossed to him and eased him down. He was as unconscious as Will and she had to get them both to the hospital in Memphis. How could she move two unconscious men? she wondered.

Major O'Brien from New Orleans. A man too bold and brash and cavalier. With a brother named Rafferty. Had the major told her about his brother because he didn't expect to survive, and she should know whom to notify? Or had he told her, so she would summon his brother? She remembered his ordering her off the battlefield, shouting with rage at her. He was no gentleman like Will.

She pushed the slouch hat off the major's head, letting his tight brown curls brush her palm, and the contact was as jolting as everything else about him. He annoyed and frightened her, but because of his concern for Will, she could forgive him his surly manner. It was a relief to have his eyes closed and not have to deal with him.

Hannah Lou was worried sick about Will. So were their parents. Mr. and Mrs. Stanton would be wild with relief. If Will lived that long. Sophia felt a pang. Could she take care of two severely wounded men?

A cold gust of wind blew through the open barn door. She closed it and walked back carefully in the dark. Removing the blanket from her saddle, she spread it over Major O'Brien. He had placed his own blanket over Will. She stretched out on hay and in minutes was shivering from the cold.

Will lay alongside the wall. She raised his blanket to lie down beside him and saw she would be against his injured leg and she might hurt him if she bumped him.

Feeling reluctant she stared at Major O'Brien. She needed a blanket. Would he waken? She didn't want him to find her pressed beside him. She slid beneath the blanket, leaving a space between them, but in minutes she was still shivering. With his fever, he would never know. She moved against him and felt the heat from his body warm her. Placing her hand on his forehead, he felt as hot as Will. Both of them were unconscious and feverish. Dear God, help me get them home, she prayed.

She had never been physically close to a man like this. He was warm, comforting. If he awakened and discovered her with him—he must not. She blushed thinking of the conclusions he would draw. Acutely aware of his every breath or slightest movement, she finally warmed and relaxed.

Groans came and she stirred, moving against a solid warmth. Drowsy, between sleeping and waking, she rubbed her cheek and pressed against his chest. She slid her arm across him as awareness overpowered sleep. Her arm circled a slender waist, a flat belly, taut with hard muscle. Her eyes fluttered open. Startled, she sat up, shocked at herself, burning with embarrassment that she had hugged him.

Major Caleb O'Brien lay with his arm outflung, his chest rising and falling with his shallow, fast breathing. Brown stubble showed on his jaw. In sleep he still exuded an aura of danger, as if his eyes would open and his hand would reach out to hold her. Yet in sleep he looked younger; his mouth was well shaped, his lower lip full; she felt a peculiar warmth as she studied him. His lashes were thicker and curlier than a woman's. His face reminded her of a painting her father had of a mariner in a storm at sea, face lifted in a defiant stare. Even in sleep, Major O'Brien had a look of determination in his square jaw. It would be a relief to turn him over to the hospital in Memphis not only for his welfare, but so she wouldn't have to deal with him.

She moved to Will who felt hotter to touch than he had

hours ago. His skin was ashen and she felt afraid. She had
to get them both to Memphis as soon as possible. Please,
Will, hang on. I'll do what I can, she vowed silently.

She stood up, cold and hungry. There was the Crawford
store at Walker Station on the way to Memphis where she
could get some food, but first she had to find transportation. She pushed open the barn door.

Thirty minutes later as the first rays of dawn hid morning stars, she knelt beside Will and stared at him, feeling
his forehead, then moving to do the same to Major
O'Brien. Will felt the hottest. She shook the major with
both hands.

"Major O'Brien! Major O'Brien, wake up!"

Even in the dusky light of the barn, she was startled by
the green of his eyes. He stared at her and he moved, then
gasped and grimaced.

"I need your help if I'm going to get you and Will to
Memphis."

He moaned and closed his eyes and she shook him.
Feeling more frightened, she debated leaving them and
riding for Memphis to get help, but both men might not
survive the wait until she could return. "Major O'Brien!"
His lashes fluttered, and he stared at her.

"You have to help me," she urged. "I've found a
wagon and hitched our horses to it. Help me get Captain
Stanton up. I can't lift either of you into the wagon." All
the time she talked, she tugged on the major to help him
sit up. Finally she slid her arm beneath him, pressing
against him. His good arm went around her, and she
pulled him to a sitting position.

"Now get on your feet." When she tried to stand and
help him up, she thought he would pull her down, but he
slid his arm around her waist and braced himself against
the wall as he gained his feet.

"Damn!" He sagged against the stall. His arm was still
lightly around her waist and she felt a wave of sympathy
for him.

"I'm sorry," she said. "I need your help. I think Will's
worse than you are."

Major O'Brien squeezed her waist as if in answer and
he swayed.

"Don't faint! Major O'Brien!"

"I'm here. Where's . . . wagon?"

"There," she said, pointing to the far end of the barn. "We have to go out that way, because they can see us from the farmhouse if we go out this end. I'll return their wagon."

One corner of his mouth lifted in a weak grin. "Get Will."

She nodded and held the major around the waist, feeling his hipbone. He gasped when he took a step, and his weight sagged on her again. She felt frightened he would faint and she was desperate to get them into the wagon. Moving would make the major's wounds worse, but there wasn't any choice.

"I'm sorry we have to do this," she said as they struggled toward Will.

Major O'Brien bit his lip, and she hurt for him. They reached Will. She knelt beside him. "Captain Stanton! Will! Please—"

Major O'Brien's hand fell on her shoulder. "Pull him to a sitting position. I'll pick him up over my shoulder."

"You can't." To her horror the bandage around his leg showed a bright crimson spot of fresh blood. "Your leg is too bad—"

"Pull him up 'fore I faint." He braced his good hand against the wall. "Can't argue."

Tears stung her eyes. She hurt for both of them. They shouldn't have to do this, she thought. Will should be home with his sister and parents. "I hate this war! I know I shouldn't, but I do."

She knelt behind Will and slid her arms around him and tried to lift him. It was like trying to lift the barn.

Major O'Brien moved closer and leaned down. His face was flushed, only inches from hers, but when she looked into his eyes, she was startled by his look of determination. With a jerk he pulled Will over his shoulder and stood up.

"Oh, damn," he said, letting out his breath.

She grabbed the blankets and jammed his floppy hat on his head, picking up Will's hat as she ran ahead. She had pulled a stone beside the wagon and the major stepped up on the rock to drop Will onto the flatbed of the wagon. As soon as he released Will, Major O'Brien slumped against the wagon.

"Major? Major O'Brien!" He was unconscious again. She climbed into the wagon. It took agonizing minutes to tug him into the wagon and cover them with blankets. The first faint graying of the sky made it light enough to see and the sweet scent of rain-fresh spring was in the air. From a nearby pen a rooster crowed. The world looked normal until she glanced over her shoulder at the two wounded officers. It bothered her that she was stealing a wagon; she had never taken anything that wasn't hers. Should she ask the people if she could take their wagon or just go and return it later?

She glanced down at the wounded officers. She would go. She knew the way home through La Grange and Germantown. She flicked the reins and they moved ahead. In minutes they circled back to the road. "Please, let them be alive when we get to Memphis," she whispered.

Three hours later she stopped to crawl back into the wagon and feel for heartbeats. Both were unconscious and at a glance, she couldn't tell if they were still alive. She returned to driving, thankful at least they didn't have to suffer with each lurch and jiggle of the wagon.

Finally she saw the spires of a church above treetops in Memphis and she urged the horses faster, praying they would get to the hospital in time.

"Thank heaven!" Sophia said as she turned on shady Adams Street. Purple lilacs and wisteria bloomed on the block of elegant houses. She tugged the reins in front of the two-story Stanton home. Help was only a few feet away now. Feeling relief, Sophia climbed down, expecting servants to come running at any moment. Dressed in a Federal uniform, she dreaded facing Mrs. Stanton who never understood Sophia's family during peacetime. The town accepted Sophia and her family, and they would have to accept her trip to the battlefield for the paper. Sophia ran around the wagon and up the stone walk to the front steps where she stopped in dismay.

Six wounded soldiers were on pallets on the front

porch. Two small servant children waved fans over the men.

"Af'noon, ma'am," a child said without a break in her fanning.

"Where's your mistress?"

"I get her," she said, setting down the feather fan and going into the house.

Flies buzzed over the wounded men and Sophia picked up the fan to wave it. In minutes the door opened and Mrs. Stanton stepped out.

"Sophia Merrick! Come in here, dear. Great heavens, you're wearing a Federal uniform! Dilcie, you get the fan."

"Yes'm," the child said, and Sophia placed it in her small hand.

"Sophia, what on earth have you been up to now?"

"Excuse me, Mrs. Stanton. I went to the hospital," Sophia said, feeling overwhelmed with relief to reach help. "They turned me away—"

"My dear, several of us have taken the overflow. Whatever are you doing in that horrible uniform? You must get it off at once! Great heavens, child, it's bad enough to be in men's clothing, but a Yankee uniform is dreadful. Your brothers would have apoplexy. I just can't—"

"Excuse me, ma'am," Sophia interrupted again, feeling desperate to get help for the men, "I have Will in the wagon and he's hurt. Doctor Perkins said the hospital is filled to overflowing. He said he would see Will here."

"You have my Will?" Mrs. Stanton asked, looking at the wagon. "Oh, my Lord!" Catching up her blue grosgrain skirt, she ran inside, calling to a servant and in seconds, servants came out along with Mrs. Stanton and Hannah Lou whose blue eyes turned to Sophia.

"Sophia, Mama said you have Will. Land sakes, you're wearing a Yankee uniform!" Hannah Lou pushed strands of brown hair from her face, and Sophia drew a deep breath. This wasn't the homecoming she pictured. Petite, with a china doll's pretty pink cheeks and blue eyes, Hannah Lou looked exhausted and disheveled, something Sophia had never seen before, not even when they were young and played outdoors. Without waiting to talk, Hannah Lou held up her skirts and ran down the steps to the wagon. Sophia went out with them as the servants lifted Will onto a stretcher to carry him inside.

"Lordy, where can we put my precious Will! Every bed is full—"

"He can have mine," Hannah Lou offered.

"Mrs. Stanton, when the servants come back to get the other officer, he is Major Caleb O'Brien from New Orleans."

Mrs. Stanton frowned and glanced at the wagon. "Hannah Lou, go with your brother. Uncle Barley and Shed, you boys come back here and bring the stretcher to help Miss Merrick. You ride to her house and carry this wounded man inside."

"Mrs. Stanton!" Sophia gasped. "I can't take the major!"

Mrs. Stanton wiped her eyes and clutched Sophia's hand. "Sophia Merrick, you're the strongest young woman I know. Your father has made you shoulder a man's burden for the past four years of your life. I'll send Doctor Perkins right over the minute he's through with Will. Jubal has midwifed and she's a good nurse. I'll send her and whatever laudanum I can spare with you."

"I think the major's arm is broken and he's shot in the leg and has a wound in his shoulder." Sophia felt as if she would burst into tears. She couldn't take care of an injured soldier. "I don't know anything about injuries. This man has lost blood and is feverish—"

"Sophia," Mrs. Stanton said, her voice firm. "All three of your brothers are fighting in this war. We have to do our part. The hospital is overflowing. I can't take another wounded man into my house. You'll have Jubal and the medication and you do the best you can." She glanced at the wagon. "At least he's not out on a battleground waiting—"

"I can't take him home. Except for servants, I'm alone. It wouldn't be proper. Even Papa and my brothers would agree about that," she said, grasping for any reason to sway Mrs. Stanton.

"Stuff and nonsense! Since when has your family ever regarded propriety as important? You know the town will accept your taking him in. Your father has raised you in the most unconventional manner possible and—" She stopped at the sound of the clop of hooves as a buggy came down the street.

"Thank God! It's Doctor Perkins." Mrs. Stanton walked away while the servants returned with a maid between them.

"Boys, you get in the wagon," Clairice Stanton called to them, waving her hand. "Jubal, help Miss Merrick until she sends you home." Mrs. Stanton turned toward the doctor's carriage. "Doctor Perkins!"

Feeling dismay and fear, Sophia stared at Dr. Perkins as he climbed from his carriage and headed into the Stanton house. Never had she felt so alone and helpless. It wasn't proper for her to be alone with the major. Papa would never approve. And she couldn't take care of a wounded man—not one wounded as badly as Major O'Brien. She glanced at the wagon. He lay sprawled in back, long ago having kicked off the blankets. The servants stared at her, waiting for her to take them home with her.

She climbed into the wagon and turned it around in the street to ride the short distance to her home on Washington.

Moving in a numbing fear, she pulled the wagon to a stop beneath branches of an oak. Three faces turned to her for instruction.

"We'll take him in through the kitchen door and I'll lead the way. Careful of his arm, because I think it's broken."

"Yes'm," one of the men said and climbed down. She watched as they moved Major O'Brien onto the stretcher. He groaned and shifted.

"This way," she said, knowing the worst was to come. Her brothers and father were robust men and never ill until the last month of her father's life, and then Dr. Perkins called constantly. Her brief nursing had been for a man confined to bed with pneumonia, not battle wounds.

She walked through the cool, high-ceilinged rooms to her brother John's bedroom on the southeast corner of the first floor. She had long ago taken over her father's room next to John's bedroom where she could work at her father's large desk. Now it would be easier to have Major O'Brien downstairs in John's bed. She rushed to turn back the counterpane as they set the stretcher on one side of the bed and eased Major O'Brien onto the horsehair mattress.

"We'll go home now, ma'am," one of the men said.

"Thank you," she answered, barely thinking about them as she glanced at Jubal. "Do you know what to do?"

"Yes, ma'am. And Doctor will be here soon. We need some clean rags for bandages and some hot water and some scissors to cut away the major's uniform."

Stretched on the bed, he was rumpled, bloody, and covered with dried mud. His face was ashen, his breathing shallow and fast. He didn't look as if he could survive the next few hours.

"I'll start water heating," Sophia said, leaving and praying Dr. Perkins wasn't called to the hospital from the Stantons'.

Two hours later she stood in her doorway and watched Dr. Perkins head toward his wagon. As she closed the door, Jubal stepped into the hall behind her.

"Jubal, how many wounded men are at the Stantons'?"

"I don't rightly know. Probably almost twenty-five now with Mister Will home."

"Doctor Perkins is sending some wounded here, but if there are twenty-five men at the Stantons', you better go home."

"Yes, ma'am. I'll tell Mrs. Stanton you're getting more men here."

"Please, do," Sophia said, still cold with fright to take care of them when she didn't know how.

She heard Mazie go out the back door and clang a kettle and Henry thrust his head into the hallway. "Ma'am, I hear we have a hurt man to care for. Do you want me to kill a chicken?"

"Yes, Henry. We have a Major O'Brien. There's a battle near Shiloh Church near the Tennessee River."

"Yes'm," Henry said, nodding. "I'll go behind the carriage house." He turned to shuffle out and she looked at his stooped shoulders and tightly knotted gray hair. He had worked for her family when her father was a boy and Henry always said he didn't exactly know his age, but she knew it had to be over eighty. He could help, but not as much as she might need. And Mazie could cook, but nursing was out. The sight of a wound or anything hurting and Mazie fainted. Henry was going behind the carriage house to kill the chicken to keep Mazie from seeing him or they would have to get out the smelling salts and revive her.

Two servants, one over eighty, the other given to fainting at the sight of anything in pain, a paper to print, wounded men to tend. Sophia felt overwhelmed. "Papa, I need your strength," she whispered. She squared her shoulders. Papa was buried at the cemetery and Amos and Morris and John were fighting for the Confederacy, and she would just do the best she could.

She glanced toward the bedroom. When Dr. Perkins worked on the major, she had almost fainted. And she felt waves of fire in her face when the doctor lifted the sheet Jubal had placed over his naked body and began to work on him without giving Sophia warning.

Three nights later she made the rounds. Lieutenant Landerson was upstairs in Amos's room with a foot wound. Sergeant Mulligan with a shoulder wound was in Morris's room. Major O'Brien was delirious and Dr. Perkins gave little hope for his survival, but as Sophia leaned over him in the candlelight and bathed his face, she remembered the determination in his eyes when he said he would pick up Will and get him into the wagon. And that moment on the battlefield when she had looked into his eyes and he could have shot her. He spared her life and saved Will's—now she would try to save his. Major O'Brien deserved to live and she would pray for him.

As she sponged his forehead, he groaned. He felt on fire to touch and was covered only by a sheet to his waist. It had been three days now and she still wasn't accustomed to his bare body. Even though he wasn't awake, she blushed hotly when she bent over him. Her gaze drifted now to his chest covered in a mat of thick brown curls. Perspiration dotted his shoulders and she bathed him with a cool cloth.

"You have to get well, Major," she whispered. "You can do it; you're tough. You brought Will home and if you did that all shot and hurt like you were, you can get over this. You—"

He groaned and turned his head, his eyes fluttering, startling her. His eyes opened to stare at her and he frowned, licking his dry lips. "Water," he whispered.

She picked up a glass and slipped her arm beneath him to hold him up, spooning water into his mouth, some of it running down his chin. When she lowered him, she wiped his chin with the damp cloth and dabbed at his parched lips.

When she looked into his eyes, she met a disconcerting, direct stare. His eyes were a crystal green with tiny flecks of gold in the center near the pupil.

His left hand reached out and caught her arm. "Amity? Amity, sure and I thought I wouldna' see ye again, lass," he said in an Irish brogue.

"I'm Sophia," she whispered, wondering who Amity was. Was he married? His fingers were strong and blunt and thick, freckles scattered across the back of his hand.

"Amity—" He turned his head and his eyes closed. Alarmed, Sophia bent over him, her hand going to his throat. His pulse coursed steady and strong, and she felt relieved.

Her relief was gone within the hour. He thrashed and moaned and then became still, his breathing labored and quick. She pulled the rocker close to the bed, afraid to leave him for fear he wouldn't be alive when dawn came, yet knowing she could do nothing to keep him from dying.

He moved, the sheet sliding off one leg that was covered in brown hair and freckles, his thigh and calf well shaped with hard muscles. She blushed as her gaze roamed over him. Henry took care of the major's private moments and bathed him. The major had scars on his ribs and back and arm and she wondered what he had done, what kind of life he had lived to get such scars. He was quick and tough and he frightened her, yet he had taken the best possible care of Will under the circumstances.

He moaned again and turned. In minutes he was shaking and she covered him with a comforter and wrapped a hot brick to place at his feet. His skin felt dry and hot to touch in spite of his chills.

Gazing down at him in the candlelight, Sophia stood beside the bed. When her legs hurt from standing, she sat in the rocker, watching him, feeling as if she could help by staying awake while he slept, yet knowing it was foolish. Later when he kicked the covers away, she stirred. His face was flushed, and he burned with fever. Sophia hurried to draw cold water and bathe him, trying to get the fever down. His curls clung damply to his forehead as she bathed his face. His lips were dry and cracked. Who was Amity? Wife? Sweetheart? she wondered.

Sophia climbed onto the high bed and sat beside him, pulling him against her to hold him so she could spoon water into his mouth. It was tedious with a few drops at a time, but gradually she got a cupful down him. She bathed his face, letting the cloth trail down over his throat to his chest. On impulse she released the cloth and moved her hand over his chest, feeling the mat of curls against her palm, feeling the heat radiate from his body, letting her hand drift down toward his belly.

Flushing, realizing what she was doing, she moved her hand away, yet she continued to study him. She had never touched a man's body like that or seen a man so bare. She knew she shouldered responsibilities few women her age were allowed to do, such as printing a paper and spying on the Federals, yet in some ways she was ignorant—she hadn't been kissed and she didn't know how to dance. With a sigh, she touched the major's hand, feeling the warm flesh beneath hers, remembering the moment in the barn when she had wakened pressed against him. When Private Crossley had grabbed her, all she felt was revulsion. It wasn't revulsion Major O'Brien stirred, but fire.

"Get well, Major. I'm sure you can," she whispered, easing him to the pillows.

Tomorrow she needed to go to the paper. It was time to get out the weekly edition, yet she hated to leave the major. She pushed his curls away from his forehead, remembering how forceful he had been at their first encounter.

Three nights later as she dozed in the rocker, she stirred and opened her eyes. Major O'Brien groaned.

"Desirée?"

Sophia stared at him in consternation. Amity, Desirée—how many women did the man have in his life? She stood up and moved to the bed, picking up the cold, wet cloth to wipe his forehead. "I'm here, Major O'Brien," she said softly. "You'll be all right."

"Water . . ."

She climbed onto the bed and pulled the major up against her, holding the cup to his lips. His head was against her shoulder, his shoulder pressing her soft breasts as he drank. He turned his head. He was inches away as his eyes focused on her and her breath caught. His gaze was clear and searching.

"Who are you?" he asked.

Chapter 3

She felt on fire with embarrassment and was acutely aware of him pressed against her; she was dressed only in her white cotton nightgown and an ocher linen wrapper. The wrapper was open and her hair cascaded over her shoulders.

"I'm Sophia Merrick," she said, trying to lower him to the bed and disentangle herself. His hand caught her forearm.

"Where am I?" he asked, dazed.

"At my house in Memphis."

As he stared at her intently, her cheeks flooded with warmth. Searching and intimate, his gaze made her aware of his hand holding her, his proximity, her knee touching his hip. The silence of the room was broken only by the steady tick of the clock in the hall beyond the closed door.

Her heart beat faster, and she felt as if she couldn't breathe. Continuing to gaze at her, he caught locks of her hair in his hand, letting the curls slide between his fingers.

"Thank you for getting us here," he whispered.

So he remembered. The fever was broken and his mind was clear.

"You shouldn't have been on that battlefield." His voice was deep and as compelling as his gaze. He reached up to touch her jaw with a faint brush of his fingers.

"I was there for a purpose. And I was trying to get away and go home when I got caught in the battle. None of the Yankees expected an attack." She lowered him to the pillows and she slid off the bed while he reached beneath the covers.

"I have my arms and legs," he said. "Will. How's Will?"

"He's going to be all right," she answered, pulling her wrapper around her and tying the sash, aware that he was watching her. "I haven't seen Will yet, because he's been sleeping when I've called on the Stantons, but Hannah Lou, his sister, said he's going to survive."

"How'd I get here?" he inquired.

"The hospital was full, and Will's mother has twenty-five wounded men now, so I brought you home with me. I have three patients here, counting you."

"Thank you," he said solemnly, staring at her with a slight frown. "So you really are Southern."

"Yes. I told you I was."

"Your family allowed you to—"

"My brothers are away fighting. I don't have any other family."

"I don't remember everything. We were in a barn?"

"Yes. I found a wagon and brought you both home."

"You saved my life," he said, in a tone of voice that made her wonder what he thought. He seemed full of disapproval of her being at the battlefield.

"I hope so. Doctor Perkins is going to be happy to see you coherent." She wondered if she sounded coherent. Major O'Brien was a disturbing man.

His gaze swept over her again and he reached out to pick up a long strand of her hair, tugging it through his fingers. "You look better this way. How long have you been sitting with me?" Beneath the covers he was naked, and only his chest was uncovered, but to her consternation, he didn't seem to notice or care. And he didn't sound like a man who had been at the brink of death for days. His voice sounded stronger with every word.

She felt flustered by his question. "You've been here over a week."

His brows arched. "A week?" He closed his eyes a moment and then looked at her again. "I'd like some water."

"Of course," she said, reaching for the half-filled cup and starting to climb up on the high bed beside him until she looked into his eyes. Before he had never been fully conscious, but now alert green eyes stared at her and she hesitated. Taking a deep breath she climbed up and slid her arm beneath him. She felt his muscles tighten as he raised up. He moved against her, his shoulder touching hers, and she was conscious again of the thin layer of her gown and wrapper between them. His body was warm, solid.

She held him while he drank. Contented, he placed his hand over hers on the cup. In seconds he sank against her, his weight a heavy pressure on her breast and shoulder. She looked down at him to protest.

His eyes were closed and he had lapsed into sleep again. She set down the cup and eased him to the bed. "You and Will are going to survive," she said softly, pulling the sheet up over his bare chest, more conscious than ever of each brush of her hands over him.

He was quiet enough now, looking pale, disheveled. How could he look so faint and weak when he was unconscious or asleep and the moment his eyes opened, he seemed to command the world? she wondered.

"Get well, Major. You can go home to your Amity and your Desirée."

Was he on the mend? Jubal said sometimes men rallied and then were gone within the next hour. Sophia reached out to touch his curls, embarrassed, yet unable to resist, because he would never know. He was handsome when he was asleep. Awake, he was too disturbing. She looked at his mouth and wondered how it would feel to be kissed. She didn't expect to marry because she had never had the social life her friends did. Helping Papa and her brothers with the paper seemed all she would ever do and most of the time she didn't want anything else, but sometimes she wondered about men. What was it like to dance and flirt and kiss? Hannah Lou loved men and loved to dance and flirt with them. Curious, Sophia reached out slowly and touched Major O'Brien's jaw, feeling the crisp stubble of his new beard.

Self-consciously she continued to let her fingers drift over his cheek, his hair. She drew a deep breath and stepped back, turning to leave the room.

The next day Mazie promised to look in on him every few minutes and when she couldn't, Henry would.

Greeting neighbors in their yards or on porches, Sophia walked the mile down Washington to Main Street to the small brick building that was the office of *The River Weekly*. Three doors from the office she saw Mrs. Ferguson and Mrs. Macon approach, a servant following, holding a parasol over their heads to shield them from the morning sun. Sophia walked faster. If only she could get to the office before they reached her.

"Sophia! Sophia Merrick!" Sophia heard Harriet Ferguson's shrill voice and removed the key from the door and turned reluctantly.

"We hear from Clairice Stanton that you have taken in our dear wounded. Now I hope you let Mazie and Uncle Henry tend those men."

"Yes, ma'am."

"Clairice said you went to the battlefield and you wore a Yankee uniform and picked up her precious Will and three other injured men. While it was fortunate for Will, that was highly improper, Sophia," she admonished.

"Yes, ma'am."

"If your brothers were here, even they wouldn't have approved of such conduct."

"Yes, ma'am," she said, accustomed to Harriet Ferguson's lectures.

"In spite of your unconventional upbringing, your father did teach you about right and wrong. Your father stood for all that is proper and tasteful and he preached and fought for temperance. I know you and your brothers are thoroughly taught about the evils of gambling and drink."

"Yes, ma'am," she replied politely.

"Those poor wounded boys at your house. Thank heavens you can trust our men to be gentlemen. The South's finest are fighting in this dreadful war."

"Yes, ma'am," she repeated. If Mrs. Ferguson spent three minutes with Major O'Brien she would revise her notion of gentlemen soldiers. "It's nice to see you both. You'll read about Will in the next issue of the paper."

"Sophia, it's scandalous for you to come down to this office and run the paper like a man!"

"Yes, ma'am, but I promised Papa I would keep the paper going and I'm the only one home to print the *Weekly* with my brothers away fighting. Good morning, ladies." She stepped inside and closed the door, thankful to escape.

She pulled on the leather apron and opened the case, her hands moving over the typefaces as she assembled the type into lines on a composing stick. The first story was an editorial about the dangers of the homemade brews beginning to take the place of regular whiskey. One good thing to come out of the blockade—whiskey is becoming as scarce as coffee, she thought.

Memphis was a river city and attracted all kinds of people from up and down the Mississippi. The saloons and gambling houses were in abundance. Her father had relentlessly preached against whiskey and cards and wrote about their evils in his paper. According to Papa, alcohol and a railroad had killed Grandpa Merrick who left a saloon and stumbled onto the tracks and passed out. Before dawn he was hit by the train.

She glanced around, thinking about Papa and her brothers. It was quiet and empty in the offices that used to be filled with her father's deep voice and John's even deeper voice while Amos and Morris were often in heated arguments. She could see Amos's thick golden hair as he bent over the press, hear John lecturing him on waste. John was the most frugal and most particular of all of them, even Papa. Brown-haired, handsome with blue eyes, John couldn't bear to see a scrap of paper go to waste. She gazed out the window at the busy office of a cotton factor across the street. Cotton prices were soaring as the crop became more scarce. She missed her brothers badly.

In the middle of the day she left to call on two businesses that placed ads in her paper. Miss Perdue's Dress Shop and Allardice's Regimental Badges took ads for the next month.

By the time she returned home, she had missed Dr. Perkins. Sophia looked in at Major O'Brien who was asleep. When she went upstairs, she met Lieutenant Landerson in the hallway. To her surprise he was dressed and carrying a small bundle, hobbling along with the aid of a cane. "Should you be up and around?"

"Yes, ma'am," he said, smoothing his straight black hair above his forehead. "Doctor Perkins said I can go home to my wife for a time and then I'll rejoin my regiment. He's written a letter for me."

"That's wonderful," she said, thinking about her brothers. "I'm sorry you're hurt. I didn't mean that—"

He smiled. "I know what you meant, and it was almost worth getting shot to get to go home. Even for a short time." His smile faded and he frowned. "The war is going to be long."

"Do you think so?" she asked, surprised. "Most people expected fighting to end in a few more months."

"That's what anyone would say who fought near Shiloh Church. I didn't think Bluecoats would fight like that." His features softened as he smiled. "Miss Merrick, thank you for all you've done for me."

"You're welcome. I didn't do anything except give you a roof over your head. I hope someone will do the same for my brothers."

"I'm sure they will. I'll be going. Henry said to stop by the kitchen and they'd have a bag of food for me to carry along."

"You do that. Are you going on foot?"

"Only as far as the train depot. Doctor Perkins said there will be a supply train through here later, and I can catch it to Vicksburg."

"I'll tell Henry to take you to the depot in the carriage."

"Thank you, Miss Merrick, and thank you for all your care. I hope your brothers are home soon."

She watched him go down the stairs and felt a twinge of hurt for him and for her brothers, saying a prayer that they were all right and would come home to her.

She went to look at Sergeant Mulligan and saw he was asleep. She moved beside the bed and looked down at him, straightening the covers, brushing his brown hair away from his broad face. Why could she touch him without feeling as if she were picking up a burning stick, the reaction she had to Major O'Brien? Sergeant Mulligan's home was Baton Rouge, Louisiana, and he wrote his parents daily; Sophia posted the letters for him. Too soon he would be well enough to go back to battle.

That night she sat down in the rocker and leaned back. Major O'Brien had slept all evening, and she wondered if he were slipping back into unconsciousness. With one small lamp burning, she rocked lightly, watching him.

Hours later she opened her eyes to find him struggling to sit up.

"If you want a drink, I'll get it for you," she said, coming to her feet and reaching for the cup of water.

"Help me sit up. I want to get up."

"Doctor Perkins said you won't be able to get out of bed for another week—" she said.

"Dammit, help me up. I'll be as weak as a kitten."

She doubted he would be that weak even as close to death as he had been. She placed the cup on the table and moved beside the bed to pull him up, blushing as she grasped his bare body and tugged. He made a sharp intake of breath and grunted.

"You hurt. Why don't you be still?" she asked.

"I won't have a muscle left if I don't move." He held her shoulder with his good hand until he sat up and she propped pillows behind him. He groaned as he shifted and closed his eyes.

"Lord, I feel as if I'm made of jelly."

"Doctor Perkins will be shocked tomorrow. You're a stubborn man, Major," she said, intensely aware of his bare chest, the sheet that rode dangerously low around his hips. He shifted and looked at her.

"I have a call of nature. Help me get to my feet, so I can get to the privy."

"I'll get Henry. He takes care of you when—" She stopped and blushed.

"Who's Henry? Your husband?"

"Heaven's no! I'm not married," she blurted. "Henry's a servant. He's been with our family since Papa was a boy."

"Just help me get to my feet," he insisted.

"I don't think you should until—" He gave her a glaring look that made her bite off her words.

"If you'll move my legs off the bed, I can get up."

"You may start your wound bleeding again."

"Miss—?"

"Merrick."

"Will you help me?" he asked, exasperated.

She took a deep breath and pushed the sheet off his feet, taking care to keep his middle covered. "Sir," she said, her face on fire, "you're not wearing anything. Let me get you a shirt."

"Damned if I know why they put wounded soldiers with maiden ladies. A shirt isn't going to cover what you want covered," he said, his voice sounding stronger with every sentence. "And I can't get into a shirt with my bad arm."

"You're with a maiden lady, because I'm the only person who'll have you!" she snapped. "I'm getting Henry." She fled the room.

"Miss Merrick! Dammit."

She hurried down the hall and into the cool night air to the second cabin behind the house. "Why do I have to have a man who is stubborn and ungentlemanly? Major O'Brien is a rogue, a mule, a varmint, a—" She rushed to the door of the cabin. She knocked and waited.

"Yes'm, Miss Sophia," Henry said, thrusting his head around the door that was open only a fraction. "Something happened?"

"Henry, Major O'Brien is conscious and wants help. You have to come."

"Yes'm. I'll be right there." The door closed, and she descended the steps. Feeling relieved she crossed the yard, the grass rustling against her slippers. Light spilled from the downstairs bedroom and the window was thrown high. As she walked toward the house, she could see Major O'Brien sitting on the side of the bed. She had seen his body before, and it never failed to make her burn with embarrassment. Now as he sat on the bed in the lighted room, she couldn't take her eyes off him. His good arm was tight with muscle, his chest covered in dark thick curls. He must have gone without his shirt often, because his skin was paler below his waist. It made a heat kindle low within her to look at him and she knew she shouldn't, yet she couldn't pull her gaze away from his strong body.

As she watched, he held the bedpost and stood up, the sheet clutched in front of him in one hand. She felt rooted to the ground. With her face burning, her gaze drifted down over his body, to his slender hips, his round, firm buttocks. He swayed and fell.

She gasped and ran for the house, racing down the hall, wondering how badly he was hurt. She rushed into the room as he straightened and turned. On his feet again, he was naked except for his bandages. His lean body was trimmed to slabs of hard muscle; the mat of brown curls on his chest tapered down in a narrow line over his flat stomach. Her gaze swept down the length of him and up.

"Oh! I thought you fell!"

He yanked the sheet in front of him and wrapped it around himself awkwardly with one hand. "I did fall. Sorry if I gave you a shock, but I guess if you've been nursing me, you're accustomed to this."

She wasn't accustomed to anything about him. And it was bad enough when he was unconscious in bed. Standing facing her, completely naked, he was a fiery jolt to her system. Why did he disturb her so? The other two wounded men didn't. She could talk to them, bathe their wounds without a qualm, but they wore clothes; one was married, and she felt as if she were with her brothers when she was with them. Major O'Brien, on the other hand, made her self-conscious and acutely aware of him.

"Come help me take a few steps and then you can leave me alone. I want to get to the washstand."

"Henry is coming," she said, her voice sounding breathless, her cheeks still feeling on fire.

"Dammit, come here. All I want is support. I can't stand much longer. My head is spinning like water in a whirlpool."

"Well, then you should be back in bed." She crossed the room to him and moved to his side, sliding her arm around his waist, feeling his warm flesh beneath the sheet, images of moments before still swirling in her thoughts. He draped his arm across her shoulders.

"I don't think you should do this, Major O'Brien."

"You might be right," he said in a tight voice. "Keep

going. We're almost there, and get Henry in here quickly. Thank God there's another man on the place."

She clamped her lips together and glanced up at him. A muscle worked in his jaw and her anger and embarrassment fled. "You hurt don't you?"

"More than I would have known possible. If I faint, just cover me. You can't lift me back into bed and Henry can't either if he's been with your family since your father was a boy."

Henry entered the room. "Miss Sophia, I can help him."

She relinquished her task with relief. "Call me, Henry, if you need me."

She left the room, remembering in vivid detail walking in on Major O'Brien. She moved to the back parlor and sat down to wait, hearing the major's deep voice and Henry's raspy one as they talked. Finally it became quiet and she moved to the doorway to see Henry approach.

"How is he?"

"He's asleep. Major's a tough man. Doc Perkins said he's mule tough and he is. He's going to make it now. Mule tough."

"Thank you, Henry."

"Yes'm. You want me to stay with him tonight?"

"No, you don't need to stay," she said, knowing how frail Henry was. "Thank you for your help."

"Yes'm." He left and closed the door quietly. She moved back to the major's room. One small lamp still burned, and she crossed the room to stand beside the bed and look at him. His color was normal and his breathing was regular. She checked his bandages and saw no signs of bleeding. Mule tough was right. And bold. Too bold. And handsome. She smoothed his curls back from his forehead. Was he married? she wondered.

She started to leave the room to go to her room, but she glanced back at the bed and could see him half in moonlight, half in shadows. He hadn't abandoned Will, and she shouldn't abandon him.

With a sigh she turned back. As long as he was unconscious or asleep, it was easier to have kind feelings toward him. She sat down in the rocker, pushing gently with her toes, rocking herself to sleep.

She stirred and moved, stretching cramped muscles, warmed by sunshine spilling through the window. She looked into green eyes. Major O'Brien was propped up in bed, gazing at her with a steady look.

"Oh!" she exclaimed, sitting up and feeling foolish, wondering how long he had been watching her.

"Have you slept there every night?" he asked.

"Yes," she answered, closing her wrapper and retying the belt. "You're hurt the worst of any of my patients. Doctor Perkins wasn't sure at first that you would make it."

"Do you have family?"

"My brothers are all fighting in the war. My parents are deceased."

"You have help besides Henry?"

"Mazie cooks for us."

"You don't have any family here?"

"No, not with my brothers gone. But they'll be back."

"How old are you?" he asked, studying her.

She studied him in return and wondered if he knew her age if she would get ordered around even more by him. She sat up straighter. "How old are you, sir?"

"Twenty-two."

"Well, I'm twenty-two, too." He was five years older— the same age as her oldest brother John. Major O'Brien looked a man, not a boy.

"You were spying for the Confederacy?"

"Yes," she answered. "I keep my father's newspaper going. My brothers will come home and run it, but I'll keep *The River Weekly* in circulation until they do. I knew there were Federals camped near Pittsburg Landing on the Tennessee River. I wanted to see what their camp life is like, what news I could gather for my paper."

"You picked a hell of a time to visit an army camp."

"The Union army has been there since the eleventh of March. I'd been to their camp once before and rode back home with news and the trip was uneventful. They didn't expect the attack, so I had no way of knowing about it. I heard a soldier say General Grant wired President Lincoln there would be no attack by the Confederates."

"No one noticed you were a woman?" he asked in a skeptical voice.

"Not the first time," she said, blushing and feeling his disapproval in his question. "A soldier noticed this time and I was running from him when the fighting started. When I met you, I was trying to find my way out of the area to go home."

He leaned his head against the headboard. "You shouldn't go to an army camp. You don't belong on a battlefield and if your father or mother were alive, they wouldn't want you to take terrible risks. You could have been shot," he admonished.

"My mother's been gone since I was small, and I think my father would be pleased. He always said the most important thing was to do one's duty. He said we were put on earth to work."

"Doesn't sound as if he had much fun," he said.

"I'm sure Papa's ideas of fun and yours, Major, were vastly different," she said, annoyed with him, thinking how much more pleasant it was when he was asleep. "It won't be long until the Yankees are whipped and life returns to normal."

Major O'Brien gazed at her. "If the Yankees fight like they did at Shiloh, it'll be a hell of a long time before they're whipped."

"Everyone says we'll outfight them," she said, thinking about reports she had heard of the thousands of injuries in the battle.

"Everyone? Men from battle?"

"Townsfolk think it'll be over soon, but Lieutenant Landerson said the same thing you did."

"Landerson?"

"One of the wounded who stayed here. He's gone home now."

"Have you heard reports of the number killed?"

"I thought they were exaggerated. They say we have over ten thousand killed, wounded, or missing. I've heard Federal losses are worse. They're saying almost twenty-four thousand men between the two armies."

"Lord. I believe the numbers."

"If that's true . . ." Her voice trailed away as she thought about her brothers.

"It's going to be a hell of a war."

"All those missing—they don't know the names of so many of the dead." She walked toward the door. "I'll get you some broth. You've barely eaten for days."

He shook his head and leaned back, closing his eyes. "I'm not hungry."

"You have to eat something." She hurried from the room and dressed in a brown muslin with short puff sleeves. Pausing in front of the mirror as she wound her braid of hair around her head, she studied herself. Papa told her it was vain to think about dresses and how she looked and next to Hannah Lou, she felt like a plain brown sparrow beside a beautiful red cardinal. Don't start worrying about appearance because of the major, she said to herself. With a shrug she went downstairs.

Later, she carried a tray with a bowl of broth and a glass of water to her patient's room. Propping up Major O'Brien, she held the bowl as he took the spoon from her.

He tried to spoon the broth with his left hand, spilling most of the liquid. Standing next to the bed, she took the spoon from his hand. "Let me do that, Major."

He nodded and she dipped the spoon into the hot yellow chicken broth and reached out to feed it to him. He patted the bed. "It'll be easier if you sit here. I know you have before."

Disconcerted, she climbed up and sat beside him to feed him. "Who is Amity?" she asked casually.

His gaze shifted to her. "Have I talked about Amity?"

"Yes, you have," she said, embarrassed by his close scrutiny.

"She's a friend. She's my sister-in-law's younger sister. Amity Therrie from New Orleans."

Sophia nodded. It was ridiculous to feel relieved that he didn't answer, "My wife."

"Who's Desirée?" Again she affected a casual tone.

He slanted her a look. "She's a friend in New Orleans. Why?"

"You've mentioned them. I didn't know if one was a wife—"

"No wife, Miss Merrick," he said, sounding amused. She felt flustered, wishing now she hadn't asked. "I'm not a marrying man. You said you don't have a husband. Do you have a beau in the Confederacy?"

"No, I don't."

Major O'Brien leaned back against the pillows and watched as she set the bowl on a table. She turned back and paused. Dr. Perkins had taught her how to change the dressings on the major's wounds, and she did so every morning and then Henry bathed him. This was the first morning the major had been conscious and alert and she dreaded working on him. She shifted the empty bowl on the tray and then picked up the tray.

"I'll be back," she called over her shoulder. She hurried down the hall, postponing the task a few more minutes.

"How's Major O'Brien?" Mazie asked when Sophia entered the high-ceilinged kitchen with its new iron stove Papa had bought before he became ill. Smells of chicken soup and hot bread filled the warm air.

"He's better. He ate most of the broth." If only Mazie could change the dressings, but that was out of the question. Henry was shaky and would have to be taught how and by that time, she might as well do it herself.

"That Sergeant Mulligan came down here to eat breakfast. He said he didn't want to leave my cooking. He asked me if you're promised to anyone, Miss Sophia." Mazie grinned, placing her hands on her bony hips, her dark eyes sparkling. "I think you could have a beau if you wanted, long as I feed the man."

"Don't be ridiculous, Mazie. He's just trying to compliment you on your cooking."

"He's in no hurry to leave here. He gets around as good as I do. You need a beau, Miss Sophia."

"You know I don't need one in wartime, and Papa would never approve."

"Course Mister Merrick would approve. He married your mama and he'd expect you to marry."

What kind of man would have won Papa's approval?

she wondered. And Papa never talked as if he expected her to wed. "Sergeant Mulligan's wound is in his shoulder, so that shouldn't keep him from getting around. And your cooking is the best in the South."

"Thank you, Miss Sophia, but you don't know anyone else's," Mazie said, turning to the stove. Sophia noticed the strands of gray in Mazie's hair were more numerous now. Both servants were getting older, and they were as much a part of her life as her family.

Sophia left the room, her thoughts on Major O'Brien. She stared at his open door and squared her shoulders. If only he would fall soundly asleep. She tiptoed to the door and peered inside. He lay sprawled on the bed, one leg half out from beneath the covers, an arm flung across the pillows, his eyes closed.

He had been sleeping through everything, but his moments of wakefulness and his alertness were increasing rapidly. She placed clean bandages on the bed and glanced at him. His chest rose and fell evenly. She moved the sheet gingerly, pushing it up to cover his body and leave his thigh bare. She remembered with total clarity his naked body, the bulge of muscles, the trimness of his waist and hips, the dark line of hair across his flat belly to his manhood. He shifted and moved his head, his eyes opening.

"I need to dress your wound. I do this every morning," she said in what she hoped was a brisk tone. Her face was on fire, and she didn't glance at him as she moved the sheet. He reached down to take the sheet from her and finish the job, bunching it over his groin.

"I'm sorry if I hurt you," she said and glanced up at him. She was doing all right until she met his gaze. He looked amused, curious, far too alert.

She bent over her task, aware of his thigh, his bare hip that showed because the sheet was pulled high. She peeled away the old bandage, her fingers brushing his thigh, touches that she was too aware of, touches that disconcerted her, stirring a peculiar warmth in her.

"You're twenty-two and unmarried and don't have a beau. I find that difficult to believe, Miss Merrick."

His observation wasn't helping. "I haven't had time for

society. I've always helped Papa and my brothers with the paper."

"Night and day?" he asked, shocked.

She gazed at the wound that was still draining, but it was clean and didn't have a foul odor. It looked offensive in flesh that was so fit and healthy. Dr. Perkins said she would know if the wound started to putrefy. She had to clean around the wound and heard Major O'Brien's sharp intake of breath.

"I'm sorry," she said. He nodded, propping his arm beneath his head to watch her.

"I'm busier than ever now. *The River Weekly* was eight pages when Papa and my brothers were home. Now it's down to four pages."

"Have you heard any war news?"

"Yes. Nathan Forrest was wounded at Shiloh, but he'll survive. Island Number Ten fell to the Union eight days ago."

"The Yankees want the Mississippi River. They're moving down from Cairo and up from the south. It's only a matter of time until they attack Fort St. Phillip and Fort Jackson below New Orleans."

"There's talk Memphis will be attacked. Some people are leaving town. The state capital and Governor Isham Harris moved here after the fall of Nashville in February. They stayed until late March and then went to Mississippi," she said.

"What about you, Miss Merrick?"

"I'll never leave. This is home and our paper is here." Finished, she reached for the sheet, pulling it down over his legs. "Now if you'll sit up, I can get to your shoulder." She grasped him, helping him to lean forward and then sit up straight. His face only inches from her, she worked in silence, feeling as if his eyes were penetrating her the whole time.

"In March there were threats that people would burn Memphis rather than let it fall into Union hands, so General Bragg suspended municipal government. We have martial law."

"Do you ever have fun?"

"Of course, I do."

"Do you like to dance?" His voice was mellow and deep; they were inches apart, her hands moving over his shoulder and chest, and she felt prickles of awareness.

"Papa always said dancing was frivolous and improper, so I don't know how." She glanced into green eyes that stared back with open curiosity. She peeled away the bandage on his shoulder and saw his flesh was beginning to heal. When she glanced at him, his mouth was clamped shut.

"I'm sorry. I know this hurts."

"Don't apologize. I thought Southern ladies learned to dance soon after they learned to walk. And learned to flirt by the time they were five years old."

"I don't know much about either." She felt uneasy and annoyed. She couldn't be more aware of him if he were a ferocious tiger she had to tend. Only he was no furry animal. He was a man, becoming stronger and healthier by the day, too bold and brash and curious.

While she sponged around the wound, she looked at him. He was only inches away, and his continual direct stare was like a touch on raw nerves.

She should have admitted she was only seventeen, but she suspected it would be better if he thought she was his age or close to it. He had freckles across his broad shoulders and his arms bulged with hard muscles, a masculine body that lingered in her thoughts and disturbed her dreams.

"Raise your arm and you can hold this bandage in place while I wrap it," she instructed.

"Where do I hold the bandage?"

"Here," she said, taking his left hand and placing it against the pad of bandages she put over the wound, noticing the warmth of his hand, the rough texture of his fingers. "You have scars."

"I grew up on a farm and I've been in fights. You don't like me, do you?" His eyes danced with mischief, and she blushed, feeling annoyed.

"We didn't meet under the best of circumstances."

He arched a brow. "You know what I think about a woman at an army camp."

"You wouldn't be alive today otherwise," she rejoined.

He caught her chin with his fingers, and her heart thudded as she met a piercing gaze. "I make you blush," he said softly. "I annoy you, but I don't scare you, do I?"

"Of course not!" she snapped, her heart thudding. He scared and embarrassed her and always—whatever the tug between them—there was an invisible, raw challenge that made her defy him. He pushed her over an edge of control no one else had ever done, and she couldn't understand her reactions to him.

"I find you too bold, too vulgar, and too arrogant!" she said with conviction.

He chuckled and leaned back. Provoked, she slapped the bandage on his shoulder.

"Ow! Dammit."

She tried to slide off the bed quickly, but he caught her, his fingers wrapping around her upper arm. They glared at each other, both breathing hard. His gaze slid to her mouth and she felt as if she couldn't get her breath. Time stopped, and she was immobile, waiting. His gaze flicked up to meet hers again, and she felt his anger. She shouldn't have hurt him like that, but she wasn't going to apologize. She jerked away, aware she couldn't have if he hadn't wanted to release her.

"Why did you take me in?"

"Mrs. Stanton made me," she said bluntly. "Otherwise, I wouldn't have."

"So why have you spent your nights in here?" he persisted. "Mrs. Stanton didn't make you do that?"

"I'm doing it because you saved Will. His sister is my closest friend."

"Are you and Will in love?"

"Heavens, no!"

He smiled faintly. "Why is that such a shocking question? Haven't you ever been in love, Miss Merrick?"

"Sir, you are forward and brash—"

"Don't forget arrogant," he said, settling back in bed and leaning against the pillows while she gathered up the discarded bandages.

Caleb shifted, studying her, noticing the faint flush still in her cheeks. She was as skittish as a new colt. And a novelty. She was dressed as plain as a guinea hen, but every time the thought came of maiden lady or stiff-necked spinster, he would glance into her deep blue eyes, thickly fringed with brown lashes and his thoughts about a spinster vanished. Or when he looked at her mouth. It was full, curved and rosy, an invitation, except she was too prim for his liking. She would be as much fun to kiss as a board, and he had never kissed an unwilling partner and he wasn't going to start with someone as straitlaced as Sophia Merrick. She wasn't going to forgive him for yelling at her on the battlefield either.

As she moved around the bed, his gaze swept over her. The pale brown muslin did nothing for her, yet it was stretched tautly over full breasts and tucked into a tiny waist. She met his gaze, and looked away quickly. He had yet to see her smile. What would make her laugh? he thought. What kind of father and brothers would raise her to be so solemn and conscientious? Lord knows, his father had known how to have fun and never hesitated to enjoy his good times with his sons. He remembered the whiskey his father had brewed in the barn and shared with his sons, making them all promise they wouldn't breathe a word about it to their mother. And the country dances—he had been only sixteen when they left Ireland, but he had known how to dance and kiss and he had been in love with Megan Pattison, even though it had been nothing more than the first crush of a young boy. He felt a rush of pity for Sophia Merrick. It passed swiftly as the longing came to get back to New Orleans, to the only family he knew.

"I sent a letter home yesterday by Henry."

Her brows arched. "He didn't tell me. I know your family will be relieved to hear from you. I haven't heard from my brothers for weeks now. They're fighting with General Lee and General Jackson."

"I hope it's not as bad as the battle we just fought."

"My brothers couldn't wait to get into battle. And they wanted to fight under Lee's command, except Amos and his friends ended up with General Jackson. Papa was alive when they left. He got pneumonia after they were gone and it was the end of him."

"I'm surprised one of your brothers didn't come back

to stay with you," Caleb said, studying her again, realizing she wasn't like any Southern women he had known, from the fallen women to the sheltered society belles like his sister-in-law. Chantal was feisty and unpredictable, but she flirted, and was aware of her beauty and ready for fun. Sophia Merrick just didn't know the meaning of fun, he concluded. And it was a wonder she hadn't fainted when she walked in on him when he was naked, he thought with relief.

"They were needed. Amos was coming back, but he was in a battle and later, when I received his letter, he said he would get here when he could. By that time, I wrote him to stay and fight, because I was managing just fine here. They know I have Henry and Mazie."

"Two elderly slaves."

"Oh, no. Papa didn't believe in slavery. I pay them to work for us."

"I'm surprised your friends approve of that," he said.

She shrugged, moving closer to the bed to place the armload of rags in a basket. "The townspeople accept us. I know they talk and said Papa was eccentric—the ones who weren't his friends and didn't share his beliefs, but he'd helped a lot of people and so some folks are friendly. I don't get invitations to parties and neither did my brothers, but Papa wouldn't have let us go anyway, so it doesn't matter. I have friends."

The town eccentric. Only it was a whole family of them. He felt another rush of pity for her. She had missed a lot of fun in life.

"You look as if you feel sorry for me. My life is fine. I run the family paper for my brothers and when this war ends, they'll come home and take over again."

"Tell me again the name of the paper?"

"*The River Weekly.* Papa started it and it's dedicated to building a strong Memphis, a city for families and law-abiding citizens."

He felt exhaustion sweep over him, hating to be hurt and weak, impatient with his wounds. He sighed, feeling as if it were a major effort to keep his eyes open. "Thanks for what you've done. I don't know how you got us back to Memphis."

"I couldn't have if you hadn't loaded Will into the wagon."

"You would have found a way, Miss Merrick."

He closed his eyes and Sophia stared at him, feeling a mixture of emotions. He annoyed her, and she felt certain there were times when he pitied her. He teased and stared and looked at her at moments as if he were imagining her stark naked. Yet he was brave and kindhearted or he wouldn't have risked his own life to save Will's. There were moments she felt his disapproval for going to the Union army camp, yet his last words left her wondering what he did think of her. Leaving the room, she paused to look back at the sleeping soldier, knowing she would never again glance at John's high rosewood bed without remembering Major O'Brien in it.

The next day she stopped first at the Stanton house on Adams and then she went to the newspaper office. She tied bundles of papers together for delivery by Henry and the young boys who had worked for her father. Some customers stopped at the store to purchase a paper or exchange a chicken or corn for a copy.

At the end of the day she wrote a story about her moments at the battlefield, and the courage of Will Stanton and Major O'Brien. It was late and dark by the time she went home with the latest edition of *The River Weekly* beneath her arm.

She paused in the doorway to look at Major O'Brien. He was sitting up, propped against the pillows, his chest bare except for the bandage around his shoulder. "They said you were getting out the paper."

"Yes," she said, waving a copy. "If you'd like, you may read it. If you'll tell me about the battle, I think Memphians would be interested in a firsthand account."

She handed him a paper and moved the lamp on the table closer to the bed, going around the bed to light another lamp.

"Are there any other papers in Memphis?"

"Heavens, yes! This is one of the smallest. Mister McClanahan joined Henry Van Pelt who founded *The Appeal* before I was born. Then Benjamin Dill became part owner and publisher. *The Appeal* is the advocate of the Democratic party. The Know-Nothing's have their *Eagle and Enquirer.* The German immigrants have had several papers. We have the *Argus,* the *Bulletin,* and the *Avalanche.*"

"What do you charge for advertising?" he asked.

"Thirty cents per line for inside advertisements and forty cents per line for advertisements on outside pages."

"It's only a matter of time until the Federals try to take Memphis. This is the main city on the river between Vicksburg and St. Louis. Do you have an active militia?"

"Most of the men who want to be involved in the war have gone to fight."

As she moved around the room, he rattled the paper. He glanced at her over the top of it. "You wrote this about the River Queen Saloon selling their own brew? You don't approve of whiskey and saloons?"

"No, I don't." No doubt he heartily approved of them. "Papa's life was dedicated to cleaning up the city and ridding Memphis of the scourges of evil. Other newspaper editors agree with him on temperance."

One corner of Major O'Brien's mouth lifted in a lopsided grin. "The scourges of evil. Miss Merrick, have you ever seen the inside of a saloon or tasted whiskey?"

"Certainly not! You know nice women aren't allowed in saloons," she admonished.

"Some of my best moments have been spent in saloons."

"That doesn't come as a surprise. Papa was dedicated to fighting gambling and drinking and sin, and he instilled that in all of us in childhood. Drink caused my grandfather's death."

"Sorry, but enjoying a drink of good whiskey doesn't mean you're going to drink yourself to death."

"Oh, no. Grandpa Merrick left a saloon and passed out on the railroad tracks. A train hit him," she said, shaking her head.

Caleb studied her. He might have guessed. A prudish maiden lady would save him. Too bad she hadn't been a camp follower—as soon as he mended a bit more, he would have to have some fun.

"A lot of townspeople take your paper?"

"Enough. Not a great number."

"I can imagine." She was getting sparks in her eyes, and he could see a lecture coming, so he raised the paper in front of his face. She had probably been raised all her life to live by her father's beliefs, just as he had been raised to enjoy a drink and a game of chance. He lowered the paper a fraction and watched her fold a blanket. Today she wore a simple blue muslin dress and he doubted if she had ever owned anything silk or satin.

"You're fighting an impossible tide."

She faced him. "Perhaps and perhaps not. Papa said there was a time in the summer of eighteen thirty-five when Vicksburg hanged its gamblers."

"That was before you and I were born. Gamblers flourish there today. And in every river city I've visited. I have firsthand proof."

"Well, it happened, and during that year the people of Memphis threatened to do the same here. The gamblers all left town or abandoned the pastime. Papa always said that day would come again."

"Did your Papa tell you how long the gamblers were gone?"

"No, I don't recall."

"If you think you'll run gamblers out of Memphis now—I'll make you a small wager on it."

Sophia knew he was teasing, because he had a faint smile, but her annoyance increased. "You know I won't wager on anything."

"What do you do for fun?" he asked playfully.

She blinked and stared at him and his brows arched. "I'll be damned. You really don't know how to have fun at all."

"Yes, I do. Right now with my brothers gone, I'm busy. I have fun. And I don't have to gamble! Gamblers heap misery on their families," she insisted.

"I'll grant you on occasion they do—that's what happened to the O'Briens. Pa gambled away our home, our land, and our livelihood."

"How dreadful!" she exclaimed, staring at him and wondering what kind of man he was. His father had lost everything gambling, yet obviously the major still enjoyed games of chance.

His chest rose and fell as he took a deep breath. His lean, dark body looked incongruous propped in the white bed with frilly covers. "My brother and I have acquired a fair amount of capital through gambling—so maybe we've evened it out for the O'Briens. Another reason to disapprove of me."

"I can forgive you a great deal because of what you did for Will."

"That's magnanimous of you, Miss Merrick," he said solemnly and again she felt he was teasing and noted the tension crackling between them as they argued.

"I'll be back shortly with your supper."

She heard a deep chuckle as she left the room. No doubt Major O'Brien was a whiskey-drinking, card-playing man who would delight in saloons and fast women.

Three days later as Sophia sat in the front parlor at the wide desk, she gazed out the window and watched a carriage slow and stop. A boy jumped out and a woman emerged behind him. She held his arm as they looked at the house, and then opened the gate to come up the walk.

Curious, Sophia stood up and went to the door. She glanced out the window and saw a pretty woman with large, black eyes and black hair. The boy had black hair and deep blue eyes. They knocked and Sophia opened the door wide.

"Good afternoon, ma'am," the woman said in a soft voice. "I'm Amity Therrie from New Orleans and this is Darcy O'Brien, Caleb's younger brother. We hear you're caring for the major."

Chapter 4

"I'm Sophia Merrick and please come in," she said, feeling awed by Amity Therrie's beauty. Her cheeks were pink; her satin bonnet was tied with a silk bow beneath her chin, and her mauve silk dress was cut in a fashionable style with full bishop sleeves. A black Chantilly lace shawl was thrown around her shoulders. One look at Amity Therrie and it was difficult to remember there was a war and goods were becoming scarce. "The major is down the hall."

"We aren't disturbing you?"

"No, not at all," Sophia said, motioning them inside the house and closing the door. With his black hair and blue eyes, Darcy O'Brien didn't bear much resemblance to his older brother.

"How is he?" Amity asked.

"He gets better every day." Sophia glanced down at the boy who was peering down the hall. "You can see him." Leading the way to his room, Sophia rapped lightly on the door frame and Caleb opened his eyes, turning his head.

"You have company," she said, ushering them into the room.

"Caleb!" Amity exclaimed and hurried across the room, her silk skirt and petticoats rustling, Darcy trailing behind her. She bent over the bed and Major O'Brien wrapped his arm around her to hug her as casually as if he were receiving guests at a party instead of lying naked as an egg beneath a few covers.

"Amity! Darcy!" he said, his deep voice changing to a tender note. He smiled, and Sophia felt a tingle of reaction to the warmth of it. Creases framed his mouth and his white teeth showed, making him more handsome than ever with a smile that was as affectionate as a hug. She felt a wave of longing as she watched him welcome them. Darcy received the next hug, and then they shifted and Major O'Brien pulled Amity Therrie close to the bed again. She stood beside him as he scooted up, tucking the covers around his hips while he squeezed Darcy's hand. He looked as if he couldn't let go of either one of them.

Feeling an intruder, Sophia slipped out of the room to leave them alone. She sent Mazie in with tea, brewed from the last they owned or could get now because of the blockade. Then Sophia went about her household tasks, aware of time passing, hearing Amity's silken laughter mix with Major O'Brien's deep chortles and she realized she hadn't ever heard a hearty laugh from him.

Another knock sounded and when Sophia opened the door, Hannah Lou stood at the threshold. Beside her was Will who was bundled onto a chaise longue. Four servants stood beside the longue, and she realized they had carried him to her house.

"Will Stanton!" She grasped his hand.

"Sophia," he said, taking her hand, "how can I ever thank you?"

"Just get well," she said, giving his hand a squeeze.

"I will, thanks to you and Caleb. And I know he was on the verge of losing consciousness when we left Pittsburg Landing. How is he?"

"He's going to be all right," she said, thinking Major O'Brien looked far better than Will whose skin was pale as snow and who looked as if he had lost too much weight, his skin pulled tautly over his broad cheekbones.

"I get word from Doctor Perkins about Caleb every day. I know you've been to the house, Sophia, but they won't wake me for guests. We brought a tiny token of our gratitude."

"Oh, my goodness!" she exclaimed, looking at two servants who stood with platters of ham and turkey and candied yams. Hannah Lou extended a jar to Sophia.

"This is for you and the men, and Will wants to see Major O'Brien."

"Come inside. I can't take all this food," she exclaimed, knowing how scarce food was becoming.

"Of course, you'll take it or you'll have to answer to Mama," Will said good-naturedly.

"Thank y'all so much," she said. "Major O'Brien has visitors—his family from New Orleans is here. His sister-in-law's sister and his younger brother Darcy."

The servants picked up the chaise longue with care. Holding Hannah Lou's hand, Sophia hurried ahead. She knocked at the open bedroom door and stepped inside.

"Major, I'm sorry to interrupt, but Will is here." She and Hannah Lou stepped aside as the servants carried Will into the room.

As Amity stood up and pulled the rocker back to make room and Darcy moved to the foot of the bed, Sophia turned to Caleb. "Major, this is Hannah Lou Stanton, Will's sister. Hannah Lou, meet Major O'Brien."

"Miss Stanton." His attention shifted to Will who motioned to his servants.

"Hold me up," Will said, his voice cracking. The servants lifted the longue even with the bed and Will leaned forward as both men embraced clumsily. Sophia looked away, noticing Amity studying the floor and Hannah Lou wiping her eyes.

When Sophia looked at Major O'Brien, she felt a tug on her heart because his eyes were filled with tears. Remembering the dreadful moments in the barn, she marveled that both men survived.

"I had to come see you," Will said. "I don't want to interrupt you and your family."

"Amity, this is Miss Stanton, Will's sister, and Captain Will Stanton. Miss Stanton and Will, this is Miss Therrie from New Orleans, and Darcy O'Brien, my younger brother."

"Glad to meet you both," Amity said while Darcy smiled and the women sat down, Amity on the right side of the bed, Hannah Lou on the left near Will.

"I'm so happy to meet you," Hannah Lou said in return, her attention returning to Major O'Brien as she gave him a smile. "Major, we can't ever thank you enough for taking such good care of my brother and bringing him home to us. You saved his life."

"Caleb, you didn't write me about that!" Amity exclaimed while Sophia looked at him. She was startled to see the sparkle in his eyes as he gazed at Amity, and Sophia felt a peculiar twist. She shouldn't care if he were engaged to Amity Therrie. His gaze shifted to Darcy and the sparkle remained, so the sparkle wasn't just for Amity Therrie.

"You saved my leg," Will said. "Doctor Perkins said I'm not going to lose it if he can help it."

"I didn't lose mine either. Darcy," he said, his voice changing again, and she wondered if a woman had ever brought that tone to his voice. Probably Amity and Desirée and a dozen others caused him to speak in such a mellow manner. "Come sit down here," he said, patting a place beside him on the bed. The boy climbed up and as Major O'Brien and Will talked, the major kept his hand on Darcy's shoulder.

"I don't remember much of that night," Will said. "Don't want to remember much either. We took a beating at the battle."

"So did the Federals."

"How did you find us, Sophia? I don't remember anything," Will said, turning to look at her along with everyone else. She met Major O'Brien's amused gaze.

"I was in the barn where Major O'Brien took shelter. He asked me to help get you both to Memphis."

"She's the reason we're here today," Major O'Brien said quietly and everyone continued to look at her, but she couldn't pull her gaze from Major O'Brien's.

"She said she was from Memphis and when she discovered you were with me, Will, she promised to get us here and she did. Without my help. I was as unconscious as you."

"Sophia!" Will exclaimed. "I owe you more than I realized. Hannah Lou told me you brought us both home in a wagon, but I didn't know Caleb couldn't help."

"Of course, he helped. He lifted you into the wagon—I couldn't have," she said, blushing. "Does your mother still have as many soldiers to care for?" she asked, wanting to change the subject from herself.

"Actually, she has twenty-seven now."

"Doctor Perkins says Mama is doing a marvelous job," Hannah Lou said, "so we have more at the house now than before. Be thankful you have your own bed, Major O'Brien. If you'd stayed at our house, you'd probably be on a pallet on the floor, sharing a room with others."

"I'm thankful every day for the care I'm receiving," he said, and Sophia blushed again, wondering if he were teasing her or if he meant it.

"I'm sorry you're not at our house after all Will has told me about you," Hannah Lou said, batting her eyes. Sophia stared at her. Hannah Lou was flirting with him. If she knew what he was like—but then Hannah Lou would probably love his rough ways and his teasing.

"Caleb is very special," Amity said softly, smiling at him. "I can tell you that, Miss Stanton. I wish we could move you home, Caleb."

"I'll be there before you know it," he replied. "Where's Rafe?" he asked Darcy, glancing at Hannah Lou. "That's my older brother who married Amity's sister."

"He's supposed to be home in three weeks." Darcy fished beneath his coat and withdrew a white object. "Look what he brought me last time. It's a shark's tooth."

"Marvelous!" Caleb said, turning it in his hand and handing it to Will to view. "And how are the studies coming?" Will passed the tooth to Hannah Lou who handed it to Sophia. She turned the jagged tooth in her hand, thinking about life on the high seas because she had never been away from Memphis, never seen an ocean. When she looked up, she caught Major O'Brien watching her.

"I can answer for him," Amity said. "I'm teaching him French and Latin now. He's a very good student except when Rafferty is home from sailing. Then I have a reluctant pupil."

"I'll do better," Darcy said swiftly, and Caleb squeezed his shoulder and nodded.

"Have you heard the number of casualties from battle?" Will asked.

"I read the figure in Miss Merrick's paper and she told me over twenty thousand."

"Could you believe the Bluecoats would fight like that?"

"No. But we gave it right back to them. It's going to be a long struggle, Will. And Amity said Farragut has commenced shelling the forts below New Orleans."

"If they get New Orleans, they'll try to take Vicksburg next."

"Enough talk about war!" Hannah Lou said. "That's all we hear all the time now. The opera is closed. The river is blockaded. I don't want to hear another word about war."

"I'm beginning to wonder if Doctor Perkins will ever let me get up again."

"He will soon enough," Major O'Brien said as if he, too, was obediently following doctor's orders. She met his cool gaze again, and then looked at Will who was already appearing fatigued. Talk swirled around her, Hannah Lou and Amity Therrie constantly flirting with the major until Hannah Lou stood up.

"My brother's been away from home long enough for his first outing. Major, it has been delightful to meet the man Will has told me so much about."

"I hope what he said was good."

"At least half was," Will answered good-naturedly, but Sophia noticed he seemed to be making an effort to keep his eyes open. She stepped into the hall and when the servants carried the chaise out, Sophia followed them to the door.

As the servants started down the walk with Will, Hannah Lou lingered. "Major O'Brien is so handsome! You're lucky to have him here."

"I'd be glad to send him to your house."

"Oh, I wish we had room. Mama said not one more soldier under her roof. I'd spend the whole day with him if he were at our house. Doesn't he make your heart flutter?"

"Hannah Lou," Sophia said, amused, "he isn't the easiest patient."

"Maybe not, but he's the best-looking one I've seen. I better go. I'll come back tomorrow."

As Hannah Lou hurried down the front steps, Sophia closed the door. She gazed at the open bedroom door, hearing Major O'Brien's voice. She should ask Amity Therrie and Darcy O'Brien to stay as long as they want. Too bad she couldn't turn the care of Major O'Brien over to Miss Therrie, she thought. Hannah Lou and Amity Therrie flirted with him as naturally as sun shining in the morning. Sophia couldn't imagine batting her lashes at him and telling him how much she enjoyed caring for him.

Five days later as she said goodbye to Amity and Darcy, Major O'Brien stood beside her. He wore her brother's shirt and pants and he leaned against the doorjamb. He hugged Amity and Darcy.

"You're coming home soon?" Darcy asked.

"As soon as I can travel," he said, giving Darcy an awkward squeeze with his good arm.

"Hurry," he said. Standing beside Major O'Brien, Sophia watched until the Therrie carriage pulled out of sight.

"Too bad Doctor Perkins said you couldn't travel home with them," she said as she closed the door.

"Sorry, Miss Merrick, but you're stuck with me," he said, sounding angry. "I'm tempted to go anyway. I hate to be away from Darcy. I feel like he needs me."

"Miss Therrie seemed to truly care for him."

"She does, but Darcy's been shuffled around since he was eight years old. Rafe is gone a lot; I'm gone a good deal of the time. Darcy deserves a home and a settled family."

Anyone who had survived the wagon ride back to Memphis from the battle should survive a train trip to New Orleans, but Dr. Perkins had been firm about no traveling. And for once Major O'Brien listened to him. Sometimes she suspected the major was in more pain than he admitted.

"I've stood on this leg all I can," he said, looking at her. "Can you help me?"

She moved closer and placed her arm around his waist,

wondering if he stayed a year if she would still feel the same tingling reaction when she touched him. He draped his arm across her shoulder and leaned on her, inhaling deeply.

"You hurt, don't you?"

"Yes."

"Why do you push yourself? You didn't have to go to the door with them."

"I want to get well."

"You have the patience of a provoked snake."

He chuckled softly. The days he had been bare, she had been intensely aware of him, thinking once he was clothed, he wouldn't be as disturbing. Glancing up at him in her brother John's cambric shirt and too-large black trousers, Major O'Brien was as unsettling as ever.

"It's a warm day, and I want to get outside."

"We can go to the front porch or into the backyard where you can sit."

"The back," he answered and she helped him to a wooden chair carved by her father that was in the shade of a tall magnolia. Major O'Brien sank down in the chair and looked around. "You have a big yard."

"Papa bought this lot and half of the next one. That gives us space to raise chickens and have a root cellar."

He leaned his head back and closed his eyes.

"I'll be right back and I'm sure Mazie will hear if you call."

"Fine, Miss Merrick."

As she entered the hall, Henry approached. "Ma'am, Miss Stanton is here to see you and the major."

"He's outside," Sophia said, looking at Hannah Lou in surprise. Dressed in pale green silk, she looked as beautiful as Amity Therrie and she looked ready for a party. Her hair was shining, parted in the center with curls over each ear. A parasol was in her hand and a wide hat was perched on the back of her head and tied beneath her chin.

"My goodness, you're dressed today, Hannah Lou. Is someone having a party?"

"No. I just came to call. How is Major O'Brien?"

"The same as ever. He's mending," she added, leading

Hannah Lou outside and realizing the reason for Hannah Lou's fancy dress. He looked up as she came through the door.

"You have company, Major."

Receiving another surprise, she watched him get to his feet with only the slightest waver and one quick grimace. She stared at both of them in consternation as Hannah Lou rushed forward and held out a jar to him.

"Will and I wanted you to have some of Mama's special jam, Major O'Brien. She makes the best in the county."

"Thank you, Miss Stanton. I'm honored," he said, taking the jam and holding her hands a moment. "Sit down here," he said, moving to an iron bench. Hannah Lou perched on one end and he carefully sat down beside her, turning to face her. "Won't you join us?" he asked Sophia, looking up at her.

"I'll come back shortly. There are some things I need to tend to in the house."

"Sophia, you'll get an invitation," Hannah Lou said, "but Mama said to tell you. Auntie Eudora and Uncle Patrick are having a ball in May to raise funds for shoes for our soldiers. Everyone in town will be there and you're to come and bring Major O'Brien. We're taking the boys from our house."

"Hannah Lou, you know I don't go to parties."

"Botheration, Sophia! Mama said you have to come and to tell you that even your papa would have approved of this party. After all, it might help Amos and John and Morris."

Felling a pang, Sophia thought about them. She missed them dreadfully and prayed for their safety every day. "I'll think about it."

"And you have to come, too, Major. I really do insist. Maybe you'll be well enough to dance by then."

He laughed and his eyes sparkled. "I'll answer for both of us. If I'm still in Memphis, I'll get Miss Merrick there. We've earned a party."

"Good! Then it's settled."

Annoyed, Sophia stared at him. He constantly took

charge, and she wasn't certain she wanted to attend a party.

"Will said to tell you that he wants you to come see him as soon as you can get around."

"If you both will excuse me, I have some things to attend to," Sophia said, knowing Hannah Lou wanted Major O'Brien to herself. Hannah Lou had already captured all his attention.

"Sophia works constantly. I like a little fun in my life."

"What's fun, Miss Stanton?"

"I love parties and dancing, men who are fun," she said. As Sophia closed the door, she couldn't hear the rest of Hannah Lou's answer, but her tone of voice was coy and as Sophia glanced out the window, she saw the major and Hannah Lou laughing. Hannah Lou's hand was on his arm and she leaned close to him. Sophia felt a pang. *What's the matter with me?* I don't care if Hannah Lou touches him or kisses him or falls in love with him. Or if he does with her. Tightening her lips, Sophia turned away. In minutes Hannah Lou would let him steal a kiss.

Sophia returned to her desk to go over her household records and bookkeeping and soon she realized her mind was back on Major O'Brien and not on the figures in front of her.

Annoyed with herself, she pushed back the chair and went to her room to get a bonnet. She paused in the kitchen doorway as Mazie bent over the stove.

"Mazie, I'm walking down to the general store for some supplies and I want to get there before it closes."

"Did Miss Stanton go home?"

"No, but she came to see Major O'Brien. She'll never miss me."

"Yes, ma'am."

Sophia left the house and hurried down the street, the disgruntled feeling gradually leaving her. She loved her city on high bluffs overlooking the river, President's Island downriver, the islands called Paddy's Hen and Chickens to the north. She enjoyed Memphis's bustling commerce, the tall trees, and the friendly people. The war, the blockade and the shortages it caused worried her. They should get through the winter with the garden

Henry planted, but would she be able to acquire paper to keep printing *The River Weekly*? she wondered.

After picking up thread and nails, she went to the newspaper office and soon she was engrossed in the paper, all thought of Major O'Brien gone.

On Friday the second of May, a telegram came. Major O'Brien lowered the message as he sat in the parlor and gazed solemnly at Sophia. "Amity and Darcy arrived safely. They wired me, because New Orleans has fallen to the Union. The Federals occupy the city."

"Oh, no! Your family is safe?"

"Yes. Memphis or Vicksburg will be next."

She nodded as she left him; she couldn't imagine her city under siege.

Wednesday afternoon of the following week she was at the newspaper office again, staring in consternation at the press. The hinge was bent on the lid to the boiler and she knelt, trying to twist a bolt free, knowing that if John were home, he could do it easily. She tugged and pulled and tried another set of pliers, but couldn't get the bolt loose. She would have to go home and get Henry and she hated to be unable to do something so simple herself.

Angrily she tackled it again, the pliers slipping. "Ouch!" She yanked her hand back; her knuckle was bloody where she scraped the skin. The tiny bell over the front door tinkled, and she looked up.

Major O'Brien stepped inside. "Trouble?"

"What in heaven's name are you doing here?" she asked in shock.

Caleb felt a twinge of amusement at the surprise in her wide eyes. His leg throbbed as he crossed the room. Her hair had come free of pins and a lock hung down her back and a smudge of grease was on her jaw.

"I've been in the house long enough. I asked Henry to hitch the horse to your carriage and give me directions to get here.

"Doctor Perkins will faint."

"No, he won't. In the first place, he won't know about it; also he's too busy with other wounded men to care what I do."

"That's true. If you can ride down here, are you going back to war?"

"Want to be rid of me, Miss Merrick?" He had to bite back a smile, because that was obviously exactly what she wanted. She blinked and closed her lips tightly and her cheeks flushed. He shifted his arm in its sling. "I'm not ready for a battlefield. Not until I can draw and fire as quickly as I did before. I'm in no hurry to get myself killed."

"I didn't want to get rid of you," she said stiffly.

"What happened?" he asked, taking her hand in his and turning it. Her hand was warm and soft, with an ugly scrape along the knuckle of her forefinger. She tried to pull away.

"I scraped my hand. It's nothing," she insisted.

He pulled out a handkerchief and dabbed at the blood. She drew her breath. He stood close enough to notice an enticing scent of rosewater. "What were you trying to do?" he asked with concern.

She motioned toward the one-cylinder press. "The cylinder isn't working. There's a bolt I was trying to loosen."

He tied the handkerchief around her hand. "There. Show me the bolt." When she pointed to it, he picked up the pliers in his left hand.

"Hold my hand steady and I'll turn the bolt."

She placed her hand over his, holding his tightly and he turned. "I hate to be so helpless." He wiggled the fingers of his right hand, jiggling the sling around his neck.

"You're not very patient, Major," she said. He turned to look at her and her face was only inches away. Her eyes were an unusual shade of blue, reminding him of spring flowers at home. Sophia was pretty, he observed. She blinked and looked down as he felt the bolt give way.

"Now I can do it," she said, taking the pliers from him.

He stood watching her work, feeling frustrated and wanting to do the task for her. His leg throbbed and he sat down to watch her. In minutes she wiped her hands on a rag. "Now I think it's fixed. I'll have to fire up the boiler. I can work with the proof press if I need to." Her eyes narrowed as she crossed the room to sit on the other side of the desk from him. "Your wounds hurt don't they?"

"A little. You print the paper all by yourself?"

"Yes. I have help with deliveries. Papa and John both belonged to the International Typographers Union, but I don't. We don't sell as many copies now and the paper is shorter."

"What's news?" he asked, studying the notepad in front of her.

"There's a growing shortage of so many supplies, pins, lard; salt is becoming more scarce. We're cut off by the Federals. I talked to Mister Qualls, a cotton factor, and in spite of the law against exporting cotton except through Southern ports, we still have a large trade in cotton."

"What's large?" Major O'Brien leaned back on his chair.

"He said over a hundred bales a day. Before the war Memphis was the largest inland cotton market. Last year four hundred thousand bales went through here. Papa said at the war's outbreak the industrial output here was valued at four million dollars."

"What's the population of Memphis?" he asked with interest.

"We're growing—now faster than ever with the factories that are going up because of the war. At the start of the fifties Memphis had a little over eight thousand people. At the beginning of this decade the population is over twenty-two thousand and it keeps growing."

"As I rode along the street, I noticed a number of able-bodied men. More than I expected to see," he commented.

"Not everyone has gone to war. Some went, some stayed." She made entries in a ledger while he sat and watched her.

"You've never been to a party?"

"No. Papa didn't believe in frivolous things." She looked solemn, facing him, answering so matter-of-factly. Hannah Lou was the opposite of Miss Merrick, he observed. He'd already tasted Hannah Lou's kisses and she loved to flirt and tease and he looked forward to the party.

"The Needham party is to raise funds for shoes for Confederate soldiers. Surely you consider that a good cause. I can promise you it is." Without giving her time to answer, he leaned on the desk. "Let's go to the party and help raise money for shoes, Miss Merrick. The shoes won't go to your brothers, but somewhere in Virginia, pretty ladies might be trying to raise funds for shoes that will go to them."

She stared past him. "It's for a good cause, but I don't know much about parties," she admitted reluctantly.

"I'll show you," he said, smiling at her. She had a faint smudge of ink on her jaw, and he reached out to rub it away with his thumb. She blinked and blushed.

"You have some ink," he explained, moving away his hand.

She looked up in surprise. She was pretty enough to enjoy parties and enjoy knowing men. He couldn't imagine a life like hers.

"I don't want your pity," she said, raising her chin. His hand was warm and rough. He met her gaze steadily, reaching out to touch her chin. "Miss Merrick, I might want to shake you or I might want to kiss you, but I don't pity you."

She blinked, still staring at him. Why had he said that to her? He hadn't ever wanted to kiss her. She was too prim and straitlaced, yet as he looked into her eyes and saw a flicker of response, his gaze lowered to her full lips and he felt a stir of desire. She was a capable, intelligent woman, but could she be any fun? Who had kissed her and had she enjoyed it? He looked into her eyes again and felt caught in a compelling stare that made his pulse quicken. She turned away, and the tension lessened.

"Since you're here, would you like to tell me about the battle?"

"If you'd like," he said quietly, leaning back and wanting to forget that day and knowing he never would. "We camped at Corinth because it's a railroad center and as long as it's open, Memphis has a line to the East. Beauregard wanted to hold it, to drive Grant back. Corinth as a rail center is vital, Memphis as a trade center and river port is essential."

"You think we'll be attacked?"

"Yes. You have the Union army only miles away. They want this town.

"I can't imagine Memphis under siege." Her gaze ran over the press and shifted to him. "Go ahead with your account of the battle."

"At Corinth we waited to attack because of weather, because our generals were trying to decide when to start the battle. Finally that April morning came the orders to attack—it was to have been a surprise and I suppose, it was. General Hardee's men were in front."

"I wish I'd known a battle was about to commence."

He caught her wrist, causing her to stop writing and look up at him. "You don't have brothers or parents here. You need someone, Miss Merrick, to tell you that you should not go to an army camp," he admonished.

"It is none of your affair whether I do or don't!" she snapped and her eyes sparked. "Tell me what happened after you and I parted."

He stared at her. Sophia Merrick was the most independent woman he'd known, except perhaps his mother who would have stood up to the devil. "The Federals dug in on a sunken road and they had a perfect defense, an open field in front of them with a slight rise in the ground that was a natural barrier." He continued to talk, remembering too clearly. Finally he stood up and reached across the desk to take Sophia by the hand.

"Enough about war. It's a beautiful spring day," he said. "Show me Memphis."

"No, I really should—" she said and looked up into his eyes.

"C'mon, Miss Merrick," he coaxed.

She capitulated and stood up, picking up her yellow straw bonnet. With green silk, the hat was frivolous unlike her plain muslin dresses, he noticed. The yellow straw framed her face and the deep green bow beneath her chin softened the harshness of her hairdo, making her look prettier. She locked the door to the office and took his left hand as he helped her into the buggy.

With a halting effort and a grimace, he climbed up beside her and urged the horses forward. "Tell me about

Memphis," he said, glancing at her. The plain green muslin had the top buttons unfastened. As prim as she was, the necks of her gowns and dresses and wrapper were always unfastened and he wondered if she was aware of leaving them unbuttoned or why she did. It certainly wasn't to entice male notice, he decided.

"The town was built on Chickasaw bluffs, so we're high above the river at this point. In the early days it was a fort and then a trading post."

"Did your brothers go to parties?"

"Yes, they did."

"Are they married or do they have women waiting for them?"

"None of them is married. Morris went to parties with Lily Mae Prentice, Amos writes to Julia Stone, and John is quieter and he never did go out much with anyone."

"So how come the brothers went dancing and you didn't?" he asked, curious.

"I'm the youngest and the only female and Papa was very particular about what I did. They didn't go to parties often, and when they did, I don't think he knew." She tilted her head to look at him. "We were discussing Memphis, Major. Three men acquired the John Rice Grant of five thousand acres. Andrew Jackson, John Overton, and James Winchester opened the land for development and General Jackson sold his interest to Colonel John C. McLemore. I've always been told Paddy Meagher's Bell Tavern, originally owned by Colonel Sam Brown, was the center of early business and Paddy Meagher was the town's first merchant."

"An Irishman," he said, grinning at her and she smiled in return. He felt better. Sophia was pretty and for the moment, good company; sunshine was bright, the sky a deep blue, and he was recovering.

"There was Ike Rawlings, a sutler, who was an Indian agent at Fort Pickering. The first blacksmith was Joab Bean, Mister Locke, the first saddlery, Mister Ragland opened a drug store," Sophia continued, "and Mrs. Fooy had the first ferry to Arkansas. And Papa said if people wanted to get married they had to go to a judge in Arkansas. Shelby County was created in eighteen nineteen. Now Memphis is the sixth largest city in the South."

"What's the fancy building?" he asked, looking at an imposing structure with a Greek Revival portico and six tall columns.

"That's one of our finest," she said with a note of pride. "The Gayoso House was designed by James Dakin and the wrought-iron balconies were added recently by local architects. It's owned by Robertson Topp. Until this year that's where the balls and the big parties were held. The Overton Hotel was under construction until the war started. It's being used as a hospital now. The war has changed so much in town. Crisp's Gaiety Theater and the New Memphis Theater are closed. John liked the theater, so I did get to see Edwin Booth perform."

The bonnet hid her face when she turned her head and Caleb wanted to untie it and take it off. And he thought about how she looked when her hair was down, a golden cascade that spilled over her shoulders and vanished all trace of primness. They turned to another street.

"This is Front Row or Front Street. A long time ago it was called Mississippi Row. Most of the cotton houses are here."

Caleb glanced at the row of brick buildings, some five stories tall with the wide doors on the ground floors to enable men to move bales of cotton inside easily. "I notice the shops are closed," he said.

"They close around two every afternoon. It's because of the blockade. So many goods are scarce and it gets worse every day. I've had Henry dig a larger garden. We're going to have to grow everything."

As they rode, she waved her hand. "Here, Front Street becomes Shelby Street. When you reach Beale, turn east and I'll show you some fine homes. Mister Littleton built there and has the largest ballroom in town."

He looked at elegant mansions built of wood instead of brick. Sophia waved her hand. "The Memphis and Ohio depot is at the north end of town. Memphis used to be divided into three corporations, Memphis, South Memphis, and Fort Pickering, developed by John McLemore. Up north the town came to be known as Pinch."

"Henry told me. He called it Pinch Gut and said that's where the Irish settled."

"They did. The three became one town and from what Papa said, Memphis began to prosper when they started charging wharfage for the boats that stopped here. Turn and we'll go to South Street," she directed. "We'll pass the Mississippi and Tennessee Railroad Depot and Memphis and Charleston. There were four railroads in Memphis by eighteen sixty. The Memphis and Charleston opened in eighteen fifty-seven. That's where they say Grandpa Merrick was killed. The very first was a short track between Memphis and La Grange."

"And it connects the Mississippi to the Atlantic."

"You sound as if you think that's grand. We were to have the Pacific Railroad Convention in Eighteen forty-nine, but a cholera epidemic caused the convention to be postponed. Town leaders hoped to get a transcontinental railroad through Memphis."

"This is the perfect city for it. Memphis is in the heart of the land and it's on a major river. This is a railroad town."

"The number of saloons and the gambling houses grow along with the railroads. Tennessee has more railroads than many states—almost thirteen hundred miles last year. Before the railroads came, the town was small. Now the population has grown and people travel through here going all directions."

"You sound as if you'd like to close it to everyone," he said with amusement.

"No. Just the bad element—the gamblers and the wild ones."

"Do I get the feeling you're referring to me?" he teased.

She smiled. She had dimples in both cheeks and he stared at her. She was prettier than ever when she smiled, but always when he thought about how pretty she was, he remembered the nights when she was in her gown and her hair fell over her shoulders. Then she was beautiful.

"What do you want to do after the war?"

"I've never given the future a thought until this battle. Now life seems more important," he replied.

"I've always known the paper is my future. Now turn and we'll go by the depot." Land was green with tall grass in vacant lots. While Sophia told him about Memphis, they passed the Memphis and Tennessee depot and turned north again on Lauderdale to pass the Memphis and Charleston depot.

"Robertson Topp, Robert Brinkley, Colonel John Trezevant were men here who pushed for the Memphis and Charleston. They promoted stock for the Memphis and Little Rock as well. Mister Winchester was behind the railroads. Mister Greenlaw helped them promote stock. While we're out, I'll show you the area of Memphis Mister Greenlaw and his brother developed. He's interested in property as much as railroads."

"Didn't your father feel he was fighting a hopeless battle when he fought the railroads?"

"I don't think he looked at it that way. He felt he was fighting for good and what's right."

"Railroads aren't the same as saloons. Railroads bring progress. If you didn't have the river traffic and the railroads, how big do you think Memphis would be now? Do you think you would have gotten to see Edwin Booth perform or had the opera here?"

She tilted her head to study him. "I hadn't thought about it that way," she said, frowning and he felt an impulse to lean forward and kiss her pursed lips. He inhaled deeply and turned his head to look away from her. Leave her alone, he told himself. She would faint. Then he felt a twinge of amusement. Sophia Merrick wouldn't faint. She might knock him out of the buggy, but she'd never faint.

As the afternoon wore on, he felt a growing liking for the city of Memphis and the railroads intrigued him. After Shiloh, he wanted something in his life and he wanted a home for Darcy. "You live in a good town," he said, impressed.

"Papa thought so," she said, looking around. "I think so, too. I like it here."

"Ever want to leave?" he asked, curious about her. Could she be fun? He doubted it. Not his kind of fun, he decided.

"Just to visit. Someday I'll get on a steamboat and go to New Orleans. Turn at the corner."

On Adams she pointed out houses to him. "There's one of the older homes, the Massey house that was built when I was a baby."

He studied the one-story house with a double portico and eight columns. They passed an elegant two-story, four-columned house while she told him about the townspeople. Finally they turned on Manassas and then on Washington to go down the alley to her carriage house.

"Sometime you'll have to see Doctor Mansfield's mansion on Lamar—it's elegant. He's a wholesale druggist here." A carriage was waiting in the alley, and Sophia gazed at it with curiosity.

Who would wait in back? If a guest came to call, she always came to the front door. Why would anyone wait in the alley for her? Or was it to see someone else?

Chapter 5

As they drew alongside, a woman leaned forward and then thrust her head through the window.

"Cal!" she cried and waved at him.

Feeling dismay, Sophia stared at her. The woman's full mouth was an eye-catching deep red, her cheeks a paler rose. A sweet scent of lilacs filled the air. The woman's low-cut green satin dress was as fashionable as Miss Therrie's dresses. And never had Sophia seen a dress cut so low. Full mounds of flesh curved above the green satin.

"Desirée," Major O'Brien said, pleasure in his voice. He glanced at Sophia. "I'll be in after a while," he said, climbing down. The woman emerged from the carriage and Major O'Brien caught her with his left arm, hauling her against his side and kissing her full on the mouth. Sophia sat up straight and turned away, driving the buggy to the carriage house and handing it over to Henry.

"Major O'Brien will be along shortly," she said stiffly, feeling a ripple of discontent and shock, feeling a mixture of emotions she didn't care to explore, knowing she was incredibly plain next to such a creature.

It was two hours later when she heard the back door slam. She stood up and left the parlor as Major O'Brien came down the hall. "That was a friend of mine from New Orleans," he said.

"So I gathered," she said, feeling her cheeks grow warm, reluctant to discuss the matter.

He looked amused as he reached out with his left hand to grip the doorjamb. He drew a deep breath, and she realized he was having difficulty.

"You're hurting again, aren't you?"

"Yes. I'm exhausted."

She moved beside him, sliding her arm around him as they had done so many times before. His arm draped across her shoulder.

"No lecture, Miss Merrick?"

"No. You've heard them all and you're going to do exactly as you please, so I won't waste my breath."

He chuckled. "I'm a bad patient."

"True enough, but you're a strong one. I know you'll survive and that's good."

"I'm glad to hear you think so. Sometimes the way you look at me, I think you'd just as soon I didn't. I want to sit in the chair."

She eased him down and knelt to pull off his boots. When she tugged on his left boot, he groaned. "Leave it. That hurts."

She looked up at him and stood up. Perspiration dotted his forehead and his color was chalky. She hurried to get a damp cloth and sponge his forehead as he leaned back and closed his eyes. A faint sweet scent clung to his clothes and Sophia stared at him, wondering about the woman Desirée. Did he love her and did he love Amity Therrie as well? She hadn't known a man like the major. He was complex and so different from her quiet brothers.

His chest rose and fell evenly. He was asleep in seconds, exhausted from the afternoon. What is he like when he's with that woman? she pondered. Feeling a strange curiosity about him, she remembered watching him wrap his good arm around the woman and kiss her, leaning over her. It made Sophia feel a yearning as she gazed down at him and she looked at his mouth. What would it be like to kiss him? She smoothed curls back off his forehead. In minutes she tiptoed out of his room and closed the door.

On Saturday she worked late at the office, arriving home at half-past ten, exhausted after a frustrating day with a temperamental press. The issue with Major O'Brien's account of the battle had gone to press that afternoon and would be delivered tomorrow morning. She paused in the front hall as she heard voices from his bedroom. A man laughed and several men's voices blurred as they talked at the same time. A cloud of smoke hung in the air. What was he doing now? she wondered.

Curious, she walked toward his room, pausing in the door as she stared. Major O'Brien was in the rocker. One of the marble-topped tables was in front of him and men sat around it. There were bottles on the floor beside their chairs, cigars in men's mouths, and cards in their hands. *Gambling.* She thought of Papa and her brothers who had never brought cards, tobacco, or alcohol to the house. She was exhausted after working late, and now to come home and find Papa's wishes violated made her feel as if she had failed her family. What would Papa do? She squared her shoulders and entered the room.

Feeling that she was carrying out her father's wishes, she crossed the room. "Major O'Brien," she called to him.

"Miss Merrick—" He rolled the cigar to the corner of his mouth and grinned.

"This is my father's house—the Merrick house—where there has never been cards, alcohol, or tobacco!" she said sternly.

"Calm down. We're just having a friendly game." Men stood up and yanked on their coats and hats.

"Sorry, Miss Merrick," Elmer Ott said, grabbing a bottle from the floor and dashing past her. Ignoring their apologies, she yanked up bottles.

"I know what Papa would do if he were here, and so do every one of you except Major O'Brien!"

"Miss Merrick, I'm sorry—" Thomas Martin said.

"Now Miss Sophia, we didn't mean any disrespect—" George Bates added as he clutched a bottle to his chest, grabbing his hat and running from the room. With the armload of bottles, she headed to the front.

Men began to scatter, gone as swiftly as windblown petals. Thad Greenly jumped off the porch, vaulting the oleanders. She carried four foul-smelling bottles across the porch and tossed them. The bottles crashed on the steps, men dodging the flying bottles and trying to catch them, yelling apologies.

Knowing Papa would say she wasn't finished, she turned back to the room to deal with the culprit. Major

O'Brien sat staring at her with narrowed eyes, the cigar clamped between his teeth.

"You mule-headed ingrate," she exclaimed, feeling her patience frazzling as she crossed the room, knowing her father would want her to be firm.

"Oh, no, you don't!" he snapped, yanking up a bottle and placing it behind his back in the chair, glaring at her with the smoking cigar pointed straight at her. A cloud of smelly smoke enveloped her.

She picked up the pitcher of water at the washstand and threw it on him, dousing the cigar. He gasped as the water hit him.

"Dammit to hell," he snapped, reaching out to yank the pitcher from her hands and catch her wrists with his left hand. He held both her wrists. "You little witch!"

Having struggled with the paper all day, and now to come home to this, she felt enraged, grappling to break free. "I've nursed you and fed you and cared for you and helped you around and I've told you how Papa felt about cigars and whiskey and gambling!" she cried, knowing the day's exhaustion was adding to her fury. She wriggled to get away, not caring if she bumped his broken arm. "This is Papa's house! How could you?" she asked, near tears.

"Keep your apron strings tied! We didn't hurt you." He released her and glared at her, running his hand over his dripping face. He studied his soggy cigar. "You managed to ruin the first good cigar I've had since I left New Orleans."

"I'm not sorry. I intended to ruin it," she yelled, knowing her emotions were on a ragged edge, yet unable to stop now. She glanced down at the money and cards on the table. "When I think how we're running short of things, having to parch rye or corn for coffee and can't get goods now and here you are tossing away real money—you have gold there—"

"Miss Merrick, you're a priggish spinster who doesn't know fun if it's staring you in the face," he said as he picked up a cloth to wipe his wet shirt.

Her rage boiled over. "Your ideas of wild, wicked, abominable fun will never be the same as mine!" She scooped the cards off the table and rushed to throw them in the fireplace.

"Hey! Stop that—"

She knelt, trying to light a match, hearing him move behind her. He caught her up with his good hand and she pushed against his chest, bumping his arm.

"Dammit," he said, shoving her back against the wall, catching her wrists behind her, holding them above her head. "You were trouble the first moment I met you and you're still trouble."

"You wouldn't be here if it weren't for me or have you forgotten?"

He pushed against her and she struggled to break free, knowing if she hit his arm, he would release her, wanting to hurt him. She was enraged with him, tugging to pull free of his grip. How could he be so strong when he had been injured?

"I'll bet the man who's kissed you almost froze from it!"

Startled, she blinked and glared at him. They gazed into each other's eyes. She felt the tug of wills between them while she strained to pull away from his hold, wiggling, aware he was pressing closer, pushing against her, his hard body turned sideways to protect his injured arm. And then her body was crushed by his, her shoulder blades and bottom against the wall, his hard chest and thigh pressed against her, their hearts racing—she could feel his as easily as her own.

"I know the type of woman you consort with!" she retorted.

"She's all woman, not a stiff-necked prim old maid."

Sophia shook with anger. His gaze lowered to her mouth and then looked into her eyes again, the question in his obvious. "I'll bet you're as much fun as watching a pond freeze and just as warm." He leaned forward. She turned her head, but he twisted, blocking her body and keeping his injured arm twisted away from her. His mouth covered hers. She clamped her lips closed, her protest muffled in her throat, fighting him with all her strength.

His mouth was on hers, warm, demanding. He lifted

his head and stared down into her eyes. "Cold as ice water—"

"You—" she began. His head dipped down again before she could say the next word, catching her mouth open, his lips pressing hers. His tongue thrust between her lips and Sophia felt a shock course through her.

She opened her eyes, to find him watching her; she closed her eyes quickly as sensations she had never experienced bombarded her and wiped out everything else. His mouth was bruising, his tongue thrusting deep into her mouth. The sensations she felt from his kiss didn't stop with her mouth, but assaulted her entire body. The resistance left her as she became more aware of what he was doing. His tongue was in her mouth, playing over her tongue! This is what it is like to kiss, she thought with awe. This . . .

He raised his head, studying her as she opened her eyes. She felt dazed, lethargic, too hot.

"You've never been kissed have you?" he asked, incredulous.

She shook her head. She felt lost, as if swirling down in green waters as she gazed into his eyes. His head tipped forward again and she closed her eyes.

His mouth brushed hers, warm lips tugging over hers, a sensual clash that radiated tingles, causing fires to leap inside her, fanning the ache low within her. His tongue touched the corner of her mouth, then played over her lips as she parted them. Then his mouth was on hers again, his tongue thrusting deep, touching her tongue. Feeling as if he would devour her, she was absorbed by sensations that stunned her.

She didn't know when he released her hands. She felt the hard bulge of muscle as her fingers played across his shoulders. His arm went around her waist and finally he raised his head.

She gazed up at him to find him studying her again. Suddenly embarrassed, realizing what she let him do, she wriggled away. He caught her arm and she looked up, ready to fight him if he intended to pull her back, yet at the same time wanting to melt into his arms again. She was battling so many conflicting emotions, which were new to her. How can I want him to continue? she asked herself. But I do. I do. Her heart thudded as she gazed into his eyes.

"How old are you?"

Surprised, she blinked and remembered she had lied to him. After a long silence she told him the truth. "Seventeen."

"Saints and angels, you're a child!" His dark brows arched.

Feeling annoyed again with him, she drew herself up. "I'm not a child," she shot back.

He blinked and stepped back and they stared at each other. What was he thinking? Did she really seem like a child to him? Her breathing was ragged and she felt shock because of his kisses. *She wanted him to kiss her.* But it was wrong to want his kisses, to get hot and weak when he touched her.

"All right, Miss Merrick, no more gambling in your house. I promise. I should be able to travel by the end of the week and you'll be rid of me anyway."

She ran her hand across her forehead. "It's been a long day and I had trouble with the press. When I came home and saw all the smoke—" She waved her hand.

He clamped his lips together and nodded. "Sorry. I shouldn't have put another burden on your shoulders. I know your father wouldn't have approved."

They looked at each other and her heart pounded as she nodded. "Good night, Major." She turned and left the room, feeling embarrassed and confused beneath his intense gaze, not knowing where she was going. Why did he set her nerves on edge and make her feel as if she were handling hot coals? And his kisses—

She touched her lips, remembering, blushing as she thought about him. His kisses set her on fire. Were all men like that? Heaven help her if they weren't and it was just Major O'Brien who stirred her in such a manner. She thought about him sitting in the rocker, glaring up at her defiantly with the cigar between his teeth, his bottle of whiskey safe behind his back. He was a rogue, yet he had sounded truly sorry and she might not have acted so rashly if she hadn't been so tired. He would be gone in days ... out of her life forever. His kisses—she would never forget them. She glanced around. She stood in the center of the darkened parlor. Why had she come in here? She turned and went to her room and closed the door, crossing the room to stare in the mirror and look at her lips that were still red from his kisses. Would she ever forget? Would any other man's kisses feel the same?

On May thirteenth, Caleb sat in the buggy at the side of the Memphis and Tennessee depot watching a train pull out of the station. Memphis was a thriving town, as bustling as New Orleans, and he liked it here. It had the Mississippi River, railroads, a gateway on the frontier with factories and a booming cotton market in spite of the war. If the war didn't destroy it, the city was filled with possibilities for a rosy future. The M&T's big engine gained speed and rolled out of sight. Memphis was the link to the south with the line to New Orleans, to the east with its Memphis and Charleston Railroad, to the north with the Memphis and Ohio, and when it was completed, there would be a line west across Arkansas to Little Rock. A transcontinental railroad through Memphis would make this a major city in the United States, of that he was certain. It set his blood racing, because he had money to invest.

When Amity came to visit, she had brought him over two thousand dollars of his money. It was in gold, which was becoming a precious commodity. Rafe was doing well with the blockade running.

Memphis held a future even if it was shelled by Federal artillery, because people would rebuild. The location was too good to abandon. Thinking about Darcy and the last letter he'd received, Caleb turned the buggy toward Front Street and the wharves. As soon as the war was over, he wanted to build a house and take Darcy to live with him. As he roamed through the town, angling his way back to the wharves, he turned on Butler and looked at the wide, muddy river. Weeds were high around an abandoned building that fronted on the water. An aged, dilapidated dock sagged into the water. A sign read MEM-PHIS & ARKANSAS.

The depot was abandoned; behind it was one train, a rusty engine, and two cars. Careful of his leg, Caleb climbed in to look at the fire gate, the smoke box, the cab, and the tender that still had coal covered with dust. He eased himself down and looked at the wheels and the connecting rods. Why was the train abandoned? Why hadn't someone claimed it or tried to buy it?

As questions swirled in his mind, Caleb felt his pulse drum. Could he purchase the depot and engine? Memphis & Arkansas. Curious about it, he climbed back into his buggy. As he drove down Chester Street, he glanced back over his shoulder at the depot. Since Shiloh, he wanted a home, and Memphis seemed a likely place, railroading an exciting business.

At the top of the bluff, he halted and sat with a breeze sweeping off the river, tugging at his curls as he watched the activity below. Men scurried about on steamboats while they mounted light cannon on the decks. Others worked to strengthen the bows with iron while stevedores loaded compressed cotton bales on board. Caleb climbed down carefully, favoring his leg as he descended the hill and crossed to the wharf to board a sidewheel steamer, the CSS *General Bragg*. A man glanced up at him.

"Getting ready for battle?" Caleb asked.

"Getting ready for the damn Yankees," he said, splicing a line and wiping his forehead.

"I fought at Shiloh."

"That's why your arm's in a sling?"

"Yes. They're tough fighters."

"We can hold our own. Should have seen *General Bragg* ram the *Cincinnati* at Plum Point. She rammed the *Cincinnati* and *General Sterling Price* rammed her. Knocked off the rudder and smashed the hull."

"Did you sustain any damage?"

"The tiller ropes had to be replaced. They have been now, and she's ready for battle."

Caleb looked the length of the ship. He thumped on a bulkhead and the man stood up. Bare-chested, his dark skin glistening with sweat, he brushed his brown hair off his forehead.

"*General Bragg* has double pine bulkheads filled with

compressed cotton to protect the machinery. There's a four-inch oak sheath with a one-inch covering of iron added to the bows. We're ready, and when we fight, our commodore won't back down."

"What's her speed?"

"Ten knots."

"What have you got to throw against them?" He gazed fore and aft. "Looks like thirty-two pounders."

"You're close, mate. Thirty-pounder Parrott rifle, one thirty-two pounder, and one twelve pounder."

"Any word on when the Union fleet will move downriver?"

Black eyes squinted at Caleb. "Soon, we think."

Caleb offered his hand. "Good luck."

"Same to you."

Twenty minutes later he sat facing Will who was on a sun porch.

"Hannah Lou will be livid she missed seeing you."

"She's not home?" Caleb asked, feeling only a slight disappointment.

"No, but she may get back before you leave."

"Have you read *The Appeal* today?"

"Yes," Will said, a frown creasing his brow. "It worries me. Father and I've discussed it. The Union army is north of here with a fleet of gunboats, and you know they're coming to attack. Memphis is a strategic point. A lot of people are packing, putting their property up for sale, and leaving town."

"I just came from the docks. They're ready or getting ready for battle. When I walked around, I saw thirty pounders, thirty-two pounders. My brother has written the Union gunboats have sixty-four pounders. And we're using compressed cotton to protect the machinery."

"We don't have the iron. The Memphis and Charleston foundry has converted into an armory to cast cannon and manufacture munitions, but our supplies are dwindling. The arsenal in the fort doesn't have enough cannon. On the other hand, remember we sunk two of their ships at Plum Point."

"Will, I'm worried about Miss Merrick," Caleb said, smoothing his trousers over his knee and feeling foolish.

Why should he care what she did or what happened? he asked himself. She wasn't his responsibility.

"Mother has already told Hannah Lou to tell Sophia to move in with us. We may leave the city. You and I have to leave. You're probably champing to get back to battle."

"No. I don't like killing men."

Will stared at him. "You? You were as eager as anyone I've known to get into the fight."

"I've hunted all my life, but war is different."

Will rubbed his leg. "We were lucky, Cal. I don't want to go back, but it's something that has to be done."

"I've talked to some of the men in town today. As you just said, a lot of property is going up for sale. I'm thinking about buying some land and coming back after the war."

"I knew you'd like my city! This is a grand place. The people are friendly and we have the best cotton market in the country. We've got more factories now because of the war."

Caleb smiled and waved his hands. "You don't need to sell me. Will, I was down near Butler and saw the abandoned depot and train. The Memphis and Arkansas. Whose is it and why is it abandoned?"

"Its owner was Phelan Leib and he gave it up and went home to Louisiana."

"Do you know if it's for sale?"

"You want a railroad? That's a giant undertaking."

"Come in with me, Will. Think what we could do! Who do I see about it?"

"Talk to Jordan Dalton. If he isn't handling the property, he can tell you who is. Cal—a railroad? Robertson Topp and Mister Brinkley, all those men have had so much difficulty with the Memphis–Little Rock."

"Look at all the railroads that have succeeded here. And the West is opening. After this war, people will move west. And into Texas. A line across Arkansas could go on to Texas."

"I'll think about it. And I'll speak to Mother again about Sophia."

"I feel relieved about Miss Merrick. If the Union occupies Memphis, she shouldn't stay with only two aging servants."

"We'll watch out for her. You and I owe her our lives. You sound as if you're leaving."

"Soon. I'm surprised the Federals haven't attacked before now. Memphis will give them control of the Mississippi River, control of all the upper valley from Memphis."

"Everyone is talking about it and getting ready for it."

Caleb stood up. "Tell Hannah Lou I'm sorry I missed her."

Outside, he climbed into the buggy, his thoughts shifting. When he asked Dr. Perkins yesterday about going home, the doctor shook his head. "Don't rush, son. You're mending fine, but let's let that leg and arm heal."

"I'll travel only to New Orleans," he promised.

"You're not a burden for Miss Sophia. She needs a man around here if you ask me. That father of hers was always thinking of his own plans."

"I can't stay here for Miss Sophia's sake. And she doesn't want me here anyway."

Dr. Perkins peered over his rimless spectacles. "I heard about your gambling party and how she tossed the men and their bottles out. Mrs. Rowntree across the street said it was a sight to behold, grown men running from little Miss Sophia as if the devil himself were after them." He chuckled and shook his head. "Her old pa probably shook his fist in his grave. That man could lecture an angel and feel righteous about it and he taught his children to be the same way. She may not want you here, but you stay for a few more days."

"Yes, sir. When will I have use of my arm again?"

"If you're patient, the time will come when you'll forget it ever happened," he said, snapping shut his black bag.

"No, Doc. I'll never forget that battle. Not ever. War isn't what I thought it would be."

"I expect a lot of men are saying that right now and a lot more will say it in months to come."

"Years, Doc."

"If we have years like this past April, I don't know how this nation will survive it, Confederacy or Union."

"I don't know either, but the Bluebellies can fight like demons."

"So can our boys. A Southern man can outshoot and outride anyone, bar none," he said. "If I were younger, I'd be out there where I'd be more help." He ran his fingers through his long white hair. "I'll be back Thursday. That leg isn't healing as fast as it was. Are you on it a good part of the day?"

"No, sir."

"See that you aren't."

Caleb headed back toward the center of town to look at the buildings and as he listened to the steady clop of the hooves of the team, he thought about Sophia Merrick. Seventeen years old. She was a baby. When he said that aloud, she had come back with a heated denial—and in some ways she was right. She ran a household, tended injured men, operated a weekly paper. He hadn't ever known anyone like her. She hadn't ever been kissed. She'd never been to a party. The fund-raiser was tomorrow night. Now that she was so angry with him over his gambling, he didn't know whether she would go or not, but Hannah Lou had come to call every day and constantly urged Miss Merrick to go.

He gazed at the tree-lined street and remembered pressing against her, bending his head to kiss her. He felt a hot stirring of desire that he knew was simply from being without a woman for so long. She hadn't kissed like ice. He had kissed Hannah Lou and Desirée—damned if it hadn't been more fun to kiss innocent Miss Merrick. He thought she would be cold and stiff and unresponsive, particularly since she was angry. But she had melted against him, yielded to him with a fiery sweetness. He remembered the surprise in her expression when she glanced up at him. She knows nothing about men, he mused, except how to get along with brothers and how to work like a man.

He thought about the enameled silver and emerald necklace he had bought at the jewelers to take home to Amity when he returned to New Orleans. He could get something else for Amity and give the necklace to Miss Merrick to wear to the party. He hadn't ever seen her wear any kind of jewelry.

What would happen to her if the Federals attacked? Mayor Park had asked for volunteers for a militia, but the men who wanted to get into the war had enlisted and left Memphis long ago. The others seemed to be avoiding it as long as possible.

He drove leisurely along Adams and looked at the houses, passing St. Peter's Church, and then trying to remember the plain house, recalling that Miss Merrick had said it was the Macgevney house and one of the older homes in town, that Eugene Magevney was Memphis's first schoolmaster, teaching in a log cabin in Court Square during the 1830s.

He went to the cotton exchange, mingling with town leaders, picking up what news he could about Memphis and the fighting.

Next he stopped at a tailor's to have a new uniform made. As Caleb stood still for a fitting, he gazed out the long window at the empty building across the street. "How is property value in town?"

"People are selling. Many folks don't want to get caught in a battle. Others don't want to live in an occupied town," the diminutive tailor said. He shrugged. "I expect my business to thrive either way."

Caleb looked down at the tailor's round, bald head. "Think they'll get a railroad going through Arkansas?"

"Mister Topp and Mister Trezevant and Mister Brinkley and some others have the land and charter. The war interfered with their plans. Now who knows how long it'll be?"

Caleb was silent, thinking about the land and possibilities. When he left the tailor's, he stopped at the general store to talk to the men gathered there. He strolled to Court Square to talk to politicians at the courthouse. Enjoying the spring day and seeing the town, he rode up and down streets, greeting people, stopping to talk.

As he recovered, he was seeing less and less of Miss Merrick. She was away from the house more and when she was home, she didn't stop to see him as she had. Was it because of the gambling? Or because of his kisses? Or because she was too busy?

He waited in the parlor that evening until she returned home.

"Miss Merrick?" he called softly.

She entered the room with papers beneath her arm. "I have this week's paper and I had a letter from Morris today and one from John. And there are two letters here for you."

"Ah, a letter from Darcy," he said, taking them from her hand, "and another one from Rafe." He looked up. "We're going to the fund-raising party tomorrow night, aren't we?"

She frowned. "I printed the programs, and I can send them with you."

"No. You need to go to give your support to the Cause."

"I don't—"

"I've been riding around town today and everyone who supports the Confederacy is going. If you don't go, it's the same as saying you are a Union sympathizer."

"Of course, I'm not!"

"Fine. We're going to the party then."

"I don't have a party dress," she said, smoothing her letter and reading.

"During wartime how many ladies do you think will have party dresses?"

"Hannah Lou will," she said, glancing up and then looking at her letter again. "Amos misses being home, but he's well and he said conditions are not bad."

"Good."

"He hasn't really fought in a big battle yet."

"Good thing he doesn't know you've been in one."

She pursed her lips and turned, leaving him alone. He grinned as she left, unable to resist teasing her.

In minutes she was back with a bag in her hands. "Where did you get this? Mazie said you brought tea and salt today."

He shrugged. "I didn't realize you were running so short on supplies. I brought a few things home."

"You can't buy tea or salt in Memphis with the blockade! Where did you get this?"

"Some things you can buy if you know the right people," he said.

"You came by them illegally." She stared at him and he stared back. Suddenly she smiled. "Thank you, Major O'Brien." She turned and was gone and he grinned. He wouldn't have been surprised if she had thrown them at him and refused the gift, but he was glad she wanted it. He hadn't realized how great the shortages were until he talked to Mazie and to townspeople and tried to get supplies.

The following night he wore a white linen shirt and dark coat. The sleeve of the coat was pinned up over his right arm. He waited for Miss Merrick in the parlor and she appeared, coming through the door, her chin lifted, her eyes glinting defiantly.

Chapter 6

Caleb's gaze swept over her. Sophia wore one of her pale green muslin dresses, with its high collar and long sleeves, and it was as plain as a blade of grass. Her blond hair was braided and wound around her head; she looked the same as she had at eight o'clock that morning.

Caleb held out his arm. "How do I look in Brother John's clothes?"

Suddenly her eyes sparkled, and he thought she was trying to avoid smiling. "I hope they don't fall off," she said, teasing.

He grinned and tugged at the belt. "I punched another hole in the leather belt and after the war, I'll send your brother a new belt." He crossed the room to her. "Now, Miss Merrick, close your eyes and hold out your hand. I have a surprise for you." He wished he could step behind her and fasten the necklace around her neck, but he couldn't use his right hand.

She tilted her head to look up at him. "What are you talking about?"

"I have a present for you. Close your eyes and hold out your hand."

"A present?"

"Didn't your father allow presents either?"

She closed her eyes and held out her hand and he wondered what her answer would have been. What kind of solemn, narrow-minded man had Thaddeus Merrick been to raise his family in such a parsimonious fashion?

Caleb placed the necklace in her palm and the moment it touched her hand, her eyes flew open, looking at it and then at him.

"I can't put it on you or I would."

"A necklace!" she exclaimed, her breath going out in a rush. He felt pleased; it was obvious that she liked it. She held it up as if she hadn't ever had a gift before. "It's beautiful! My goodness, thank you."

She hurried to the mirror, and he silently cursed the sling around his arm, because he wanted to fasten the necklace on her. She held the oval twists of enameled silver with a glittering emerald in the center. Her eyes sparkled, and he was surprised how much the gift pleased her.

She turned to face him. "It's beautiful!"

"It looks very pretty," he said, thinking about her, still wondering how she would look in a silk dress with her hair in a more fashionable style. He remembered her in the white nightgown sleeping in the rocking chair with thick golden tresses spilling over her shoulders. She looked beautiful then with her pale skin and thick lashes, her full rosy lips. He longed to reach out and unwrap the braids from around her head. "You wear green often, so it should go with your dresses," he said softly.

"It'll remind me of your eyes," she said and then blushed.

"Miss Merrick, I didn't know you noticed," he said, grinning.

She smiled at him. "Of course, I've noticed. They're unusual."

He wondered if she knew what flirting meant. Smiling, he offered his good arm. "Ready? I told Henry I would drive the buggy."

"How kind of you. I worry about him; he's getting old."

"He worries about you, too."

"Henry?" she asked, sounding surprised.

"Of course. He remembers when you were born. So does Mazie. They've told me." Outside the air was cool. Magnolias were in bloom, large waxen white blossoms showy against the dark green leaves that blended into the night. "This is as close as you'll get to a coming-out, Miss Merrick. Of course, you're young for a presentation party."

"I never would have one. I think to the town, my family is an oddity. Eccentric is what I've heard some people say."

"Did they say that to you?"

"No. I've overheard conversations. I don't get invited to parties, because I don't move in the circles of people who have parties. Hannah Lou and I became friends because she lives only a short distance away and when I was small, I roamed around the neighborhood while Papa was busy preaching and getting out the paper."

"I didn't know your father was a preacher."

"Not officially. Not with a church. He simply preached temperance and what he thought the world should do. But Papa helped people who needed help and so townspeople have tolerated us. Except on occasion."

"What occasion?"

She shrugged as Caleb helped her into the buggy and climbed up beside her. "Once he tried to destroy a saloon on Whiskey Chute—that's the street of saloons between Main and Front. Some ruffians were going to hang him. The sheriff came to his defense and brought him home."

Caleb glanced at her. What kind of childhood had she had? he wondered. A father who was almost hanged for his preachings, a man who demanded constant work from his children. As they drew closer to the Needham house where the party was held, she became quiet.

When they entered the house, Sophia took a deep breath. Lights blazed from every room, and in spite of shortages and the war, the ladies were dressed in green and red and golden dresses of satin and silk. Sophia started to panic. *I shouldn't be here. They won't want me and I don't know what to do.* Major O'Brien linked her arm through his, moving so she was on the side of his good arm.

"Major, I don't belong here," she said solemnly, feeling cold with fear. To her amazement he flashed a broad grin. In an instant he generated so much warmth that she completely forgot the crowd and her fears.

"Sophia," he said, the word causing a tingle in her. "Can I believe my ears? You who have dressed in a Yankee uniform and spied on General Grant; you who have thrown men twice your age from your house and smashed

their whiskey and tried to burn my cards and defy me;
you who brought two unconscious men miles across open
land and saved our lives—you're afraid to walk into a
house filled with people you know? I never thought I'd
see the day. Sophia, shaking in her shoes! There is something that frightens the intrepid, self-sufficient Miss
Merrick."

"Stop that!" she said, annoyed with him in spite of his
dazzling smile. She lifted her chin. "This is entirely different, and I'm sure you don't understand because you
have the manners and the constitution of a jackass!"

He chuckled and squeezed her hand. "Ah, me. I knew
you were only teasing me. I thought I'd found something
that stirs fear in even as dauntless a heart as yours—
here's our hostess. Good evening, Mrs. Needham. How
I've looked forward to this night. It has been a thousand
years since I've been to a party or to a fete given by such
a beautiful hostess."

"Major O'Brien, how you do tease! Miss Merrick, I'm
so glad you talked him into coming. My, we're all going
to hate to see the major go. We almost wish you wouldn't
get well so you would stay with us."

"What's that, Eudora?" Patrick Needham asked, coming to stand beside his wife. "Good evening, Miss
Merrick. And Major O'Brien. Everyone has asked about
you, and Doctor Perkins assured us he gave us permission
for you to attend tonight."

Sophia stared at him. How had he won over the
Needhams in such a short time?

After a while they excused themselves from their hosts
and moved into the ballroom. When he paused every few
seconds to greet someone, Sophia stared at him in amazement. When had he met so many Memphians? How did
he know people better than she or just as well? she wondered. In minutes she relaxed. No one knew she was present. Major O'Brien was the center of attention, charming
them all. To her amazement when she tried to withdraw
to join some of the ladies at the refreshment table, Caleb
held her hand tightly against his side and turned to her.
"You can't leave me. I might fall down without your support. My leg hurts."

He was lying blatantly. She had stopped changing the dressings on his wounds since Dr. Perkins told her they were healing nicely. Now it was only the broken arm that was taking time to heal. Major O'Brien could stand and walk without the slightest aid.

Hannah Lou joined them and took every advantage to flirt with the major. While they talked, Sophia noticed so many men in uniform with bandages, arms in slings, men leaning on crutches. Injured men seated in chairs lined one side of the room where they could watch the festivities. Many of them had been brought over from the hospital.

"Sophia," Will Stanton called out as he approached them. He was gaunt and pale, but he was standing on his own and she was delighted to see how well he had progressed.

"Will Stanton!" she exclaimed. "You're better."

"Finally. Look at this," he said, pointing at Major O'Brien. "He's as tough as old leather. You don't look as if you've ever fought a battle, except for your arm," he said, grinning at Caleb.

"You look great."

"I know better, but I'll make it. I wrote your sister-in-law."

"Chantal?"

Will laughed. "Your body may be fine, but your mind is cotton. No. Miss Therrie. Amity."

"Did you now?" Major O'Brien asked and Will blushed, grinning at him. Would such a question ever make the major blush? she wondered. She couldn't imagine anything that would bring a blush to his cheeks other than anger. And did he care if Will wrote Miss Therrie?

Musicians strummed a few notes and noise of the crowd lowered as everyone turned toward the stage at one end of the ballroom. Mayor Park stepped to the edge of the stage. "Ladies, if you will line up along this side of the dance floor, the gentlemen will pay to dance with you. The money must be in gold please, and we can melt down watches and rings. We'll have all the aldermen—Samuel Tighe, Mister Morgan, Mister Merrill—lined up beside the stage. Find your alderman who is ready to take payment. Any contribution you can make will buy you a dance with a beautiful lady." He paused while there were cheers and applause. "All the proceeds from tonight will go to buy shoes for our glorious Confederate army."

Another rousing cheer came. As soon as it died down, Mayor Park raised his hand.

"Now step right up, gentlemen, for a dance and for a good deed in helping our fighting men. We want them home by Christmas."

Hannah Lou batted her eyes at Major O'Brien and turned to leave.

Will nodded to Caleb. "Let's pay and see if we both can do ten steps without collapsing. You'll probably do a hundred."

"However many, I'm going to enjoy them." He looked down at Sophia as she stepped back. "Sophia, join the ladies."

She shook her head. "You know I don't dance. I'll wait with the matrons."

"No, you won't. I'll dance with you, and we will barely move. Everyone will know it's because of my injury. Now go join them or I'll drag you there."

"There is something about you, Major O'Brien, that is both kind and extremely irritating," she said lightly.

"That's my natural charm," he replied, and she capitulated.

"You always get your way!"

"Maybe on the dance floor. Unfortunately on the battlefield, I don't get what I want at all," he said solemnly and she realized just how deeply the memories of the battle continued to plague him. But at that moment she was overcome by her own worries as he left her with a slight push and she had to join the group of beautiful women lining the side of the ballroom. She felt plain and out of place. Hannah Lou was far up the line and gave her a surprised look. Sophia stood between Lydia Hobson and Eunice Mott who glanced at her without speaking. They chatted constantly to each other across her and to the women standing beside them. She knew who both of them were, but years ago they had ceased speaking to her.

"Who do you think will claim you?" Lydia Hobson

asked, fanning herself until the pink rosebuds began to flutter in her black hair.

"With Ronald away fighting, the only men I want to dance with are Major O'Brien or Captain Ainsley or Major Tischler," Eunice Mott replied.

"We'll see which one of us gets to dance with them first."

There were lines of men making payment and the first men claimed their partners and moved to the dance floor. Major O'Brien headed toward her and Eunice leaned forward, the wide hoop beneath her green satin dress bumping against Sophia. Sophia caught the scent of hyacinth and looked at Eunice's shining blond hair and pink cheeks.

"Here comes Major O'Brien," Eunice whispered to Lydia Hobson. "I wonder which one of us he'll dance with."

Sophia wanted to get out of the line. Everyone would watch them and she would gladly hand him over to the other women. And then he was in front of her, looking only at her.

"Good evening, Major O'Brien," Lydia said, smiling at him. He returned the smile and shifted his attention.

"Miss Merrick, may I have this dance? I'll have to favor my wounded leg."

"Of course, Major O'Brien," she answered, moving with him onto the dance floor aware of the stares from the women. He placed a hand on her waist.

"She saved his life," came a loud whisper from behind them.

"Then he has to dance with her."

"No, I don't," he said with amusement to Sophia, looking down into her eyes.

"Lydia Hobson was dying to dance with you. So was Eunice Mott," she said, feeling more relaxed.

"I doubt that. There are other dances. Put one hand on my arm. Now we'll take four steps like this in a square. You follow me. One, two, three, four. Very good. Do it over again. It would help if I could use both arms."

She watched his feet, trying to follow his lead. "Why

are you doing this? There are some ladies here who want desperately to dance with you. I'll let you go."

He cocked his brow, looking amused. "Want to be rid of me, don't you?"

"No. I just think you could have more fun."

"I'll take care of fun. I'll dance with others. This first dance is with you. It's time you learn how."

"Papa would have apoplexy."

"Your father is gone and you have to live your life. And I can tell you Sophia," he said, his green eyes sparkling, "that you are far too lively to go through life without learning to dance. You're doing splendidly."

"Thank you," she said, feeling a rush of pleasure and looking up at him. He watched her while they danced, and she smiled at him. "I'm dancing!" she exclaimed softly, beginning to enjoy herself.

"I'm afraid, Sophia, that after this dance, I won't find it so easy to get the next dance with you."

"Why not?"

He gave her a look that was amused, yet didn't answer. Was he thinking she would have others claiming her for dances? "I don't think I'll be in demand. Look at my dress and hair."

His gaze drifted over her hair and then down, slowly, languidly perusing her full length. This unexpected gesture made her remember his kisses, remember that night when he had been nude and she had walked into the room, remember his coppery body. A sticky, lethargic heat engulfed her, making her feel weak and trembly. *How could he do this to her by a look?*

Just as leisurely as his gaze lowered, it drifted up until he looked into her eyes. "You're a beautiful woman."

Her pulse fluttered. Just words, yet the compliment wasn't like any other she'd ever received. Did he really think she was beautiful? This man who had dazzling women fawning on him? Who had women like Desirée and Amity Therrie travel from another state to see him? His words were scalding, stirring that low, aching warmth in her the same as his kisses did. *You're a beautiful woman.* The compliment became a treasure to keep in memory, to hold forever.

"Thank you," she answered, knowing she sounded breathless, feeling foolish for her reaction to the simple compliment, yet he watched her solemnly and looked at her as if he meant it. "You're very nice."

His hearty laugh was deep, rolling up out of his throat, his eyes sparkling, white teeth showing, a warm laugh that coaxed her to smile in return. "Nice? Sophia, you have called me many things, but never did I even come within a mile of *nice*."

She blushed, feeling foolish, suddenly sorry she had been cross with him so often. "You have your moments. You've been very nice tonight. The necklace is beautiful. I love dancing, and that was nice of you," she finished, thinking about the compliment.

"What was nice of me?"

"To give me the compliment."

The music ended and she wanted it to go on forever.

"Ladies, line up for the next dance," Mayor Park announced. "Gentlemen, get ready. We're off to a fine start! Over five hundred dollars in gold, plus some fine gold watches."

"Thank you, Major O'Brien," Sophia said.

"Get back in line and we'll dance one more."

"No. You have too many pretty ladies waiting for you to ask them to dance. As difficult as it is, I'll share you," she said solemnly, and he grinned.

"I'll be back and I expect to find you and to have another dance."

She nodded and moved away, sitting down in a chair near a cluster of matrons. She watched Major O'Brien ask Hannah Lou to dance. In minutes Will Stanton was in front of her.

"Sophia, I'd be honored if you would dance with me."

"Will, how nice," she said, surprised and standing. "Do you feel like dancing?"

"Only for a few minutes and then I have to get off my leg. But I want to dance. I saw you with Caleb."

"That's the first time I've ever danced in my life, so I'm not very good at it."

"Well, we'll be evenly matched, because I can barely

hobble around," he said, placing his hand on her waist and taking her other hand in his.

She looked at his feet to concentrate on following him, but in minutes she realized he was the one having difficulty keeping in step.

"You dance divinely," he said. "And I'm glad you're here tonight. Mama said it's high time you join the rest of Memphis at a party."

"Will Stanton, I think you should stop this and sit down."

He smiled and headed toward the edge of the dance floor. "I agree. My leg feels like it's on fire, but I'm so thankful to have two legs and two feet that I just had to get out here and dance even for only a few minutes."

"Thank you, Will, for asking me to dance," she said, pleased, realizing she didn't feel the same disturbing reaction to dancing with Will or talking to him as she did with Major O'Brien. She watched him waltz past with Hannah Lou whose eyes were sparkling. He laughed at something she was saying, and he looked handsome, debonair. Papa would never approve of him. Not ever in the next hundred years. Nor would John or Morris or Amos. For that matter, *she* didn't approve of him. He smoked and gambled and swore and was rough and wild and sometimes quite ungentlemanly. Yet . . . She drew a deep breath. She would not think about his kisses.

"Do you mind if I sit with you? It may keep someone from asking you to dance," Will said.

"Of course, I don't mind! I'll be happy to sit with you," she said. "Want a chair to prop up your foot?"

"That would be nice."

She pulled a straight-backed chair closer and lifted his foot to place it on the chair, and then she sat beside him.

"Tell me about that night in the barn," Will said. "When I ask Caleb, he says he doesn't remember."

She related all she remembered, leaving out that she had slept beneath the same blanket with Major O'Brien. The music ended and Mayor Park called for the women and men to line up for the next dance, reminding them that in a few more dances, they would be treated with a song from Miss Henrietta Claypool. People applauded and then left the dance floor to line up again.

She saw Major O'Brien dancing with Eunice Mott who was smiling up at him, no doubt flirting with him.

"Miss Merrick." A tall, brown-haired officer wearing rimless spectacles faced her.

Startled, she looked up. "I asked someone your name. I'm Lieutenant Oakley. May I have this dance?"

She glanced at Will. "Go ahead, Sophia."

"Yes," she answered, still surprised, suddenly uncertain again about her dancing, yet biting back the fact that she didn't know how.

"I'm from East Tennessee, ma'am. Up in the mountains. I fought at the battle near Shiloh and was wounded and I'm just getting well."

"So many are here tonight who were wounded in that battle and are recovering. I know you want to go home."

He placed his hand on her waist and took her other hand in his and she made an effort to follow him, but in moments she was moving with ease and realized Lieutenant Oakley wasn't as expert at dancing as Will and Major O'Brien.

"I've never seen so many beautiful ladies in my life as here in Memphis," he said, and she smiled. "And that includes you, Miss Merrick."

"Thank you," she said, thinking he was unaccountably polite. Her plain muslin dress couldn't be described as beautiful in a room filled with ladies in silks and satins. "Have you ever been away from home before?"

He grinned and shook his head. "No, ma'am."

"You're a lieutenant. That's a high rank for a man from the mountains who hasn't been away from home before and is so far away now."

"I got my officer's rank because of my shooting. That's one thing you learn at home. I've heard about you, Miss Merrick. All the men are talking about how you wore a Yankee uniform and rode into that battle and brought five wounded men back to the hospital in Memphis."

She laughed and shook her head. "No, Lieutenant. I only brought two men back to Memphis and one of them helped me with the other."

"Five or two men, what you did was brave. I admire that, Miss Merrick. I like a person with grit."

She danced with him, talking to him about his home and family, noticing that she couldn't spot Major O'Brien and then she saw him coming through the door to the outside with Eunice Mott. Her lips were red and she gazed up at him with a look that was adoring. He had kissed Eunice. Sophia felt annoyed with him and then with herself. She didn't care who he kissed or what he did. He didn't care that he had kissed *her*. She was so inexperienced where men were concerned. No doubt he hadn't enjoyed kissing her. She shifted her attention to Lieutenant Oakley, giving him a broad smile. Concentrate on what Lieutenant Oakley is saying. Forget Major O'Brien, she told herself. He can kiss anyone he pleases. It doesn't matter. Lieutenant Oakley was smiling at her, his brown eyes friendly above narrow cheeks covered with a smattering of freckles.

"Thank you, Miss Merrick, for the dance," he said as he left her beside Will.

"How I wish my leg didn't ache! Except I'm so thankful to still have two legs," Will said. "I'm going to lose you again."

"What—" She followed his gaze and looked up at another soldier. He had black hair and blue eyes and reminded her of her older brother.

"Miss Merrick," Private Gates said, his face flushing, "I don't know how to dance and if you want to go back and sit down so you can dance with someone else—"

"Of course, not. I'll show you," she said, biting back a smile. "You follow my steps and we'll step in time to the music; just do these four steps and repeat them. Look now. One, two, three, four."

He followed, stumbling and slowly getting it, looking up and smiling broadly. "Thank you so much! I watched you, ma'am, and you looked like you'd be nice. I was afraid some of the ladies would laugh at me."

"No one would do that," she said.

"Oh, my. Sorry," he said as he stumbled and stepped on her toe. For the first time she saw the bandage sticking slightly above the collar of his coat. Was every soldier there wounded? She glanced around the dance floor for Caleb and couldn't find him, but when she turned and looked toward Will Stanton, the major was seated next to him, arms folded across his chest. He was talking, Will turned toward him, but as his gaze met hers, the contact was as tangible as a touch. She turned to look up at Private Gates. "Where are you from? Not Memphis."

"No, ma'am. I'm from Chattanooga. I've never been away from home before and I've never been to a dance before. For that matter, I've never been in a hospital before, but I have now. Or a war."

"I wish all of you could go home. I hope it doesn't last long."

"Do you have men in the war?"

"Yes. My three brothers are in the East fighting with Lee and Jackson."

"I hope they get home soon. Miss Merrick, I heard you saved six men from the Shiloh battle."

She laughed. "Each time I hear about that night, the number of men I saved grows. It was only two."

"Well, it's still an amazing thing you did. I wish I'd found you. I had to ride the train with all the wounded men and it was pure he—. Sorry. It was bad."

"Tonight is the first dance I've attended, too, Private."

"Pshaw, ma'am. You're saying that to make me feel good. But it's nice of you. All the ladies in Memphis are nice. And they're the prettiest women. Makes me homesick. There are some pretty women in Chattanooga, too."

"Did you leave a sweetheart behind?"

"No, ma'am. But when I go home, I'm going to get me one and if I survive this war, I'm getting married and start my farm."

They danced and when the music ended, he led her back to the sidelines where another officer stepped to her side. "Miss Merrick?"

She looked up at a tall, dashing officer in the newest uniform in the room. Brass buttons gleamed against a gray uniform with gold braid and gold stars on his standing collar. "Good evening, Private," he said. "I'm claiming the next dance with Miss Merrick."

"Thank you, Private Gates," she said, smiling at him and turning to the major.

"I'm Major Tischler. May I have this dance?"

"Of course," she said, amazed, a fluttery feeling coming as she gazed up at the blond officer who looked as commanding as Major O'Brien. In minutes they were dancing and she realized that Major Tischler was an excellent dancer and the first man who seemed to have escaped being wounded. "Were you in the battle near Shiloh?" she asked.

"No. I'm just passing through Memphis to catch up with General Beauregard. I've been transferred to his command. Now I wish I were staying longer in Memphis."

"I wish you could," she said.

"Everyone is talking about you and your daring rescue of six men."

She laughed again, looking up at him. "Only two, Major. The story grows."

He grinned and they spun around. His long legs stretched out and she enjoyed herself, delighting in dancing, feeling air rush against her, loving every moment until the music finally stopped.

She looked up at him and laughed. "That was fun, Major."

"The pleasure was all mine. May I call before I leave town, Miss Merrick?"

"Of course," she said as she walked beside him.

"I think that's our last dance until the singing is over," he said.

"And I need to return to my seat. I was with Captain Stanton and Major O'Brien."

Major Tischler led her to her seat and turned away as Major O'Brien stood up and gave her his chair, pulling another one up next to hers.

"You look as if you're having a good time," Major O'Brien said quietly.

"I agree with you that dancing is fun."

"Will and I are having a discussion about the city."

"Caleb already knows everyone in town," Will said.

"I've learned how much Memphis has supported the

railroads. Will just told me that the state of Tennessee, after urging by Memphians, endorsed a three hundred and fifty thousand dollar bond issue to finance the Memphis and Louisiana Railroad."

"They backed the Memphis and Charleston with five hundred thousand," Will added. "This is a railroad city. They hoped to get the route to the West Coast."

"I know how the city has supported the railroads. But look how many saloons have opened since some of the railroads have come into town," she said. "And I know, Major, you think that's just dandy. You're as happy with the saloons as you are with the railroads."

Cutting into conversations, Mayor Park rapped a gavel for attention and the room quieted.

"Ladies and Gentlemen, I hope you enjoyed the dances. Tonight has been good for all of us and for the Confederacy. So far this evening we've raised over two thousand dollars."

Everyone applauded while soldiers cheered the news and one of the councilmen waved a fistful of gold in the air.

"Now a special moment for all of us. Miss Henrietta Claypool will sing for us."

With her golden curls piled high on her head, ringlets curling on the back of her neck, Miss Claypool held her pink satin skirt and stepped forward. When the applause died, she began to sing. As Sophia listened and watched her, she looked down at the emerald necklace, the deep green catching the light. She touched it, picking it up. The silver felt warm from lying against her. She held it in her hand and gazed at the emerald. She turned her head to meet Major O'Brien's cool green-eyed gaze. What was he thinking while he studied her?

They applauded and then Henrietta Claypool held out both hands. "If all of you will join me," she said, and the musicians began the stirring notes of "Dixie." Everyone who could stand came to his feet. Sophia sang, hearing Will's tenor and Major O'Brien's baritone, glancing at them to see tears in Will's eyes and a solemn expression on the major's face. The musicians went from that to

"When This Cruel War Is Over," and she noticed several soldiers wiping their eyes.

Finally the musical interlude was over and the dancing began again. Mrs. Stanton appeared, dropping her hand on Will's shoulder. "We're taking this soldier home before he wears himself out. Sophia, I'm glad you're here."

"Thank you, Mrs. Stanton. I'm glad to be here."

"Can you believe the amount of money we've raised tonight? Two thousand dollars for shoes for our boys. And Major O'Brien, we have to thank you for your generous contribution."

"Yes, ma'am. Glad to do it. Sophia," he said, shifting his gaze to hers, "if I can tear you away from the dancing, I think we'll go home. My leg aches."

"Sophia," Mrs. Stanton said, tapping Sophia on the arm, "take this man home, and you insist he stay off his injured leg. These boys never know what is good for them."

"Yes, ma'am," she said, aware Major O'Brien linked her arm through his. They moved through the crowd toward the front door.

"Why does she give you instructions to take me home with you when she knows you're unchaperoned and she wouldn't under any circumstances do the same with her daughter?" he asked, and Sophia felt a ripple of surprise at the brusqueness of his voice.

"Because they all know no man has ever shown any interest in me and I have never shown any interest in a man. I think they long ago decided I was a spinster."

"A spinster! Hell, you're only seventeen! And you've danced all evening!"

"Lower your voice," she retorted, blushing and glancing around, grateful that no one seemed to have heard him.

"If I went home alone with most of the females in this room it would start a rumor the moment we walked out the door," he said gruffly. She turned to face him.

"But the matrons and the ladies and my friends all know that I'm a spinster and I'll observe decorum. And they know a man as experienced and appealing as you will not be tempted by someone like me. We are not well suited, Major."

He drew a deep breath and his green eyes seemed to drive her back. She raised her chin, feeling caught in another silent contest with him.

"The whole town and Mrs. Stanton in particular shouldn't hand you over to me as if—" He snapped his mouth closed.

"But you see, they know. As if I couldn't possibly be compromised."

He leaned closer, his hand on her forearm. "But suppose you are? You know I'm no gentleman."

She felt closed in, buffeted by his anger, unable to fully understand why he was aggravated. "I won't be. Neither of us wants that," she said and hoped she sounded calm and cool and as self-possessed as he always was.

"I can't stand here arguing. My leg hurts," he said, taking her arm again and continuing to the door.

They thanked the Needhams, Sophia pausing as Major Tischler came up to tell her goodbye, glancing at Major O'Brien as he talked. Finally they were in the buggy, and she took the reins to drive.

"I'll do this. You look as if you've pushed yourself enough."

He reached over and took them back, holding them in his left hand. "I can manage and now that I'm sitting down, I'm fine. If I didn't know better, I would think you had been going to dances for years. You danced constantly."

"It was delightful. Thank you for teaching me how to dance. I really had a good time and I met the nicest men."

"Did you now?"

She glanced at him, noticing a sharp note in his voice.

"Yes. Lieutenant Oakley, whom you met from East Tennessee, and Private Gates. And Major Tischler. He asked if he could come calling tomorrow, so we may have a guest. You enjoyed yourself, I'm sure."

"Yes, I did. Except I intended to dance with you again and we didn't get to."

"You did your duty teaching me to dance and it was marvelous. I know Papa wouldn't have approved, yet I don't see any harm in what I did tonight and it raised all that money for shoes. I suppose he might even have approved if he knew it went to help the Confederacy." She hugged her knees and hummed the tune to one of the waltzes while Major O'Brien rode in silence. They pulled into the carriage house and he climbed down, offering a hand to her. She jumped down.

"I'll unhitch the horses, Major, so you don't have to stand on your leg. I don't want to wake Henry."

"I can help," he said tersely, and she wondered what had happened to his good humor.

Caleb moved to catch the harness, frustrated that he could use only his left hand. His leg throbbed, his shoulder hurt, and he felt a tight knot inside. And he knew why he felt it. He hadn't liked watching Sophia dance with the other officers. And it was the first time in his life he had ever experienced jealousy. He didn't like admitting it to himself, but he knew what he felt.

She was a baby. A seventeen-year-old child. And she was prim and proper and not the type of woman with whom he wanted to be involved. All the town trusted her to care for a man and keep him in her house unchaperoned. They knew she was too prudish to become involved; they thought she was too plain to attract a man. But she wasn't plain. Sophia was a beautiful woman. But oh, so proper. If a man kissed her three times, he would be on the way to the altar. She was innocent, unprotected, and he wouldn't be the one to take advantage of her. She had opened her house to him, nursed him, and he would be the lowest sort of scoundrel to court her. Women like Sophia Merrick lost their hearts too easily and she didn't have any womenfolk to explain men and life to her and she didn't have any men to protect her.

She reached up, standing on tiptoe to remove the harness and he wanted to catch her around her tiny waist and yank her to him and kiss her. But he wouldn't. She was too young and too innocent. It wasn't right. She took to dancing like a bird to flying, spinning around the dance floor with soldier after soldier. He ground his teeth together. *I don't give a damn who she danced with tonight!* Let her dance with every man in Memphis.

"My leg hurts," he said, knowing it wasn't his leg that was bothering him.

"As soon as the horses are taken care of, I'll help you inside. Until then, sit down, Major."

He helped with the horses, and finally they closed the door and stepped outside and she slid her arm around his waist.

He drew his breath sharply. "I can make it," he said tightly, afraid if he put his arm around her, he wouldn't stop there, but would pull her against him to kiss her.

Inside the house he paused in the hall where a lamp burned.

"Major O'Brien," she said, her eyes shining as she gazed up at him with a smile, her dimples looking adorable, "tonight was marvelous fun. I'm so glad you talked me into going and thank you for the lovely necklace."

"You're welcome. I'm glad you went." He jammed his fists into his pockets to avoid reaching for her.

"Whenever I dance, I'll remember you and this night."

"I doubt that, Miss Merrick."

"Of course, I will. It was wonderful." She turned away, spinning around with her arms held out, her skirts swirling out away from her as she went to her bedroom. He watched her and as she closed her door, she looked at him, her brows arching.

"Do you need help?"

"No," he answered gruffly.

"Good night, Major," she said and closed her door. He wanted to hit something. He would pack and go to New Orleans and to hell with Dr. Perkins. He needed to get back where he knew other women, where he could kiss Desirée and forget Sophia Merrick. He realized he was standing in the center of his darkened room, staring at the rocker and remembering the nights when he had stirred and looked up to find her sleeping in the chair. He yanked off his collar and shirt. Tomorrow men would call on her. Caleb paused, his belt unbuckled and pulled partially free. If soldiers came to call, she wouldn't have anyone here except Henry and Mazie.

A man could easily take advantage of her, and some soldier would when he learned she didn't have any family.

"Brimfire and damnation." Caleb sat down on a hard chair and stared into the darkness in front of him. He couldn't just abandon her to the soldiers who would call. She needed someone, but he wanted and needed to get home. He rubbed his neck, feeling ridiculous, annoyed by Sophia and himself. It was the fourteenth of May and Sophia was able to get along just fine without him. Tomorrow he would go home, he promised himself.

The next morning when he dressed and went for breakfast Sophia was already seated in the dining room. She wore a deep blue cotton that made her eyes seem more blue and was the prettiest dress he had seen her wear. The emerald necklace was around her neck and the top two buttons to the dress were unfastened.

"Your dress is pretty," he said as he sat down to her right.

"Thank you." She smiled at him, her eyes shining while her hand went to her collar and she fidgeted with the two buttons, fastening the lower one. He caught her hand. "Leave them alone. It's buttoned almost to your chin anyway," he said, feeling amused.

She blushed and moved her hand away.

"Why do you always leave those top buttons undone?"

"I don't give it much thought and I feel confined—" She shrugged. "I don't know why. A foolish habit."

"I think there's a whole side to you, Sophia, that you're trying to repress," he said softly, leaning closer to her over the table.

She laughed. "That's a ridiculous assumption, Major, and you wouldn't recognize repression if it came up and bit you!"

"Today I'm not going to get into an argument with you." Her eyes sparkled, and he felt a strange mixture of emotions. "I'm controlling myself right now."

"Good heavens, over what?"

Before he could answer Mazie came from the kitchen and placed a steaming cup of dark brew before him. "Major, I'll have some grits for you right away."

"Thank you, Mazie."

Sophia waved her hand toward his cup. "There's no

more coffee. I think everyone in town is out. That's parched rye."

"I wonder if supplies are as scarce in New Orleans?"

"It's the essential things that are worrisome. Doctor Perkins is worried about quinine; I worry about paper and ink. I have shoe blacking or berry juice if I can't get more ink. I'm running out of buttons, and we've run out of soda. People all over town are using different kinds of substitutes."

He gazed at her, thinking it would be a blessing if she ran out of paper. It would keep her out of danger if the Union captured Memphis.

"Now, Major O'Brien, what's disturbing you this gorgeous morning?"

"You shouldn't live here alone. You need someone here to protect your reputation," he insisted.

To his annoyance her smile deepened, and she waved her hand as if dismissing his suggestion. "Major, if my good name has survived staying here alone with you—and it has—it will survive visits from men I met last night. You know no matron in this town would allow you to be alone very long with her daughter—so it's how they view *me*. You're worrying over something that didn't bother Papa or my brothers."

"The only damn reason your papa and your brothers didn't worry was because they didn't let you out of their sight. You weren't having gentlemen callers."

"My, you're a grouch today," she said airily, increasing his annoyance. "It's entirely too nice a day. Maybe you should call on Eunice Mott or Hannah Lou or any of those beautiful ladies who dote on you."

"You're changing the subject. There should be some spinster in Memphis who would gladly move in—"

"Major, I can take care of myself. Don't you try to entice some fussy spinster to chaperone me!"

Mazie's usually delicious breakfast lost all appeal to him and he tried to curb his temper. "You're enjoying your damned independence!"

"Do you swear that much around Hannah Lou or Eunice?" Sophia asked sweetly.

"No, I damned well don't, because they don't provoke it!"

Sophia's blue eyes twinkled and she pursed her lips, and his anger boiled. "I provoke your anger? Go visit Hannah Lou and she'll calm you."

"I'm calm," he shot back. In spite of his annoyance, Sophia looked gorgeous and he wanted to yank her into his arms and shake her and kiss her until she agreed with him and stopped urging him to see other women. And he wished she wouldn't see other men today.

His feelings shocked him. He had never been so intense about a woman before.

"Sophia—"

"Relax, Major O'Brien," she said, standing, "you're not my father, and no one will hold you responsible. If I lose my good reputation over Major Tischler or Private Gates or anyone else, it'll be all my own doing." He was bestowed a sparkling smile with dimples, and she turned and left the room.

Sophia seldom wore hoops and crinolines, and he watched the sway of her hips. Did she know she had a provocative walk? Did she know she was provoking him?

He pushed his chair away in anger, coming to his feet, struggling to keep from going after her. He clamped his lips shut.

The minx! She took to dancing last night like a bird to flying, and men took to her like plants drawn to sunshine. They not only were charmed—he heard all the talk about her daring at Shiloh. A captain from Louisiana tried to tell *him* how she bravely rescued six wounded men. He swung his fist through the air.

"Major, are you all right?" Mazie asked, coming from the kitchen.

Embarrassed and annoyed, he nodded. "Just angry over being so incapacitated."

"Miss Sophia had the best time last night. I'm glad you took her to that party. It's time she meets some nice gentlemen, and she's just blossomed this morning."

"I'm going out," he snapped, striding from the room. He left the house to ride out past the mouth of Wolf Creek and Cochran's Mill to practice shooting with his left hand. After thirty minutes attempting to shoot a tree stump, he quit in disgust. He couldn't hit the courthouse with his left hand.

It was noon by the time he stopped at the newspaper and the door was locked. He rode home and a block from the house saw the Merrick buggy. He caught up to ride alongside it. Sophia gave him a breathtaking smile of dimples and even white teeth.

"Good afternoon."

"This is a beautiful day," she said happily. "Major Tischler stopped by the office this morning and I showed him all around. His uncle owns a paper in Bowling Green, Kentucky."

"How nice."

"You still seem out of sorts."

"No. It's a spring day and I've bought a train ticket and I'm going home tomorrow."

"Are you really? I thought Doctor Perkins said not to travel."

"Doctor Perkins will adjust to my leaving." He watched her. "I'll be back. I've bought land here."

"Why would you buy land in Memphis?" she asked in surprise.

"I think it's a good investment. One of the best. This city is poised for bigger things. You told me yourself how the population is growing and that it was the largest inland cotton market in the country before the war. I've talked to men in town, to Robertson Topp, to John McClanahan, and Benjamin Dill. I think the opportunities are great."

"You're coming back here after the war?"

"Don't look so shocked. Yes, if only to sell my holdings. I've got funds available. I've invested my money in my brother's blockade running—"

"Great heavens, your brother is a blockade runner? No wonder everyone in town loves you."

"Everyone? You, Sophia?" he asked, arching his brow, wondering how she would answer.

"You know you've won the friendship of people here," she said.

"My saints, if only I'd known. Sometimes you look at

me as if you'd like to take your papa's rifle to me," he said, beginning to enjoy himself.

"Will you stop teasing! In a minute I will want to take Papa's rifle to you. You're full of devilment, Major."

"Someone's at your house," he said, feeling annoyance return. Another one of the damned officers she met last night, no doubt. "Miss Merrick, you were quite a success at the dance."

"Thank you. You can't imagine what a delightful time I had. I do like dancing, Major. I wonder who that is." She turned the buggy to stop and climb down. Caleb saw a man in a dark suit standing at the door talking to Mazie who was dabbing at her eyes.

Sophia went up the steps and Caleb dismounted, tying the reins to the hitching post and following. As he climbed the step, he saw Mazie's stricken look. His insides knotted and he felt cold, looking at the man who faced Sophia. Caleb walked faster.

Chapter 7

The man turned to Sophia. "Miss Merrick, I have some names of Memphis men who were with General Jackson in Shenandoah." Sophia heard a roaring in her ears and she could barely hear the man's next words. Major O'Brien moved to her side and she was dimly aware of his arm around her waist.

"These men were killed at the Battle of McDowell. Ma'am, I'm contacting the families. These are the casualties. I'm sorry."

With stiff fingers Sophia took the list from him. She didn't need to read it to know what she was going to find, but her gaze went to the paper and the name leapt up at her. *Amos Merrick.*

She wanted to faint, to lose consciousness and not feel the pain that enveloped her heart. She felt Caleb's arm tighten around her waist. "No," she said, tears filling her eyes.

"I'll go tell Henry," Mazie said and went inside while Caleb held open the door and pushed Sophia into the hallway. Caleb pulled her against him and held her while she cried quietly, dimly aware of his hand stroking her head. "Amos, Amos," she cried. "I hate this war!"

"I'm sorry, Sophia," he whispered. "War is pure hell. So many hurt. I'm sorry."

She sobbed and Caleb wanted to scoop her into his arms and silently cursed his inability to do so. He took her by the arm and led her to the parlor where he sat down and pulled her onto his lap and pressed her against his chest.

In minutes there was a knock at the front door and Henry shuffled into view. Sophia stood up, wiping her eyes.

"Miss Sophia, sorry about Mista Amos."

"Thank you, Henry," she said.

Another knock sounded and Henry moved haltingly to the door and opened it. Caleb heard voices, and Clairice Stanton swept into the room with Hannah Lou. "Sophia! We just heard about Amos."

Mrs. Stanton wrapped Sophia in her arms while Hannah Lou dabbed at her eyes and looked at Caleb. Then Mrs. Stanton moved away and Hannah Lou hugged Sophia.

"We just heard," Mrs. Stanton said to Caleb. "The lists are in and several local boys were on the list. Carson Brenner, James Whiteman—"

"James and Carson and Amos?" Sophia said, tears still coursing down her cheeks. Caleb wanted to put his arm around her, but stood where he was. She didn't need any rumors that might sully her reputation.

Another knock sounded and the Hamptons entered. "Major O'Brien. Clairice and Hannah Lou," a tall woman said. She turned to Sophia to hug her. "Sophia, I'm so sorry."

Caleb stepped back, and Hannah Lou moved to his side. "It's so terrible," Hannah Lou said.

"Every battle will be terrible. We had some battles at first that were routs," the major said, "but after the fighting I saw near Shiloh, I don't think there'll be many more routs."

"James and Carson and Amos and there are others. William Spencer and Dade Waterford. They all wanted to be together and they joined at the same time," Sophia broke in. When she cried softly, Caleb patted her back and she leaned against his shoulder.

In minutes the room was filled with people and Caleb saw dishes of food go past in the hallway as people brought steaming platters and bowls of food.

Later, Dr. Perkins stepped in front of Caleb and shook his left hand. "Glad you're still here. She's going to need someone the next few days. And she'll need help next week when it's time to get out the paper."

"I had planned to leave tomorrow—"

"Son, you listen to me. You can't fire a gun, and there's no rush to get yourself back onto a battlefield. You don't have parents or a wife waiting for you. You stay right here. She saw you through a tough time. Now you see her through one. I like Miss Sophia and I don't want her left alone yet."

"Yes, sir. I'd already decided to stay for a few more days."

"You stay until she's more herself. And knowing Sophia, it won't be long."

Late that night when he closed the door behind the minister and the entire Stanton family, Caleb turned to her. "Will Stanton brought over a bottle of brandy. Sit down in the parlor and I'll pour you a glass."

"I've never had brandy in my life."

"It's like dancing. You'll love it."

She gave him a faint smile, and then it faded and he saw the hurt return. In minutes he sat down next to her on the faded rose horsehair sofa. He handed her the brandy and after the first sip, she coughed.

"Ugh! You like this?"

"Keep at it. It'll do you good tonight. You might even feel like sleeping."

"I don't now. And you don't have to sit with me."

"I know I don't. How old was Amos?"

"Eighteen. Morris is twenty and John is twenty-three. I don't even know if Morris and John know yet."

"You said Morris and Amos were together."

"The last letter from Morris said Amos was fighting with General Jackson, and Morris hadn't been in a battle. The last I heard from John, he hadn't been in battle either. John's with General Lee.

Caleb settled back, pulling off his boots and stretching out his long legs. "Did Amos look like you?"

"Others would probably say he did. Morris and I resemble each other the most. John is taller and heavier and darker. He doesn't look like the rest of us. Amos had the same color hair I do, but he was very tall and thin. He was closest in age to me, and we played together often as children."

"You're still a child. There are children fighting in this war. Other than the generals, I didn't know anyone over twenty-two years old and I knew plenty who were only eighteen. Most of them were eighteen. Except Will."

"Amos was so young. He was the best help at getting

the paper delivered. And he could fix anything around the house or at the paper. You have two brothers?"

"I had three. We were coming to the United States from Ireland and our ship wrecked. We were separated and I kept Darcy with me. Later I found Rafe in New Orleans and I settled there. We never have found Fortune. We were headed for New Orleans when the ship went down. After all this time, I can finally accept that Fortune drowned."

"I'm sorry. I didn't know. How old was he?"

"I was seventeen. Fortune was fifteen, Darcy was seven. Rafferty is the oldest. He was twenty-two."

"You've finally stopped hurting?" she asked, studying him, and he reached out to wipe a tear off her cheek with his thumb. Her skin was soft, smooth as satin.

"Sometimes it hurts, but not like it did the first few years. We were close."

"So were we. I always tagged along with my brothers and our father took us with him to the paper from the time my mother died when I was nine."

Caleb sipped his brandy and watched her while she talked. She stared ahead, seeming to forget his presence, reminiscing about her brother while she unwound one of her braids and ran her fingers through her hair to loosen the plait. He set down his glass and reached to take down the other thick braid to undo it. Her hair was silky sliding over his fingers. When it fell over her shoulders, he turned her slightly and kneaded the muscles in her back with his left hand.

"Does that help you relax?"

"I don't think anything can help, but thank you."

He wondered if she knew he was present. She seemed lost in her thoughts, continuing to talk about her brothers. Finally he sat back and poured more brandy for both of them.

It was almost dawn when she looked drowsy. He took the brandy glass from her hand and set it on the table, pulling her against his left side. "Go to sleep, Sophia," he said softly, keeping his arm around her. In minutes he felt dampness against his chest and knew she was crying again. She wiped her eyes and then became quiet. Her hand shifted across his thigh. Her breathing was even and she slept. He leaned closer to kiss the top of her head. So many men killed. And so many more would be killed. She had only two brothers left now. He prayed they would come through the war.

"Tough little Sophia," he whispered, remembering that moment when he had faced her over the muzzle of her rifle on the battlefield. She would survive this, too, but he knew how she hurt. Losing Fortune had been gradual, no abrupt message saying he had drowned at sea, but it hurt so badly. For years he couldn't accept it, still searching crowds for sight of him, Rafferty running ads and haunting the docks at New Orleans to ask about Fortune. Looking down at Sophia, Caleb felt a yearning and he cursed his injury, wishing he could pull her onto his lap and hold her close. And kiss her. He pushed images from his mind, staring into space, knowing he couldn't leave Memphis tomorrow as he had planned.

A memorial service was held Sunday afternoon at the Cavalry Episcopal Church for all the men lost in the latest battle. Monday morning Caleb unpacked his things and told her he would help print the Thursday edition of the paper. She went with him and he knew she was better off, because work would take her mind off her loss.

Grief insulated Sophia from the rampant speculation about the Union army and each day Caleb's worries for her safety grew. And land was available, people putting it up for sale at giveaway prices to get out of town and escape a conflict. He had bought five lots and he intended to buy more land before he left Memphis. And there was a prize he particularly wanted.

On the second of June as Sophia sat over breakfast in the dining room, Major O'Brien came through the door.

"Sophia, I want to talk to you."

"Yes, Major?"

He sat down to her right, pulling his chair close, and she caught a clean, soapy scent. His hair was damp and he wore a cotton shirt and new black cotton trousers. "You said once that your father left you comfortably fixed and the paper brings in a revenue."

"That's right."

"If you have funds available, there's land going up for sale here every day and the prices are good. I'd advise you to buy some land. After the war, it should be worth more."

She gazed beyond him. "I hadn't thought about it. I know people are leaving Memphis and I know I plan to stay. I suppose John would want me to purchase some land if I can get it at a good price."

"You know I've bought several lots and I intend to buy some more before I leave. I'm going to look at some today if you want to come with me."

"You're definitely coming back?"

"I might settle here. Why does that surprise you?"

"I can't imagine you settling anywhere. You look like the type to roam."

He leaned back on the chair and stretched out his long legs. "I worry about Darcy. I want to own a home and give him a more settled life. In not too many years, he'll be grown. And as for selecting Memphis—the business possibilities are endless. I'll start a business here.

"What kind of business?"

He was staring at her throat, and she realized she hadn't fastened the top button. She tugged it into place while he watched her. "I want to build a railroad."

"A railroad!" she exclaimed, feeling annoyed with him.

"I know how your father felt about them, but that's progress, Sophia. You should fight saloons and support the railroads. After the war, railroads ought to spread across this nation like birds in springtime."

She frowned. "You know they bring all sorts of troublemakers and wild people into town."

"Maybe they bring wild women and gamblers, but they also can haul cotton and machinery and travelers easier, more conveniently, and faster than stages or horses or wagons. Have you ever ridden on a train?"

"You know I haven't."

"If I had the opportunity, I'd take you on one. Memphis is on the river and it's only a hundred miles from the frontier. When this war is over, I think more people will head West and many will come through Memphis. I've talked to men in town and I know they tried to get the connection for a railway between the East and West coasts to come through Memphis."

"That will depend on the outcome of the war. I'd think you'd want to live in New Orleans. You call it home."

"I want to get out on my own instead of working with my brother. And business prospects look enormous here. I want to settle and have a home for Darcy."

Sophia studied him. "I can't imagine anyone, including your older brother, telling you what to do and succeeding in getting you to do what they say."

He laughed. "I've done some things you asked."

"Only when it suits you."

"I've bought the old Memphis and Arkansas line from here through Arkansas. I'm acquiring the land in Arkansas. Jordan Dalton is my lawyer and agent."

"The Memphis and Arkansas never did run!" Astounded, her thoughts swirled. *He was returning to Memphis.*

He touched a stray wisp of hair that escaped her braid. His gaze searched her face, and she felt her pulse race as he leaned closer. As his eyes met hers, he looked solemn.

"I didn't come in here to discuss business. There's something else. You're here alone, and the city may be under siege soon. Everyone expects an attack. I've talked to Will and his mother said you can move into their house."

Sophia shook her head, feeling a twinge of annoyance.

"Don't argue, Sophia. You can't face an army alone," he insisted.

"I'll manage," she said. "I've gotten along just fine here and I have Mazie and Henry."

"You take care of them as much as they take care of you. If an army occupies this town, you're a woman alone and soldiers will soon know it and take advantage of you."

"I've taken care of you and other soldiers, run the paper and the house, and I have no intention of moving in with the Stantons. You take care of yourself, Major O'Brien," she said firmly.

He studied her and she could feel the tug start again between them, an invisible clash that set every nerve on edge, that made her watch him warily even though he was sitting still doing nothing.

"You don't know anything about soldiers far from home."

"I'll remember the Stantons' offer." Their words were polite but the tension between them wasn't. She didn't want him telling her what to do when he was leaving and she wouldn't see him again for years if ever. "There may not be an attack."

"Everyone expects it soon. General Thompson says he can hold back the enemy if he has a militia, but so far, he has only a handful of volunteers. Not enough to protect the city. And if the city falls to the enemy, you'll have to sign an oath of allegiance to continue printing your paper."

"Never!" she exclaimed.

He ran his hand across his brow. "Sophia, you have a stubborn streak in you that will get you into trouble."

"I'll bring the small press home and hide it here. I'll put it in Amos's room," she said defiantly.

"You can go to prison for that! They won't allow you to print a paper that supports the Confederacy. *The Appeal* is all set to move their presses out of town. They'll put them on the railroad and go."

"How do you know they'll flee Memphis?"

"Benjamin Dill told me about the possibility." Caleb stood erect, showing how much he had recovered. "Want to look at property with me?"

He towered over her and she felt uncertain about him. "Yes, Major. I'll get my bonnet."

Three days later he walked into the office while she worked. It was early afternoon and Sophia looked up as the bell jingled over the door. Her pulse skipped as she gazed at him. His brown unruly curls were windblown and he wore a Confederate uniform and he looked different. And then she saw his arm.

He paused and held out his arms.

"My goodness—your arm is healed!"

"I've told Doctor Perkins goodbye. Look here—" He waved his arm and winced, grinning at her. "My arm is weak and it hurts to move, but I'm out of the cast."

"Wonderful!" she exclaimed, standing up as he approached the desk. His green eyes sparkled, and she remembered that night in the barn. "I didn't think I could get either one of you to Memphis in time."

"But you did," he said, holding his arms out and then dropping them to his sides. "And now I'm going to ride out of town and practice shooting. Come with me."

"You just said you're weak and you hurt."

"I do, but I have to start sometime."

"I need—"

"Tomorrow I'll be on my way to New Orleans. Come on, Sophia. Shut the office."

She stared at him. He was really leaving now. She nodded, feeling a strange sense of loss. She had become accustomed to him at the house.

She put her bonnet on her head and he reached out, taking the ribbons from her hands to tie it beneath her chin, smiling at her. Gazing into his green eyes, she smiled in return.

"It's the first week of June and it feels like June," he said in his deep voice. "Summer in the South. Hot, and at home the steamy afternoons were lazy, clouds so white in the sky and bees buzzing around the flowers and the smell of grass in the air."

"Home? New Orleans or Ireland?"

"New Orleans. I stopped thinking of Ireland as home a long time ago. It seems like forever since I left. My ties are here now. I think this country is magnificent. I love the hot days and warm nights of summer. I love the railroads and their big steam engines. I love Memphis with its bluffs high above the Mississippi and the steamboats that stop here and the people who pour in and out of here. It has beautiful homes, beautiful trees, and beautiful women," he said, gazing down at her with his brow arched.

"Hannah Lou and Lydia Hobson are very beautiful."

"You know I'm not talking about them," he said quietly, turning her to face him as they reached the buggy.

She gave him a wide-eyed stare, feeling warm, thrilled by his words while at the same time, knowing she shouldn't give them much heed. He helped her into the buggy.

She glanced at him as they rode along Front Street. He was handsome and she didn't want to think about his leaving or about his going back into battle. "I suppose I shouldn't worry about you returning to fight. You're so tough."

He glanced around. "The most rugged man on earth can't stop a minié ball."

They rode out Chickasaw Street past the saw mills and the gas works, crossing Gayoso Bayou to turn east on Mill and back north on Main until they were out of Memphis. Pulling off in high grass in a field dotted with trees, Caleb climbed down and offered his hand to help her.

Holding his revolver with both hands, he fired at a dead tree. Within seconds pain shot like fiery arrows through the muscles in his arm, but he clamped his jaws together and continued to fire. To his relief he began to hit his target. All too soon his arm tired. Sophia sat on a tree stump watching him, and he glanced at her.

"Want to try?"

She stood and walked over to him. She had shed her bonnet and unbuttoned the top buttons of her black dress and the tiny glimpse of flesh drew his attention. She wore the emerald necklace daily. "Come here and I'll show you how to fire this. It's already loaded and this has a repeating action."

She smiled and took the revolver from his hand. "You forget I have brothers." She held the weapon with both hands. "I'll shoot at the end of the lowest branch," she said, aiming at the same dead tree he had used for a target. She missed the first time, but the second was on target. She returned the revolver to him. "It's been a long time since I practiced."

"I should have known. Will you write to me?" he asked, looking down at her.

"If you'd like."

"I'd like it very much. I'll worry about you. When I come back to Memphis, I expect you'll be married to some Confederate officer."

She smiled, her dimples showing, the wind blowing her hair. He thrust the revolver into the gun belt he wore and placed his left hand on her shoulder. "If the city falls to the Union, close your paper and move in with the Stantons. Promise me that you will."

"I'm sorry. You're going back to war and you can't promise me you won't go into battle. If I don't move in with the Stantons, it won't mean I'm in danger."

"You father didn't know he was going to die and leave you alone and your brothers left when your father was still with you. They didn't know you'd be alone. I'm sure they worry, too."

"Don't you worry about me. I'll get along. Look at how well our fleet did last month at Plum Point. They disabled two gunboats and didn't receive any significant damage or injury."

"This may be different. They caught the Union fleet by surprise." He looked annoyed as he took her arm and they returned to the buggy to ride home.

As they reached Union Street and neared Court Square, men ran back and forth across the street.

"Something's happened," Major O'Brien said. Her pulse beat faster. Was Memphis under attack?

Thad Greenly waved at them. "Major, word is the Union fleet is moving downriver! Our River Defense Fleet is ready. We're going to be attacked!"

The paper! She felt a ripple of fear for *The River Weekly.* She had heard stories of presses burned and confiscated in Nashville. She remembered holding her father's hand that last afternoon and swearing she would protect the paper and keep it going until her brothers returned. She lifted her chin and glanced at Major O'Brien, who was watching her intently. "I'm not letting the *Weekly* fall into Federal control!"

Major O'Brien clamped his jaw shut and looked ahead. "I'm going to ride upriver until I can see the enemy. Do you want to come or should I take you home?"

"I'll go with you. I can't believe the Union can take Memphis. We have ships to defend the city."

"You have cottonclads—that's what men are calling them. Instead of steel to protect them, they have bales of cotton. It's not the same. And there's no real army here."

"I wonder if I should move my press now."

"Dammit, you're going to get yourself in trouble. Just

wait. They're not going to take Memphis quickly. There will be a battle."

They rode north, winding along the river, and she became silent, worrying about her press, thinking what supplies she wanted to move home and wondering when Caleb would leave town. If there was going to be a battle, would he leave as soon as they returned to her house?

Shadows were beginning to slant across the river's surface when they turned a bend. She felt another ripple of fear as five boats steamed into view. They looked squat and cumbersome with fat smokestacks belching clouds of black smoke and the Stars and Stripes fluttering in the breeze. Huge cannon projected from the front and sides and she thought of drawings she had seen of alligators from swamps down South.

"They look dreadful."

"They're floating gun carriers. My brother has seen one in action and he wrote me about it. The paddle wheel is inside where it's protected by armor."

"They go so slow, like huge drifting monsters."

"They're heavy. It's a miracle they float. There are only five of them. We'll have eight. It looks like transports coming behind them."

"If we have them outnumbered, we should win."

He sat in silence. Sunlight sparkled across the water and glinted on the dark metal plating of the boats. As the fleet slowly drifted past, the sight of the dark snouts of cannon and the heavy plating sent a chill through her. Caleb turned the buggy and they followed alongside the gunboats and she wondered how soon the battle would start. The gunboats stopped four miles upriver from Memphis. The major halted the horses and they sat again watching the boats until the shadows were long, then he turned toward the city. Hundreds of people lined the banks of the river and roamed along the levee, watching for the boats.

"Look at everyone," she cried.

"They know the battle is coming."

They stopped behind the carriage house. As he helped her down from the buggy she rested her hands on his forearms until her feet touched ground. The last dusky light of day played over his features, highlighting his broad cheekbones. "Are you leaving Memphis now?"

"I ought to leave, because I'm an enemy of the Union. Instead, I'll stay until the attack to see what happens."

"You're not staying because of me." she blurted.

"Yes, I am."

"I can take care of myself," she said, feeling a mixture of emotions. She didn't want to move to the Stantons' and she didn't want Major O'Brien telling her what to do; on the other hand, all she could think of was, *he's leaving*.

"Will you pack and go to the Stantons' tonight?"

"No, Major. It may not be necessary." His fingers locked around her upper arms and he held her.

"Dammit, you're in danger. And don't tell me again that you can take care of yourself."

Feeling the tension grow between them, she yanked away from him and strode toward the house. When she thought about his leaving, she felt overcome by loss. Foolishness. Once he's gone, the empty feeling will go away, she told herself. The house was empty before and if it's too bothersome, Dr. Parker will send some more wounded over to nurse. If there's a battle, the house may be full of injured men again. She entered the darkened house and lit a small lamp on the table in the hall. Caleb followed her inside and she looked up at him. The soft glow of the lamplight was reflected in his eyes. He was solemn while he watched her.

"If a soldier comes in this house, you won't be able to stop him from doing anything he wants to do," he persisted.

"Of course I can. I can get Papa's rifle. Major O'Brien, I don't want to hear another thing about what I can and cannot do!" She started to pass him to go to the kitchen. He caught her arm and spun her around.

She tugged, trying to yank free and then she looked up. The hungry look in his eyes scalded, burning every raw nerve. His gaze was on her mouth, his intention plain to see in his face.

He slid his arms around her, hauling her hard against his chest, crushing the breath from her lungs. "I've wanted to do this for a long time," he said in a husky voice.

She couldn't get her breath, and her heart pounded violently as she lifted her face to his. She wanted him to hold her, to kiss her. He groaned and bent his head, his mouth coming down on hers, his tongue thrusting over hers as he leaned back against the wall and spread his legs and held her pressed against him.

She melted against him, feeling hot, breathless. His kisses were all she remembered and more. So much more this time. With a shock she felt his hard erection press against her; she moaned softly, her hips shifting against him. She shouldn't kiss him and allow him to kiss her, she told herself. It wasn't proper, and he soon would be out of her life forever. This meant nothing to him. How much did she care? Thought stopped as she ran her hands along his strong shoulders. She felt lost, torn with longing, wanting him. Finally with a gasp, she pushed away.

"Stop it, Major!"

"Sophia—" he said.

"No. Don't kiss me. You know we shouldn't. You're leaving and we may never see each other again."

He stared at her as if he hadn't heard her. What was he thinking? He looked angry, *so handsome*.

He turned away and walked past her, stopping to glance around. "I'm going to the Stantons' to talk to Will once more. You keep your father's rifle and pistol handy all the time." He strode out and slammed the door behind him and she clenched her fists. She shook and felt assaulted by longing, fighting what her heart and body clamored for—a man who was as volatile to her beliefs as fire mixing with gunpowder.

Remembering his strong arms around her, she placed her hand against her heart. "No," she whispered. "No, Major."

Closing her eyes, she thought about his kisses. She couldn't fall in love with a man like Major O'Brien. And he would never love her in return. Not with women like Hannah Lou and Amity Therrie and Desirée hanging on his every word.

She carried the lamp to the parlor and held up her father's rifle, checking that it was loaded. Was Memphis going to be attacked and could the Confederate fleet crush the Federals?

She was in bed when she heard Caleb come into the house. He was far noisier than her father or any of her brothers, his boots scraping the hall floor, his door banging closed. Every footfall seemed to echo in her heart. He was going to bed. Images came to mind of his standing nude, his long, coppery body, his maleness. She groaned and tried to stop thinking about him.

After a restless hour, she got up and pulled on her wrapper, lighting a lamp and carrying it with her. She went to the parlor, crossing the room to the desk.

"What the hell are you doing?"

She almost dropped the lamp. Spinning around, she peered into the darkness. Caleb was seated in the wing chair, a cigar in his mouth, the tip glowing.

"Sorry, about the smoke," he said quietly. Bare-chested, he wore his dark trousers and boots.

"I couldn't sleep, so I thought I might as well get ready for tomorrow."

"Come sit down," he said, motioning to her. He picked up a glass and finished the contents, then poured another one.

She felt uneasy, aware of his bare chest, of her wrapper that she pulled tightly beneath her chin.

"Sit down, Sophia," he said more forcefully and she moved to the sofa to sit on the edge and face him. He leaned forward. "Have some brandy."

"No, thank you."

"Always the prim and proper miss."

Angered by him, she accepted the glass to take a sip, feeling the warmth of the brandy course down her throat.

"Will said everyone he knows is going to the river at dawn. We might as well join them and see what Memphis's future will be."

"You're angry."

He looked at her, his gaze intense and she drew a deep breath.

Caleb studied her in the dim light from the lamp. He wondered if she had any idea how beautiful she looked. Her hair was down, a pale silky cloud spilling over her shoulders, the top of her wrapper unfastened and the top of her white nightgown unbuttoned only enough to show her pale throat. He fought the impulse to get up and pull her into his arms and kiss her. He wanted her. It wouldn't be right. He wasn't ready for marriage and he had to return to fighting eventually. And Sophia Merrick wasn't the woman for him. As much as he admired her, because she was braver than soldiers he had known, he didn't share her views on anything. She disliked railroads, disapproved of his whiskey and cards, and she was as independent as a well-fed cat.

"I would feel a lot better leaving here if you would stay with the Stantons."

She lifted her chin and he wanted to shake her, yet if he reached for her, he would kiss her. He remembered her pressed in his arms, her full breasts soft against him.

"I've been thinking about it. If Memphis falls, I want to move the small press home. If I go to the office now, there are materials I can pack to get ready. If the Confederate cottonclads beat the Federals, I'll have to unpack everything. On the other hand I can have my supplies ready to move. I came to get the office key from my desk. Then I was going to get dressed and call Henry and ask him to hitch up the wagon and go with me to the office."

"I'll hitch the wagon. I'll go with you," Caleb snapped. All evening he had fought the temptation to go to her office and smash her presses so she couldn't print a paper if the Union captured Memphis. "They send women to prison, you know."

"I'll take my chances. I'm keeping the paper going for the memory of Papa and Amos, for John's sake and Morris's sake. It's the least I can do."

"I think all of them would want you to give it up if they could discuss it with you."

"You don't know my family. My father would want me to keep it going." She stood up and thrust the glass toward him. "Here's your brandy, Major," she said scathingly.

His temper frayed and he stood up swiftly, taking the glass and downing the contents. She turned away and he drew a deep breath, reaching for her against all good judgment, against reason.

He yanked her back to him and she resisted.

"No, Major. You're all the things I don't believe in and don't like.

He tossed the cigar into the fireplace and tightened his arms around her, holding her head with one hand, his left arm around her waist. "There are some things about me you damned well do like!"

She closed her mouth and fought against him and he knew they were fighting more than just the words spoken between them this evening. He wanted her; he was infuriated by her. And the disparities were mutual. *At the same time . . .*

She wore only the cotton wrapper and her nightgown and he could feel her supple body, the warmth of her, and his heart hammered in his chest. He throbbed, aching for her warmth, wanting to push away the wrapper and gown, wanting to kiss every inch of her silken skin.

Her hair spilled over his hands as he held her. Her struggles ceased and she yielded, standing still while he bent over her until she had to wrap her arms around him. He thrust his tongue deep, wanting her warmth and fire, drowning in her passionate responses.

He untied the wrapper, then fumbled with the buttons of the gown, pushing both garments away, cupping her full, soft breast. He felt on fire with need. He ran his thumbs over her taut nipples, bending his head to kiss her, aware of her soft moans, of her hands playing over his shoulders and back. He pushed the gown to her hips, kissing each breast, feeling her tremble. His pulse roared in his ears. His erection was hard, throbbing, and he felt he would burst. "Sophia," he whispered, "I want you."

He slid his fingers beneath the gown to push it away, but her hands caught his, holding his wrists tightly.

Sophia gasped for air, aching, her hips moving, burning with longing. She had to face facts, she told herself. He was going to leave her and they were so different. She couldn't lose her heart to him. She wouldn't!

"Stop, please," she whispered, moving back. He raised his eyes slowly, giving her the same searing, hungry look that always made her breath catch. His gaze roamed over her bare breasts and she was torn between reaching for him and yanking up her gown. She wanted him, yet she tugged up her gown and stepped back out of his reach. "I'll get hurt," she whispered, turning away. She rushed to the desk and picked up the key, hurrying out of the room without looking back, afraid if she turned around, she would run straight into his arms.

Caleb tugged the reins and they sat at the edge of the bluff. It was almost half-past four in the morning. Wagons creaked and harnesses jingled as buggies and wagons and men mounted on horseback lined the bluffs to watch the battle. There was a steady buzz of voices while people unpacked baskets of food. The stars and bars waved all along the riverfront.

"Major O'Brien! Sophia!" Hannah Lou waved and Will motioned to them.

"Come join us," Will urged, climbing down out of his buggy to offer his hand to Sophia. They climbed up to squeeze close on the driver's seat with Caleb between Hannah Lou and Sophia while Will sat on Sophia's right. Hannah Lou looked radiant in a deep blue poplin and Will looked healthy and strong for the first time since the Shiloh battle.

"Commodore J. E. Montgomery is commanding the Confederate fleet," Will said. "Father said Montgomery issued a proclamation to the people of Memphis that he has no intention of retreating. He said he has come here so that we can see Lincoln's gunboats sent to the bottom by our fleet."

Hannah Lou wriggled in the seat, placing her arm on Caleb's. "I hope it's over quickly and none of our men are hurt. Mama said she couldn't possibly come watch, but Papa thinks we'll whip them easily and send them to the bottom of the river."

"We have the advantage of being on the downstream side," the major said.

"What difference will that make?" Hannah Lou asked, gazing up at him. He looked down at her. While he explained that the current made it easier for the Confederate boats to retreat and maneuver, Sophia thought about his kisses only a few hours ago. Had he kissed Hannah Lou like that? And others? She was sure he had, that the kisses and women meant nothing to him. Don't lose your heart to him, she told herself. He wouldn't care and he will leave Memphis and kiss other women.

Moving slowly against the current, Confederate gunboats formed two lines of four each.

"The big cannon are in the front line," Caleb said.

"That's the *Jeff Thompson,* the *Sumter,* the *General Lovell,* and the *General Beauregard,*" Will commented.

"Here come the Bluecoats."

"Their transports are following."

She glanced around. Thousands of people lined the bluff, which gave a panoramic view of the river. Sunshine glinted on the spires of the churches and over the rooftops of the tall buildings on Front Street. She felt a shiver run down her spine as she remembered the commencing of the battle at Shiloh. Cannon blasted and she jumped. Caleb looked down at her, and she wondered what he was thinking.

The Federal fleet responded. Shot clanged when it hit armor plating, splintering through exposed timber. Black smoke pouring from smokestacks thickened and mingled with smoke from cannon, obscuring the view.

"Lord, look," Caleb said and pointed at the battle. At first she couldn't decide what had caught his attention, but then she saw two of the Federal boats charge past the advance Federal line. Throwing up plumes of spray and creating high waves, the boats sped through the water.

"Those aren't transports," Caleb said.

"What in blazes are they doing?" Will asked.

"They're charging. They're going to ram the *General Price.*"

Sophia watched in horror as the Federal ship struck the *Price* broadside. A clang echoed over the bluff, sounding above the blast of cannon as the ram crushed the *Price*'s wheelhouse. Hannah Lou screamed and slumped against Caleb. He caught her, sliding his arm around her waist and patting her hand as her eyes fluttered.

From age twelve Hannah Lou fainted or pretended to faint when it suited her, but as Sophia watched Caleb hold her friend, she felt a strange twist of annoyance. *Jealousy.* She shouldn't be jealous of anything Hannah

Lou did with the major. She looked at the battle and tried to forget Caleb O'Brien talking softly to Hannah Lou.

"The *Price* is heading for the Arkansas shore," Sophia whispered and then realized she was gripping Caleb's arm tightly as he covered her hand with his. She glanced up at him to see him watching the battle with narrowed eyes.

"The *Beauregard* is going to ram one of theirs," Caleb said, and she followed his direction, watching it strike the Federal *Queen of the West* aft. "There's another!" he exclaimed.

She heard the clang as a ram struck the *General Beauregard* on the bow. While the ram towed the *Queen* toward the Arkansas shore, the *Beauregard* was swamped. Men went into the river from the smashed *Beauregard* as it sank.

"They can't all get off," Will said and she stared with horror as the *Beauregard* disappeared into the river, water swirling over it.

A ball hit the *General Lovell,* striking aft and tearing a gaping hole. Water rushed in as the *Lovell* sank.

"We got one of theirs. It's heading for the Arkansas shore," Caleb said excitedly.

The air reeked of gunpowder and noise was deafening. She wanted to place her hands over her ears as she heard cries from injured men and remembered too clearly the horror of Shiloh.

"Three of ours are already out of the battle," the major explained.

It suddenly hit her that when the Federals claimed the city, her paper would be lost; she couldn't move a press to her house in a Union-occupied city. She glanced up at Caleb, who was engrossed in the battle while Hannah Lou constantly talked to him. Sophia tapped Will's arm urgently.

"Excuse me, Will," she said in a low voice. "I'll be right back. I want a handkerchief." He jumped down and helped her from the wagon. When she reached the ground, she saw out of the corner of her eye that Caleb turned to look at her. Another clash from the river caught his attention, then he shifted his gaze to the battle.

Will helped her up onto her wagon. "Go back, Will. I

feel faint. This reminds me of the battle at Shiloh. I may just lie down in the wagon."

"Sorry, Sophia." He looked sympathetic as he turned away. She sat on the wagon seat. When Major O'Brien turned to Will, who leaned close to talk to him, he looked past Will at her and she put her head in her hands. In minutes when she glanced back, he was watching the battle. She picked up the reins. With a flick the team moved forward and she headed through the crowd, people parting to make way for her. She glanced over her shoulder to see Caleb jumping down from the wagon. Her heart pounded. If she didn't get through the crowd, he would catch her easily.

She saw Caleb running toward her. She skirted a carriage, people moved out of her path, and then the way was clear. She urged the horses on, her heart pounding as they broke into a run.

The major was only yards behind her.

"Sophia! Sophia, wait!"

She turned and leaned forward, wind blowing her hair as the horses tore around a corner and down the street. Her heart pounded as she heard the sounds of battle behind her. She had to save Papa's press. In minutes she slowed and stopped behind her office, backing the wagon to the door. With shaking hands she unlocked the door. Henry stirred and stood up.

"Miss Sophia?"

"Henry, the Confederacy is losing the battle. Help me move this equipment," she ordered, rushing past him.

"What will happen to us?"

"I don't know, Henry. Hurry." She lifted the boxes she had placed by the door last night, feeling a sense of desperation to get everything moved. Then she turned to face the major. He stood in the doorway with his arms akimbo, staring at her. With the light behind him, his lean body and face were shadowed. He took the boxes from her hands and passed them outside to Henry.

"You're going to do this?"

"Yes. I have to."

"Henry and I can load the rest. Get in the wagon."

One glance into his green eyes, and she closed her mouth and held back an argument. She climbed into the wagon and

watched, hearing sounds of battle. Black smoke drifted overhead and the smell of gunpowder was strong. She shivered
and looked past the men at the dark interior. Would the Federals destroy her big press and office?

Major O'Brien swung a carton onto the wagon. How
could he lift even the small press with his weakened arm?
she wondered. He looked pushed to the limit when he
told her to get in the wagon. She gripped the seat and
watched him work.

Finally he and Henry came out carrying the proof press
and hoisted it into the wagon. It landed with a thud and
Henry climbed up behind it. As Caleb closed the office
door, she had one last glimpse down the darkened office.
Her gaze ran over the red brick building, and she felt a
twist of pain in her chest. Papa was gone, Amos was
gone, now the paper might be lost. She watched the major
come around the wagon and climb up beside her. He
would go now, too.

Tears stung and she looked down at her hands folded
together in her lap. She wasn't going to cry. The paper
was a tie to John and Morris and she would keep it going,
she vowed silently.

Major O'Brien placed his arm around her shoulders and
pulled her closer to him. She didn't think she could bear a
word of sympathy or she might lose control and burst into
tears. She sat looking at her hands, trying to think about
something else so she wouldn't cry. If Memphis fell, what
would happen to everyone? To Mazie and Henry?

"What happens when an army takes a city?"

"They've taken New Orleans, and in many ways, life goes
on," he said, looking away and she suspected he was keeping
some things from her. "My family is fine."

Were they really fine, or was he just trying to reassure
her? She didn't want him to leave, yet it was time for him
to go. He would be taken prisoner if he stayed.

"A woman alone is damned vulnerable," he added.

She drew a deep breath, knowing he didn't approve of
what she was doing.

They pulled the wagon as close to the back door as possible and she climbed down to help them unload. Mazie

came out to carry boxes. As she passed the major, Sophia caught his arm.

"Can you and Henry carry the press upstairs, or should I get someone else to help him?" she whispered.

"We'll manage," he said, gazing at her solemnly. "The moment we bring it into your house, you're placing yourself in jeopardy. When you print a paper, you'll commit sedition."

"I have to do this." She went downstairs to get another box. Trying to control her emotions, she felt as if the slightest mishap would push her over the edge. She heard the grandfather clock chime nine o'clock. It seemed more than a few hours ago when they left to watch the battle. The boom of cannon still carried from the river. Did Memphis still belong to the Confederacy? she wondered.

As she passed Major O'Brien in the doorway, a deep-rolling boom rocked them. She felt a vibration in the air and looked at him in question.

"What was that?"

"Something just exploded." He turned away, and she went outside to pick up another box, looking at the darkening cloud spreading overhead.

The men carried the press upstairs and finally all the boxes were in the house and Henry led the team away. Mazie returned to the kitchen and when Sophia looked around, Caleb came down the hall with his broad-brimmed hat on his head.

"You're leaving?"

"I'm going back to the bluffs to see how the battle is progressing. Want to come along? I told Henry to hitch the team to the buggy."

She nodded and they headed for the wagon. As they drove toward the river, they heard shouts and a commotion and the major turned toward the courthouse. In minutes they saw a crowd and he slowed the buggy at the edge of hundreds of angry people while they watched the Stars and Stripes go up over the post office.

"Memphis belongs to the Union," Major O'Brien proclaimed, picking up the reins. "We'll see what the damage is."

They sat on the bluff and saw the crippled Union ships. "Where are our boats?"

"They've sunk or we'd see them. They weren't going to retreat," he said grimly, and she hurt over the loss.

As they returned home, he stopped in front of the Stantons'.

"I need to go home," she insisted.

"We'll just pay a short visit," he said, standing on the ground and looking up at her. "Climb down," he ordered and offered his hand.

"You've brought me here, because you know Mrs. Stanton will urge me to move in with them now. I want to go home, Major O'Brien," Sophia repeated, annoyed with his cavalier manner.

He reached up, his hands closing around her waist and swung her to the ground. She looked up, ready to protest, but the anger sparking his green eyes made her keep quiet. She lifted her chin and turned toward the Stanton porch.

It was late afternoon when they left the Stantons' and returned home. Mazie served dinner and afterward, Caleb went to his room. Sophia went upstairs to unpack boxes. She wanted to get out an edition tomorrow.

As she bent over a box, she heard a knock at the open door and turned to see the major.

"Come in. I can't find the things I need."

"I'll help. What are you looking for?" he asked.

"You're not leaving?" she asked in surprise.

"Not unless you want me to go. The Federal forces will be moving in and getting settled. I'm in no danger tonight or for the next few nights for that matter."

"You don't know," she said, frightened for his safety.

"They won't search houses. They'll issue proclamations and warn people to leave town, but not tonight. They're getting established."

She thought of her brothers and grief threatened to overcome her. "How long will this go on?"

"Unfortunately, the war is just getting started."

She turned away. "I've looked for my containers of shoe blacking and I can't find them. My ink is almost gone, so I need the shoe blacking, and now it's gone."

He came up behind her and turned her to face him. "I won't leave you alone yet, Sophia."

She drew a deep breath and he pulled her into his arms to kiss her and she wrapped her arms around his neck and clung to him. She needed his strength.

When she pushed against him, Caleb released her. He felt torn in two. He needed to leave town. If the Bluecoats caught him, he would be taken prisoner. Yet he didn't want to leave Sophia alone. For all her independence, she was in danger and didn't realize how grave it was. He was safe tonight and tomorrow he would see what changes the Union would initiate.

He gazed into her eyes, looking at her full mouth. She hadn't kissed anyone except him and she shouldn't hold his interest at all when he thought of the women he had known and the ones in his life now. Hannah Lou flirted constantly and whenever they were alone, she allowed him to kiss her. Desirée gave her body willingly and knew all sorts of ways to charm a man, yet it was Sophia who set him on fire in a way no other woman had. This afternoon at the Stantons' for a few minutes, he had been alone in the sunroom with Hannah Lou and she had moved close, raising her face, waiting for a kiss and he hadn't wanted to respond. He had kissed her, but it was nothing. He didn't want to go home to New Orleans and find that only one woman's kisses set him aflame. He clamped his jaw shut, desire making him ache, worries for Sophia's safety plaguing him.

"If your brothers knew you were here alone, they'd come home."

"No, they wouldn't," she said calmly. "We were brought up to do our duty."

They should have been brought up to give some protection and attention to their little sister, he thought, but he didn't say that to her. Mrs. Stanton sat down with him yesterday morning and told him about Sophia's family and her eccentric father and how Sophia had been treated the same as the boys.

He watched her stand on tiptoe to place a box on a high shelf. He crossed the room to her and took the box from her hands, swinging it up easily. He turned to face her, placing his hands on her shoulders. The faint scent of tea roses came and he wanted to pull her closer and inhale the fragrance, taste her sweetness. Instead he studied her. "Come with me to New Orleans," he urged. "My family will let you stay there."

"Thank you, but I can't. It isn't necessary and I won't leave."

He looked at the dark press, squat and still, and he wanted to take an ax and smash it so she couldn't place herself in danger. He had spent sleepless nights thinking of returning to New Orleans and worrying about Sophia's safety. He turned to walk out of the room before he pulled her to him to kiss her. Any moment he would have to flee. He had told Henry to keep a horse ready all the time.

Later in the night Caleb waited until the house was quiet. Wrestling with his conscience and his heart, feeling angry and worried, he stared into the darkness. Finally he stepped out of bed and pulled on his trousers. His feet were bare as well as his chest. Picking up pliers, he stepped into the hall, going soundlessly to the stairs. Halfway up a stair creaked and he froze.

Nothing stirred, so he continued to the second floor, moving without a sound to the room with the printing press. He opened the door and when it squeaked, he stopped, glancing over his shoulder at the darkness at the top of the stairs. Sophia slept in the bedroom next to his, so it wasn't possible for her to hear a tiny squeak from the second floor. He opened the door.

The press was outlined against the moonlit window. He crossed the room to it. He had spent yesterday afternoon at the office of the *Appeal,* talking to a journeyman typesetter, who told him what screws to remove to make the press inoperable. She would rage and hate him for it, but she wouldn't end up in a Union prison.

He crept across the room and knelt beside the press. He began twisting a bolt. It dropped off into his palm and he reached up to pull out a rod. Something rustled behind him and cold metal pressed against his back.

"Get your hands in the air."

Chapter 8

He stopped and raised his hands slowly. "Sophia?" he asked, shocked that she would threaten him.

"I'll shoot if you touch that press. Get away from it."

He had been in enough fights to know when someone was in earnest, and the realization that she would actually shoot him because of her press, made the last shred of his temper snap. He came up in one motion, spinning around and swinging his arms to knock the pistol from her hands.

The blast was deafening in the small room.

"Dammit!" he snapped, slamming into her and they both went down.

Sophia fought him, pounding him with her fists, furious that he would destroy her press. "I saved you and kept you alive and nursed you back to health and you want to destroy me!" she cried, beating against him.

With a bellow of rage, he rolled on top of her, catching her hands and holding them with his, pinning her wrists to the floor on either side of her head. His full length pressed her into the hard floor and they both gasped for breath as they glared at each other.

"Dammit, you would have killed me for a printing press!" he yelled.

"I took care of you, and you turn against me!"

He stared at her and the look made her shake. His weight was heavy. And then she felt his body change; she knew the moment desire stirred. He bent his head and feeling furious with him, she tried to turn away.

"Get off—"

His mouth covered hers and she closed her mouth, pressing her lips together, feeling the hot touch of his tongue, a slow, sensual wet sliding across her lips. Her

heart thudded against her ribs. He was leaving her forever. With a sob her lips parted and the searing invasion
of his tongue made her writhe beneath him. And when
she moved, she was assaulted by tantalizing sensations
throughout her body.

"Sophia," he whispered, raising his head, and then lowering it to kiss her throat.

"Caleb," she responded. "Caleb." She wound her fingers in his hair, feeling the tight, silky curls. Her heart
thudded against her rib cage and she ran her hands across
his shoulders as she returned his kiss. His erection thrust
against her and she moaned, her hips moving beneath
him. *This is what loving is. Caleb, Caleb.* She ached,
wanting him.

His hands framed her face, his fingers winding in her
hair until he shifted, sliding his arms beneath her, turning
them both and rolling to his back while holding her
against him. She lay against the length of his lean body.
Her wrapper was open, her cotton gown and his trousers
the only barrier between them. He ran his hands the
length of her, sliding over her back, over the curve of her
bottom. She felt lost in a maelstrom of sensation and
emotions. She wanted to hold and kiss him forever. She
didn't want him to leave Memphis. She didn't want to
feel this way about him. He was going to destroy her
press tonight. That was like destroying her.

Caleb ran his hands down her thighs, catching the
gown and tugging it and the wrapper up until he felt her
bare legs. She moaned as he slid his hands up, feeling the
curve of her bare bottom, sliding his hands higher to her
satin-smooth back. He was on fire with wanting her, feeling as if he would burst with need. He wanted to roll over
again and move between her legs.

He turned on his side, holding her with him, shifting to
kiss her throat while he tugged free buttons on the front
of her gown. He pushed it open, cupping her soft breast.

She gasped, clinging to him, her hips moving against
him and her fingers stroking his back, winding in his hair.
He touched her nipple with his tongue, feeling the taut
peak, taking it in his mouth.

With a sob Sophia pushed against him and scrambled

away, coming to her feet. He rolled up, standing, and they faced each other in the darkness.

"There's a world of differences between us," she said, gasping for breath. "You'll go and I don't want to be in love with you when you leave."

"I don't want you to go to a Federal prison," he said, his voice deep and raspy, his hands clenched at his sides. "You print a paper that's loyal to the Confederacy, and that's what will happen."

She stared at his broad, muscular chest. Her gaze lowered, seeing the bulge in his pants. She yanked her gaze up to his face. If he touched her, she would be in his arms and she couldn't tell him to stop again. He could break her heart so easily. "Just leave!"

He stared at her and turned away, striding out of the room, and she felt as if all the strength went out of her. She clutched her middle, unaware what she was doing. She was falling in love with him and she didn't want to love him. He would ride away and she wouldn't see him again. And he was all the things her family disliked and didn't approve of. Things she didn't approve of. She leaned back against the wall and anger and hurt vanished as she remembered his kisses, his hands on her body. "Caleb," she whispered, knowing it was best to send him away, wanting him back, wanting to be in his arms. *I love him.* Heaven help her, she loved him. How long would it take to get over this feeling for him? she wondered.

Midmorning Caleb walked along Front Street. Uniformed men filled the Court Square and walked the streets. Colonel Fitch was in charge of the city and Union soldiers were everywhere.

Will strode beside Caleb. "My family is going to stay in the city as long as there's no danger. I'm able to return to fighting, so I'll go soon. Father wanted me to wait and see if we have to get the family out of town. I worry about them, because Father is showing his age. He seems frail."

Caleb glanced at him. "I've been thinking about it, Will. There are other Confederates still in town, and they'll have to leave. We could find a place and fight our own battles and still help the Confederacy."

"What do you want to do?"

"We can raid Memphis, take Federal arms, and send what we garner to our men. We'd help the Confederacy and still be close to home."

Will stopped walking to stare at him. "We could join Bedford Forrest if that's what you want to do."

"No. I want to be on my own, able to get back to Sophia if she needs me."

Will tugged at his earlobe as he stared at Caleb. "I'd be willing to try."

"I'll find a place where we can camp, and we'll have to get some supplies."

"My uncle Morton has a farm outside Germantown. He'd like to join the Confederates, but he can't leave the farm. Maybe we can stay there and the men can camp on his farm. There won't be Bluebellies on his farm. How long do you think we can stay in Memphis without drawing Union attention? The Federals don't seem organized yet."

"I'd guess a day or two. Proclamations will probably be issued soon and every man who stays in town will have to take a loyalty oath."

Will shook his head. "They'll have a time enforcing that. They don't seem to take any notice of us."

"The town is still full of able-bodied men. Not everyone went to war. They may conscript the qualified."

They reached the corner of Main and Madison. "Father wants me to come to his office," Will said, motioning toward the buildings of cotton factors. "Most of the merchants have closed their businesses rather than have dealings with Yankees. There might not be any open hostility, but there's going to be a lack of cooperation."

"If Forrest attacks, there's no militia to give him support."

"Bedford Forrest was wounded at Shiloh. He won't raid anything for a time." He paused. "We might have to leave town on a moment's notice. Any Yankee discovers we're in the Confederate army, we'll be wanted. Caleb, I'll make some discreet inquiries. I can think of four men who might ride with us. If we have to flee, meet at my uncle's. It has a sign on the fence, MORTON STANTON. It's west of the Germantown Road and south of the Wolf River."

"Good. I'll draw up a list of supplies." Caleb grinned, placing his hands on his hips. "We may have to ride back and steal them—if we do, we'll get them from Yankees, not our own stores."

"I don't want my family to know. I don't want them to worry."

"They're going to worry, Will, the minute you ride out of Memphis. I worry, because I know Sophia is going to print that damned paper of hers until someone forcibly stops her."

"She's like her father. My father always said Thaddeus Merrick was the most stubborn, hardheaded man he had ever seen. You know where to find me if you need me." Will turned and strode up the street and Caleb remembered that dark night in the rain. Thank heaven Will survived, but he would go right back into danger again.

Caleb turned to walk back toward Sophia's. He looked at the Federal gunboats along the wharves. The docks teemed with uniformed men. The Stars and Stripes flew over Memphis now and he wondered what changes would occur.

Caleb changed course to walk past Court Square. He glanced at the statue of Jackson where Memphians had scratched out the words cut into the marble proclaiming the need to preserve the Union. Oaks gave cool shade as he looked at the clusters of officers, the Federals coming and going at the courthouse. He crossed the street, his thoughts shifting to Sophia. Lord, he didn't want to leave her alone, yet each day he placed himself at risk. He didn't want to fall in love with her, but he couldn't stop thinking about her. He couldn't remember any woman who had constantly invaded his thoughts.

His lips firmed. Leave Memphis, he told himself. See how he felt when he was away from her.

He strode across a street, pausing to let a buggy pass. A group of Federal officers stood on the corner, and one faced Caleb. Taller than all the others, the captain was bareheaded, the breeze tugging at locks of his wavy black hair. His blue eyes met Caleb's and narrowed. Caleb's heart slammed against his ribs and his breath caught in his throat.

"Fortune," he whispered, feeling shock course through him as he stared at his brother.

Chapter 9

Caleb realized he was staring and would draw attention to himself. The officer was coming toward him. Caleb jerked his head, motioning to the officer to follow. He rounded a corner behind a building, stopping in the alley.

In minutes a tall, black-haired Union officer came around the corner. Caleb felt as if a fist clenched his heart; he moved forward, enveloping his brother in a hug, forgetting the Union uniform, overwhelmed by joy.

"Fortune, thank God, you're alive!" he said, squeezing Fortune, feeling a knot in his throat and tears sting his eyes.

They moved apart and looked at each other and both grinned as they wiped their eyes. "Where the hell have you been?" Caleb asked.

"Where have I been? Where have you and Rafferty been? Where's Darcy and Mother?"

Caleb's smile vanished. "Mother died that night," he answered solemnly. "The rest of us are fine and live in New Orleans."

"I really didn't think she would survive the sea. And New Orleans! Lord, I placed ads in the paper there!"

"The hell you did! So did Rafe. He placed ads for you, but somehow we missed each other. Come with me. I'm staying at a house here. I want you to meet someone and we can talk more freely without worrying about a Union officer coming around the corner."

"You don't like Union officers?"

"I'm a major in the Confederacy."

"My God, Caleb, why?"

"Lord, you're tall. You're the tallest one of us," Caleb said, grinning and studying him. "For that matter, why are you a Bluecoat?" He waved his hand. "Come home with me and we'll talk."

Fortune fell in step beside him. "Why are you a Reb? You're no slaveholder."

"No, but when we arrived in New Orleans, Ormonde Therrie gave Rafe and me jobs. The Therries are a second family, and now we're related. Rafe married one of the daughters, Chantal Therrie."

"French and Irish? Why are you living in a home here if you're from New Orleans?"

"I was wounded at Shiloh. The hospitals were overflowing, so men were placed in homes. I'm trying to get my aim back before I return to fighting. Now where have you been since the night of the shipwreck?"

"I was picked up by a ship headed for Brazil. When I got a ship back to the United States, it docked in Baltimore. I needed to work before I could do anything else, so I stayed in Baltimore. I met someone there and married—"

"Married!" Caleb stopped in shock and turned to his brother. "Fortune, you're nineteen."

"I'm not married now," Fortune said, and Caleb felt surprised by the harshness in his voice. "We were seventeen." They commenced walking again while Caleb listened. "Marilee Wenger was from a plantation south of Atlanta, Georgia. She was in Baltimore with an aunt who approved of me and we eloped. Her father had planned to wed her to an older man in Georgia."

"Lord, I hate that custom. What happened?"

"We had a baby boy, Michael. Shortly after Michael was born, Marilee's father came while I was away. Trevor Wenger took Marilee and our son and started back to Georgia. Along the way, Marilee and Michael contracted pneumonia and they died."

"I'm sorry," Caleb said, feeling solemn and realizing how much Fortune had changed. Tall and broad-shouldered, he had filled out. His face was broader than Rafe's yet there was a strong family resemblance in their jaws and straight noses, their blue eyes and black hair.

"I intended to go to Georgia to kill Trevor Wenger, but I received a letter from him from New York. He was on his way to England after the deaths. Then the war came along. Trevor Wenger is the South to me. That's why when the war started, I enlisted. Every Southerner I face, I think of Trevor Wenger." He glanced at Caleb and his eyes were cold. Caleb felt a twist of sympathy as he met his brother's gaze. "Until now. If you're a Reb, I guess I won't be so eager to fire. I may face you across gun barrels."

"I hope not! I've had enough war to last me a lifetime. It's senseless killing."

"It's not really our war. I'll get Wenger if I have to wait until the war's end and go to Georgia. I don't know if he's sitting out the war in England or if he's returned. I keep hoping I can get to Atlanta."

"The way you Bluebellies fought at Shiloh, you might do it." Caleb took his arm, feeling the solid muscle beneath the sleeve of his uniform. "Turn here."

They crossed the porch and Caleb stepped into a cool hallway. Sophia was at the head of the stairs. "Come down, Miss Merrick," Caleb said, "there's someone here I want you to meet." As he stared at her, he felt surprise.

He studied her, momentarily forgetting Fortune. Her hair was a different style, curled over her forehead, fastened in a full, low chignon behind her head. The emerald necklace glinted against her black poplin as she moved, and the three top buttons were unfastened. He felt his pulse drum. He realized he was staring. She carried her bonnet in her hands and she placed it on the newel post as she stepped down into the hall.

"Miss Merrick, I want you to meet my brother Fortune O'Brien," Caleb said perfunctorily, still captivated with her new hairdo. Why had she made the change? She looked prettier than ever. Poised, smiling at Fortune as he greeted her, she glanced back and forth between them.

"The brother who was lost at sea?"

Fortune grinned with a flash of white teeth. "I wasn't any more lost than they were. I settled in Baltimore and couldn't find them."

"How wonderful you've found each other now," she said, yet Caleb detected a solemn note. "You're a Yankee officer."

"Yes, ma'am."

"He's not the enemy," Caleb said. Was she alarmed about her printing press? How deep would Fortune's loyalties to the Union go?

"Come sit in the parlor," she said, leading the way. Both men followed her and she tugged the bellpull to summon Mazie.

"Miss Merrick saved my life at Shiloh. She brought Will Stanton and me home from battle."

"Then I'm doubly glad to meet you, Miss Merrick," Fortune said, smiling at her. "And I can't acknowledge you on the street," he said to Caleb. "You know what will happen if word gets out you're a major in the Confederacy."

"As long as he stays here, Captain, you're welcome to come call and see him here. No one will know what happens in my house."

"Thank you. We're going to be deeply indebted to you." He looked at Caleb. "Tell me about Rafferty and Darcy," Fortune said as he sat down on the wing-back chair and stretched out his long legs.

"Rafe is a cotton factor and has his own ships. Right now he's running the blockade."

"For the Confederacy?"

"For the O'Briens. I've put my money in his ship business and he's sailing back and forth between here and England." While he talked, Caleb glanced at Sophia. The open windows and sunshine were behind her, highlighting her golden hair. She looked beautiful and he yearned to move across the room and sit beside her.

They drank substitute coffee and talked. Fortune looked at Caleb. "You're going to have to leave town, Cal, or go into hiding. You're the enemy."

Caleb nodded, glancing at Sophia and she looked down at her fingers locked together in her lap.

"Miss Merrick, do you have a husband or father in the war?"

"Neither one, Captain O'Brien. I'm not married and my father died shortly after the war started. He printed a newspaper here, *The River Weekly*."

"I know that government will require all editors to take

an oath of allegiance if they continue to print their paper," Fortune said.

"I've closed the office of *The River Weekly*. My father is no longer alive, so now I'm out of the newspaper business."

Fortune nodded as he stood up. "I need to get back to headquarters, Caleb."

"It was nice to meet you," Sophia said.

"It was my pleasure, Miss Merrick. I can't thank you enough for saving my brother."

She remained in the parlor as Caleb walked to the front door with Fortune where they stopped to face each other. "She said you can come call and see me here."

"You can't stay in Memphis long without taking an oath of allegiance."

Caleb glanced over his shoulder and lowered his voice. "I worry about her. She's alone except for two elderly servants."

"There's no family?"

"No. The brothers are fighting and her father is dead. One brother was killed in Shenendoah."

"You're staying here and she has no family?"

"Yes, but her reputation is intact. You'll hear about her from someone if you're in town long enough. The Merricks were the town eccentrics. I think the dowagers view her as a spinster already."

"Miss Merrick?" Fortune said, arching his brows and sounding so skeptical Caleb had to laugh.

"She's grown up with a father who preached temperance and fought saloons and she's his daughter."

Fortune studied him. "She probably doesn't approve of gamblers either then. I'm surprised she gave you shelter."

"Drinking, wild women, gambling, and railroads. Doctor Perkins made her take in some wounded."

"You're not that wounded now. Are there other wounded staying there?"

"Not any longer."

"Be careful, Cal. You can get hurt falling in love."

"I'm not in love," he said, feeling a strange sense of lying to Fortune with his statement. "I worry about her because she's alone. I'm leaving town, but I won't go far.

I'll come back at times, so if you want to get in touch with me, contact Sophia."

"I thought it was Miss Merrick," Fortune said, studying him.

"It's Sophia."

"I'll try to call often and see if she's all right."

"Thanks, Fortune. That means a lot. She saved my life and she needs someone now. I'm writing Rafe about you today. Darcy will be overjoyed. You won't know him when you see how he's grown."

"I hate that we're on opposite sides."

"You can change," Caleb said with a grin.

They looked at each other a moment and Caleb reached to hug Fortune again. "God, it's good to find you!"

"I'm going to try to arrange a trip to New Orleans as soon as possible. You take care of yourself. You're running risks staying close in enemy territory." He stepped back, his gaze sweeping over Caleb. "You would have to be a damned Rebel!"

They stared at each other. "Take care of yourself," Caleb said solemnly.

"You do the same," Fortune replied, and Caleb walked down the front steps with him.

"This street seems quiet enough," Caleb said, glancing around, "but I know it won't do for people to see us talking. You'd get asked questions."

Fortune strode away, and Caleb watched him, still unable to believe they were finally reunited and Fortune had survived the shipwreck. He had grown taller. Caleb's gaze ran across Fortune's broad shoulders and down his long legs. He turned and Caleb waved to him. Fortune grinned and returned the wave.

Caleb went up the walk and into the house, strolling into the parlor. Sophia was nowhere in sight. Mazie was in the kitchen with smells of peas cooking and ham baking.

He turned and strode up the steps to the room with the printing press. The room was empty but he saw a paper with wet ink and he crossed the room to read, drawing a sharp breath.

Anger stirred and beneath it, he felt a cold fear for Sophia's safety.

CITIZENS OF MEMPHIS—Memphis falls to Federal forces! General Van Dorn escapes with thousands of dollars of property! RESIST the Federals and their influence. The Loyal Memphian will take up the banner of free press and our Cause and carry it as long as possible while other papers have had to close or flee. Resist the tyrants, pray for our brave men, and know that someday we will once again see the stars and bars fly from Court Square!

"Dammit," he swore, striding downstairs. "Sophia!"

Mazie came from the kitchen wiping her hands on a towel. "Major O'Brien, she said to tell you she'd be back in a few hours."

"All right," he said, experiencing a cold fear for her safety. Glancing at the newel post, he remembered the bonnet in her hands when she had come downstairs. While he had been in front talking to Fortune, she had gone out the back to deliver her inflammatory papers. Feeling a panicky sense of urgency to find her before a Union soldier discovered the papers, Caleb paused in the kitchen doorway. "Where's Henry?"

"Miss Sophia sent him on an errand."

"Do you know where they've gone?"

"No, sir."

He left, saddling his horse, feeling a tight knot of fear for her safety. Where should he go? North or south? He prayed that he was in time.

Freshly printed papers were stacked on the floor and the back seat of the buggy. Covering them were blankets and several packages of material, two sewing baskets, a shovel, a pitchfork, and a scythe.

Sophia picked up the reins to ride down Washington, turning onto Second Street. She stopped at the back of a tall brick house and knocked at the back door. A servant opened the door.

"Is Mister Martin home? I'm Miss Merrick."

Auburn-haired Edwin Martin and his thirteen-year-old son Aaron came to the door.

"Mister Martin, I brought the tools you lent my father so long ago. They're in the buggy."

"Fine, Miss Merrick. Aaron, come along."

At the buggy, Martin lifted the tools off the blankets, moving aside the packages of material and the folded blankets.

"Did anyone stop you or question you, Miss Merrick?"

"No. The Union soldiers I passed on the street glanced at me, but no one asked what I was doing."

He handed his son a stack of papers and picked up another. "We'll get these distributed after dark."

"Please be careful. I don't want anyone hurt."

"Damn the Federals. Anything we can do to oppose them is fine with me. I just wish I could—"

He bit off his words and she saw the worried look in his brown eyes. He had six young Martins to care for and Elmer was only a month old or Edwin Martin would have gone to fight. "You're needed here," she said softly and he stepped back.

"Miss Merrick, everyone will be anxious to get a paper that isn't under Federal control, but this can't be safe for you."

"So I've heard, Mister Martin, and if I don't get by your house with my papers, you'll know something has happened. I'll print copies as regularly as possible."

"Your father would be proud of you and your brothers."

She nodded and climbed into the carriage. The next house she stopped at was the Weatherbys', leaving one stack with Morton Weatherby. She also went to Silas and MaryBelle Silvertons', and MaryBelle insisted she come inside and have some corn bread that was freshly baked.

Shadows were long by the time she had only two stacks to go and she rode out of town past Federal pickets. To get to the Garners' house, she had to pass through Nonconnah Bottoms between Coldwater River and Nonconnah Creek. Fourteen-year-old Chadwick Garner was one of her most reliable delivery boys.

As she rode along, two Union officers on horseback

approached. They slowed from a trot, and her pulse quickened when she thought about the three stacks of newspapers in the floor of the buggy behind her.

The two men moved apart and blocked her path. She was in an isolated area, thick trees closing out late-afternoon sunlight. She slid her hand beneath the folds of her skirt to her reticule, feeling the solid weight of the Colt revolver.

She tugged the reins and halted facing the men. An officer turned his horse to ride up beside her. He was startlingly handsome with deep blue eyes, thick blond hair, and a mustache. He tipped his hat and even white teeth showed in his smile.

"Major Dunstan Trevitt, ma'am," he said in a deep voice. "You're—?"

"Miss Sophia Merrick," she answered, her heart pounding as he leaned forward in the saddle to look at the seat behind her.

"Looks as if you're carrying a cargo."

She smiled and waved her hands. "Major, just days ago a steamboat brought yards of beautiful material. I'm taking some to a dressmaker and I have some tools to return to a friend of my father's."

"Your father isn't in Memphis?"

"He died," she said, looking down and winding her fingers together in her lap.

"I'm sorry about your father," he said, sounding sincere. "It isn't be safe for you to ride out here alone. There are a lot of soldiers around Memphis now."

"Thank you for the warning Major," she said politely. "As soon as I take the material to my friend and the tools back where they belong, I'll go home."

"Where's home, Miss Merrick?"

"On Washington Street."

He rode closer and his voice lowered. "We're far from home, and it's nice to see a pretty lady. Do you have a beau in this war?"

"I have some dear friends who are away fighting."

He smiled. "You said 'Miss', so you're not married or promised."

"No, Major," she said, torn between telling him he belonged to the side that had killed her brother and being nice to him so he would let her go. She drew herself up. "If you'll let me pass, my friends are expecting me."

He tipped his hat again and waved his hand to the other officer who moved out of the way. As she drove off, she glanced around and saw Major Trevitt watching her and she felt a flutter. If they followed her, she would have to leave Papa's tools and the packages of material.

Within minutes she fought the urge to turn again and see what the Union officers were doing, but rode staring straight ahead. When she turned into the Garners' lane, she glanced over her shoulder and didn't see any sign of the officers.

On the return trip they were waiting in the same place. Now her heart didn't pound with trepidation, because she had distributed all the newspapers. As a precaution, she left the tools and the material. When Major Trevitt rode up beside her, he glanced into the empty buggy.

"Evening again, Miss Merrick. I think you need an escort home. A lady shouldn't be out alone. This is a deserted, dangerous spot."

"Thank you, Major Trevitt. I know the way home and after all, you are the enemy."

He smiled. "Ma'am, I'm never the enemy of a beautiful lady.

"Thank you, Major," she said, slightly amazed. She was unaccustomed to men paying her compliments or flirting, but from the moment Caleb O'Brien had come into her life, she had received attention and flattery and it surprised her. She glanced at the Yankee. He was handsome, with thickly lashed blue eyes, a ruggedness to his facial structure that made him interesting. He turned his head, and she was embarrassed to be caught staring at him. He leaned closer.

"Miss Merrick, may I call on you?"

She felt caught in a dilemma. She didn't want him to call, but she didn't know how to say no. She was unaccustomed to dealing with men and he was a Federal and she was printing a rebellious newspaper. If she said no, would he retaliate?

"Major Trevitt, we're on different sides in this war. I think that ends all socializing."

"There are some barriers that were meant to be broken," he said and smiled.

"I'm afraid that North and South barriers are impossible to surmount."

"Not so. You've given me a challenge, and I'll have to prove to you that North and South aren't irreconcilable. I'm from Kentucky. That's not so far north."

"Major, you could be from Louisiana, but your uniform indicates the Union and that is a world away."

"Surely not. I'll have to prove it to you. It's a challenge I look forward to. What business was your father in?"

"My father owned a newspaper, *The River Weekly.* It's closed now. He died shortly after the war started."

"I'm sorry, ma'am, about your father. My family is in Louisville. Memphis is a beautiful city," he said as they rode past the intersection of Adams and Manassas streets and turned onto Washington. Dusk was settling and light spilled from windows of houses until they reached hers. It stood in darkness and she glanced at the windows. Where was Caleb?

"Here's my house, Major Trevitt." She tugged on the reins, praying he would ride away. Suppose Caleb came to the door? "Thank you for accompanying me home."

"My pleasure, Miss Merrick."

Major Trevitt swung down out of the saddle and hitched his horse to the post. He held out his hand to help her down.

She alighted from the buggy. "Once again, thank you, sir."

"Yes, ma'am," he said, smiling at her. "Miss Merrick, I wish you would give me half a chance to make you forget I'm wearing blue."

"I'm sorry, sir."

He doffed his hat. "And I regret that I couldn't persuade you that I'm not your enemy. Perhaps I'll have an opportunity to escort you again. Good evening, Miss Merrick."

"Goodbye, Major." She went inside, moving to the window to gaze out as he rode away. The other Union officer caught up with him to ride beside him and both men turned the corner and were lost to sight.

"Who's the Union officer?" Caleb asked from the darkness.

She spun around. "You startled me!" He struck a match and it flared. His green eyes were fiery. He turned to light a lamp and then he faced her. The faint smell of sulphur hung in the air from the match.

"You didn't answer my question."

"Major Trevitt. He escorted me home, because he thought I shouldn't be out alone."

"Dammit, Sophia! You shouldn't live alone, you shouldn't ride around town alone, and you damned well shouldn't print that newspaper that will get you a prison sentence!"

She felt her temper rise. "You can stop your swearing, Major. I loathe profanity and what I do is—"

He stepped forward, gripping her upper arms. She faced him, looking into eyes filled with sparks. "Unhand me!" she snapped, aware he was worried about her, yet angry that he wanted to interfere with her paper.

"I rode all over town looking for you. Where were you?"

"I delivered my papers!" she said disdainfully, yet her heart leapt when he said he had looked all over town. Did he *care* that much? "Papers you don't like, because they preach against your way of life. Release me, Major!"

They looked into each other's eyes and she felt the fiery tug of wills, the sparks that made her shake with fury, and the undercurrent that was always there with him. His gaze lowered to her mouth and her pulse jumped; she felt caught between anger and desire, enveloped in his heated look.

"Dammit," he whispered, pulling her to him. His arms went around her and he bent his head, his mouth coming down on hers. She fought him because she was angry with him and his cavalier manner, because she was terrified she was falling in love with him so deeply she couldn't survive when he left.

He raised his head. "I'm going tonight."

The words fell like a blow to her heart, and she wanted

to cry out in protest. It sounded so final. "Where? You're going to New Orleans?" And the real terror. "Are you going back to battle?"

"You care?" He frowned, watching her. She gazed back, feeling loss swamp her. Anger drained away in longing. She swayed, standing on tiptoe and he groaned, his head coming down to kiss her again. She felt his fingers in her hair and in minutes the pins went flying, her hair spilling down over her shoulders.

"Sophia," he said, all the anger leaving his voice. His hungry tone made her heart lurch, and she pulled back to look at him.

"I don't want you to go," she whispered, touching his cheek. He turned his head to kiss her palm and she hurt, wanting him to stay, knowing she did love him and she would never know another man like him, knowing he should go because he couldn't be part of her life.

"I'm not going far. I won't stay here; I can't risk arrest. It creates risk for you, and any day now, the matrons in this town are going to realize how well I am and how long I've stayed at your house. I've found a place near Germantown. I'll come back to town at night."

"You're doing this for me," she said, feeling awed, staring at him.

He wound his hands in her hair, his gaze sweeping over her features with a fierce look that made her pulse drum. He bent his head to kiss her, molding her against his body, crushing the breath from her lungs.

His fingers went to the fastenings of her dress and in seconds he pushed the dress off her shoulders, tugging away her chemise and bending his head to cup her breasts and kiss her. Sophia trembled in his arms, torn between wanting to give herself to him completely and knowing what a disaster it would be.

His hands were everywhere, moving over her hips, her thighs, at her waist, touches that were ecstasy, that she wanted. She felt wanton, lost, and she tried to cling to reason. She should say no, but she knew he was going back to fighting. She caressed him, touching him, sliding her hands over his back and broad shoulders, winding her fingers in his soft hair. Heaven help her, she wanted more of him. Remembering the moments when he had been nude, remembering nights when she had touched his furred chest, she wanted to feel his body bare against hers.

"Sophia," he said, his voice a husky rasp. His fingers slid between her thighs and she gasped at his touch. Stop him now before you end up hurting forever, she screamed at herself. He'll leave and go to New Orleans, back to the women in his life.

"I have to stop, Caleb." She moved away from him and pulled up her dress, holding it in front of her. He gasped for breath as if he had been running.

"We don't belong together, you and I. I'll get hurt and I don't want to be hurt that way. Just go."

He winced as if she had dealt him a blow. He clamped his lips together and clenched his fists and she knew she was doing the right thing. This worldly, experienced man would not fit in with her simple life and he would break her heart.

He strode past her, his boots loud as they scraped the bare floor in the hall. In minutes she heard the back door slam and she crumpled on the settee.

He's gone. I sent him away. I told him to go. Caleb. Caleb, I love you. He'll go back to the war. Back to Desirée and other women. It hurt so badly. "Oh, Caleb . . ." she whispered as she put her head in her arms and cried, feeling lost and alone and wishing she hadn't told him to go.

The house had never seemed emptier. She couldn't sleep, finally dozing near dawn and waking to move restlessly through the house. Upstairs she crossed to a window to stare over the treetops. She could get a glimpse of the silver thread of the river in the distance. Where was he? Had he really gone to Germantown and stayed? She didn't think so. Her head throbbed and she rubbed her temple. It will be better tomorrow, she thought. Maybe days from now it won't hurt so badly. Yet, she knew it would.

When Mazie came Monday morning, Sophia had a fire built in the stove.

"Henry said Major O'Brien left last night."

"That's right."

"Henry said he'll be safer away from Memphis, but he don't look like a happy man. Henry said something is on that man's mind."

"Probably the war, Mazie," Sophia answered, wishing Mazie would talk about something else.

"Miss Sophia, I've known you since the day you were born. You don't have a mama or papa and Mister Amos isn't coming home. You need a man and the major was worried into a fit yesterday when he didn't know where you'd gone. You've had two gentlemen under this roof who'd court you if you'd let them, and I think it's time you let someone!"

"Mazie!" Sophia stared at her in consternation. "Both men are gone now. And Major O'Brien is a gambler and a whiskey-drinking man!" Both equal sins in Mazie's eyes who had never touched a drop of liquor in her life and was proud to say so.

"Both those men were fine men, Miss Sophia. And the major cared for you. And 'sides, he told me how his daddy raised him to enjoy good liquor."

Sophia stared in amazement unable to believe she had heard correctly. Mazie was almost as antiwhiskey as Papa had been. Had Major O'Brien won Mazie over to his views on liquor?

"He's gone now, so it doesn't matter."

"Someday he might be back. He told Henry he owns land here now. Miss Sophia, you want to end up like old Miz Kressen?"

Eliza Kressen was a spinster schoolteacher who lived in a small house at the end of the block. She was afraid of the dark and wouldn't venture out after sundown. She was thin as the porch rail and even Papa had been impatient with her in spite of her loyalty to all his causes. She was scared of everything and often spent Saturdays on the street corners predicting the end of Memphis for its wicked ways.

Sophia laughed, momentarily amused. "Mazie, I'm not sure a man could have changed Miss Kressen!"

"Yes'm, he would. Man changes a woman just as much

as a woman changes a man. Miss Sophia, if the major comes back, you need to be nice to him."

Sophia felt amused, her spirits lifting for a moment because of Mazie's admonition. Caleb had won over Mazie and probably Henry. A knock sounded and Sophia wiped her hands on a towel and went to the front. Through the beveled glass she could see a man and as she drew closer, she saw the blue uniform. She opened the door to face Major Trevitt.

"Good morning, Miss Merrick," he said, doffing his hat.

"Good morning, sir," she replied coolly, standing in the doorway with no intention of inviting him inside. Every time she saw the blue uniform, she thought of Amos and of Caleb's injuries and Will's wounds. She remembered Shiloh and Private Elwin Crossley and her distaste grew.

"The army is contacting anyone connected with a Memphis newspaper," Major Trevitt said courteously. "May I come inside?"

Feeling reluctant, she ushered him into the front parlor. Settling on the settee and crossing his long legs, Major Trevitt looked at the room. "You have a nice home, Miss Merrick."

"Thank you. We enjoy it."

His gaze swept over her in an impersonal manner. "You're wearing black for your father, I see. It seems as if all the ladies in town are dressed in black."

"So many have lost family in the war."

He smiled disarmingly and glanced at the door as if he expected someone to come walking through. "Do you have any errands to take you on a buggy ride today? I'd be delighted to escort you and give you my protection. You or any of your family."

"Thank you, Major, but we feel quite safe. Memphis is my home. And I carry my father's pistol."

He laughed and then he leaned forward, lowering his voice. "Miss Merrick, I intend before my stay in Memphis is finished to find some way to make you smile."

"You seem to keep forgetting the war, Major, yet it's something I can't forget for a moment."

"Someday it'll be over, and differences will fade. Miss

Merrick, I'm captivated by the beautiful women in Memphis, particularly one on Washington Street. When I look into your blue eyes, I forget I'm a soldier and I forget there's a war. I haven't been in a battle and I haven't killed anyone. I may not survive the war. Surely you can tolerate my presence for a few minutes."

She wanted him out of the house. But she realized the cooler she was to him, the more he persisted, so she smiled. "I'm not so aloof; we're just on separate sides."

"Ahh, there," he said, placing his hand against his heart in a mock gesture. "Already the snows of winter thaw a fraction."

She shook her head. "Major, such nonsense! Now what's the purpose of this visit?"

"We're talking to townspeople about the newspapers they print, and your father's name was on the list. When I saw Merrick on Washington, I asked to take this street."

Feeling cold, she thought about the room at the head of the stairs and the press and her equipment. And one copy of *The Loyal Memphian* on her desk.

"The more I see of Memphis, the more I like the town. Have you lived here all your life?"

"Yes, it's the only home I know. My grandfather printed a paper, and then Papa took it over."

"Now *The River Weekly* is closed. Is that correct?"

"Yes, Major. I closed the office the day before the battle. I won't open it again until the war's over."

"So this decision is yours, Miss Merrick?" he asked, studying her. He glanced around. "I thought perhaps your mother was the one who decided the paper's future."

"My mother is no longer living." His gaze shifted to her and his eyes narrowed, his pale brows arching.

"I'm sorry to hear that. You've lost both parents, so who lives here with you? An aunt?"

"I have two servants," she said, feeling as if a cold wind had blown across her nape as she watched a change in his expression. His eyes narrowed again, and he tilted his head to study her.

"You live *alone*?"

"Sir, that isn't why you came calling? The paper is closed, so is there anything further you need to know?"

He settled back on the settee and studied her. "I find it distinctly difficult to believe that you reside here alone, Miss Merrick. You're a very beautiful woman."

"I have two servants with me and until the Union army arrived, there has been no problem," she said, growing nervous. The polite tone was gone from his voice.

"There won't be a problem now, I promise you," he said. "I'll personally see to your protection. If any soldier gives you trouble, you let me know at once. Send one of your servants and I'll come immediately."

"And if you're the problem, Major?"

He laughed and leaned forward, reaching the short distance to take her hand. "Miss Merrick, I promise you, I won't be a problem."

She tired to withdraw her hand, but his fingers held her firmly.

"Sir—"

"Do you hate all Federals so much?" he asked softly, releasing her hand.

"Yes. My loyalties to the South run deep. I had a brother killed in a battle in Shenandoah."

He shook his head. "My regrets on your losses. A brother and a father. Tell me about Memphis. I know nothing about the town."

"We're the major city between St. Louis and Vicksburg. This is a large cotton market, even with the war. *The Appeal* was our largest paper, but it's gone now."

"There are wild rumors circulating of a woman who was from a Memphis paper and donned a Union uniform and was in our camp at Pittsburg Landing." He tilted his head to study her. "They said she had blue eyes."

She gazed back at him. "And was she caught?"

"No, so it makes no difference now, except she must be exceedingly daring."

"I haven't heard any such rumors. Perhaps it was one of those stories that circulates without basis in fact. Sir, if you've finished your questions, I must ask you to go. I wouldn't want to harm my reputation by having neighbors talk about a Union officer staying unduly long."

He looked amused and made no effort to move and she felt a flutter. "Miss Merrick—what's your full name again?"

"It shall always be Miss Merrick to you, sir," she snapped and then realized she might goad him into causing her more trouble. "Sophia."

"Ah, that's better. Sophia. A beautiful name, as lovely as its owner."

"And a name you wouldn't use if father or brother had been home," she said, angry with him.

He shrugged. "No, perhaps not. Someone in Memphis is printing a paper, and we can't locate the office. *The Loyal Memphian.* Do you know anything about it?"

"I've never heard of it," she said, hoping she sounded convincing, thinking again of the copy on the desk upstairs.

"Have you seen the area around Pittsburg Landing, Sophia?"

Suddenly she laughed, relaxing a fraction. "No, I haven't, Major, but even if I were your elusive woman who visited the battlefield, what would you expect me to answer?"

His brow arched. "Finally. I feel as if my morning is a success. I coaxed a laugh from you."

"Major, Memphis is filled with pretty ladies who might be happy for your attention."

He leaned forward, his elbows on his knees. "Perhaps we always want what we can't have," he said softly.

"I'm not a challenge to you, Major. I must ask you to go," she said, standing, praying that he would get up.

He stared at her, an amused look on his face, and then to her relief, he stood and picked up his hat. As she started for the door, he moved beside her. Without warning his arm went around her waist and he swung her around against his chest.

Her hands came up against him and she pushed. "Stop it, Major. I'm not alone and I can call my servant."

"Sophia, I don't want to hurt you. I can't resist a challenge like you."

"I imagine, Major, that my biggest charm is the fact that I live alone. Otherwise you wouldn't dare this." She was furious, struggling in vain, aware of the lust in his gaze.

He bent his head and in the fraction of time before his mouth touched hers, she thought of Caleb, the only man she had ever kissed. She twisted, and Major Trevitt's arm tightened. He stopped only inches away. "Sophia, I don't want to use force."

"Then release me," she said, pushing against his chest.

"There's no beau who's away to war?"

"No."

The dim sound of voices startled her, and relief washed over her. His hands fell away. "I want you, Sophia."

"You don't know me, Major, and you never will," she said emphatically.

His smile broadened as someone knocked at the front door.

Chapter 10

Sophia smoothed her dress and opened the door to face Hannah Lou and Mrs. Stanton.

"Come in," she said, stepping back and holding the door, thankful to see them. Both entered and looked at the major.

"Mrs. Stanton, Hannah Lou, may I present Major Trevitt. Major, this is Mrs. Stanton and her daughter, Miss Stanton."

"I'm charmed to meet such lovely ladies," he said politely, giving Hannah Lou a broad smile. "I was leaving, so I won't intrude on your visit."

"You won't intrude," Hannah Lou said, gazing up at him and returning the smile. Sophia stared at her. Had she forgotten Will's injuries from the Yankees? How could she be so polite?

"No, Major, you're not intruding on us," Mrs. Stanton said in a cool voice. "Actually, Sophia, we need Henry to go get our other carriage. Something happened to the wheel and our buggy is at the corner in front of Eliza Kressen's house."

"Ma'am, let me look," Major Trevitt offered politely.

"I wouldn't want to trouble you, Major," Mrs. Stanton said. "We'll have it fixed in no time."

"It's my pleasure, ma'am. Which corner?"

"Right there, Major. I'll show him, Mama," Hannah Lou said, taking his arm and stepping onto the porch with him while Mrs. Stanton frowned.

"Come sit down, Mrs. Stanton. I'll have Mazie bring us glasses of water."

"Thank you, Sophia." Frowning, she stared at Hannah Lou.

"I'm so glad you came when you did," Sophia said.

"That Yankee wasn't giving you any difficulty, was he, Sophia?"

"No, ma'am," she said, having no intention of alarming Mrs. Stanton about Major Trevitt. "I'll get the drinks if you'll excuse me."

When she returned, Mrs. Stanton was the only one in the parlor. Her bonnet was beside her on the settee. "Is Hannah Lou still outside?"

"Yes. The major asked her to accompany him to the buggy so your neighbors wouldn't think he was doing something to property that didn't belong to him. I can't believe we have Yankees in Memphis."

Sophia sat down, picking up a fan. "How is Will?"

"Will left last night with Major O'Brien."

"I didn't know they went together," she said, feeling surprise.

"Yes. I hate to see him go back to fighting. I feel we've had one lucky escape and I wish I could just keep Will home now."

If Caleb had gone with Will, they probably were on their way to rejoin General Bragg and his officers. Sophia drew a deep breath and felt another pang of loss. When would she see Caleb again? she wondered.

"Sophia, we can never forget or repay what you did. I do wish you would move in with us."

"Thank you, but this is home. If something threatens me, I'll come stay."

"You do that at once. Just send Henry over to tell me, and we'll come and get you."

"I plan to put up some watermelon pickles. If you'd like, I can share a few jars. It's so easy."

Sophia tried to look attentive, but her mind was on Caleb. Where was he? Was he on his way back to New Orleans or back to battle? She never really thought he would stay in Tennessee once he left her house.

It was another thirty minutes before Hannah Lou and Major Trevitt came through the door. He was laughing; he dropped his hand from holding Hannah Lou's arm. "Your buggy is fixed, Mrs. Stanton."

"Why, thank you, Major."

"Would you like a glass of tea or water?" Sophia asked. He had shed his coat and hat and had his shirtsleeves rolled up. His forehead was damp with perspiration and in spite of his disheveled appearance, she had to admit he was handsome. His blond hair was thick, slightly awry from the wind.

"I'd be grateful for a glass of cold water and to join such lovely ladies for a moment before I return to headquarters," the major said. "This is a beautiful city, you have, ma'am," he said to Clairice Stanton.

"We love Memphis very much and hope the war won't destroy it."

"Unless the Confederacy attacks us, you should be safe now from any major destruction."

"You mean your officers won't cause any harm?" Hannah Lou asked, batting her eyes at him.

Could Hannah Lou look at any handsome man without flirting? Sophia felt mildly annoyed with both of them. He was back in her parlor. She had no intention of letting the Stantons leave him alone with her. If he didn't leave first, she would go home with them. He flirted with Hannah Lou, laughing at something she said, his gaze going to Sophia.

"Why don't we all go for a short ride to see if your buggy is fixed?" the major suggested. "You can show me part of Memphis and tell me about your town, and I'll make certain that wheel is in place. Mrs. Stanton? Can you forget for a few minutes that I'm wearing blue?"

"I'm afraid—"

"Please, Mrs. Stanton," he said quietly, looking her in the eye. "I'd rather be home. This isn't what I want either, but I have little choice. For a short time, can we forget the war?"

She sighed. "Very well, Major Trevitt. But only briefly. We are of different persuasions."

"I'm glad you stopped to see me," Sophia said to Mrs. Stanton, standing when they did.

"You have to join us, Miss Merrick," Major Trevitt said. "Mrs. Stanton, can't you persuade her to come for a ride?"

"Of course. Sophia, come join us."

Sara Orwig

Hannah Lou linked her arm in Sophia's. "You have to come with us."

"Good," Major Trevitt said, taking Mrs. Stanton's arm and holding the door. As Sophia passed him she glanced up to see him watching her, a faint smile on his face. Sophia sat beside Mrs. Stanton while Hannah Lou rode next to Major Trevitt. He drove and Sophia wondered what gossip they would stir by riding through town with a Union officer.

Mrs. Stanton directed them east and in minutes they were riding away from the residential area, and Sophia realized that Mrs. Stanton had no more desire to be seen with the Union major than she did.

An hour later they returned home. Major Trevitt jumped down and offered his hand to Sophia. "If you ladies will wait while I walk Miss Merrick to her door, I'll accompany you home. The town if filled with soldiers, and I'd feel better if you let me see you home."

"Thank you, Major," Hannah Lou said quickly.

He took Sophia's arm and helped her down, cupping her elbow as they went up the walk.

"I seldom have found myself in the position of being unwanted and rejected," he said lightly.

"Sir, Miss Stanton is quite happy to talk to you and she is a lovely person," she said as they climbed the porch steps.

"I find a challenge exhilarating," he said, rubbing her arm with his fingers until she pulled away.

"Goodbye, Major."

"Until next time—"

He went down the porch steps and she closed the door. She rubbed her forehead and prayed she wouldn't see him again. Hannah Lou flirted constantly with him, but Hannah Lou had a father and mother at home and servants. Sophia remembered the afternoon and when she told him her mother wasn't living. From that moment he had grown more bold. She went to the parlor and picked up her papa's revolver to see that it was loaded. His silver letter opener lay on the desk, and Sophia touched its sharp point. She didn't want to move to the Stantons', but now soldiers would know she was a woman living alone.

Two days later she was in the general store. "Mister

Haskins, thank you for sending word that you'd open the store this morning," she said, leaning close and whispering to him, because Union soldiers were in the front of the store.

"Yes, Miss Merrick. When you get what you need, you better go home."

"What's happening?" she asked, thinking of the streets filled with soldiers on horseback, men rushing past in buggies.

He glanced toward the front. "There was a raid on Memphis last night."

"What kind of raid?"

"Our men. They hit the Federal arsenal in the fort and stole rifles and ammunition."

"Was it Nathan Forrest?"

"No, ma'am, not this time." His eyes sparkled as he looked at her through rimless spectacles. He pushed them higher on his thin nose. "Word has it that the raid was led by one of your soldiers."

She felt a cold touch of fear. "My soldiers?"

"That Major O'Brien. They say the Stanton boy was with him. They had over twenty men. Bluebel—Sorry, the Federals are fired up this morning. There are a few ladies out, but later when the stores close, you need to be home."

"Thank you, Mister Haskins," she said, barely aware she answered him. Caleb in a raid. She felt torn between terror for his safety and joy that he was still in the area. *He hasn't gone home.* He must be near Germantown at Will's uncle's farm just as he said he would be. She gathered her packages and left.

Within minutes after she arrived home, she heard a knock at the front door. When she saw the blue uniform, she squared her shoulders. The pistol was in the drawer in the front parlor. She opened the door expecting to see Major Trevitt. Instead Captain O'Brien stood before her with a large basket in his hands. He removed his cap.

"Good morning, Miss Merrick. I was in the neighborhood and wanted to say hello."

"Come in, Captain," she said, closing the door behind him, still unable to see much family resemblance between him and his older brother. Caleb's face was broader, his eyes green, his hair brown, and his skin darker. The moment the door closed behind him, Captain O'Brien turned and his smile vanished.

"Have you seen Caleb?"

"Not since he left the evening after you talked to him here. Come into the parlor, Captain."

She sat down on the settee. He followed and held out the basket. "I brought these to you."

She took the basket and removed the cover, looking at an assortment of boxes and bottles. "Oh, my goodness, coffee! Real coffee." She picked up a bottle. "Vinegar. And flour!" She looked up at him as he moved to the hearth. "Thank you, Captain. This is wonderful! Oh, and buttons! What a treasure."

"I know there are shortages. Have you heard the talk around town?"

"Yes," she answered, turning a large bottle of ink in her hand, thankful for the gifts. "I was told it was possibly your brother."

"Someone saw the band of raiders and they have a description of three of the men. One of them is Cal. It's just a matter of time until they get his name."

"Will this cause difficulty for you?"

He blinked and then to her surprise, he laughed and she felt a clutch to her heart as his features softened. For the first time, she saw a family resemblance and she ached to have Caleb back in her life. "No, Miss Merrick. There are so many O'Briens in the Union army and the Confederacy, I don't have to worry about anyone realizing it's my brother. We don't look alike either." His smile disappeared. "I'm worried about him if he intends to stay near Memphis and make more raids. You haven't seen him?"

"No, I haven't," she said, wondering when she would.

"At least he isn't running needless risks coming back to town. If a good description of him is passed around, it'll be dangerous every time he comes to Memphis. If he hit and left and has gone south, then it won't matter." As Captain O'Brien stood at the hearth with his elbow on the mantel, he ran his hand through his hair, again reminding her of Caleb.

"If he does contact you," Captain O'Brien said, "tell him that security is strongest to the south and southeast.

They've placed more pickets to the south. There's no way to watch all six miles of Memphis's border, so that's where pickets are concentrated."

She nodded as he moved away from the hearth. "Won't you sit down, Captain?"

"No. I need to get back. I'll call again, Miss Merrick."

"I hope you do," she said, following him to the door. "Thank you for all the wonderful things."

He stopped to face her. "I was so busy thinking about Cal, I almost forgot. Someone brought a Rebel paper to headquarters. All editors have had to take a loyalty oath, but someone in town is circulating a paper secretly, urging residents to resist and not cooperate with the Union. Copies of *The Appeal* have appeared, too, but we know who's printing that paper and we know they've left Memphis and gone to Grenada, Mississippi. The other paper is *The Loyal Memphian* and a search is on for the publisher. If it's one of your friends, pass along a warning. Whoever is printing the paper is breaking the law."

"I'll remember," she said, gazing into blue eyes that looked at her intently. At the door Captain O'Brien paused. "Do you need anything?"

"No, thank you for your generosity."

"I think some of the shortages here will ease, because we'll get supplies sent in from the North. Of course, if merchants here won't cooperate or open their businesses, it may take a while before you'll see the goods on the shelves. If you see Cal, tell him to be on his guard. I don't want to lose him now that I've found him," he said tensely.

She nodded and watched him go down the front walk, his long legs covering the distance swiftly. He was taller, less thick through the shoulders than Caleb. Captain O'Brien seemed a lean, solemn man and she wondered if it was the war that made him that way. She closed the door, picking up the basket to take it to the kitchen. While she seldom drank coffee, Mazie and Henry thrived on it and they would be happy.

"Miss Sophia," Mazie said, stepping to the kitchen door, "was that Yankee officer back to call? Did he bother you?"

"No, Mazie. This is a different Yankee officer."

"I don't know why Yankees are coming to this house. Mister Merrick would send them packing. They have no business here."

"He brought us some food and supplies," she said, placing the basket on the table.

Mazie stood with her jaw thrust out and her hands on her hips as her gaze went to the basket. "Humph! We don't need Yankee goods."

"Mazie, it's Major O'Brien's brother, and he brought us coffee."

Her dark eyes widened. "Major's brother? *Real* coffee?" She moved to the basket. "I guess if he's related to Major O'Brien, he's a good man. Here's vinegar and soda. Real soda!" she exclaimed, picking up a box. She laughed. "The Yankee O'Brien is as nice as his brother!"

Sophia placed the coffee and vinegar on the counter and looked out the window. When would she see Caleb again? she wondered. Would he make another raid on Memphis?

Moving in dark shadows, Caleb dismounted and waved his arm. Men mounted on horseback reined while Will caught up with Caleb. They moved forward with only the slight sound of footsteps as twigs snapped. They ran in a crouch to a wagon, ducking down to wait as a guard rounded the corner of the armory that had been the Memphis and Charleston foundry. He walked past only yards away and turned the corner out of sight.

"It'll be three minutes before he's back," Caleb said. "C'mon." They rushed to the building where Caleb hoisted Will to his shoulders. Will yanked tight the leather gauntlet and then wrapped his hand and arm with a scrap of woolen blanket. He slammed his fist through a high window.

Glass shattered and tinkled inside as he hit the window again. Unwrapping his hand, he tossed the blanket over the window ledge and scooted inside.

Caleb drew a deep breath, his thumb on the trigger of his Colt revolver. Had anyone heard the glass break? It was almost time for the guard. *C'mon, Will.*

Caleb ran to the back door, waiting, hearing Will strike the lock inside. Another blow. Three minutes should be up. Caleb squeezed into the slight indention of the doorway and waited, holding his breath, his hand held high, revolver ready. Another clank came from inside the building.

He heard the footsteps. *Stop, Will.* The footsteps were louder and Caleb held his breath, pressing his back against the door. The guard strode in front of him, only a few feet separating them. He turned, and they looked into each other's eyes.

As the guard swung his rifle, Caleb lunged and they went down. Caleb swung the revolver, bringing the butt against the man's head. With a grunt the guard fell back, resistance going out of him. Caleb yanked off his belt, rolled the guard over and trussed him, dragging him out of the way of the door. He picked up the rifle as the door swung open.

"Lord, Will, that took forever," he said as he pulled out a match and struck it, waving it in the air. Men rode forward and Caleb turned to light a lantern. He waved his arm as the men neared.

"Get rifles and get out of here! Thad, John, Charles—stand guard." The men fanned out, riding around the corner of the armory while Caleb ran inside, picking up a crate, looking at a nest of rifles on a shelf.

"Get ammunition," he called as he picked up the crate and heaved up to the wagon bed.

"The guard's stirring, sir," a man said to Caleb.

"Place a gun against his head, but don't shoot. That'll keep him quiet until we go."

"Yes, sir."

Men ran through the armory, gathering what they could. In minutes Caleb placed another load of ammunition in the wagon as the driver looked down at him.

"Get this wagon the hell and gone!"

"Yes, sir!" Lawrence flicked the reins and the team moved forward, the wagon lurching over the rough ground.

"Grab what you can carry!" Men scurried through the armory.

A man ran around the corner of the building. "Yankees! Yankees!" he yelled.

"Get out!" Caleb called, waving his arm. "Get out. Ride!"

Men scrambled on horses and wheeled away. Caleb and Will ran, men offering them a hand as Caleb threw himself up behind Charles Thibodeaux and clung to the eighteen-year-old's slim waist. A shot rang out and Caleb heard shouts. More shots came and he felt a sharp bite in his arm. He glanced down and saw a stain on his shirt. Yanking off a neckerchief, he wrapped his arm, and then tied a knot with his teeth.

Glancing over his shoulder, he fired his revolver. Federals came on horseback, pounding after them. They neared Caleb's horse and he jumped into the saddle, yanking the reins, spurring his horse, and firing behind him.

Will rode beside him and Caleb waved his hand. The men divided, some riding with Will to the south, others turning north with Caleb. More shots rang out and John Roland slumped in the saddle and then straightened. Caleb spurred his sorrel, feeling it stretch out as they galloped away. He held a bag of gunpowder. He struck a match, jammed it into the neck of the bag and tossed it behind him. It swung in a high arc, the bag catching fire in a tiny, bright glow that reached the gunpowder.

It exploded as it fell in front of the Yankees. Horses reared, giving Caleb and his men a bigger lead. They splashed through a creek and hit level ground, letting the mounts stretch out. Caleb was thankful he had insisted every man have a good steed, because now it was a race to the swiftest. With the horses they rode, he felt they could outrace the Yankees.

In another quarter of an hour, their horses were lathered. He glanced back and felt a leap of satisfaction. They were losing the Yankees. The distance was great and he spurred his horse, knowing he was running a risk with a good animal, yet a few more minutes at a gallop might lose the Federals completely.

For another hour they rode north and when he was satisfied they had lost the Yankees, they stopped to water their horses and then turned south.

When they passed Memphis, Caleb waved and left them. Glancing at the moon that was high overhead now, hanging like a sliver of steel against inky darkness, he became aware of his arm for the first time. It throbbed and burned and he wondered how badly he was hit. Judging from his injuries at Shiloh, this wound was superficial. His thoughts shifted to Sophia. He wanted to see her and to hold her. He knew he shouldn't jeopardize her by going to her house, but he felt an overwhelming need to be with her.

He slowed, riding with caution. He couldn't call on his horse for another pounding run tonight; he was wounded, carrying a rifle and revolver. If a Union soldier spotted him, he would be arrested. He shouldn't ride into Memphis, he told himself. *I have to see her.* His pulse raced as images of Sophia in her bed danced in his mind. He felt his body respond, and jerked his thoughts back to the raid. He prayed that Will lost them and that the wagon had enough lead, and Lawrence had gotten safely away.

Caleb turned on Pigeon Roost Road, the horse's hooves loud in the night's silence. His nerves became raw as he constantly scanned the road for soldiers. Finally he rode into the yard behind her house. His pulse pounded. He wanted her so badly. It seemed like an eternity instead of only fifteen days since he had last seen her. He had never felt this way about a woman before and he didn't want to feel this way about Sophia, but he couldn't ride away without seeing her. At the back door he paused. *She's young, innocent, not my kind of woman. Leave her alone.*

He stopped arguing with himself and turned the knob; nothing yielded. Thankful she was locking the doors, he pulled out his knife and thrust the tip into the lock. In seconds, the door swung open and he stepped inside, closing the door behind him. He struck a match and as soon as a lamp was lighted, he carried it with him. Sophia knew how to shoot and she was in the house alone. He stepped into the hallway.

"Sophia?" he called. There was no answer. With his pulse drumming, he walked toward her darkened bedroom.

Chapter 11

Sophia stirred, opening her eyes, staring into the darkness. The boards in the hall creaked and she sat up, the sheet falling over her lap. Light shone in the hallway. Footsteps came and she felt cold with fear. She reached for the revolver on the bedside table.

"Sophia?"

"Caleb?" The sound of his voice washed over her, sending waves of heat in its wake. She threw aside the covers and the revolver and climbed out of bed, running across the cold floor.

He stepped through the doorway. Looking lean, disheveled, dusty, *so marvelous,* he had a second to set down the lamp before she was in his arms. Her heart thudded as his strong arms crushed her to his broad chest. He kissed her, and she returned his kisses, pushing his hat away, winding her fingers in his hair, clinging to him, joyous he was with her.

He raised his head and frowned. "Tears?" he asked in a husky voice, wiping her cheek with his thumb. She brushed at her eyes, her gaze sweeping over him. She couldn't get enough of him, wanting to kiss him and hold him and look at him all at the same time. She ran her hands over his shoulders and arms and gasped.

"Caleb, you're wounded!" Terrified for him, she burst into more tears.

"Lord, Sophia, stop crying. I'm all right. It's not bad. Not like before."

"I've been so scared for you." Smelling of leather and gunpowder, he had a faint stubble of a beard and now he had a mustache. His curls were a thick tangle, and he had a smudge of black on his cheek. She felt as if she wanted to devour him; she stood on tiptoe, pulling his head down to her.

He groaned, his arms tightening around her as he shifted and moved, leaning against the wall and spreading his legs, pulling her between them. She felt his throbbing arousal press against her as he kissed her and unfastened the buttons of her gown. Feeling on fire, she raised her head to look at him while she tugged his shirt free of his trousers. He pulled it over his head and tossed it away.

"Your arm—" She looked up and forgot his wound.

His green eyes darkened, filled with a blatant desire that made her tremble as he pushed away her gown. Even though the air was cold against her skin, the room felt as if it heated to summer steam. He placed his hands on her bare hips and pushed her back to look at her.

She felt weak in the knees, shy, yet she wanted him to love her. She loved him, and he was risking his life daily. This moment she had him in her arms and she wanted him to kiss her. "Caleb—" she whispered.

The scalding look in his eyes took her breath as he met her gaze. He bent his head to kiss her breasts, cupping their fullness, taking a rosy nipple in his mouth, turning his head to kiss the other, his tongue flicking over her nipple.

Feeling hot fires of desire start low inside her being, she ran her hands over him. She ached, wanting him, sliding her hands over his hips, shyly touching the bulge in his trousers.

He inhaled deeply and groaned, tugging free his belt.

Without taking his eyes from hers, he swung her up in his arms and carried her to the bed. With a soft rustle as his weight came down on the horsehair mattress, he lowered her to the bed and leaned over her. "I want you, Sophia. I want to make you tremble and cry my name." He framed her face with his hands, holding her still while he studied her. "I want to love you until all your reserves are gone, until you give everything to me, until you're mine completely. . . ."

"Caleb," she whispered, shaken by his words.

He stepped back to unbutton his black trousers and shed his boots and the rest of his clothes.

She couldn't breathe as she looked at him, remembering when she had seen him nude before, never seeing him aroused, ready for her. He came down beside her, his lean body against her. She closed her eyes, her hands roaming over him as he kissed her breast, his tongue trailing over her stomach. He picked up her foot, caressing her leg, moving between her legs to kiss her knee. "You're so soft . . ." he whispered. "I've dreamt about you, Sophia. You can't imagine how I've missed you," he said, his voice a rasp. He kissed her inner thigh, his hands moving in feather touches.

She was aflame as his tongue flicked over her moist warmth. She gasped and moved her hips, her hands winding in his hair. "Caleb, please. You mustn't . . . oh, please," she whispered, pulling him closer, raising her hips to meet him, feeling his tongue washing over her.

Caleb's heart pounded against his ribs. He felt he would burst with need for her, yet their joining would be painful and lovemaking would be the first time for her.

Her skin was softer than anything. He wanted to know every inch of her, to love her and to drive her to frenzy. Finally he couldn't wait as her hands caressed him. He was on his knees between her thighs. She gazed up at him, her golden hair spread on the pillow, her eyes dark with passion. "Sophia," he whispered, unable to say more as she raised her slender arms to him.

He was hot, hard, ready for love. He came down and Sophia closed her eyes, her hands sliding over his strong shoulders. This man was all she wanted ever. He made her faint with passion, made her tremble for his touch. All their differences were nothing, vanishing in her need for him.

He thrust into her, his voice a whisper in her ear. "Sophia, love, you're mine now."

She clung to him, sliding her hands over his body, relishing the flat planes and smooth contours, the silky feel of his bare back and firm buttocks as she tugged at him and raised her hips to meet him. "Caleb, I want you," she whispered and then thought spun away as he plunged deeper. He felt big and hard, as he thrust slowly.

She felt caught, impaled. A surging need made her

move her hips and added need to need, building while her pulse roared in her ears and she heard his raspy breathing. And beneath it all, while sensation rocked her and she clung to him and rose to meet him, she was aware of his deep voice.

"Sophia, Sophia, Sophia," he murmured.

Then all sound was gone, pain vanished, replaced by consuming desire until he shuddered, his heat spilling inside her. She held him tightly, wracked with spasms. Ecstasy came. *Caleb is mine. This moment is forever mine. He wants me as I want him.* The roaring in her ears faded and the blinding light behind her closed eyes vanished as she relaxed.

His body was heavy on her and he raised his head to kiss her damp forehead. He shifted, brushing tendrils of hair away from her face.

He was solemn, his brown hair curling over his forehead as he studied her. "I have ached with need for you."

She touched his lips with her fingertips, smiling up at him, looking into his eyes and seeing the same love mirrored in his expression that she felt. Her smile vanished as he groaned and wrapped her in his arms to crush her to his chest. She clung to him, her ear pressed to his heated flesh, hearing the steady thud of his heartbeat, wishing she could hold him this way forever and never have to let him go back to danger. Her fingers drifted down over his back and hip to his thigh where rough curls tickled her palm. His body was a marvel and she blushed as she caressed him, wanting to touch him all over, still aching to have him as close to her, as much a part of her being as possible.

"Oh, great heavens!" she exclaimed, pushing him away.

"What's wrong?" he frowned, holding her with his hands on her waist.

"Your wound!"

"You startled me. I thought I'd hurt you."

She stood up and grabbed the counterpane to wrap it around her. He stretched on the bed and reached out, catching a handful of material to tug it away. The cover fell to the floor and she stood naked before him as his gaze roamed over her.

"Caleb," she said, blushing. Every inch of flesh felt as if his fingers caressed her instead of merely his eyes looking at her.

"Yer a beautiful woman. I want to look at ye," he said in a husky voice, his brogue surfacing. They gazed at each other and she wanted to fling herself back into his arms. Instead, she drew a deep breath and stepped backward, trying to take her gaze from the length of him. His broad shoulders and muscular chest made her want to feel her flesh against him again. She turned abruptly and went to get water and a cloth and clean rags to bandage his arm.

To her relief the wound wasn't deep. "This isn't as bad as the ones you received at Shiloh."

He was silent, still nude, his hands playing over her and it was difficult to concentrate, to keep her gaze from drifting to his body. Suddenly she felt swamped by fear for his safety and she turned to look at him.

"I'm so scared when you're gone," she whispered.

She wrapped her arms around him, clinging to him, struggling to control her emotions and unable to stop tears that spilled over her cheeks.

"Sophia," he said, his voice filled with tenderness that made her ache more. "Don't cry, lass. I'm fine." She tried to turn away and wipe her eyes while he picked up a cloth to wipe away her tears, turning her face to him.

"I'm frightened for you. Look how badly you've already been hurt. I don't want you in a war!"

He gazed at her solemnly. "And I don't want you in a Union prison, and they do put women in prison. You don't have to print a newspaper, but you know I have to fight. Would you want me to quit?"

She firmed her lips and drew a quivering breath. "Everything in me cries yes."

"You mean what we feel for each other makes you want to say yes. Otherwise, you would want me to go, because you love your home and your family and your beliefs. I hate the war and I hate the killing, but I'll fight. When it's over, I'm putting my gun away." Caleb thought about the guard he had encountered at the armory. Before Shiloh he would have stabbed the man and all of them would have been less likely to be discovered or identified, but now he couldn't kill unless he or his men's lives depended on it. He wiped her tears, running his hand over her golden hair, feeling desire stir again for her.

She bent her head to finish wrapping his arm, fastening the bandage in place.

"Sophia," he said, his voice a rasp as he cupped her breasts, caressing her nipples with his thumbs, his pulse roaring. She moaned and closed her eyes. Her lips parted while her hands slid over his chest and down to his thighs, moving over him.

She slid her hand between his thighs to touch him, hearing him draw his breath. "Sophia—"

"I want to know you," she whispered, her cheeks burning even while her hands played over him.

"I thought ye were prim—Lord, was I wrong!"

She raised her face, leaning forward to kiss him, pushing him down on the bed while she wriggled and shifted until she was on top of him. She felt his manhood throb with hardness as he kissed her.

She wound her arms around his neck, pulling him closer. "I want you, Caleb."

He groaned as he trailed kisses over her breast, starting fires again until he entered her slowly, filling her. "Caleb, please," she urged.

"Put yer legs around me, Sophia," he whispered in her ear, turning his head to kiss her as another giddy spiral started and she felt consumed by flames of love for him.

Spent, she lay in his arms and stroked him, marveling at him, blushing, yet amazed and reveling in recollection of everything he had done, every inch she had caressed. She couldn't bear to think about parting and it hovered in her mind like dark storm clouds on a distant horizon.

Dawn lit the room. Caleb studied her asleep in his arms, her leg thrown over him, her long hair spread across his chest. He wanted her again, but he needed to get out of town before it became more dangerous.

"Sophia," he whispered, kissing her lightly, trailing

kisses to her throat, aching with desire. He pushed away the sheet to look at the curve of her hip. Her breast was pressed against him. His gaze drifted up and met hers. She shifted, raising her face to his as he rolled over her and kissed her and he forgot time, wanting to lose himself in her softness.

Hours later she moved away. "I need to dress; someone might come to call. You can't go now because it's daylight. You know it'll be dangerous to leave town."

He grinned and nodded, placing his hands behind his head and watching her. "It's so difficult to stay, but I will," he teased.

She blushed. "Caleb—"

"I like to look at you."

"I won't ever get dressed at this rate. Soon Mazie will discover you're here."

He frowned and sat up. "Dammit, I forgot about Mazie and Henry."

"So?"

He turned to her, scowling. "I'm not compromising your reputation! I'll move to the other bedroom until Mazie is gone."

He gathered his things while she watched him. *I'm already compromised. More than compromised.* Her gaze roamed over his lean, hard body. Her pulse began to race as she studied him. *I love you, Caleb O'Brien. You've possessed my body and you have my heart. It's yours and it always will be. "I'm not a marrying man . . ."* She remembered him saying and felt a stab of hurt. She turned away. He saw too much when he looked at her.

He yanked on his trousers and carried his things to the door. "Sophia, tell her I rode in last night because I was injured."

"You can't hide much from Mazie or Henry. Get one of John's shirts. I'll wash yours."

He frowned and glanced into the hallway, and then he was gone. She gazed after him, wishing she could keep Caleb with her forever, knowing that he would go and someday he wouldn't come back to her.

Half an hour later she entered the kitchen to find him seated at the table talking to Mazie when Henry entered.

"Mornin', Major," Henry said. "I saw your horse." Henry placed a stack of wood beside the stove. "Folks talking about soldiers riding in town last night and taking guns from the Yankee men."

"What are they saying?" the major asked.

Sophia sat at the table and Mazie place a plate of grits and a sliced fresh peach from the tree in the backyard. Henry straightened up and frowned, running his hand over his head.

"Well, sir, word's out it was you. I think Yankee soldiers heard you stayed at this house."

Caleb glanced at Sophia, his forehead creased in a frown. "They'll come question you about me."

She felt a numbing fear for his safety. He should have gone before dawn. A loud knock sounded at the front door, and Sophia jumped. Panic enveloped her. "Hide somewhere."

Caleb stood and picked up his revolver. "Where's my shirt? It has blood on the sleeve."

"I put it in the backyard in the washtub."

He picked up a gun belt and strapped it around his hips, jamming his hat on his head. "I'll go out to the carriage house. Send Henry if I need to get out of here."

She nodded and hurried to answer the front door while Caleb strode across the yard. He stood in the shadowed carriage house, sunlight slanting through a high window. In minutes he heard footsteps and voices and he drew his revolver.

"Sir? Major?" Henry's soft voice called.

"I'm here," Caleb said, stepping out, his Colt in hand. He gazed at Henry and Fortune and relaxed.

"Here he is, sir," Henry said and turned back toward the house.

Caleb leaned against the rough wall of the carriage house. "You gave me a hell of a scare."

"You need to be scared. I can't keep calling here. Right now no one has mentioned we have the same name. They know you're a Major O'Brien and they know you stayed here when you were injured. Someone will come question Sophia about you today."

"I want her left out of this."

"Then you shouldn't have come back to raid," Fortune said solemnly. "A guard at the armory gave a good description of you. One of the saloon owners was in the crowd and he said you stayed here after the battle at Pittsburg Landing. Why did you let the guard live to give a description, Cal?"

"I had enough killing at Shiloh to last me forever. I'll go back to war, and I'll kill if I have to, but not otherwise."

"I came to warn you." Fortune's gaze was cool, his voice harsh. "You should get out of Memphis and stay out for your sake and hers."

"I was waiting until dark to leave."

Fortune rubbed the back of his neck. "I don't think they'll search the house. She wasn't the only one to take in the wounded, so no particular attention has been given to her."

"I don't want to cause her trouble."

"Sooner or later something will happen if you stay. Someone will see you, or you'll encounter Union soldiers." Fortune faced him. "I won't come again, because it might jeopardize her safety, but I'll keep watch. I can talk to Henry and see if she's all right."

"She told me about your bringing food. Thanks."

"I think the shortages here will ease as our boats come downriver. If shopkeepers will cooperate. Right now we're a bunch of damn Yankees they don't want to associate with even if it means starving."

Henry came out of the house and trotted across the yard. "Sir," he said, looking from one to the other, finally focusing on Caleb, "there's an officer coming up the front walk."

"I walked here," Fortune said. "I'll go down the alley."

"They didn't waste any time checking on her."

"Same one's been here before," Henry said, turning to go back to the house.

Caleb frowned, wanting to call to Henry. "He's been here before." He took Fortune's arm. "You know why?"

"It was about the newspaper. We've called on everyone who had a paper. If they continue to print, they have to take a loyalty oath. She said her father died and she closed the paper."

"Now this officer is back." Caleb glanced at the house.

"I'll go. I don't want them to think about two O'Briens at the same house," Fortune said.

Caleb watched him stride away down the alley. He ran to the house and stepped inside. "Mazie," he whispered.

Her eyes became round. "Major O'Brien," she whispered, "that Yankee man is here again."

"Where are they?"

"In the parlor."

Caleb pulled off his boots and tiptoed into the hallway.

Sophia made every effort to appear relaxed and be attentive, but all she could think about was the two O'Briens somewhere behind the house. She had sent Henry to warn them and she hoped they took it seriously. Caleb was unpredictable and too fearless for his own good, she thought unhappily. She sat in the rocker while Major Trevitt stood in front of the hearth, his hands behind his back and his feet spread apart.

"I'm glad I have a reason to come calling so soon," he said, and she was thankful Caleb was outside out of earshot.

"I'm not publishing *The River Weekly,* so I don't understand the reason for the call."

He smiled and crossed the room to touch her chin. "It didn't occur to you," he said in a soft voice, "that I might be here solely to see you?"

"No, Major. Would you state your business," she said, pushing his hand away.

He stood close enough that his knees pressed against hers and he looked amused. "Sophia, you're a fiery little beauty and I'm intrigued."

"Either state your business or leave my house."

He laughed and leaned down, placing his hands on both arms of the rocker, his face inches from hers. "I told you, I don't like force—I don't need to use it. You're an irresistible challenge, Sophia Merrick, and I intend to win you over until you come into my arms willingly." His blue eyes were wide and clear, his white teeth even, and he was handsome, but all she could feel was burning anger at his taking advantage of her situation.

"Sir, I am irresistible only because I'm unchaperoned and you know you can make advances without an irate father challenging you, but don't push. I'm known in this town and I have friends."

"I won't push," he said, sliding his hand over her throat, and letting it drift down across her breast as he straightened up and moved away to sit down facing her on the settee. He tossed his hat down beside him and crossed his legs. "You had a Major O'Brien who stayed here after the battle near Pittsburg Landing."

"Yes, I did. He's been gone weeks now."

"Do you know where he went?"

"I imagine he's gone back to fighting," she said, praying her voice sounded casual. "Major O'Brien could have gone home to New Orleans. I had several men here after that battle and when they left they said they were going home or back to their regiment."

The floorboard in the hall squeaked. It was a slight sound; Major Trevitt never glanced around, but Sophia felt as if a cold wind had blown across her nape. She fought the urge to glance toward the hall, because if Caleb were listening, she didn't want Major Trevitt to discover him.

"He was with you much longer than the others."

"His wounds were worse. Doctor Perkins didn't expect him to survive."

"I've talked to Doctor Perkins. He said Major O'Brien could have gone sooner than he did. Why did he stay?"

She rubbed her fingers together, weighing how best to answer him. "For a time I continued my father's paper. The day Major O'Brien planned to leave Memphis, I received word that my brother Amos had been killed in the East. I suspect the major pitied me and stayed longer than he needed to. He helped with two issues of the paper before I shut down the press."

"Of course," Trevitt said softly, "I would stay if I had a chance. The two of you here all alone—I can't imagine that didn't compromise you with townsfolk."

"They know my family's standards and mine," she said

with a lift of her chin, praying Caleb couldn't hear the conversation. "I was aiding wounded men, and Southerners are gentlemen."

He chuckled. "No offense, Miss Merrick. I haven't heard a breath of scandal about you. You haven't seen Major O'Brien since he left?"

"No, Major, I haven't."

"Would you tell me if you had?"

She shrugged. "I see no reason not to tell you. Is there one?"

"We think O'Brien is still in this area. Rebels raided the armory last night and stole weapons and ammunition. We have a description of a man, and it sounds like your Major O'Brien." Trevitt studied her. "But enough about him for the moment. There'll be a dance Saturday night at the hotel. I'd be honored if you'd allow me to escort you to it."

"Sir, I have no inclination to attend any party with a Union officer. If we've finished discussing Major O'Brien, I need to get back to my tasks."

Major Trevitt stood up and moved toward the door. When she didn't get up, he gave her a languid smile. "Afraid to walk to the door with me, Miss Merrick?"

"You gave me just cause last time," she snapped and stood up.

"It's the first time in my acquaintance, I've had a woman fear me. And the first I've had one so completely reject me," he added softly, still smiling at her.

Feeling angry with Trevitt, she was frightened what Caleb might do if he overheard their conversation. "I don't fear you, Major. And I regret you feel a challenge. I find it difficult to imagine every woman you encounter eager for your attention."

He laughed. "Perhaps not, but often I'm not interested either. It's the first time I've been interested, that I've encountered such a cold reception. If you had a sweetheart, I would understand your response, but you say there's none."

"That's right."

"I've asked a few townspeople and they've said the same. You have Memphis friends and those who don't particularly like the Merricks. You haven't won the endearment of the tavern owners with your father's stand against them."

"My father was a man of principles." She halted out of arm's reach and Major Trevitt looked amused. His gaze roamed over her boldly, studying her breasts before glancing up.

"I could show you excitement, Sophia, and make your life easier."

She held her anger in check. "I must get back to my washing," she said.

"Still afraid to come too close." Suddenly he stepped near, his arm sweeping around her as he yanked her to him and kissed her. His mouth was bruising and she pushed against him. She hated his mouth on hers, his tongue sliding into her mouth, yet she was terrified to make noise. If Caleb heard her protest or heard her cry out, he would attack Trevitt.

Major Trevitt released her, looking down at her. "I'll win."

"Find a woman who is attracted to you!" she said softly, wanting to avoid her words carrying to the back of the house.

She hurried to throw open the front door and step onto the porch. He put on his hat, turning to look at her. "You're a beautiful woman, Sophia."

"Goodbye, Major Trevitt."

He left, striding down the walk and mounting his horse to ride away. She stepped into the house and closed the door. With a revolver in his hand, Caleb stood in the parlor doorway, his eyes stormy with rage. He motioned to her.

"Come here, Sophia."

Chapter 12

She stepped into the parlor and Caleb closed the door, placing the revolver on a table. He turned around, holding her upper arms. "I wanted to come in here and pound the man through the floor," he said, his Irish brogue becoming apparent as he rolled the words off his tongue.

"I'm so afraid for you," she said softly.

"For me!" He tilted her chin up, looking at her mouth, his green eyes blazing with anger. "Sure and damn him to fires of hell, he kissed ye, didn't ye?"

"I'm all right."

"Dammit. Ye shouldna' live here alone, and there's nothing I can do to keep ye from it!"

"Stop swearing, Caleb."

"Sophia, he knows ye're a lass who lives alone. And he's takin' advantage of it."

She raised her chin and looked him in the eye. "Major Trevitt hasn't hurt me, and I have a revolver and know how to use it. He probably won't be back again."

"Ye know he damned well will be back!" Caleb strode to the window as if to give vent to his fury by some kind of action. As he moved Sophia looked at his broad shoulders, her gaze drifting down over his narrow hips and long legs.

"If I could only get my hands on him for a few minutes—" Caleb said. She moved behind him, coming up against him, running her hands along his thighs and pressing against him.

He turned, all anger leaving his expression. "Sophia," he said with such tenderness, her heart contracted. He tilted her face up to his. "I worry about ye, I'm afraid for ye. And I love ye," he whispered. "I want ye, love." He bent his head, his mouth covering hers as she wound her arms around his neck and he pulled her close to him.

He picked her up and carried her to her bedroom, closing the door behind him. He carried her to the bed, bending his head to kiss her.

Hours later he shifted in bed and turned on his side, propping his head on his hand. He toyed with long, silken strands of her hair. "Sophia—"

"That tone means you want something."

He arched his brows. "How do you know that?"

"I've been around you enough now to know when you're trying to coax me to do something you want. In anger or passion, your Irish shows. When you coax, you get that honey tone to your voice that would melt snow."

"I don't coax."

"No, you don't if you don't have to. Most of the time you bully."

"You have to live with the Stantons," he insisted.

"You won't be coming back to Memphis?" She studied him and saw the flicker in his eyes as he gazed back.

"Yes, I'll come back, but I'll give this up if it means your safety."

"I'm safe. I promise you."

"When I think about Trevitt putting his hands on you, I want to smash him."

"You're too fierce, Caleb." She snuggled up against him, kissing his throat, inhaling the clean scent of soap on his skin. "I should get up and see about our supper."

She slid out of bed and gathered her clothing, turning to look at him. He lay stretched on his side, unabashedly naked, gazing at her with a fatuous smile. She smiled in return, feeling her heart lurch, because when darkness came, she would lose him to danger.

"Stop worrying about me," he said softly.

"I'm terrified for you," she whispered.

He came off the bed, crossing the room to pull her to him and in seconds her clothes fell from her hands and she wrapped her arms around him to return his kisses.

That night while they ate, she listened to him tell her tales about Ireland and his brothers and his childhood. She knew he was being his most charming to keep her from thinking about his leaving. Mazie and Henry had gone to their quarters and the house was quiet except for Caleb's deep voice.

And finally they were silent looking into each other's eyes. She felt overwhelmed with desire and love as he stood up and led her to her bedroom.

She fell asleep in his arms, held tightly against him, only to awaken in the night. Moonlight spilled over him and she rose up slightly to look at him, letting her fingers trail over his bare thigh, feeling crisp hairs against her palm, watching his body respond to her strokes. Coming awake at once, he turned his head to kiss her fingers, and then he pulled her down to him to love her again.

The next time she stirred, she ran her hand over the bed and came awake. She was alone.

"Caleb!"

"I'm here," came a deep voice from the dark. He moved into the moonlight and she gasped. He was in uniform and his voice was solemn. His gun belt was buckled around his hips. With a cry she flung herself out of bed to run to him.

He held her tightly, his belt buckle cold against her skin, the gun belt cutting into her flesh. She tried to hold back tears, knowing she had to let him go.

"Come back to me," she whispered.

He pushed her away a fraction and tilted her face up to his. "Don't be afraid. I'll be careful." He kissed her and then pulled her to him, his mouth covering hers, his tongue thrusting deep as if he could consume her and make her part of him so there would be no separation. His strong arms crushed her to his heart until he finally broke away.

"I'll be back," he said. "If you have trouble, you promised to go to the Stantons." As he strode away, she caught up her wrapper to throw it around her and run down the hall after him.

"Caleb!"

He kissed her again at the back door and then he was gone, striding across the yard while she hurt so badly. She held her fists clenched against her heart as tears streamed down her cheeks. *I love you, Caleb O'Brien.* She wondered if she would ever see him again.

Then she saw his dark shadow as he rode toward the alley and turned the corner and was gone from sight. She closed and locked the door and walked back to the bedroom in the dark. The house was empty, the bed still warm, still holding his scent and she ran her hands over the pillow and then threw herself down to cry. *Please take care, Caleb. Caleb....*

As Caleb rode out of the alley and turned the corner on Washington, a shadow shifted behind him.

Major Dunstan Trevitt sat up in bed and threw back a sheet. "Confound it, just a minute!" he bellowed as pounding came from the front door of the small house. The woman rolled over and sat up, pulling covers to her chin.

"What is it?"

"Someone to see me, I'd guess." He yanked on pants and went to the door to throw it open.

A soldier stepped into the room and saluted. "Sir. I waited as you ordered. A man just rode out of the alley and down Washington and turned the corner heading south."

"Could you see him?"

"No, it was too dark to see his features."

"But he came out of her house?"

"Yes, sir."

Dunstan felt a wild surge of triumph. He hadn't expected to gain anything from having two men watch Sophia Merrick's house, but he had nothing to lose by stationing two privates where they could see if anyone came or went from the front or back doors. "Good work, Haines. That's all for tonight. Do what you want for the next twenty-four hours. I'll station someone else on watch tomorrow night."

"Yes, sir. Thank you, sir."

Dunstan returned the salute and closed the door behind him, his thoughts shifting to Sophia Merrick. Caleb O'Brien had to be the man who left her house tonight. And she had said there was no sweetheart! he thought angrily. So Sophia Merrick wasn't the innocent, prim woman the town thought. She was in love with Major Caleb O'Brien, the Secesh who was leading the raids into Memphis! He was relieved that Rebel Forrest was occupied with fighting farther east, else if the two paired up, it would be a bigger disaster than the Union already had.

He remembered the tavern owners he had questioned: "She's a cold one—cold as icicles in January," said one. "Doesn't believe a man should drink or socialize or have fun. Old maid spinster who would faint if a man wanted her," said the other. Or when he had asked that Haskins fellow at the general store: "Miss Merrick is a fine person. Very high principles."

He remembered leaning on the counter, lowering his voice. "Who's the man in her life? Miss Merrick is very pretty."

"Miss Merrick?" Mr. Haskins frowned. "There's no man in her life. Her father wouldn't have allowed it. Doubt if Sophia Merrick has spent five minutes alone talking to a man unless it was about her family's newspaper or to the wounded fellows she cared for after Shiloh."

And when he asked Jorgenson, the blacksmith, he shook his head. "Spinster, she is. Raised to work like her brothers." He grinned and licked his lips. "Just as soon kiss a wooden doll, Major. If you're looking for fun, go over to Miss Pearlie Marie's. There's fun. Ask to meet Abigail."

Trevitt struck a match and put it to the tip of a cigar, inhaling, puffing, and blowing out a stream of smoke. He thought about Hannah Lou Stanton, riding in her carriage to the general store, flirting with him and making eyes at him. Too bad she wasn't the one who lived alone, he mused. His pulse raced at the thought and he savored memories of the afternoon, thinking of when he had climbed into the Stanton carriage. Hannah Lou had scolded him in her little-girl voice, telling him he must go, all the time letting him pull her into his arms. His body responded to erotic thoughts as he remembered kissing her, sliding his hands over her breasts until she finally scooted away.

"Sir, you'll give me a dreadful reputation, and my father will be livid! You must go," she said, pouting, straightening her rumpled blue silk dress.

"I'll go, Hannah Lou, but when can I see you again?"

"I might take my carriage out tomorrow and ride along Fort Avenue, east of Fort Pickering about three in the afternoon," she said slyly, her voice changing to a sweet note. "Perhaps if you're in the area, you could ride with me for a time."

He smiled and stroked her throat, watching her inhale, her breasts straining against the fabric. He reached into his pocket and withdrew a small box. "I've had this a long time to take home to my mother, but I can find something else to give her. It looks as if it belongs on you, Hannah."

"For me?" She gazed at the box and he had to bite back his amusement as she was obviously torn between accepting the present or politely refusing as she had been taught to do. Southern women and their genteel manners made him impatient. Beneath the courteous manner, Hannah Lou was hungry for a man.

She accepted the gift, lifting out the gold and ruby necklace. "Oh, great saints! My mother wouldn't allow this—"

He took it from her. He had won it in a game of faro and he had a long chain made for it. He fastened it around her slender neck, kissing her below her ear.

"Major Trevitt, it's gold. I can't take—"

"Hannah," he whispered as he faced her. "Someday I want you to meet my mother. She would think this necklace perfect for you." He held the winking ruby in his hand and watched Hannah Lou as he tucked it into the neck of her silk dress, his hands moving over her bare breasts. His arousal was hard, swift. He wanted to yank the silk down and kiss her full breasts. He moved his fingers to find her taut nipple.

"Oh," she breathed, closing her eyes. He leaned forward to kiss her, cupping her breast, feeling its lush fullness, expecting her to stop him any moment. When she didn't, he shifted, keeping one hand on her breast while his other slid beneath her skirts.

"Major—"

"Dunstan. Call me Dunstan. I want to hear you say it," he said, trying to keep her mind from what he was doing as his hand stroked her legs and moved between her thighs to touch her.

"Major!" She flounced away, looking hot, flushed, petulant, yet she wanted him. How long would it take to seduce her? he wondered. She wasn't dealing with one of her Southern gentlemen who held her in high regard, and he hoped she didn't realize it until too late.

"I must say goodbye," she said breathlessly.

"As difficult as it is, I'll go, but I'll dream about tomorrow, Hannah. And I'll dream about kissing you." Her expression made his pulse throb. She was ready for seduction, looking as eager as he felt. He climbed out of the carriage and smiled at her before he closed the door. He moved away, going to the blacksmith's, hoping no gossipy matron had spotted him coming out of the Stanton carriage to report it to Hannah's parents.

"Dunstan, what is it?" came a soft voice and he turned. Verna Mae was a wench who had worked in sporting houses. She was beautiful and more pleasure to a man than most of the women he had known.

"Military matters, hon," he said, reaching for her, thinking she would be twice as much fun as Hannah Lou, but he liked the idea of possessing the fancy Miss Stanton. He'd grown up in a shack along the Chicago waterfront and he intended to come out of the war a rich man and he liked seducing Southern belles. Most of them he met were spoiled and sheltered and inexperienced; it was a tiny victory to wield power over them, aware if they knew the truth about his past they would loathe him and never speak to him. And he liked to do things to them that their prissy Southern gentlemen wouldn't do to the women they loved.

Verna Mae came into his arms and pressed against him. He forgot Hannah Lou as he bent his head to kiss Verna Mae.

An hour later he lay smoking in the dark. Verna Mae was wrapped against him, her arm and leg thrown over him. Major Caleb O'Brien was Sophia Merrick's lover, and no one in the entire town suspected it.

Major Caleb O'Brien from Louisiana. It would be a
medal or promotion for him to catch O'Brien. And Sophia Merrick. She had no protector except O'Brien. And
someone was printing a small paper loyal to the Confederacy. She'd lied about O'Brien—she could easily lie
about the paper. She had just shut her *River Weekly* down
after the battle for Memphis. Was there a press at her
home? He'd had men watching her newspaper office and
it was closed just as she had said. No one came or went
from there. He remembered their first meeting out on the
road beyond the edge of town. Had she just been deliver-
ing tools and material—or had there been newspapers in
her buggy? He wished now he had searched it that day,
yet if he had found the papers then, he would have had to
arrest her. This way, he might use threats about Major
O'Brien or the paper to get her to do what he wanted.

He blew out a stream of gray smoke. Sophia Merrick.
She was feisty, a real challenge to him. He intended to
possess Hannah Lou Stanton and Sophia Merrick before
the month was over. And he wanted to catch O'Brien
sooner. His pulse raced at the thought. Catch O'Brien and
reveal that Sophia was his mistress. What would she do
to keep that from the public? He wanted to bring her to
her knees, the insolent Miss Merrick.

He puffed the cigar and grinned. He wanted more than
bringing her to her knees.

The next morning in his office at Union headquarters,
he faced Sergeant Howden, a man who was using the war
for personal gain.

"If you see any man go in that house, come get me at
once. Contact me no matter where I am or what I'm
doing," Trevitt said.

"Yes, sir."

"I want to catch this Rebel. We can hang him and make
an example of him. Don't let those Southern neighbors of
hers see you and don't draw Miss Merrick's attention."

"Yes, sir," Howden responded.

"Southerners are loyal to their cause and they'd do
anything to protect him. The man who brings me word of
the Reb will get a promotion."

"Yes, sir."

"Howden, what about that load of iron at the armory?"

"It was taken to the address you gave me."

"Who knew about it?" Trevitt asked. Even Verna Mae didn't know what he had locked in her shed. He told her to stay away from there, and she obeyed him like a trained dog.

"No one, sir, except me. I had it loaded on a wagon and I took the wagon myself. As far as any officers are concerned, it was taken by the Rebs." His black eyes had a sly look. "I got two wagonloads moved. No one the wiser."

"Good," Trevitt said grinning, opening the drawer and unlocking a metal box. He withdrew gold coins and placed a stack on the desk. "Every time the Rebs hit, we should gain, too. Just keep your mouth shut, Sergeant."

"Yes, sir. Thank you, sir," he said, pocketing the coins.

"This is the only reason to go to war as far as I'm concerned. Both of us ought to come out of this wealthy men."

"Yes, sir. I've heard a man just east of here who's looking to buy iron for the Rebels. I think he has the money."

"Let me know. Dismissed, Sergeant."

Trevitt sat back in his chair and gazed out the two-story window at the view of the Mississippi. He knew life on a river and he liked it. River towns had more opportunities and right now Memphis was filled with them. He could easily acquire land. He had bought land in Kentucky and Tennessee and north of here in Illinois. Whenever he could steal something, the Southerners were fair game. He'd found Howden a year ago and they had worked together as a team since. The market for iron was getting better with every day of war.

He hoped O'Brien would come back to town tonight. The sooner they had him under arrest, he reasoned, the sooner it would give him control over Sophia Merrick. Tomorrow afternoon he would be with Hannah Lou.

Twenty-six hours later he climbed into the buggy with Hannah Lou and took the reins. "How did you get away from home all alone like this?"

"It's wartime and Mama is so busy. She still has six wounded to care for. I told her I was going to call on Sophia. Sophia is all alone and Mama worries about her. We might do that on the way home."

He smiled, driving the buggy northeast, heading along the road where he knew they would soon be in an isolated area. His gaze ran over her rose silk dress. "You look beautiful today, Hannah Lou," he said and meant it. Her cheeks were rosy, her skin pale, and her full red lips inviting. The dress wasn't the latest fashion, but it was costly. He looked at the pair of matched bays harnessed to the buggy, thinking about the shortages of fine horseflesh in the field. Kentucky and Tennessee had the best horses he had ever seen. And the Stanton carriage was as elegant as the horses. Velvet seats, the springs giving them an easy ride.

She smiled at him and flashed him a flirtatious look. "Thank you, Major. You look rather dashing yourself. I never thought I'd see the day when I'd ride alone with a Yankee officer."

"Your mother wouldn't allow it now if she knew. And your papa would call me out."

Hannah Lou wriggled on the seat. Evidently she liked doing something daring and forbidden. His pulse jumped; it would make seduction easier.

"I'm not so different from men who are on the Confederate side," he said. He had ridden out to seduce her, but now as he looked at her, another idea came. What if he won her hand? He didn't want to live in the North when the war was over. He was wanted for theft in Chicago and couldn't go back there. He hated the cold winters. And he didn't want the deep South. He had heard stories of their steamy summers and bugs and indolent ways. But the border states and a border city suited him fine. Hannah Lou was wealth and society. And ripe for picking.

"You said you're from Louisville, Kentucky. Do you have brothers and sisters?" she asked.

"I had three brothers, but two have been killed in the war. The other is fighting in the East," he said, hoping the lie would stir her sympathy.

"I'm sorry. Two brothers killed is terrible. So many we

know have been killed. Papa never thought it would last this long. I imagine you miss your family."

"Yes, I do, but when I'm with people like you and your mother, I forget the separation. You're mother reminds me of home."

"When the war is over, you'll go home to Kentucky?"

"Yes, I will," he lied. He had no ties in Kentucky. The idea of winning Hannah Lou in marriage seemed better the more he thought about it. The Stantons were one of the wealthiest families in town. He had seen their home and he knew Carlton Stanton was actively buying and selling cotton and increasing his fortune. There was only one son who had gone back to fighting and it would be easy to eliminate him if the war didn't. Hannah Lou would inherit a fortune and society would accept the man she married.

"Major, we should turn around and head back toward town."

"Let's give the horses a drink." He turned off the road, going across flatland to a meandering creek. Trees lined its banks and he halted between willows. He jumped down and swung her down, pulling her into his arms.

She came willingly, winding her arms around his neck while he kissed her. Even when he plunged his hand beneath the neck of her dress, her protests were feeble and she clung to him. While he kissed her throat, he unfastened the dress and pushed it down around her waist damning the hoops and corset. He bent to cup her breasts and kiss her through her thin, lacy chemise, hearing her quick intake of breath.

While he kissed her, he slid his hand beneath her skirt along her thigh. She moaned softly and pulled at his hands. "Major, we have to stop."

"Hannah, you set me on fire. I've never known a woman like you," he whispered, cupping her full breasts to kiss her. He was aroused, wanting her, torn between seduction or trying for marriage. "Tell me it doesn't matter that I fight for the North. What I feel for you makes me want to burn this uniform."

"Oh, Major Trevitt."

"Dunstan. You're to call me Dunstan." He slid his hand

between her legs and for a moment she yielded, letting him touch her while she kissed him. Finally she pushed away and fumbled with her dress.

"Major, we have to stop," she said, watching him and he realized she was deliberately waiting to pull her dress up until he looked at her.

He fought for self-control, because he wanted to throw her down in the grass and take her, but other possibilities loomed. No need to act in haste, he reminded himself. He could go home and bed Verna and get relief. He reached out to stroke Hannah Lou, watching her eyelids come down, her lips apart.

"Hannah Lou, you're the most gorgeous woman I've known," he said in a husky voice.

She smiled and pulled up her dress. "Major, now I'm rumpled and I don't know what I'm doing or saying."

He raised her face in his hands. "Dunstan. I want you to call me Dunstan now. We're going to know each other intimately, Hannah Lou. I love you."

"Dunstan," she whispered, her eyes going wide and looking up at him. "Dunstan." She stood on tiptoe, and he leaned down to kiss her, thinking about Sophia Merrick who wasn't fun yet, but the time would come when he would destroy her resistance.

While he drove Hannah Lou to town, he continued to mull over whether to win Hannah Lou in marriage or seduce her. Marriage didn't appeal to him except for the money it brought, yet Hannah Lou could open the door of Memphis society, and she could give him a fortune. Lord knows, he had no intention of ever being tied down to one woman, but that was no problem.

Hannah Lou continued to fuss with her clothing. "I declare, Dunstan, you crushed this dress into a million wrinkles. Mama will take one look at me and ask me what I've been doing."

"Can't you slip into the house and change your dress before you see her?"

"Yes, I can, but next time—"

"Next time, I'll take your dress off first thing so it won't get a wrinkle," he said in a husky voice, caressing her thigh.

"Oh, Dunstan!" she said in a breathless tone, gazing up at him and he felt a surge of exhilaration. Could he win her parents? What could he do to win over the stiff-necked Southerners enough to get her father to say yes to marriage between them, a Yankee and a Rebel?

A quarter moon was visible high overhead three nights later when Caleb and Will, dressed in blue Union uniforms, moved from building to building with stealth. Lawrence Martin and Charles Gibson followed. Caleb paused to study the shadowed building on Main street that still had the Rivermen's Hotel sign over the door. Two guards stood in front and one in back. Lights burned in two upstairs rooms. Will had learned that the Union payroll and money supply was under a guard in a safe in the front room on the southeast corner of the hotel the Union had taken for part of their headquarters. Before heading for their target, Caleb and Will crept to the opposite corner of the building, the darkened northwest room of the hotel.

"Think Ethan has held up the Memphis and Charleston train yet?" Will whispered.

Caleb glanced at the moon and calculated the time. "It's too soon. Once he takes the Memphis and Charleston, he has to head out of town."

"He better not leave us holding the money."

"We have to get it first."

Caleb nodded to the others and moved away, staying in shadows, trying to slip behind the guard. He reached the side of the building and risked looking around. The guard leaned against the wall, a cheroot in his mouth. Caleb pulled a rock from his pocket and tossed it. It sailed in a high arc and landed with a clatter in the street beyond the building.

Peering into the darkness, the guard turned toward the sound. Caleb threw another rock. The guard shifted his rifle and walked ahead cautiously.

Caleb rushed behind him. As the man turned, Caleb hit him with the gun butt and the guard sank to the ground. Caleb waved his arm and men moved out of the shadows, Lawrence leading horses to the side of the building.

Feeling a sense of urgency, knowing they had only minutes before discovery, Caleb broke a darkened window. While Lawrence and Charles stood guard, Caleb and Will climbed inside. He and Will walked down the hall to the southeast corner room. The guard saluted.

"General Sherman wants the guard changed. You're to report to him at once," Caleb said.

The man frowned. "At three in the morning?"

"Yes. You're Dalton, aren't you?" Caleb said, praying the saloonkeeper had the name right when he heard the soldier complain about standing guard in the hotel all night.

"Yes, sir."

"Get your friend. General Sherman is waiting."

"Yes, sir. As soon as you give me the password, sir."

Will moved to the left. Watching Will, the man raised his rifle. Striking the rifle, Caleb hit him. Caleb swung his revolver and caught the man on the side of the head. The man slumped to the floor.

"Pull him into the room." They closed and locked the door.

"Hurry! It's a matter of minutes," Caleb said, picking up a chair and smashing a window. The window breaking should have been heard by someone, and Caleb fought the urge to flee. He drew his pistol and fired at the squat safe, blasting the lock. Yanking open the door, he scooped up sacks of gold.

Caleb tossed the bags to Will who tossed them outside through the window. The heavy weight of the bags and the clink as he shifted and moved them made Caleb's pulse beat with satisfaction.

"Hurry, Cal!"

Overhead feet pounded on the floor, and men yelled.

"Someone's coming!" Will said. "Hurry!"

Caleb yanked up three bags, tossing them swiftly.

"Let's go, Cal."

"Wait, there's more. We're taking it all," he said. He heard feet in the hallway and he grabbed two more sacks.

Feet pounded toward the door, sounds growing louder. Caleb snatched up two more bags.

"Caleb, for Lord's sake—"

Will climbed out of the window. Caleb ran and jumped as someone smashed the door behind him. He was in the saddle, the horse running as soon as he threw his leg across it. They raced away down Main Street.

Shots came from behind and he glanced over his shoulder. A dozen soldiers were behind, only a block away. "Ride for the river!" he yelled, waving his hand. He tore ahead to lead and they pounded through town. He passed Court Square and turned the corner. Federals rode toward him. Caleb headed down Whiskey Chute with the Union coming behind. Charles and Lawrence turned to fire behind as they galloped along narrow Whiskey Chute. Men came out of saloons to watch, some running out of the way. Suddenly a dozen riders loomed up at the end of the street and Caleb yanked on the reins. They were boxed in with Federals in front and behind them.

Chapter 13

Caleb glanced around and wheeled his horse. "This way!" he yelled riding over the boardwalk and into a saloon. Women screamed and men jumped out of the way, some laughing.

"Help 'em out, boys!" someone yelled, and a window crashed. His horse knocked down tables and chairs as they plunged through the building. Caleb ducked riding through a doorway into a back room where men jumped from their chairs. A man yanked open the back door and waved his hand.

"Over here, Reb!"

Caleb waved and went through the door, spurring his horse and turning east on Madison. Men shouted, waving them on.

They raced past the M&CR depot along Pigeon Roost Road, galloping over the Deaderick plantation. Caleb heard the train whistle above the pounding hooves of the horses.

Veering across open ground he raced along the tracks and in minutes saw the lantern on the caboose. A white plume of smoke trailed behind as the engine gained speed. Caleb raced alongside, watching for the open boxcar. The third car from the caboose was opened wide, a man standing inside. Riding alongside the open boxcar, Caleb and his men tossed the bags of gold.

The Confederate waved at them. Caleb felt a surge of elation. How long would it take the Union to realize their train as well as their money had been taken by Rebels? Outside of La Grange Caleb's raiders would stop the train, unload the gold, and destroy a railroad bridge and the train. A shot rang out behind him.

He yelled and waved his arm and men followed him to the east. Will and the others turned south. Caleb still had one bag of gold over his saddle. If he was caught with it, it would go harder, but he wasn't going to give it up. There was enough in the bag to cover his men's expenses for months, and he intended to keep it.

He leaned over the horse, urging it on, feeling a wild surge of exhilaration. They had the Yankee gold! They had succeeded and as far as he knew, his men were safe.

He let out a yell. They had outridden the Bluebellies before and they would again.

Caleb slept through the morning and then he stirred and sat up. Frowning, Will sat in a chair across the room. "What the hell is wrong?"

"We should move somewhere else today, Cal. Germantown is a small community and a Union camp. We're in the middle of Yankees."

"I don't want to jeopardize your uncle, because he's been good to let us stay here."

"It isn't my uncle. He rides with us and he hates the Federals. Germantown is Union now. They've already burned the public buildings except for the Presbyterian church and the Masonic lodge. If they find we're staying in the area, they may burn houses."

"We'll go. We can camp out."

"Here's a poster they've put up around town. And last night Charles stabbed the guard outside and killed him."

"Dammit, I gave orders not to do it."

"We should have killed the guard inside," Will added solemnly. "He probably gave a good description of you."

Caleb pulled on his pants and stood up, crossing the room to take the drawing of himself from Will's hands.

"Wanted, dead or alive. One thousand dollars reward. I thought I might be worth more than that."

"You stirred everyone up, taking the Yankee's gold, riding through a saloon, commandeering the train, the whole city is talking about the raid. The Yankees are in a rage; one of their supply lines is cut, because of the railroad bridge destroyed by our men. They say it was a million dollars. One million, Cal. The Memphians are ready to make you the town hero. Federals want to hang you. What we're doing is no longer secret."

Caleb let the paper flutter down on a table.

"All right. We break up. Some of the men will join Nathan Forrest. Some will go back to their units. I'll join Bragg, because he's taken Beauregard's command."

"I'll go with you. We did a good job while we were here, Caleb, but it's time to move on."

Caleb crossed the room to the washstand, pouring water into the basin to splash it on his face. Holding the wide leather razor strop, he whisked the blade back and forth and then began to shave.

"Round up the men and we'll ride out by noon."

"Make it an hour from now, Cal. There's a thousand-dollar reward for you. In wartime that's a fortune."

"I'm going to see Sophia today."

Will's mouth dropped open. "You can't! Dammit, you can't go into Memphis. That's suicide. You want to hang? They're enraged over the raid."

He shrugged. "I'll wait until dark."

"It won't matter. You know they'll watch her house."

"Why would they? Just because I stayed there while I was recuperating."

"Dammit, don't go. You're issuing your own death sentence."

"I have to see if she's all right," Caleb said quietly, turning to look at Will who rubbed the back of his neck.

"You're a fool. You won't come back."

"Yes, I will. There's a Union major who wants her and he knows she lives alone."

"So what can you do about that? You can't move in with her and you can't protect her." Will studied him. "I can't believe Sophia Merrick can hold you here."

"She isn't holding me here, but if she were the reason, why would it surprise you?"

"Sophia Merrick and you? She's innocent and inexperienced and so prim. Hannah Lou said Sophia wouldn't let a man kiss her."

Caleb tucked his shirt into his pants and grinned. "She's not so prim, Will."

"Sophia? Miss Proper?" Will tilted his head to study

him. "I wouldn't think she could put up with your cigar smoking, whiskey drinking, card playing ways. And why would Sophia interest you?"

"I just want to make certain she's safe."

"Cal, Sophia is a fine person, even if she is straitlaced. Don't lead her astray," Will said softly.

"I won't hurt her."

"See that you don't. I feel an obligation to Sophia, because we both owe our lives to her. I don't want to lose a friend, but if I find out you've hurt her, I'll call you out."

Caleb was buckling his belt and he looked up. "I have no intention of ever hurting her," he answered calmly. "Far from it. That's part of the reason I'm going to Memphis. She's in danger from the Yankee major and I'll beat that son of a bitch to a pulp if he hurts her."

"Don't take advantage of her innocence."

"Will, stop being such an old maid. I won't hurt her. Ask her yourself. Does that suit you?"

"Well, if you're so damned hell-bent to see her anyway, you better warn—" He broke off and rubbed his jaw.

"What is it?"

"Nothing." Will stood up. "I'll gather the men and we'll ride out of here. Someone could come after us any minute now."

As he started out of the room, Caleb caught him by the arm. "What the hell did you start to say—what's wrong? Has something happened to Sophia?"

"You're too much of a hothead and I should have kept my mouth shut."

"But you're into it now. Tell me what you started to say or I'll flatten you, Will."

With his mouth in a set line and his brow creased in a frown, Will reached into his pocket. For a moment Caleb felt mystified until Will unfolded a newspaper. "If she doesn't stop printing this paper, she'll be in prison. I've heard the Yankees are combing the town for the publisher."

Caleb picked it up and glanced at black letters: "*. . . daring raids that make the Federals look inept and foolish. They can't guard the guns they have taken from*

*Memphis. They should see they can't win the war. Resist.
Don't open your shops to the Federals."*

"Dammit," he said, crumpling the paper and throwing
it down. "I can't make her stop printing the damn paper
and I know she's in danger of prison."

"Well, well, so that's how it is," Will said in a soft
voice, placing his hands on his hips. "A woman who
doesn't melt when you look her way and doesn't obey
your every command? Hannah Lou almost faints when
you walk into the room. And I've seen other women
around you. That's why you're interested in Sophia.
You've met your match."

"What are you talking about?"

Will grinned. "Little green tadpoles! Sophia Merrick
has you dancing a jig."

"The hell you say! I just don't want to see her go to
prison."

"C'mon, Caleb, admit what you feel," Will said,
chuckling. "You've found a woman you can't control and
she's won your heart." He laughed and Caleb felt angry,
embarrassed, foolish. And he knew Will was right.

"I can't get her to stop publishing the paper. I can't get
her to move in with your family. I'm worried sick about
her, Will."

"Well, you poor soul. *You* worry about a woman? It's
always the other way around. They throw themselves at
you, and you go blithely on your way and are barely
aware of them. Well, maybe more than barely, but you
take what you want and do what you please. And now
you've met one who doesn't faint if you look at her and
one you can't control, and she has you tied in knots." He
laughed and shook his head, turning to go. "I'll see you
in Mississippi, Cal. Try to survive so you get there."

"Dammit," Caleb said, watching the door close behind
Will. Sophia did have him tied up in knots. And Will was
right that they needed to leave Memphis, but he couldn't
leave Sophia with a Union major determined to take advantage of her and with her printing an inflammatory
newspaper. He kicked a cushion and turned to pull on his
boots.

The moment the sun slipped below the horizon, he was

riding in to see Sophia. He knew the house might be watched, but he would be careful; he had to know if she was all right.

One hour after dark he urged his horse forward. The night was warm and still, the scent of summer roses in the air. He could hear crickets and the croak of frogs and the steady clop of the hooves of his horse. He skirted town and came in from the north. Along Washington he dismounted and moved quietly down the alley, taking his time, sitting on the ground. Over an hour later, he saw a shadow shift. Inhaling deeply, he rose to his feet, pulling out his revolver and turning it in his hand. Soon the shadow moved again, revealing the outline of a man's shoulders. Taking care to avoid making noise, Caleb crept up behind the man.

Standing only yards behind the soldier, Caleb stepped forward and the swung the revolver through the air.

"What—"

The soldier turned. Caleb caught him on the side of the head, a blow that was a dull thump and the man sank to the ground. Yanking rope from his pocket, Caleb rolled the man over and tied his wrists behind him, next tying his ankles and binding them to his wrists. He yanked loose a neckerchief and tied it over the man's mouth, then secured him to a tree. Someone would find him in the daylight hours. He moved through the yard pausing beneath an oak at the side of the house. Light spilled from the front parlor and he walked closer to see if Sophia had company.

Hoofbeats stopped and footsteps crossed her porch. Caleb hurried to the next tree, pressing close until he heard Sophia's voice. He stepped away from the tree and saw Major Trevitt go inside.

Feeling disturbed, Sophia gazed up at the major. "Sir, it's late; rumors will start if you're in my house."

He reached out to stroke her throat. "Sophia, this is a friendly visit. I'd think you'd be terribly lonesome." He gazed past her. "This is a big house for one woman."

"I have brothers who are away in the war and will come home. There were four of us plus my father."

"And now there's only you," he said, his gaze lowering to her breasts.

Annoyed by him, Sophia moved to the parlor, stopping near the desk where she could get to the drawer with the revolver. On top of the desk lay Papa's silver letter opener that was honed as sharp as a dagger.

The major followed her into the room and glanced around. "I'd like you to show me your house. I've never seen all of it."

"I'm sorry, Major. I see no need to show you my bedroom or the other bedrooms." He stood between her and the door and her heart raced. Why did he want to see the house? Did he suspect the newspaper?

He took off his coat and dropped it over a chair while he watched her. Dropping his hat on top of the coat, he stood facing her. "Sophia, I can't believe a woman like you enjoys being alone. But of course, you aren't always alone. When will Major O'Brien be here again?"

Her pulse jumped with fear as he unbuttoned his shirt at the neck.

"I don't know anything about Major O'Brien," she said stiffly, feeling afraid for Caleb, amazed Major Trevitt knew about them. "I told you he left a long time ago."

"But he comes back. And when he comes, he stays. And he's seen your bedroom."

"Major, I have to ask you to go. If you don't, I'm going to get my neighbor to come ask you to leave."

He smiled. "Does your neighbor know you're the major's mistress? Does anyone in town know this?" he asked, unbuckling his belt.

"Sir, stop undressing!" she snapped, feeling afraid, flustered by his questions about Caleb. *How did he know?* Was he guessing? Was Trevitt having the house watched? "Sir, if my father were alive, you wouldn't dare do such things."

He came toward her, and she backed against the desk, scooting toward the drawer that held her pistol. "You're a beautiful woman, Sophia. And you know where the man is who has our gold. He's stolen almost one million dollars in gold from us. If he thought you were in danger, I think he would come into town to protect you."

"Get out of my house," she screamed.

Trevitt stood only yards away and he looked at her with smug satisfaction. She felt shivers of fear, because she was alone. Screams wouldn't stir anyone because no one would hear. The street was wide and the houses sound.

Suddenly Trevitt reached out and yanked her to him, pulling her against him and bending his head. He held her head as he kissed her while she fought and struggled uselessly. The pistol was out of reach.

She hated Trevitt, hated his hands on her, his mouth on hers. He ran his hand over her breasts, and Sophia beat against his chest and pushed to no avail. Backing her, he pushed her down over the desk, forcing her legs apart and moving between them. She struggled in silence, knowing she couldn't fight his strength, feeling him push up her skirts.

Outside Caleb moved from the tree to a window. A wing chair partially blocked his view, and he couldn't see anyone in the room. Where the hell were they? Had Trevitt forced her to a bedroom? Caleb moved to another window, his gaze sweeping over the empty settee, the empty chairs. His breath caught in his throat. Sophia was sprawled on the desk, her legs spread with Trevitt between them bending over her as he tugged at her skirt. Burning with rage, Caleb turned.

A pistol jammed into his stomach.

"Don't move, Major O'Brien, or you're a dead man." He faced a Union soldier. "We're going to headquarters. Thrown down your gun and get your hands behind your head."

Caleb swung his arm, coming up and hitting the man's arm. The Yankee's revolver flew out of his hand as Caleb hit him again, plunging against him and dropping his gun to pull his fist back and hit the man on the jaw. The soldier's head snapped back; he staggered, fell to the ground, and lay still. Caleb yanked a knife from his boot and stabbed the man.

Sophia groped behind her as the major slid his hand beneath her skirt. His weight held her pinned down while he pulled open her dress, his hands sliding over her breasts. "We have all night, Sophia."

Her fingers closed on the letter opener, and she swung it with all her strength.

It stabbed into his shoulder and he gasped, staggering back. She yanked open the drawer and spun away from him, raising the revolver. "Get out of my house or I'll shoot," she yelled.

"You stabbed me, you baggage!" he said, pulling free the letter opener and gasping again, holding his hand over the wound. "Damn you, you little bitch. You'll be sorry."

"Get out, Major, or you'll be sorrier," she threatened.

They faced each other, both breathing hard, and then he yanked up his coat to hold it against his bleeding shoulder. He strode out the door and slammed it behind him. Running after him, she turned the lock and sagged against it, buttoning her dress when she heard the back door splinter.

She spun around, raising the revolver, wondering if it was another Union soldier.

Boots scraped as someone ran across the kitchen. Gun drawn, Caleb stepped into the hallway and they looked at each other over pistols.

Chapter 14

"Caleb!" She tossed down the revolver. It hit the boards with a clatter and fired, the shot taking a chip out of the newel post inches from Caleb as she ran to him.

He caught her against him and thrust his revolver in his holster, holding her tightly. "Where's the bastard?"

"He's gone."

"How'd you get rid of him? How'd you get the gun?"

"He knows about you," she said. "You've got to go. They must watch the house. Please get out now. They have a reward for you." She turned her face up to him, and he bent his head, his mouth covering hers as his heart thudded and he kissed her hungrily, wanting her more than ever. His arousal was swift, yet he had to know what happened to Trevitt.

"Sophia," he said, "where is Trevitt? How did you get him to go? How'd you get a gun?"

"I stabbed him. There was a—"

"You *what*? Caleb asked, pushing her away to look at her, bending his knees so he could look her directly in the eyes. "What did you do?"

"I stabbed Trevitt because he wouldn't stop," she said, crying. "I'm so scared for you. There was a letter opener and I stabbed him in the shoulder and got my gun and ordered him out. But it's you, Caleb. They know about us!"

"Great saints in the morning," he said, terrified for her safety, aware of the dead soldier in her yard. "You're getting out of here right now. You're coming with me. Get some clothes and be quick about it."

"What are you talking about?" she said, her eyes going wide.

"He'll be back to arrest you. He may search the house."

"Why would he arrest me?"

"You stabbed him."

"He attacked me," she protested. "He won't want to make that known."

"He'll probably deny that he attacked you, but he'll come back and arrest you," he said impatiently. While they argued, Trevitt could be riding back with a dozen men. "If they know you're seeing me, he won't let this go by. They'll question you about me. You're not running the risk."

"I'm not leaving my home and paper," she said, backing away from him.

"That damnable paper," Caleb snapped, patience gone. "You're not safe, Sophia." He passed her going into her bedroom and throwing open the armoire. "What clothes do you want to take?"

"I'm not going anywhere," she said, lifting her chin and getting the fiery look that made him want to shake her. His pulse raced with fear for her safety. He looked at the clothes and began yanking things out.

"Caleb, stop it! I refuse to go with you."

He saw a valise beside the armoire and picked it up, setting it on the bed and jamming clothes inside. He threw in her brush while she pulled at his arm.

"Stop taking my things. It won't do you one bit of good, Caleb O'Brien, because you can't force me or bully me or frighten me into leaving my home and my paper. I won't go to the Stantons' house. If I move in with them, I'll have to give up my paper and my freedom."

He yanked her nightgown and wrapper off hooks and tossed them in the bag and then he picked up two pairs of slippers and a pair of boots and crammed them inside. He struggled to close the bag and turned to face her.

She had spots of color in her cheeks and sparks of fire in her eyes and he wanted to yank her into his arms and kiss her until she melted, but he couldn't take the time. Any moment now escape would be impossible.

"Is there anything else, Sophia, that you don't want to leave home without?"

She glanced at a picture on the dresser. "I'm not going." He picked up the picture.

"Who is this?"

"My mother."

Caleb opened the valise and squeezed the picture inside and closed it again. "Anything else?"

"No." She stood with her hands on her hips and her chin lifted. "Caleb O'Brien, I refuse to leave!"

"Sure and I'll not stand by and see the woman I love go to prison just because she's so damned stubborn." He locked his fingers around the valise and crossed the room.

Sophia watched him, her heart pounding. He would leave now and he was angry. She remembered the moment on the battlefield when he tossed away her rifle and yelled at her. He was hotheaded, unpredictable, and fiery, making a brash raid on the Union, stealing their gold and riding through downtown Memphis, racing horses through a saloon to escape. She didn't know what he was going to do next, but she wasn't leaving home. She braced her feet and gazed into his eyes as he came closer.

He stood yards away. "We have to go."

"No. Absolutely not!" Her heart pounded, because he looked fierce.

Suddenly he stepped forward and swung her over his shoulder. She realized what he was going to do and tried to jump out of reach, but he caught her. She beat against his back and struggled uselessly. His arm was like iron holding her as he strode out of the room. He bent down and scooped up her revolver.

"Caleb O'Brien, I hate you for this! Put me down! I'll run away the first moment I can!"

He didn't answer but strode outside across the yard. He went up on Henry's porch and kicked the door.

"Yes'm?" Henry's sleep-filled voice came from the other side of the door. It swung open. "Major?" he said, sounding shocked.

"Henry, stop him!" she cried.

"Henry, Miss Sophia stabbed that Union officer tonight. I'm taking her where she'll be safe. And I've killed a soldier near the front of the house. Get Mazie and go to friends."

"Henry, stop him!"

"Yes, sir, Major. Miss Sophia, begging your pardon, but Major's right. You go with him. He's a good man."

"Henry!" She shook with rage, hanging helplessly over Caleb's shoulder.

"While I saddle a horse, Henry, run to the house and throw some food into a bundle for me to carry. Be quick about it."

"Yes, sir," he said, hurrying out.

Sophia beat against Caleb as he strode to the carriage house and set her on her feet, dropping the valise to hold her with both hands, gripping her upper arms.

"I'm wanted and I'll hang if they catch me. Now you stop yelling and making noise, because we have to get out of Memphis."

"I'll scream at the top of my lungs if you take me out of this yard."

"Oh, you will?" He swung her around, pinned her arms behind her and tied them swiftly with a piece of rope.

"Caleb O'Brien, I hate you!"

He looked around, spotted a rag and pulled it from a hook. He threw it over her, pulling it tight over her mouth and tying it behind her head. He saddled the horse, hooking the valise on the saddle. He swung into the saddle and lifted her easily, placing her before him.

Henry ran across the yard, Mazie coming behind him and both had bundles tied in cloths they handed up to Caleb.

"Miss Sophia, you let him take care of you," Mazie said and stood beside Henry as Caleb turned the horse.

"Henry, you and Mazie, take what you can and get out. They should be here any time now." He flicked the reins, and they rode out of her yard.

Sophia tried to cry out, the sound muffled by the rag over her mouth. He turned her head against his chest to muffle her cries.

She tried to kick him and his arm tightened around her waist.

"Stop that, Sophia, or I'll throw you across this horse like a sack of flour."

Enraged with his cavalier handling, she kicked his shin.

Suddenly she was on her stomach across the horse as they rode down the alley. She bounced against him, feeling as if she would fall. Every trot of the horse hurt and she cried in outrage and indignity and loss. She didn't want to leave home. Where was he taking her? They slowed and she didn't know what he was doing until she heard another horse. He had his horse tied somewhere else. She kicked her feet and tried to cry out in protest. He swung her up.

"Now if you'll ride quietly and won't kick, you can sit up."

She turned to glare at him, looking up at him. She wanted to claw him and hit him and tell him to go to the devil.

She rode breathing raggedly as they turned east. Suddenly he yanked the reins to ride behind a house. She heard the jingle of harness.

"Not a peep out of you," Caleb whispered in her ear, pressing her face against his chest. "Our lives are in danger."

She struggled to break free, wanting to yell. Let him go to jail! If Union soldiers started after him, he would have to let her go and race for his life.

She struggled and tried to scream, the sound coming out muffled. Instantly she was crushed against him so tightly her head swam and spots danced in front of her eyes. In seconds he released her and leaned close to her ear. "Not a sound from you," he warned.

She glared at him as he urged the horses forward. They circled the house and continued out of town. Passing familiar landmarks, darkened houses, the hoofbeats and crickets the only sounds in the night, she felt torn from her family.

When they were away from Memphis, he rode to a creek to let the horses drink. He climbed down and reached for her.

"Sophia, we're going to settle this right now."

Her pulse pounded at the harsh note in his voice. He pulled her down and turned her, yanking loose the rope around her wrists and removing the gag.

"I hate you for what you've done!" she gasped, touching her lips.

"You would have given me to the Federals back there if you could have," he said with rage in his voice. His hands were on his hips and each word was clipped.

"No, I wouldn't have. If they had heard me, they would have come after you and you would have ridden away and escaped and left me to go back home."

"No. I wouldn't leave you to go to prison. I would have been taken prisoner and so would you and I'd hang. Is that what you want?"

"Damn you, Caleb O'Brien! You've taken my house and my paper and—"

"Sophia, you're too independent for your own good," he snapped in a cold, quiet voice, interrupting her. "I'm going to protect you unless I know in your heart you want to be rid of me and that you truly hate me. Now tell me you hate me, Sophia, and I'll let you do what you damned well please."

"I hate you, Caleb O'Brien!" she said, her voice a rasp as he came closer and she backed up. "You stay where you are. I hate you!" she cried, her voice rising and she felt all control slipping.

"I'd like to shake you; I wish I could ride out of here and forget you," he said, grinding out the words, "but the last thing I feel toward you, Sophia, is hatred. I won't let you go to prison even though you're hell-bent on it."

"You leave me alone!"

"No. If you don't mean what you're saying, then I'm going to keep you out of trouble if I lose my life trying!"

"Get away," she said at the edge of the creek. He moved closer and she turned to run. His arm snaked out and caught her and swung her around, yanking her against him.

"You think you can kiss me into submission, Caleb. Well, you can't—"

"I just want to see how deep *hate* goes," he said, bending his head. "You're going to do what I want, Sophia."

"No, I'm not," she argued, her heart pounding and her pulse roaring as he bent his head. She tried to twist away and he wound his fingers in her hair and held her head as he kissed her, and in seconds she could no longer resist. With a sob all her defenses crumbled; her anger evaporated, transforming into hurt and need as she cried. He pushed her down, moving between her legs and she struggled, not wanting him to touch her intimately, wanting to stay aloof from him, trying to keep him from winning their struggle.

His hands drifted beneath her skirts, pushing them up, unfastening her drawers and sliding them over her hips.

"No, Caleb—"

"No, Sophia?" His hand played over her and she gasped and raised her hips to meet him.

"Yes, I want you," she responded, forgetting her loss. He thrust into her softness. Sophia reached for his shoulders, pulling him close as he turned his head to kiss her passionately.

Sophia clung to him, moving with him, feeling a desperate urgency. Worries and fears vanished; all thought was gone. Wave after wave of exquisite sensation washed over her, taking her breath as she held his strong shoulders and moved her hips with his until they both cried out.

"Caleb, please!"

"I love you, Sophia," he proclaimed in a husky voice. She barely heard the words as she felt caught in an overwhelming urgency, and then his body shuddered and he relaxed.

She gasped for breath, sounds and thought returning, remembrance settling on her like a heavy winter cloak. Her defenses were down, the barriers gone, demolished in the past few minutes when she had given herself wholeheartedly to him. She burst into tears and held him. "I've lost everything, Caleb. My home and my family and our paper. Amos is gone. Papa is gone. I don't know that Morris and John will ever come home. Can't you see if I lose the house and the paper, I have nothing?"

He rolled on his side, holding her close, legs entwined, stroking her head, letting her cry. "Begorra, Sophia, yer two brothers may come home to ye."

"Everything else is gone," she sobbed.

He stroked her hair, her throat. "And ye don't hate me, Sophia."

"I hate your taking charge of my life! You do things your way, Caleb O'Brien."

"And sure 'tis good I do, or ye would be in prison, lassie, my love. Yer a stubborn one, Sophia Merrick. Now don't cry. Yer not in a prison and ye can start another paper again someday."

She shifted to look into his eyes. "Bully," she said softly.

"And ye need bullying, love. Duty has to stop somewhere and common sense take over."

"So whenever you want your way, is this how you intend to get it?"

" 'Tis not a bad way."

"I still want to go home."

"And I still am not going to allow it." His voice was gentle, but Sophia heard the note of steel as he stroked her hair away from her face. "And if you run away, I'll tie you up again."

She moved away from him and went to the creek to wash. Caleb followed, stripping off the rest of his clothes and wading into the cool water. She felt torn emotionally. She watched him splash in the water and drop down to swim away from her. As passion cooled and Caleb's strong arms were gone, she wanted desperately to go home. Suddenly she ran for one of the horses, swinging up into the saddle, hearing splashing behind her.

She paused to glance around and see him racing toward her. He reached out as she flicked the reins. His hand jerked the reins and his arm locked around her waist and pulled her down. She fought against Caleb's wet, slippery body.

"I warned you, Sophia."

"What are you going to do? Where are you taking me? You have to go back to battle."

"I'm taking you home to New Orleans," he said, facing her, his hands on his hips. He was wet, nude, masculine, and she tried to keep her gaze from lowering, but she couldn't resist. His body made her pulse pound as she looked at him.

He turned away to dry himself with his shirt and yank on his clothes. In minutes she was seated before him on a horse. "We have a long ride. You cooperate or I'll tie you again. We're still in enemy territory."

She bit her lip and kept silent, angry again with him, feeling defiant, wanting badly to go home. They rode in silence back to the road and she turned for one last glimpse of Memphis, knowing at night all she would see would be a few twinkling lights on the horizon.

Along with the lights she saw a plume of gray smoke spiral into the air. "Something's burning, Caleb."

He shifted and looked back in silence. When he turned around his arm tightened around her and he kissed her forehead. "Sophia, stop fighting me. You're safe and that's what matters," he said in his tender tone of voice that always made her heart melt.

"You murdered a soldier?"

"A Yankee who was watching your house. He caught me and was taking me in."

She felt uncertain over her future, hurt by her losses. After a short time, she raised her chin and gazed ahead. "What will Miss Therrie think about your bringing me to New Orleans?" Her cheeks burned at the forwardness of the question, but she was curious about his answer.

"Amity?" he asked, sounding amused. "She'll be delighted; Amity and I are old friends, nothing more."

"I find that difficult to believe. She seemed to hang on your every word when she visited," Sophia said stiffly.

He chuckled. "No, Sophia. You're wrong. I know that Will and Amity correspond regularly."

"Will Stanton?" she asked, twisting to look up at him.

"Yes," Caleb replied, catching her chin with his finger. "That's better. I don't like your anger."

"You always do something to stir it!"

He chuckled again. "You're a feisty one, Sophia Merrick, and you need a strong hand to keep you out of trouble."

"There's a world of difference between having a strong hand and being jackass stubborn!"

He laughed. "I think you need my stubbornness. If I

heeded your words, you would be in a Yankee prison tonight."

She became quiet and after a mile he lifted her chin to him. "Why so quiet, love?"

She felt on edge, hurt and loss threatening her control. She didn't have anything or anyone until John and Morris came home and at the moment she didn't know if they were still alive. Caleb would leave her with strangers in New Orleans and go back to battle. "Leave me alone. You've done enough this night."

He hugged her to him and his voice was deep and gentle. "Stop worrying. Someday you'll go home again and you'll have your paper and your house. Right now, you're safe, love."

She didn't feel safe. She felt lost and alone. She stared into the darkness and wondered what lay ahead. "Caleb, are we riding through Yankee-held country?"

"We'll leave the road and skirt the towns until we're on Confederate ground. Grenada is still Confederate. From there south we can try to go to the river and hitch a ride on a boat."

They rode in silence and she wiped away tears, trying to cry in silence so he wouldn't pity her. She slid her hand over her valise. It was all she had. She had no money—the family money was in the bank in Memphis except for the bit of gold in her reticule.

Caleb tugged on the reins and dropped down to the ground, swinging her down in his arms.

"Put me down, Caleb. I can walk."

"I thought you were asleep. We'll stop and sleep here for a few hours and then ride on." He hobbled the horses and unsaddled them and spread two blankets. It was a warm summer night and he pulled her down on the blanket. She lay stiffly against him as he stroked her hair away from her face.

"Sophia," he said softly, "you'll see it will be better to leave Memphis. There will be a time to go back."

She cried quietly and felt his fingers slide over her cheeks. He leaned forward to kiss her tears away. "You'll have your house again and your paper. I promise you."

"You can't promise what you don't know! I've never

been away from Memphis except the times at Shiloh. Never!" She buried her head against his chest, sobbing, unable to stop once she let go.

He held her tightly against him while he gazed beyond her into the darkness. Sophia was so young in some ways, and tonight she had lost everything that was a tie to her family. She needed to cry and to vent her emotions, but anyone nearby could have heard her. His Sharps was ready, beside him on the blanket. He stroked her as she trembled and finally wrapped her arms around him. Her sobs diminished and faded and then she became still and he suspected she was asleep. Kissing her temple, he strained to hear any disturbing sounds, knowing they were still in Union-held country. He held her tightly, stroking her, thankful he had ridden into Memphis tonight and brought her out, because if he hadn't she would be in prison now. He thought of the plume of smoke rising above Memphis and wondered about her house.

The first faint rays of dawn came and he shook her awake, watching her as she moved around, amazed at the depth of his feelings for her. He had been terrified for her last night and he was thankful they had escaped. Her hair cascaded over her shoulders and he watched her braid it. After a moment he crossed to her and took a thick plait in his hand. "Let me, Sophia." He stood quietly behind her, feeling the silky locks, wanting to lean forward and kiss her nape, but knowing they had to get going because they were in dangerous territory.

Finally he helped her mount, giving her waist a squeeze. She looked down at him solemnly. He hated that she was hurting; he wished he could do something to stop it.

"Ye're brave, lassie," he said softly, and she looked away, her gaze going to the horizon. He mounted and moved beside her. "Listen for anyone approaching, Sophia."

Later in the day he motioned to her to ride ahead so he could watch and listen. He rode with his rifle ready and Sophia held the colt. Her back was straight, her golden braids trailing on her back and as he rode, he stared at her. He loved her wildly and he wanted to marry her and his life would never be peaceful again, yet he couldn't imagine living without her. She was a bright flame in a dark world at war. He needed her warmth and laughter. Her feisty nature was part of her appeal, even if it meant storms in his life. And in moments of passion she was the most sensual, exciting woman he had ever known. He hated that he would go back to war, and leave her facing uncertainty, because in spite of all his reassurances, she had lost her home and paper and friends.

At least he knew she was safe from the Federals and prison. He hadn't planned on marrying for years, but she could be carrying his child right now—something that didn't seem to have occurred to her.

The sun rose high and he motioned to her to leave the road and turn west. When he found a creek, they dismounted. "We're stopping. It'll be safer to sleep now and travel after dark. Less chance of encountering soldiers."

In minutes the horses were unsaddled and he had spread blankets, pulling her down into his arms and holding her. At dusk they ate cheese and apples and thick slices of ham. He untied another bundle and pulled out a bottle. "Bless Henry!"

She gazed at the demijohn of brandy and frowned. "Where did that come from?"

"I had some at the house. I got it from one of the saloons," he said, wondering if she would demand he dispose of it, but she merely continued eating.

"When this war is over," she said wistfully, "I want to have a dinner with hot biscuits and thick honey and a juicy roast. And I want to eat an orange."

"Maybe you won't have to wait until the end of the war. With Rafe running the blockade, perhaps he can get things."

When they finished, Caleb saddled the horses. "Ready to ride?"

"How do you know where you're going in the dark?"

"I'm accustomed to this. If I tell you to get off the road, do so at once. We're still in Union territory." They headed south and he angled back to the road, where they could make the best time.

He judged it was near midnight by the white moon rising overhead when he heard a hoofbeat. For a quarter of an hour, Caleb rode with his rifle in hand. Finally he caught up to ride beside Sophia.

"Someone's following us," he whispered, leaning close to her. "I'm dropping off the road to wait and see who it is. You ride ahead and keep your pistol drawn. If you hear shots, ride for a town. I'll catch up with you. I'll whistle if everything is all right."

"Please be careful," she whispered, touching his arm, and he drew a deep breath. One minute she seemed to care and to love him and the next she was angry and wanting to get away from him, yet he knew what an upheaval it had been to leave her home.

He rode to the west into dark shadows, halting to wait, his rifle cocked and ready.

Chapter 15

In a few minutes he heard a rider approach. The man rode into moonlight and Caleb stared at the broad shoulders and shadowed profile.

He wasn't certain, so he raised his rifle. "Halt and raise your hands!"

"Caleb?"

"Fortune! What are you doing here?" He rode forward. "Sophia's ahead and I don't want her to be alone. Let's catch up, and then you can explain."

Fortune caught his arm. "Wait a minute. You might not want to tell her. The Federals burned her house last night."

Caleb felt a ripple of worry. "Damn, I was afraid something like that would happen. I don't want her to know."

"You need to get off this road. Our army uses it and the price on your head has gone to ten thousand."

"Well, damn. I don't know whether to be scared or flattered."

"You damn well better be scared. There's an arrest warrant out for her."

"I guessed there would be. How's Trevitt?"

"Angrier than a sore-tailed bear. He wants her."

"That's why I took her away. Let's catch up with her."

They broke into a gallop, pounding down the road until Caleb guessed they should be drawing close. He motioned to slow and when Fortune did, he rode closer. "I don't want to frighten her. I'm going to whistle."

The whistle was clear in the quiet night, and in minutes he saw a figure ahead waiting on a horse by one side of the road.

"There she is." He waved. "Sophia." As they reached her, he waved his hand. "Look who's here."

"Miss Merrick," Fortune said, greeting her.

"How did you find us?"

"I found someone who talked to your Henry. I took a chance on this way. This is how I would go if I were heading to New Orleans."

"How'd you know we were going to New Orleans?" she asked, looking at Caleb.

"We probably think alike," Fortune answered. "I have to get back to Memphis. They've increased the price on your head to ten thousand dollars," he repeated to Caleb and then he looked at her. "The Provost Marshal has issued an order for your arrest, Miss Merrick, for aiding the Rebellion and for sedition against the United States government. They've learned you printed *The Loyal Memphian*."

She raised her chin. "And Major Trevitt? Is there a charge for attacking an officer?"

"Major Trevitt's in a rage over the paper. I don't know what you mean, attacking an officer."

"He isn't injured?"

"Yes. His shoulder is bandaged. Trevitt said he had an accident on board one of the ships at the dock." Fortune looked back and forth between them.

"He doesn't want to tell people," Caleb said. "Sophia stabbed him because he attacked her."

"Lord, that's all the more reason for you two to get out of Tennessee. Cal, I have to get back. Get off the road. We'll have soldiers along here tomorrow."

"Come with us to New Orleans," Caleb insisted.

"I can't. The army would have a price on my head. But I can't wait to see Darcy and Rafe. Tell them I'll be there the first chance I get."

"You take care of yourself," Caleb said, halting and turning so he faced Fortune. He stood in the stirrups and leaned over to hug his brother, who hugged him in return.

"Be careful. You're the wild man running risks," Fortune said. He turned his horse and waved, vanishing into the night, and Caleb wondered when he would see his brother again.

Sophia rode in silence beside him. "Is that all he told you?"

"Yes," he said, having no intention of burdening her with the news about her house. She had suffered too much from war.

"If they know I printed *The Loyal Memphian*, they must know about my press. Did he say?"

"No. I think we should get off the road and go across country. You follow me." He moved in the lead and veered west, thinking if they could ride along the river, they might find a boat that would take them south.

The next day they rode into the small river town of Chestnut Grove. Caleb learned it was still a Confederate town and within the hour he boarded the horses with the blacksmith until he could come back and claim them. Then he took Sophia to a small one-story hotel near the river where he registered them as husband and wife and was shown to a room.

As soon as the door closed behind them, she turned to look at him. "Caleb, I can't stay here with you."

"Yes, you can," he said. "Porters will be right back, because I ordered a tub of hot water so we can bathe. It may be hours or a day before I can find a boat going south that will be safe, so you might as well wait in comfort."

"Do they think I'm your wife?" she asked, blushing.

He tried to bite back his amusement as he reached for her. "Yes. This may be our last time alone. When we get to New Orleans, we'll be with my family and we won't be alone, and then I have to get back to fighting. I'm going down to the dock and ask questions about steamboats. You bathe or whatever you want."

She frowned and he caught her chin. "No worries now," he said softly.

She nodded, and he kissed her until he heard a rap on the door.

Minutes later Caleb told her goodbye and closed the door. She looked at the tin tub with steaming water and unbuttoned her dress, thankful to sink down in the hot water.

She washed her hair and then climbed out to dry. Then she washed her clothes, hanging them on the window ledge to dry. She opened the valise and pulled out a cotton chemise and a wrinkled blue muslin dress, shaking out her clothes and remembering Caleb throwing them inside while they argued.

She heard the door and Caleb entered. "There may be a boat in two hours," he said.

Dressed all in black, he was rumpled, dusty, his curls a tangle and a dark stubble on his jaw, yet he looked appealing. This man had become so important to her, so much a part of her life. His gaze lowered, and she tingled as he came toward her. Her pulse raced when Caleb reached out to slide his hand around her waist and draw her to him.

"We have to get farther away from Memphis, love," he said softly, looking down at her. "Otherwise, I'd like to keep you here for days. The risk is too great though, and we better be at the wharf in two hours to catch the boat." His gaze drifted over her face while she ran her fingers over his shoulders. "You smell sweet and you're clean and I'm dusty. I'll bathe," he said, brushing her cheek with a kiss and turning away.

He unbuttoned and pulled off his shirt, the muscles rippling beneath his coppery skin. He unbuckled his belt, dropping it on the floor, and unbuttoned his pants to pull them off. When he glanced at her, she walked toward him languidly, feeling hot as she unfastened her dress. In minutes she was in the water with him, his strong body wet, slippery and warm. He settled her on him, his hands cupping her full breasts as he leaned forward to kiss her.

Two hours later she waited on the wharf while Caleb talked to the steamboat captain. In spite of her losses, she felt a tremor of excitement. She had never been on a steamboat, never been anywhere away from Memphis and Germantown and Shiloh. She looked at Caleb standing in the sunlight talking to the captain. Caleb's hat sat squarely on his head, hiding his brown curls. Her gaze ran down his lean form and long legs and she knew she was indebted to him for helping her even if it wasn't what she had wanted to do. In minutes he motioned to her and came striding down the plank to pick up her valise and take her arm. "We're passengers. We'll be in New Orleans tomorrow."

"New Orleans is held by the Union. How can we get into town when you're wanted?"

"We'll get off upriver and I'll get horses. I know how to get to Rafe's without being discovered. New Orleans is a seaport city with crowds, and we'll be far from Tennessee. There won't be posters with my picture all over town."

She gazed up into his green eyes, remembering his determination that morning in the barn when he had picked up Will and carried him to the wagon. She smiled at him and placed her hand in his, knowing that she could trust him to get them to New Orleans. His brows arched and his warm fingers locked around hers, giving her hand a squeeze.

She stood at the rail as the whistle gave a blast and water churned and they moved away from the small dock. She could see the hotel and she felt as if she were leaving another part of her life behind. Soon Caleb would leave her to go back to war. She glanced up at him. He stood with his arm touching her, his profile to her. His jaw was clean shaven now, curls showing beneath his hat that he had pushed back on his head. The thought of parting with him was as terrifying as giving up her home. How had this man become so much of her life? What would she feel about him after a long separation? What would she feel for him if times were normal? Were her feelings influenced by the turbulent circumstances? She didn't know the answers, but she couldn't bear to part with him. She placed her hand on his arm and he looked down at her, his green eyes darkening.

"Come here, love. We'll go to our cabin." He led her to a small cabin and closed the door and dropped the valise, pulling her to him. "I have you to myself for just a little while longer."

"Caleb, your family may not want me," she said, new worries surfacing.

"Don't be ridiculous. Amity and Darcy already know you."

"I'd feel better staying somewhere on my own. If there was some way to get my money from Memphis, I—"

"Sophia, you're staying with my family. I don't want to go off to war while you're alone in the city. Stop worrying, because when you meet them, you'll like them." He raised her chin. "Until then, let's forget families and war and problems," he said softly, bending his head to kiss her.

That night as she lay in his arms, she tried to stop worrying about his family. "Caleb?"

"Yes," he said, turning locks of her hair in his hand.

"This is the first time I've been on a steamboat. There were so many that stopped at Memphis, but I've never ridden one," she said as she listened to the deep chug of the engine and felt the constant movement of the boat.

"I want to take you to Ireland, Sophia. It's beautiful, just like Tennessee. And sometime I'll take you on a train ride and you'll see what a wonder they are."

His voice was a deep rumble. Her shoulder was against his bare chest and she could feel a slight vibration when he talked. She rolled over to look at him. "If only I could keep you from going to war!" she said, holding him tightly, the cold fear washing over her as she thought about him in battle.

"Don't worry. Tonight, I'm here in your arms." He raised up and looked down at her. "Sophia, love," he said softly, while she tangled his brown curls around her fingertips, "I wanted to wait until we were in New Orleans where I could take you to some fancy restaurant and buy you something pretty and make it special, but I can't wait until then. I have to ask you now. Will you marry me?"

Chapter 16

Sophia gazed up at him, her heart drumming as she pulled his head down and kissed him long. He finally raised slightly.

"Will you marry me?" he asked again.

She caressed his cheek and felt her heart torn between two answers, between reason and love, between what she knew and what she felt. He frowned and raised up higher.

"Begorra, lass, what's this? You don't love me?"

"Yes, Caleb, I love you," she said, tracing her finger along his full lower lip.

"Then why no answer?"

"Because you're going to war. I'm away from home. We're both in desperate times and we're so terribly different. We can't go through life fighting."

"I have no intention of askin' a woman to marry me so I can fight with her," he said gruffly, his brogue thickening as he studied her.

"I think we should wait until the war is over."

"Sophia, I love ye and I want ye, and I don't want to wait. And ye may be carrying our child now. Have ye thought of that?" Caleb asked, frowning. Her damnable independence was coming between them, and it hurt.

She blinked and he realized she hadn't given it thought and he wanted to groan. "If ye're with child, lass, we're going to a preacher."

"I'll know soon and if I'm not, I think we should wait until the war's over, Caleb," she answered solemnly. "You're rushing into something that you might feel differently about later. And we're not in ordinary circumstances. And I feel your conscience is making you ask."

"Then ye know damned little about me!" he said. "If I

ask for ye in marriage, then I love ye and want ye to be my wife."

She rolled over, stretching the length of him. "I love you, Caleb O'Brien, and I always will. When you leave me to go to war, I think my heart will break." She kissed his throat, sliding down to trail kisses to his bare chest, moving off him to continue to kiss and stroke him until he caught her hands and swung her down to lean over her and kiss her, taking her breath and making her pulse pound. He paused and raised up.

"You'll be my wife, Sophia. If we love each other, nothing should stand in our way. Not doubts and fears."

He kissed her hard, his hands moving over her and Sophia yielded to him, returning his caresses and kisses, feeling her heart burst with love for him and wanting to cry out, *"Yes! Yes, Caleb, I will marry you."*

On Wednesday Sophia felt swamped with uncertainty as she stood beside him at the rail and watched as the boat turned toward a private landing. Caleb shook hands with the captain and jumped to the dock, taking her hand and pulling her alongside him. The captain tossed him the valise, and men came forward across the dock. Approaching them was a tall, thick-chested man with deep brown eyes and graying sideburns.

"Caleb!" he cried, hugging Caleb and turning to her.

"Sophia, this is Ormonde Therrie. Ormonde, this is Miss Merrick from Tennessee."

"Caleb!" came a cry as a buggy stopped near the dock and Amity Therrie hurried to hug him, her pale green dress rustling, and then she turned. "Miss Merrick!" she said, her dark brown eyes going wide with surprise and she stepped up to hug Sophia.

"Come up to the house," Ormonde Therrie said.

"Hey, Mister O'Brien," a grinning servant called, and Caleb stopped to greet three men before turning to take Sophia's arm and walk with them to Amity's buggy.

"I want to hear all the news," Ormonde said.

"Yes, sir. And then I'd like to get horses from you to ride into town."

Ormonde smiled. "I suspect we'll lose you all too

soon. You want to see Rafe and Darcy, I know. Let's go up to the house."

Caleb helped Sophia into the buggy and he sat between Amity and her, taking the reins from Amity.

"You're well," Amity said. "I'm so glad. Will wrote to me that you both stayed near Germantown. He said that's only a few miles from Memphis."

"He's fine, too, Amity. He plans to come to New Orleans."

"Will does? How soon?"

"I don't know with the war, but I think soon."

"I'm so glad you're home. Darcy talks about your coming home all the time."

As they approached Belle Destin, the Therrie home, Sophia gazed up the slope through the tall oaks at the most magnificent house she had ever seen. Tall columns surrounded the house and the galleries were wide with a fan transom over the front door. She felt more lost by the moment even though Amity seemed warm and friendly. As they entered the wide hall, Caleb held her arm.

"You must want to freshen up," Amity said. "You know where your room is Caleb. Sophia, come with me, and I'll take you to your room. A servant will bring your valise."

Amity took her hand and Sophia glanced at Caleb. Before she turned away, he winked and she felt better.

"I'm so glad you're here!" Amity exclaimed. "We've been terrified for our home, but so far, the Yankees have left this house alone. Sometimes I think Rafferty may have paid someone to get them to do so, but Papa says he'd have to pay the whole Union army to get that. And that dreadful Butler man! He's in charge in New Orleans and he is the worst man to ever walk this earth."

Sophia relaxed more as Amity talked and realized that Caleb must not have been exaggerating when he said all that was between them was friendship. Amity led her into a large, sunny room filled with pink cushions and a frilly pink counterpane on the canopied bed. The servant placed her valise on the floor.

Amity's dark eyes sparkled. "Tell me about Will

Stanton! Is he really well? Have you heard him talk about coming to New Orleans?"

"No, I haven't," Sophia said, taking off her bonnet. She looked at Amity whose hairdo was fashionable and whose dress was beautiful. "Miss Therrie—"

Amity laughed. "You have to call me Amity! I'm so glad Caleb is home. If only you'd brought Will with you."

"Amity, would you show me how to comb my hair so it's—" She felt foolish suddenly, wishing she hadn't asked. She had just arrived and she was asking her hostess for something quite personal.

"Your hair? Of course. I'll get Loretta, and she can do your hair for you. She does mine. And I know you'd probably like to change and freshen up before you come downstairs."

Sophia opened the valise and shook out a dress. It was her brown muslin and full of wrinkles. Amity crossed the room and took it from her hands. "Let's see if you can wear one of my dresses or Chantal's and we'll get your dresses pressed."

"I don't want to be so much trouble. I should wear mourning, but I had only one black dress and it didn't get packed," she said, remembering Caleb yanking up her things and stuffing them into the valise.

"That's no trouble," Amity said, her eyes sparkling as she studied Sophia. "I never thought I'd see Caleb bring a woman home with him."

Sophia blushed, wondering what Amity would think if she knew all the circumstances of their flight from Memphis. "I had to leave Memphis." She gazed at Amity who looked friendly and curious. "I stabbed a Yankee officer."

"Stabbed! Great heaven!"

"He'll live. I didn't kill him. I stabbed him in the shoulder and Caleb—Major O'Brien—thought I would be arrested if I stayed in town."

"Stars in heaven, you stabbed a Yankee! Papa will be so pleased with you, Miss Merrick."

"You have to call me Sophia," she said, warming to Amity and thankful to have found a friend. Suddenly she felt tears well up. "You're so nice. I didn't want to leave home, but it's very pleasant here."

Amity hugged her. "You're with friends." She stepped back. "I'll get Loretta and we'll surprise Caleb and then, may I tell Papa what you did?"

"Oh, please, I'll be embarrassed and it was terrible—"

"Papa will think it brave. And wait until Chantal hears. I'll be right back." As she left the room, Sophia looked around again, her spirts lifting and her fears diminishing. The Therries were warmhearted, and the house would cheer anyone.

Two hours later, Sophia stared at her image in the mirror while Amity clapped her hands.

"You look ravishing and you have to wait until I get downstairs before you come down. I want to watch Caleb when he sees you."

"I'm not certain it's me," she said, amazed by the transformation Amity and Loretta had wrought. Her hair was turned under behind her head in a full, low chignon with crimped curls over her forehead and braids looped over each ear. Emerald earbobs dangled in her ears and she wore the emerald necklace from Caleb around her neck.

The dress was a dream. The silk felt marvelous against her skin and the dainty batiste chemise was a whisper. The dress had a low neck and tiny puffed sleeves with rosebuds and lace against the green silk. She touched her throat and felt daring and unclothed. Never in her life had she worn a dress that didn't have a neckline covering her collarbones and yet she had to admit, she liked the way she looked. Papa wouldn't have approved, but Caleb would approve and Amity was delighted. And Sophia loved the dress.

She moved away from the mirror, and then stepped back for one last look, still amazed she was looking at herself. She left the room and moved to the top of the stairs. Amity and Caleb stood in the hall below and Sophia was certain Amity had brought him there on purpose. She started down the stairs and Caleb turned to look up at her.

His expression changed to one that she knew—solemn,

bold, filled with desire as his gaze lowered and then raised. She forgot Amity standing to one side and then Amity was gone and she was alone with Caleb as she came down the steps and he came forward to meet her.

"You look beautiful, Sophia," he said seriously, his voice deep and husky.

She felt half naked and touched the necklace. "Thank you."

Caleb came up a step so she was at eye level. His voice was a whisper. "Right now, I would give a fortune to be alone with you and take that dress off you."

She tingled all over, feeling breathless, wanting him.

"Lord, you're beautiful, Sophia."

"Thank you. You were right. Your family is nice."

"Miss Merrick," Ormonde Therrie said, coming into the hall from outside. Caleb took her arm and they moved forward to meet Ormonde. "Caleb, both of you come into the parlor. I have to hear all the news."

"And you have to catch me up on New Orleans," Caleb said.

"This is a special occasion. If it weren't for Rafe's daring and ingenuity, we'd be suffering more. He gets supplies to us that make me feel ashamed and I think he's the reason our house still stands. I suspect it would have been burned if it hadn't been for him. All our neighbors' houses are gone."

Caleb frowned and paused. "Burned?"

"Yes. Now I want to hear about Memphis and what news you can bring," he said as they entered the parlor.

"Maybe Memphis was more fortunate than I realized," Caleb remarked.

Amity was seated on the settee, and Sophia sat down facing her. Caleb sank down beside Amity as she smiled. "Sophia told me I could tell you, Papa. She stabbed a Yankee officer."

Suddenly embarrassed, Sophia's cheeks flamed as all of them looked at her and Caleb smiled. "So you told Amity," he said softly.

"Good heavens, child, you stabbed a Yankee! We'll drink the first toast to that!" Ormonde Therrie said.

"He'll live," she answered. "I stabbed him in the

shoulder, but that's why Caleb thought I should leave Memphis."

"Enough reason."

"Actually, sir, we're both wanted by the Federals, but I don't think we'll be in danger in New Orleans. I brought Sophia, because she has no family in Memphis. Her brothers are fighting in the East and she's wanted by the Yankees for sedition. She printed a newspaper loyal to the Confederacy."

Ormonde Therrie smiled at her. "Miss Merrick, I admire your abilities and spirit! We're honored to have such a guest."

"Thank you, sir. I kept the family paper going for my brothers."

"Miss Merrick, our home is your home," Ormonde Therrie said. "And anyone who is brave enough to stab a Yankee is always welcome here. I heard that you wore a Yankee uniform to Shiloh and you brought Will Stanton and Caleb back to Memphis when they were wounded."

"Yes, sir. And thank you. Both of you have made me feel so welcome," she said, seeing the pleasure light Caleb's eyes.

"What's the war news in this area?" Caleb asked.

"We have Beast Butler in charge in New Orleans. The man is impossible," Ormonde replied. Sophia listened as he told about the assault on New Orleans by Admiral Farragut and the wild night when the Union seized the town. While he talked, she glanced at Caleb and caught him looking at her, his gaze sweeping over her. When he met her eyes, he winked and turned back to Ormonde.

"You have to stay at least one night with us before you go to town," Amity said.

"I insist, Caleb. I know you can't wait to get back to your brothers, but we want to spend some time with you, too."

"I'd planned to stay here tonight, and tomorrow if you'll give us horses, we'll go to town."

"We'll take you if that's all right with you," Ormonde said. "Rafferty just returned home two days ago, so this will be a wonderful homecoming and what a surprise."

Sophia felt compelled to turn and caught Caleb studying her again. She blushed and faced Ormonde.

"Where's Blaise?" Caleb asked and Ormonde frowned.

"She stays at her house in town. She's rarely here anymore." Ormonde glanced at Sophia. "My wife," he said stiffly, and Sophia realized something was wrong between Mr. and Mrs. Therrie.

They sat and talked for the next two hours and then Amity said she wanted to show Sophia the house.

Sophia felt overwhelmed as they walked through the spacious rooms filled with treasures. "This is so beautiful. Thank heavens it wasn't burned."

"Papa says we still may not be safe. We don't go into town often. Twice Yankees have come and taken horses and livestock, but Papa said let them have anything they want. Once one came in the house and Papa made me hide. The soldier took silver candlesticks and Papa let him have them without protest. He said we'd get along better that way. Some things are buried in the yard now. I hate this war. I don't want Will to go back to fighting. I don't want Caleb to go either."

They ate in the large dining room while a servant pulled the rope for the punkah, stirring a cool breeze and afterward they sat on the upstairs gallery. A breeze came off the river and crickets and frogs were a background chorus.

"You have brothers away fighting don't you? Was it three brothers?" Amity asked.

"Amos was killed in Shenandoah," she replied. "Morris is with General Jackson and John is with General Lee, but I haven't heard from either of them for months. Now their letters won't get to me."

Caleb reached out in the dark to take her hand and lace his fingers through hers.

Ormonde stood up. "I'll bid you young folks good night. I'll see you in the morning, Caleb. Miss Merrick, we're so happy to have you here."

"Thank you, sir, for welcoming me into your home."

Amity rocked. "Now you can almost forget the war. It's so quiet and peaceful and still here. Caleb, how soon are you leaving?"

"I haven't decided. I'll stay for a time."

"I wish you'd never go back. I wish none of you would go. Papa says our lives are all changed now anyway. He doesn't think it'll ever be the same again. He thinks Rafferty is right to build a future and avoid battles. Of course, he's in as much danger running the blockade. He's lost one ship."

"I didn't know that," Caleb said, stroking Sophia's knuckles with his thumb, a sensual slight stroking, yet stirring longing in her.

While they talked, Sophia was intensely aware of him, wanting to touch him, wanting to be in his arms. All evening long he had watched her.

Finally Amity stood up. "I'm going to bed. If you want me, Sophia, my room is next to yours."

"Thank you," she said, standing. "I should go to bed, too."

"Wait a minute, Sophia," Caleb said quietly. "We need to make some plans for tomorrow."

She sat down again as Amity left them. He stood and pulled her up and went to lean against the wall, pulling her against him between his legs.

"Caleb, we're not alone!"

"I know we're not, dammit. You're the most gorgeous woman I've ever seen," he said softly, wrapping his arms around her and kissing her. She clung to him, leaning against him, returning his kisses.

He bent his head, trailing kisses along her throat down to the neckline of the dress, his tongue touching her bare skin, inflaming her.

"Caleb, I love you," she whispered. "But we're not alone and Amity could come back out and I'd be so embarrassed."

"It would make it a lot easier if I could tell everyone we're going to marry."

She framed his face with her hands. "I love you and I need your strength and if I could hold you here forever I would, but you may feel so differently when you come back. Reason says to wait. And I better go to my room before you destroy my good name."

"I'd like to destroy it," he said, sliding his hand beneath the neck of her dress over her full breast. His touch made her ache for more, for a night in his arms.

She drew a sharp breath and allowed him to caress her for minutes before she caught his wrist and turned it to kiss his hand. "Oh, Caleb. I want to be with you." Knowing she should go, she left him.

The bed was turned down for her with one of Amity's fancy gowns laid out. When Sophia slid against the cool sheet, she lay in the darkness, thinking about Caleb's proposal, wondering if she could survive when he went to war. She wanted to be his wife, wanted to marry him, but did he truly love her or was it the wild circumstances they were caught in? Would he come home and feel differently toward her? Would he return and wish he hadn't married in haste? She wanted to marry him, but nagging doubts continued to pursue her. Would he change with a long absence? Could they get along for a lifetime when they had so many differences? Yet how big were the differences? Already she took an occasional sip of brandy. Now she could see why he thought the railroads were good for Memphis. She thrashed in bed, feeling uncertain, worried, fearful about his going. But she was certain of only one thing: she loved him completely.

She hadn't had a chance yet to ask him about being wanted for sedition. Would she ever be able to go back to Memphis?

After lunch on Thursday she climbed into a buggy beside Amity with both men in front and they headed toward New Orleans. When they rode into the city, she was entranced with the shuttered houses and the ornate wrought-iron balconies, the narrow streets and fancy buildings. The afternoon was steamy hot, and she dabbed at her forehead with a handkerchief, yearning for a breeze. Union soldiers were everywhere and Caleb wore civilian clothing with a broad-brimmed hat pulled low over his eyes. Finally they turned into a carriage house and he helped her down.

"We made it here," he said, giving her hand a squeeze.

Darcy came running from the house and threw his arms around Caleb who hugged him in return. "Cal, you're home. Did you bring Fortune?"

"No, but he's promised to come soon. Darcy, you remember Miss Merrick. Sophia, this is Darcy, my youngest brother."

They were in a palm-filled courtyard with a fountain splashing in the center. Through a doorway, a woman emerged, smiling and walking toward them. She was round with the expected baby, but when Sophia looked at her face, she thought Chantal O'Brien was the most beautiful woman she had ever seen. Her golden hair was shiny, her black eyes sparkled.

"Caleb!"

"Chantal! You're beautiful."

She laughed and patted her middle. "And very big!"

"Chantal, this is Miss Sophia Merrick. Sophia, this is my sister-in-law, Chantal O'Brien."

"I'm so happy to meet you," Chantal said. "Come inside. Rafferty is at the office, but he will be home soon and we have such a surprise for him."

They went through a cool shadowed hallway and upstairs to a long parlor with a view of the city. As soon as they were seated, Amity glanced at her. "Sophia, I have to tell Chantal—Sophia stabbed a Yankee officer!"

"My word!"

"He's still alive. It was in the shoulder, but I had to leave Memphis," Sophia explained.

"I'm so sorry," Chantal said.

A door slammed, and Darcy jumped up to run from the room. Sophia's curiosity arose about the oldest O'Brien. Caleb had talked about Rafferty often. She heard boots on the stairs and then a tall, handsome, black-haired man entered the room. His eyes were as blue as Fortune's, his face thinner. All three older brothers had the same charming smile as he looked from her to Caleb.

"Caleb!"

Caleb crossed the room to hug his brother and she still couldn't see much resemblance between them beyond their smiles. Caleb was inches shorter, thicker through the shoulders with a squarer face. Caleb's skin was darker, his hair lighter, tightly curled, and brown.

"Sophia, meet my oldest brother, Rafferty O'Brien. Rafe, this is Miss Sophia Merrick from Memphis."

"She had to leave because she stabbed a Yankee," Darcy said, studying her.

"Welcome to New Orleans. You're a brave lady."

She blushed as she greeted Rafferty, and then he turned to welcome Amity and Ormonde. Before long they were all seated talking, Caleb listening to Rafe's tales about the blockade.

It was almost time for dinner, and Chantal showed Sophia the room that she would share with Amity. As they left the room, she heard Rafe call Caleb aside.

Caleb followed his brother downstairs to the long room that Rafe used for an office. As soon as they were alone, Rafe opened a drawer and pulled out a paper.

Caleb glanced at it. "I'm wanted for leading Confederate raids into Memphis."

"You rode right through town to come here. That's wild, Caleb."

"This is a busy seaport. No one paid any attention to us."

"And Miss Merrick stabbed a Yankee?"

"He attacked her, and she defended herself. That's why she left Memphis. She was printing an inflammatory Confederate paper at her house and the Federals have been searching for the person who's been printing it. I knew they'd be back to search her house and they'd find the press so I took her with me and left."

"Then you're both wanted."

"Yes. Fortune caught up with us on the road south to tell me. She's subject to arrest and prison. I have a bounty on my head. I don't think I led anyone here."

"I'm not scared for my sake. What are your plans?" Rafe asked.

"That's what I wanted to ask you. Sophia doesn't have a price on her head, and there won't be any posters here. The arrest warrant is because of the paper she printed. The Yankee hasn't told anyone that she stabbed him. He said he was hurt in an accident. I want to return to the war. The only family she has are two brothers who are fighting in the East. Can she stay with you?"

"Of course. We're not suffering badly from shortages because of my running the blockade. We're making a huge profit, Cal, and I'm still selling some things to the Confederacy, some to the highest bidder, and some things I've given the Confederacy. I've given things to the Federals, too. I don't think the South will win this war."

"I haven't thought so since Shiloh," Caleb agreed.

"Most of our money is in a bank in England, because it's safe there. Blockade running exceeds my wildest dreams and we'll come out of this war—if we survive it—rich men."

"How much danger are you in?"

"How much are you in on the battlefield?"

Caleb glanced out the long windows at people passing on the street. "It was hell at Shiloh. I never knew war could be so bad. So many men I knew killed." He looked at Rafe. "There were over twenty thousand wounded or killed or missing in the two days we fought."

"I heard. I wondered if the figures were correct. I'm in danger, but not as much as you. It's dangerous when we reach our coast and try to land and unload; sometimes it's dangerous sailing, but most of the time we have the sea to ourselves and have hours when there's nothing to worry us."

"I've asked her to marry me," Caleb said abruptly.

Rafe's head came up and he placed his hands on his hips and grinned. "I never thought I'd see the day! Congrat—"

"Wait a minute," Caleb said, moving around the office restlessly. "She thinks we should wait until the war is over and life if normal."

Rafe frowned. "Sorry, Cal. When I think what I went through to win Chantal—I'm sorry."

"She thinks we may feel differently when life settles again. If it ever does. I hate what people may think about her traveling here with me."

"You didn't ask her for that reason, did you?"

Caleb turned to look into Rafe's eyes. "What do you think?"

"No. Sorry. We'll take care of her, and she can stay at Belle Destin with Amity part of the time if she likes. You'd be safer at Belle Destin."

"I don't want to cause trouble for either you or Ormonde."

"Don't worry. You won't if you don't roam through town," Rafe warned.

"I've heard Beauregard was replaced by Bragg."

"That's right. You can always sail with me if you'd rather get into blockade running."

"No. I'll join Bragg's men again."

"Cal, who's this Will Stanton? Amity writes him regularly and talks about him often."

"Will is a fine person. Sophia saved both of us as Shiloh and took us to Memphis. Will recuperated at home and I was at Sophia's. Will and I hope to go into the railroad business together after the war. We've bought an old depot and a railroad."

"You're not coming back to New Orleans to live?" Rafferty asked, studying him.

"No, I plan to return to Memphis. It's not so far when the trains are running. I like Memphis, Rafe, and I think I can build a railroad that will be important."

"I hate to lose you, and you may change your mind. If you have a sound proposal, I'll invest in it."

"When the time comes, you'll hear about it in great detail. You'll like Will, too."

"I'm glad to hear. It worried me because he lives away from New Orleans and it's wartime and people do foolish things. You'd be safer if you'd sail with me."

Caleb watched a buggy pass in the street and turned around. "I think the Confederacy is important to Sophia. I feel I need to fight for her sake, for the Therries. It seems something we're all caught in and can't stop."

"It's not our fight."

"It's mine now because of Sophia."

Rafe nodded. "Just try to survive."

"When are you going out again? Where'll you go?"

"I'm not going until our baby is born. Chantal's time is only two months away, and I won't leave her. How's Fortune? When is he coming to New Orleans?"

"He said as soon as possible. You won't know him. He's taller than you are. I guess he wrote you about his marriage."

"Yes. I can't imagine him having a wife and child."

"They're no longer alive."

"He wrote all about it. I just pray you both don't end up on the same battlefield. I hear from Tobias Barr. He's fighting for the North. He had his own furniture business in Chicago before the war started."

"I hope I don't face him in battle either. It was so bad, Rafe. I never dreamed it would be that bad."

"I never would have guessed fighting would be difficult for you. You're a hunter and a fighter."

"Not like this. Wholesale senseless slaughter." He moved away from the window. "I'm going to bathe and change. Thanks for taking Sophia into your house. She's never been away from Memphis."

"She's beautiful, Cal."

"I think so." He left, climbing steps to his room.

That night as he sat across from Sophia, he couldn't take his eyes from her. Beneath Chantal's and Amity's guidance and wearing their silk dresses, Sophia blossomed into a breathtaking beauty. She was in a scarlet silk dress, her blue eyes sparkled and her cheeks were rosy. Her hair was the latest fashion, parted in the center, turned under behind her head. She turned to look into his eyes, and he saw the flicker in the depths of hers as she gazed back at him.

He ached to pull her into his arms and he knew he wouldn't get her alone in this house filled with people.

As they sat and talked the third night, he was tense, anxious for dinner to end. He was going back to battle and he wasn't leaving without getting to be alone with Sophia. Before dinner Caleb had made plans to get Sophia to himself as soon as they were finished eating. Dining at Rafe's was usually long, leisurely, and enjoyable, but tonight Caleb couldn't wait to finish.

"The Fourth of July came and went with no celebration by loyal Confederates," Rafe said.

"Your brother shot his share of firecrackers today," Amity said, glancing at Darcy who grinned.

"The big news in town," Rafe said, looking at Caleb, "should interest you since all you talk about is railroads. Today President Lincoln signed the Pacific Railroad Act. I've heard he wants the eastern terminus to be Council Bluffs, Iowa, but that's not settled yet."

"The war took it away from Memphis. It'll be a northern route."

"I don't think anything in the South will ever be the same," Ormonde added.

Talk swirled around them, but Caleb found it difficult to pay attention. Finally they moved from the dining room to the parlor, and he took her arm.

"If you folks will excuse us, I'd like to take the buggy and show the Vieux Carré to Sophia. We should be safe enough if we go out at this hour."

"Fine," Rafe said.

"We can go—" Chantal said, and Rafe placed his arm across her shoulders.

"No, we can't. Let them go. You don't need a bouncing buggy ride. Just be careful," he said, looking at Caleb, who took Sophia's arm and ushered her out of the room before Darcy or Amity said they wanted to go along.

"Caleb, go back and ask if Darcy or Amity want to go with us."

"Not for the world will I go back," he said tersely, descending the stairs. "I asked a groom to hitch up the team hours ago. Hurry, Sophia." He helped her into the carriage and left to get a driver. In minutes he climbed in beside her and lowered the leather flaps, not caring how hot it became inside.

"Finally, I have you all to myself," he said, pulling her onto his lap, her bottom soft on his legs.

"Caleb, I'll be all wrinkled!"

"Then we can solve that right now," he said, his fingers working swiftly at her buttons while he kissed her throat. He didn't want to go back to battle, yet he had to, and he wanted memories to take with him through the bleakness of war.

"Caleb O'Brien! Stop that. I'll be disheveled—"

"I want to tell you goodbye. I have to leave, Sophia," he said gruffly, and Sophia turned to look at him. The horses' hooves clopped on the cobblestones and the buggy swayed while her heart seemed to careen and lurch against her ribs. Fear was a suffocating blanket that suddenly took her breath. She rested her hand on his hard shoulder.

"You're going to war."

"Yes. Rafe asked me to sail with him, but I feel an obligation for both of us to fight for the Confederacy."

The words hurt so badly. She cried out and threw her arms around him, clinging to him. This moment in time he was hers; she ran her hands over his strong shoulders, down over the muscles in his arms. *The last time together.* Her lips covered his warm lips; her tongue thrust into his mouth as his arms wrapped tightly around her and he kissed her back. Her fingers worked at his cravat, tugging it free, pulling his linen shirt out of his trousers and over his head. She kissed his chest, the hairs tickling her while the buggy bounced and swayed and she felt as if every roll of the wheels took her closer to losing him.

He pushed away her dress and silken chemise and pulled her close, stroking her while he kissed her, unfastening her drawers. Finally he eased her back on the length of the seat and moved between her legs, thrusting into her softness.

Sophia clung to him, her hips moving as she pulled him closer, wanting to make her part of him forever. She was jammed against the seat of the rocking carriage, clinging to his hard, lean body as he thrust into her. She held him tightly in desperation.

"Sophia! Love," he cried as he shuddered in climax and she held him and moaned.

"Caleb, don't leave me," she begged.

Their breathing was ragged and she ran her hands over him, feeling the hard muscle, knowing she might lose him forever.

"Caleb, I love you," she whispered, kissing him. Finally she sat up, reaching for the dress that was a silken cloud on the floor of the buggy. "I'll look so rumpled; it'll be scandalous to go home."

"You might have to marry me, Sophia."

He leaned back in the carriage, his chest bare. He had pulled up his trousers and buttoned them and he reached for her. "Leave the dress. We'll ride around until everyone at home has gone to bed and no one will see you."

"We'll do no such thing. I'm not riding through the streets of New Orleans naked as a snake! Suppose someone stops us."

He chuckled and pushed the dress out of her hands. "No one will stop us."

"And we'll go back at a decent hour. Your family is very nice and I don't care to have them thinking I'm some sort of . . ."

"They won't."

"No, they won't, Caleb, because I'm dressing and we're going back when we should. I'll be living with them while you're gone."

"Sophia, marry me. If you'll marry me, I'll wait another week to go."

She placed her hand on his cheek. "Caleb, you and I have such battles. I love you, but this is wartime and nothing is sane and normal. And we have such differences."

"If you're carrying my child—"

"I'll write you. And if I am, you can come home to me and we'll wed."

"Then I pray you are," he said in a husky voice. His arms tightened around her. "I want you, Sophia, and someday you'll be mine. You and your fierce independence."

Her heart pounded as he kissed her and she forgot the dress, letting it slide from her hands.

It was after midnight when she finally kissed him goodbye in the hall. She lay staring into the dark. Was she making a terrible mistake by not marrying when she loved him so completely? Yet how they fought! John and Morris certainly wouldn't approve of Caleb. It would cause a rift in the family.

Shortly after noon Caleb told the family goodbye. She walked to the alley behind the carriage house. She gazed into his green eyes. "Please, come back to me," she whispered, moving into his arms, feeling terrified for his safety. He caught her up, crushing her to him to kiss her.

He released her and mounted, riding down the alley, sitting straight and tall, his broad shoulders squared. He didn't look back. And then he was gone. She felt as if her heart were shattering like fragile crystal against stone. "Caleb . . ."

She felt swamped with loss, praying that he would be safe. Finally when she had her emotions under control, she returned to the house.

For the rest of the day, Ormonde and Amity and Darcy showed her the Vieux Carré, taking her to a fancy restaurant, showing her shops filled with delights in spite of the war, melons at the market, the thick hot chicory that people were substituting for coffee.

The family kept her busy, and she bought yarn to knit a blanket for Chantal's expected baby.

Two weeks later, Darcy ran in waving letters. "From Cal!" he exclaimed. "Here's one for Sophia, one for you," he said, handing it to Amity. "And one for me."

Everyone sat to read and Sophia went to her room to tear hers open, looking at his bold scrawl:

My love:
    I've caught up with Will now, and we'll soon be with Bragg's forces. With a brother who is a blockade runner, I haven't suffered privations, but the farther north we go, the worse and more desperate things are. Shoes are a precious commodity. Uniforms are patched and worn. I'm not in the fighting yet. I miss you more than I would have thought possible. I want you in my arms, Sophia. I dream of you, yearn for you, want to kiss you. Time is short, so I must close.
    All my love, Cal

She held his letter tightly in her hand, running it against her cheek. She wiped away tears. She missed him dreadfully and she wanted to write to him and wondered if her letter would ever reach him. She unfolded the letter to hold it against her heart and remember Caleb.

Finally she sat at the desk and wrote:

My dearest Caleb:
    I just received your letter and can't bear to think about you returning to battle and being without things you

need. It is comfortable here with your family, but Rafferty has warned all of us that shortages will grow and he won't be able to get things to us as easily as in the past. The prices are soaring now. I miss you, too, unbearably, and dream about you and think about you until I'm certain your family must think I'm daft, because I'll think about you and forget that someone is talking to me. They are so kind and Amity has been a love, trying everything to keep me from pining for you. And she wants to know everything about Will and she looks forward to each letter from him as I do from you. Please take care of yourself and come home to me. Even though I am not carrying your child, I am ready to marry. You'll just have to adjust to my brothers and they'll have to adjust to you.

All my love, Sophia.

Two weeks later on August fourth, Sophia sat knitting with Amity. Chantal napped and they heard Rafe's footsteps coming up the stairs.

"You're home early," Amity said. "Chantal is asleep."

"Let her sleep. I had some business to take care of this way, so I thought I would stop at home. Sophia, if you'll excuse Amity and me for a few minutes, I need her opinion on something," he said as he escorted Amity from the room.

"Of course," she said, bending over the knitting and then stopping to look out the window, gazing north. She still missed Memphis and she felt at a loss. Here there were servants to take care of her every need and after spending years working on the paper and helping Mazie and running the household the past year, she felt restless, wanting to keep busy partly to fight the steady cold fear she had for Caleb.

She heard Rafe returning and looked around to see him come into the parlor without Amity and close the door. She looked into his eyes when he turned around and her heart turned to stone.

Chapter 17

She dropped the knitting as she stood up, unaware of the ball of blue yarn unrolling away from her. She felt cold as ice and her head spun. "It's Caleb, isn't it?"

Rafe stopped a few feet from her, his brow furrowed and his expression solemn. He held out a letter to her. "No. Sophia, it's not Caleb."

The first wild rush of relief was gone as swiftly as it came as she looked at him and took the letter. He was too solemn.

He took her hand and held it. "I'm sorry. It's one of your brothers."

She winced as if from a blow and felt pain knot her chest. "No."

"Fortune sent me a letter and he has one for you. It's your brother Morris."

"Morris!"

She tore open the letter and held it with shaking hands. It was a letter within a letter. The first was from Fortune and she raced over it:

Dear Miss Merrick:

I have watched for any mail to you. First, let me say, your servants Henry and Mazie are with friends and they are fine. Your office is just as you left it. I've had one letter from Cal, and he's fine. Now, the real reason for this letter.

The enclosed letter is from a Major Tomlison. I regret to tell you that your brother Morris was killed in battle. I send my deepest sympathy for this great loss of yours.

Fortune O'Brien.

She opened the second letter that was faded and wrinkled and brushed her cheeks as tears fell on the letter. She scanned how Morris had died so bravely fighting for the Confederacy. She let the letter flutter to the floor.

Rafferty stepped to her and gently pulled her into his arms. "I know we're little more than strangers, but you'll have to let us be family to you now. I'm sorry for your loss."

She was in pain. "Morris was so far from home on a battlefield without any family."

"He had family of sorts," Rafe said quietly. "His comrades have to be family for each other."

She barely heard what Rafferty said. "He's in a grave somewhere and I don't even know where." Hurting, she felt swamped with loss. Amos and Morris both gone. "I wish I could just know where he's buried."

"I'm sorry, Sophia."

Tears fell, splashing on her hand and she wiped her eyes while Rafferty patted her shoulder as he released her. "I've told Amity and I need to tell Chantal."

The door opened behind him, and Amity crossed the room to take Sophia in her arms and hold her while they both cried. "I'm sorry," Amity said. In minutes Chantal hugged her and Darcy came into the room, sitting quietly, his expression solemn.

That night as conversation was carried on around her, she thought about Caleb who was with Bragg's Army of Tennessee near Chattanooga. She had no idea where John was fighting or if he were alive. She hadn't heard from him for months now. Morris was gone, buried on a battlefield without prayers or service or Memphis friends to mourn him. She dabbed at her eyes, and Amity squeezed her arm. She was thankful at least to know about him, because so many men who were killed were unidentified. She longed for Caleb's strong arms and she knew his family was being as helpful and kind as they possibly could.

As the days passed, Sophia felt the pain lessen. On the third of September, Chantal gave birth to a dark-haired baby girl, Daniella Marie O'Brien. Chantal and Rafferty looked as if they would burst with joy. He couldn't keep from constantly touching Chantal or looking at tiny Daniella with her black eyes and dark hair. When Sophia held the new baby, she was caught up in a wave of longing for Caleb. The baby was precious, and Sophia lay awake that night, missing Caleb, wishing she hadn't been so logical to wait until the war was over to marry him. She wished she was carrying his child.

By the third week after Daniella's birth Sophia, Amity, and Darcy packed and rode back to Belle Destin. Sophia hadn't heard from Caleb since the first letter and every night she lay staring into the darkness, filled with worry about him.

Chapter 18

July 1865
Memphis, Tennessee

The door swung open. "Hannah Lou?"

"Sophia!" Hannah Lou stepped forward to hug Sophia. "You're home."

"I saw your mother," Sophia said, gazing beyond Hannah Lou, dreading going inside the house. "I could hardly believe it when I learned you married while I was away."

"I wish you could have been here," she said. "Come inside. I'm so glad to see you. I want to show you my house. Isn't it gorgeous?"

"Yes, it's one of the grandest in town," Sophia said with sincerity, admiring the brick Italiante with its arched, narrow windows and high ceilings.

"Hannah Lou?" called a male voice.

In the middle of the morning, Sophia thought she would miss Hannah Lou's husband because he would be at work. His deep voice rang with familiarity even though it had been three long years since she had last heard him speak. Dunstan Trevitt stepped into the hall. He was more handsome than ever. His gaze settled on Sophia, and he smiled.

"What a surprise! Don't tell me. Let me conjure up the memory of one of my wife's best friends. Miss Merrick," he said, walking up to her and hugging her.

She stiffened and moved away. "I was surprised to learn about your marriage."

He gazed at her with a look of amusement, yet she felt chilled in his presence and the hug had been uncalled for. "And you've come back to Memphis to start your paper again. They don't require women to take the oath of allegiance, so you're free to do what you want. Military rule ended the third of this month."

"Yes."

"Well, I've been told you're a staunch opponent of railroads, so we're still on opposing sides, Miss Merrick, because I'm building a railroad," he proclaimed.

"I doubt if our paths will cross often," she said, wondering if Hannah Lou knew the full reason she left Memphis.

"I'm leaving now. I'm late," he said, turning to Hannah Lou. He slid his arm around her waist and kissed her full on the mouth.

"Dunstan!" Hannah Lou exclaimed when he released her.

"Come back again, Miss Merrick. I know what close friends you and my wife are." He strode to the hat rack and removed his hat. As Hannah Lou turned toward the parlor, Sophia glanced back at him and Dunstan winked.

She felt a swift rush of dislike and knew she would seldom come back to this house. She followed Hannah Lou into the parlor that was filled with mahogany Victorian furniture and potted palms. Gilt mirrors decorated the walls and heavy wine-colored satin draperies were pulled back from the long windows.

"Your home is beautiful," Sophia said, thinking it too elaborate for her taste.

"Come see all of it," Hannah Lou urged, taking her hand and chatting steadily until Sophia realized Hannah Lou had changed. She seemed nervous and on edge.

Upstairs she paused in front of a large bedroom. "I've lost two babies," she said abruptly, staring at Sophia with wide eyes.

"I'm sorry. I didn't know," Sophia answered.

Hannah Lou bit her lip. "This is our room."

Sophia didn't want to go inside. She could see the four-poster bed, the glass lamps on marble-topped tables flanking the bed.

"You have a beautiful home," she repeated, wanting to get away, wondering if Hannah Lou were happy.

"Where will you live, Sophia? I know your family's home burned."

"How did it burn?"

Hannah Lou looked away. "I didn't know for a time. They said the Yankees did it. Dunstan doesn't want me to call them Yankees. I'm to say the Union or Federals. They said you were printing that paper that was against the Union."

"Yes, I was."

"Thank heaven the war is over and all that is behind us now. I'm so thankful. Memphis is changing. Come down to the parlor and we'll have a sip of brandy."

"Hannah Lou, it's morning."

"Just a sip. It helps brighten the day. Where did you go when you left Memphis?" Hannah Lou asked. Her pale green silk dress was the latest fashion, yet it hung on her thin frame.

"To New Orleans. I stayed with the Therries and with Caleb O'Brien's family."

"You traveled with Major O'Brien all the way to New Orleans? We thought maybe you had an aunt in the East."

"I do. She's no longer alive."

"Major O'Brien. Are you married to him?"

"No." Sophia felt an ache. "I haven't heard from him in a year and I haven't heard from John in over two years. Caleb fought with General Bragg and then with General Johnston."

"So many men died without anyone knowing their names."

"I expect both of them to come home," Sophia said stiffly, refusing to think they wouldn't.

They sat in the front parlor and Sophia didn't touch the brandy, but Hannah Lou drank two small glasses and by the time Sophia left, she was thankful to step outside into the sunshine.

"Come see me, Hannah Lou."

"I will." Suddenly she grasped Sophia's hand. "Please come back soon."

"Hannah Lou, are you all right?"

She batted her eyes and looked down the shady street, blinking and looking uncertain. "Yes. I'm fine."

"We're friends if you want to talk," Sophia said softly.

Hannah Lou looked down the street again, and Sophia wondered about her marriage.

"I'm all right. Come back."

Feeling concern for Hannah Lou, Sophia climbed into her buggy. Whatever was bothering Hannah Lou, she wasn't going to talk about it. Sophia shivered. How she would hate to be wed to Dunstan Trevitt.

The Weekly office was one of the two familiar things in her life where so much had changed. Besides the newspaper, there was Mazie who worked for her again. Henry died in 1864. As she sat behind the desk, the bell tinkled over the door, and she looked up.

Her pulse skittered, and she slid open the drawer beside her where her reticule held a Colt revolver.

Smiling, Dunstan Trevitt crossed the room, and sat down across the desk from her. "So you're back in Memphis, in business again, and still not married."

"That's correct. And I'm still close friends with Hannah Lou."

His blue eyes were cold in spite of the smile on his face. "Sophia, I figure we have an old matter to settle between us."

"The war is over, Major Trevitt—or do you prefer Mister Trevitt?"

"People call me Major. You may call me Dunstan."

"The war is over and I'm clear of the charges now," she insisted.

"And I have a scar on my shoulder that Hannah Lou thinks I received in an accident on board a ship here at Memphis."

"I prefer to forget that night," she said firmly.

He leaned forward and she slid her hand to the reticule. "Reaching for a pistol, Sophia?"

"Perhaps."

"You can relax. I'm here today to talk."

They faced each other in silence, and she could feel his anger.

His voice dropped lower. "I've waited all these years. You're back. Either pack and go, or know you'll have to answer to me for that night. Next time I'll make certain those pretty little hands of yours are tied."

"Sir, will you leave!" she shouted.

"You don't want to hear about it do you? Then I'll let

you think about it." His voice was soft and his smile vanished. "You live alone in that little house you bought on Washington. You're all alone at night, Sophia." He leaned closer. "I'll tie you and I'll finish what I started so long ago."

"Get out, Major," she said, standing and aiming the pistol at him.

He rose and brushed off his hat. "I'll go. Put your pistol away." Suddenly he moved with lightning speed, knocking the pistol from her hand and catching her wrist, twisting it until she cried out. He caught her other hand and held her. "See," he said, his voice cold and quiet, "I could take you to the back right now and tie you up and when I got through you'd be polite to me and you'd do what I want."

She looked him in the eyes and saw his fury. He released her.

"But I'm going to wait and let you worry about it. It's too fast and easy now. No, I want you to think about it every time you come down here and when you're lying alone in your bed at night, because I'm going to take you, Sophia, and I'm going to make you pay for that night."

"And I'll shoot," she said angrily.

He shook his head. "You'll never have a chance to touch your pistol."

"You'll get caught. I'll tell people how you've threatened me."

"And they'll laugh at you and say you belong in the lunatic asylum. My reputation in Memphis is good and I have friends among the matrons. I've been careful. No one will believe you. I'm married to a beautiful woman— why would I do something like that?"

"Because I stabbed you."

"No one except you and I know that. It would be your word against mine. I have a man who says he was with me when I was hurt in an accident. I have a doctor who tended my shoulder who will verify my story. Go ahead, tell people. You know they've always thought your family a little mad." He placed his hat on his head and went to the door, turning to look at her. "Maybe tonight, Sophia. Or maybe months from now. I'll get my revenge. The time will come when you'll do exactly what I tell you to, and you'll tell no one." His blue eyes were cold and his voice was low. He closed the door behind him, and she slumped in the chair, feeling shaken and vulnerable.

Sophia thought about her small frame house on Washington where she lived alone. Mazie came to work in the day, but she was getting deaf and would be no help even if Sophia paid her to stay at night. She ran her hand across her forehead. No matter what precautions she took, there would always be times when she was alone.

She could hear the controlled fury in Dunstan's voice, see the determination in his icy gaze and she believed him.

She picked up the revolver and studied it. She needed something smaller she could carry all the time. If she shot him, he would have to explain to people.

Her gaze rested on the Hoe press and she stared at it. Dunstan Trevitt was buying land and soliciting investors to build a railroad through Arkansas to Springfield, Missouri. She straightened in the chair. If she fought his railroad with her paper, everyone in town would know they were enemies and it might be more believable to people if she accused him of harming her.

She rubbed her brow again, worry returning in full. If she fought him about the railroad, people might think any accusations against him were false, that she was merely trying to ruin him because of the railroad. Whether they thought that or not, she intended to fight Trevitt.

"Fight the saloons, not railroads," she remembered Caleb saying. Men were still returning home from the war and she still hoped that Caleb and John would return. She refused to think about the hundreds of unknown soldiers buried in mass graves in battlefields all across the land. Caleb's last letter had come over fourteen months ago. He was a colonel, fighting in Georgia. The letter was yellow and faded now, always on her bedside table.

She pulled a piece of paper in front of her and tried to concentrate on work, but her mind constantly jumped back to Dunstan Trevitt and his quiet threats. Her wrist had dark bruises from his fingers, and she wondered if anyone would believe her if she told them.

She struggled to work and finally succeeded in getting

stories written. She left early to go to Court Square and make inquiries about the new railroad through Arkansas and Missouri.

That night every sound in the house seemed magnified. She checked all the locks on the windows and doors and drew the drapes, but she still felt vulnerable and exposed. She didn't think Dunstan would do anything soon, because she expected him to torment her. She moved through the house and paused in the bedroom to pick up the derringer she had purchased in the afternoon.

A slow kindling rage burned toward Dunstan Trevitt. Just when she was beginning to consider some of Caleb's arguments about railroads helping build the city, now she was locked into a bitter struggle with Trevitt.

She lay awake in bed, listening to noises, knowing that she couldn't spend every night in fear. The dresser was pulled in front of the closed and locked bedroom door. She had the windows closed and the room was stifling. Furious with Trevitt and herself for fearing him, she turned on her side and closed her eyes.

The following Friday late in the afternoon when Sophia was reaching for her bonnet and ready to close the office, the bell over the door tinkled and she turned. Her breath caught and she slid her hand into the folds of her skirt to the shallow pocket that held the pistol while Dunstan Trevitt crossed the room. His fist was closed over a copy of *The River Weekly*.

She stepped to the desk, opened the drawer and picked up the big Colt revolver and raised it. "Stop where you are."

He halted and held up the paper. "I don't know what you think you have to gain by this!" he snapped shaking the paper and she saw her article against another train through Missouri.

"My small paper and my influence won't ever hurt you," she said, hoping she sounded calm. Her pulse raced, and the revolver was heavy.

"I don't need any arguments against my Memphis and Springfield train, particularly that we already have one going to St. Louis."

"Get out," she spat. She stared at him, wanting the conversation to end, wanting him out of the office.

"People will know you hate me. Later if you try to tell them I've hurt you, no one will believe you. They'll think you're making it up because of this." He shook the paper again.

She raised her chin. "People have always thought the Merricks eccentric, but they know we're honest. My paper is too small to hurt you, and you have influence in this town that I can't change."

"You'll regret this," he said quietly, dropping the paper on the floor. His blue eyes held bits of fire that stabbed at her. He moved forward, and she pulled back the hammer of the revolver.

"I'll shoot. You know that."

He stopped. "There will come a time when I'll get even, Sophia, and I'll enjoy every minute of it." He turned and left, slamming the door with a crash that made her jump violently. She took care to release the hammer and lower the revolver. Her palms were damp and she shook. There was no mistaking his rage. She couldn't protect herself from him constantly. Feeling weak and terrified, she sat in the chair and stared at the door. A copy of the paper was on her desk and she glanced at the article.

Does Memphis need another train through Missouri? The Memphis–St. Louis line will be sufficient to convey goods and people to Missouri and points north and west of Memphis. The city has just pledged fifty thousand dollars to get the Memphis–Tennessee running again. Memphis had trains in all four directions before the war, north, south, east, west. Use the funds to get these lines running again instead of building a second line through Missouri.

She stopped reading, knowing the article from memory. She hadn't expected such a violent reaction from Dunstan Trevitt. She needed someone to talk to about what was happening, but she could no longer confide in Hannah Lou.

She closed the desk drawer, felt the small pistol in her pocket as she stood up and reached for her bonnet. She locked the office and climbed into her buggy. As she passed Main and Adams, the Stanton buggy passed in the opposite direction and she waved at Clairice Stanton, longing for the friendship she once had with Hannah Lou.

Clairice Stanton turned her head and raised her chin, coldly avoiding Sophia's greeting. Shocked, Sophia stared at Mrs. Stanton and then the buggies were apart, traveling their opposite directions. She felt a crushing blow over Mrs. Stanton's treatment and she wondered if Will would ignore her in such a manner also. She thought about Will who had been taken prisoner the last year of the war and now was home recuperating. She had gone to visit him once and learned he hadn't seen Caleb in over a year.

Whenever she had a letter from the Therries and the O'Briens, they refused to give up hope that Caleb was alive even though they hadn't heard either.

On impulse she turned at the corner and went to Adams to call on Will again. Usually the shady streets with the elegant houses gave her a sense of peace, but Dunstan Trevitt and his threats had changed her world to menacing shadows and she felt tense about him.

At the Stantons' a servant showed her into the parlor and Will came in, crossing to her to take her hands.

"Sophia, this is a welcome pleasure."

"I wasn't sure it would be, Will," she answered solemnly. "I just saw your mother."

He frowned and rubbed his neck as he sat down facing her. "Mother's angry over your stand about Dunstan's train, but she'll calm down. She should remember you've always opposed the trains."

She felt an enormous relief that she still had a friend in Will. "Will, you know why I left Memphis that night."

He looked solemn. "Yes, I do. At the time I didn't know Hannah Lou would marry him. She doesn't know what happened and neither do my parents, because I felt it would only worry them." He frowned and stared at her, and she wondered how he felt about Dunstan.

"I haven't told anyone else," Sophia said carefully, "Dunstan has threatened me since I've come back to Memphis."

"Dunstan?"

"Yes," she said. "That's why I wrote the article about

his plans for a rail line. I wanted people in town to know there was a bitter feeling between us."

"How has he threatened you?" Will asked, his sandy brows arching.

"He's told me he'll get even for that night."

Will's lips firmed and he rubbed his hand on his knee. "The devil. I'll speak to him about it."

"I'm sure he will deny it."

"I don't think Dunstan will do anything, Sophia. He wanted to scare you."

"I think he meant it."

Will's frown vanished and he shook his head. "No. Dunstan wants people's support in Memphis. He's working to win everyone over and he wants this train to Missouri. Try to forget his threats. Are you going to tell Hannah Lou?"

"No, I don't want to worry her with it."

"I'm not sure Hannah Lou is happy being married. Mama says Hannah Lou hasn't adjusted to no longer being a belle with so much attention. I hope that changes. I know she values your friendship, so please call on her."

"He's threatened me. I can't go to his house often."

"Go when he's not there. The threats are simply threats and no more. I can't imagine Dunstan jeopardizing his place in society, and there isn't a breath of scandal about him."

With a sinking feeling of disappointment she stood up. "I must go now."

"Thank you for stopping. Don't worry about Mother. She'll calm down and so will Father."

"Good day, Will," she said.

In the buggy she glanced around the street. She felt as if she were being watched and she knew it was a ridiculous notion. Dunstan couldn't trail around after her, yet she couldn't shake the nagging feeling. Will hadn't believed Dunstan would be any threat or ever cause her harm, yet he and Caleb were the ones who knew what Dunstan had done that night so long ago. If Will didn't think Dunstan meant any real harm, who else would believe her?

Feeling more alone than ever she drove home. Her

heart began to pound in her chest as she looked up to see Dunstan Trevitt sitting on her porch.

She slowed and climbed down from the buggy, walking to the foot of the steps and gazing up at him. "Does Mazie know you're here?"

"Of course. I told her I wanted to see you and I would wait here on the porch."

"All my neighbors will see you sitting here and know you have been to my house."

"Yes. And they'll see I haven't gone inside. They can see us talking now. And they know what you've written about me—"

"Not about you. About the Memphis and Springfield train." Her hand was on the small pistol in her pocket and she wondered what he wanted in coming to her house.

"Your servant is deaf. I don't think she could hear if you called to her."

"What do you want, Major?"

"I want you to know that there better not be another article against that train. You'll only make things more difficult for yourself." His voice was soft, barely audible to her and if anyone were around, they couldn't hear what was being said.

"I just came from the Stantons. Will Stanton knows what happened when I left Memphis and he knows about your threats now."

There was no change in Dunstan's expression as he stared at her. "He'll stand by me if anything ever happens because of his sister. I have the Stantons' support. Did he give you sympathy?"

"No, he didn't, but he heard what I had to say."

Dunstan's lips thinned and spots of color appeared in his cheeks. He stood up and crossed to the steps, and her pulse pounded in fear. She backed away from the steps as he descended slowly.

"I have a pistol in my skirt," she said. "Don't touch me," she warned.

"I'm not going to touch you—now," he said quietly in a voice that made the hairs on her nape stand up. "Sophia, I will make you pay for stabbing me and for this article."

She didn't want to hear his threats, but the only way to

avoid them was to turn her back and walk away and she was afraid what he might do. She stared at him, raising her chin and looking him in the eye, hoping he couldn't hear her heart pound.

"You look pale. Soon your paper will support my railroad. I promise you that you'll be eager to endorse it. Tonight when you're alone, think about me," he said seductively. He turned and strode to his buggy.

She rode her buggy to the back and unhitched the horse. When she entered Mazie turned to her.

"There's that Major Trevitt in front, Miss Sophia."

"He's gone now, Mazie," Sophia replied. In her bedroom she stared at her reflection in the mirror. How long before Dunstan carried out his threat? she wondered.

The next week Sophia moved through the throng on the wharf. Boats lined the docks, one coming in, churning water in its wake. She pulled her deep green moire skirts close around her.

"Miss Sophia, we don't belong down here. We need to go home now," Mazie complained. "This is no place for a lady." A shrill blast shattered the air from a steamboat.

"I've been told the *Bluebell* is carrying paper among other goods, and I'm not going home until I find out whether that's true or not."

"Miss Sophia, if Mister John or Mister Morris or Mister Amos or your papa were here, they'd want you home!"

"You stay right beside me. I have a pistol in my purse."

"If you pull a pistol, no telling what will happen. Please, Miss Sophia."

Sophia scanned the boats, watching the *Contessa* maneuver to get up to the wharf and unload. Ragged men stood at the rails. Another shipload of men returning to the South from prisons and battlefields. For days after the war's end she would come down to the wharf and watch boats unload, praying for sign of Caleb or John, disappointment overwhelming her until finally she stopped watching the boats arrive.

Telling Mazie to wait, she pushed her way on board the *Bluebell* and in minutes found Captain Aguila.

"Ma'am, come to my cabin."

Inside she sat facing him. "I'm Sophia Merrick, Captain Aguila. I've been told you're carrying paper and I want to purchase some if possible. I have a newspaper, *The River Weekly.*"

"Yes, ma'am. You've heard right. With the war, everything is scarce, but it won't be long until all sorts of things start flowing back to the South and factories start up again. In a few months, I expect to get paper from Georgia. They're rebuilding already."

She spent the next hour with the Captain, finally making arrangements for the paper to be delivered to her newspaper office.

"Now, Mazie, it's all done," she said as they left the *Bluebell*. "I have enough paper to last me for months."

"Yes, ma'am, and we're going home. This place is filled with thieves and murderers."

The most danger wasn't from anyone on the wharf, Sophia reflected. It was from someone like Dunstan Trevitt, a man who was admired as a pillar of society. A few families wouldn't accept his Union affiliation, but many of them chose to forget now that the war was over. Men brushed against Sophia, causing Mazie to mutter and push some out of the way.

Sophia looked at the milling crowd along the wharf, the promenade, and the levee. So many coming home. At the Jefferson dock, a man, taller than many, a battered, broad-brimmed hat on his head, caught her attention. She studied him and her gaze slid away and then returned. His back was to her and he was shoving through the crowd. Sometimes she had thought she'd glimpsed Caleb or John only to rush after a man and be disappointed. It was probably the same now as she watched the soldier who was too thin to be Caleb, yet the stride was familiar. He glanced around. He was too far to see clearly, but her heart missed beats and she grabbed Mazie's arm.

Chapter 19

"Mazie!"

"Miss Sophia, what's wrong?"

He pushed out of the crowd and began striding away. Her heart pounded. *Caleb!* He looked leaner than ever, his gray trousers were faded, the gray shirt wrinkled, his hat battered, but there was no mistaking the familiar long stride, his broad shoulders, the thick curls on the back of his neck. She tried to push through the throng. She was a block away from him.

"Miss Sophia!"

Sophia knew Mazie was calling her name, but she couldn't go back. Caleb was probably headed to her house. She wanted to cry with frustration trying to get through the crowd. She should get the buggy and find him, but she didn't want to turn back. She had to catch him.

Finally she broke free and spotted him striding up Jefferson. She ran, feeling her bonnet slip behind her head, holding up her skirts, oblivious to people turning to stare.

"Can I help you, miss?"

"Miss—?"

She ignored the questions and offers, barely hearing them as she ran. "Caleb!" she shouted, feeling tears on her cheeks, not caring. "Caleb!"

He glanced around and continued walking, and she dashed across the intersection, running around a buggy and scared she had lost him when he was out of her sight. Then he was in front of her again. He carried a satchel and his long legs covered the distance swiftly. She gasped for breath. "Caleb!"

He turned around.

She waved at him as her heart pounded. He dropped the satchel and came toward her, his green eyes seeming to engulf her. He had a curly beard and a mustache and he looked so *thin*. He was dusty, disheveled, and she felt as if she would burst with joy. He broke into a run, and then she flung herself into his arms as he clutched her in a hard embrace that took her breath away. She raised her lips as he crushed them in his kisses.

"Sophia," he said, his voice gruff. Her heart pounded, thudding against her ribs. He looked at her and she thought she couldn't ever get enough looking at him or touching him.

"I saw you and I've tried to catch you. Oh, Caleb—"

He kissed her again. He smelled of smoke and his breath had a trace of whiskey and his whiskers tickled her, but she relished everything about him.

He released her and looked down at her with a hunger that made her feel hot and weak. "Lass, I've dreamt of ye for three long years," he said, his brogue thick and his voice rough. "We go somewhere or I'll take ye here on the street."

"Oh, Caleb. You're home," she exclaimed.

"Sure and I am to stay, love."

"I have a house on Washington. They burned my house that night."

"I meant it, lassie. Find a place for us to be alone."

Her pulse skittered and raced. "The buggy is back— heavens, I left Mazie in all that crowd."

"Mazie? I want ye to myself," he insisted.

"You'll have me to yourself," she said, breathless at the passion in his voice. "Your valise, Caleb—"

"Damnation. I'll get it and we find Mazie and then we're alone. Do ye understand?"

She felt giddy with joy. She wanted to pull him into a darkened doorway and run her hands over him. At the same time, her emotions were ragged. She had waited so long. And been so alone and so afraid for him. Tears of joy threatened.

"Hurry, Caleb. Get your bag," she said breathlessly.

"Oh, lass, my love. Ye canna' know."

"Yes, I do know, Caleb," she said solemnly. "I've waited for you.

"There's been no other woman," he said solemnly. "And there never will be. No cryin' now, lass," he said, wiping tears off her cheeks with his thumb. She twisted her head to brush his hand with a kiss.

"Caleb, get your satchel," she whispered, "so we can *go*."

He ran the distance to pick up his belongings and then came back and she couldn't stop looking at him, wanting to be in his arms. He gazed at her with a scalding, blatant desire in his eyes that made her yearn to be home with him. He draped his arm around her shoulders and she slipped her arm around his waist. If anyone who knew her well saw them, it would start a storm of gossip, but at the moment, she could no more stop touching him than she could stop breathing.

"Ye look beautiful in green. I think New Orleans has changed ye."

"Oh, Caleb, I'm so afraid you'll disappear!"

"I'm home. I'll not disappear and within this hour, ye'll know how real I am." He looked down at her and gave up holding her around the waist as they strode along together. "Yer damned crinolines. I may burn them and to hell with fashion."

Laughing, feeling joy bubble inside, she had to stretch her legs to the fullest to keep up with him.

"Mazie and I were going to the market."

"We'll take Mazie to shop at the market and you and I will go home. *Alone*."

"Mazie may have gone to the buggy. It's this way," Sophia said, tugging on his arm.

Mazie was seated in the buggy and as they walked up, she looked at them and her eyes became round. "Lordy, Major O'Brien! Thank the Lord, you're home again!"

"Hello, Mazie," he said, grinning at her and giving her a squeeze. "Sure and I had to fight all across the U.S. to get home to your cooking."

"Yes, sir. Looks as if you could use a little of my cooking."

He helped Sophia up beside him and he stopped in front of the hotel. "Sophia, wait while I get a room."

"You can stay at the house," she said softly, and he shook his head.

"It would start gossip," he said solemnly, his green eyes telling her what he really wanted. He jumped down and strode into the lobby.

"Miss Sophia, if you'll get Major to kill a chicken for us, I'll get to cooking as soon as we get home. Are we still going to the market?"

"We'll go. Here he comes."

Caleb climbed up beside Sophia, and she touched his arm again, wanting to hold him and not let go. "We were going to the market," she said.

He nodded. "We'll take Mazie and let her shop and you take me to your house so I can wash up. You can go back and pick her up."

He helped Mazie out of the buggy, and she beamed at him. "I'll get you something you can't resist! I know how you like my chicken," she said, adjusting the basket on her arm. Sophia handed Mazie the list and money.

"I'll be back to get you. You can wait in the shade there where you can sit down," Sophia said, pointing to benches across the road beneath a line of oaks.

Caleb drove to her small house. He swung her down from the buggy and lifted out his satchel, taking her arm and walking into the house. They stepped into the kitchen and he kicked the door shut behind them and dropped the satchel as he reached for her.

"Ah, Sophia, lass, how I've waited . . ."

She was in his arms, her heart feeling as if it would pound through her chest while she ran her hands over Caleb and clung to him, wanting to kiss and hold him forever.

His kisses were searing, dreamt of so many nights and now real, devouring her as he thrust his tongue deep into her mouth and crushed her to him. He held her away, trying to unbutton her dress, fumbling and yanking it open to shove it over her hips and unfasten the crinoline. He peeled away the chemise and pulled off his shirt, unbuckling his belt as she ran her hands over his chest.

His green eyes held her gaze, the hungry expression in them making her pulse race as he pushed her to the kitchen table. With a sweep of his arm he sent a cup and a bowl of fruit flying and pushed her back on the table, moving between her legs and unbuttoning his pants to free his throbbing manhood.

"I have dreamt of ye night upon night. Ye are why I kept going and why I survived, love. Ye are all to me forever and I want ye now. I will kiss you, every inch of you, later, but now, I canna' wait."

He thrust into her softness as he pulled her to him and kissed her. Sobbing with joy, wanting him desperately, Sophia wrapped herself around him, clinging to his hard body while they moved in wild abandon. She felt consumed, and she wanted to be part of him. He was big and hot, driving into her with a frenzy of need. She felt as if she spun into dizzying darkness and then wave after wave of sensation washed over her, ecstasy pounding her.

"Sophia, my lassie," Caleb cried, kissing her deeply, passion engulfing her.

She stroked him and then was lost in blinding waves as she held him tightly and cried out. "Caleb, please, oh, love, my love!"

They moved together, the climax ripping through her, and then he sagged against her while she held him tightly and ran her hands over him, continually reassuring herself that he had finally come home to her safe from war. "I knew you would come home. I knew you would. I've watched for you and prayed for you."

"And I've dreamt of you and needed you and wanted you and thought about you constantly when I wasn't on a battlefield facing cannon. God, it's good to be here and hold you."

"Caleb." She wanted to touch him, to say his name, to constantly reassure herself he was home.

He kissed her temple, trailing kisses to her ear, to her throat and shifting away, helping her up. "I have to wash," he said. "I'd rather not let go of you for even a few seconds." His gaze roamed over her bare breasts while she caressed his chest and shoulders, sliding her hands down over his hips. She ran her hands along his ribs and felt a ridge that suddenly made her heart lurch. "Turn around."

"I'm all right."

"Turn around, Caleb," she said, pushing him. He turned and she looked at the red scar that cut across his flesh from his ribs up across his shoulder blade. "Oh, Caleb!" she gasped, kissing his back. "You were hurt!"

He turned around. "It's a saber wound and I'm over it and I'm all right. Let's forget the war, Sophia," he said solemnly. "I don't want to think about war now. It's over."

She stood on tiptoe and brought his head forward to kiss him hard, to move her hips against him and hear him groan.

"I'll have to go back to get Mazie before long."

"I like Mazie, and my stomach is protesting not eating any decent food since the war started, but I want you all to myself."

"I suppose we need to build a fire in the stove to heat water for your bath."

"You can't imagine how good that sounds. I'll build the fire, but I don't want to let go of you."

"I think you have to make a choice," she said, looking up at him, feeling his body respond to her as his arousal came, pressing against her.

"Sophia, I want ye and want ye and want ye," he said, lapsing back into the brogue. He kissed her as hungrily as the first time. He picked her up in his arms and strode across the room. "Where's the bedroom?"

"Down the hall," she whispered, kissing his ear, trailing kisses over his temple. He placed her on the bed, his weight coming down beside her and then he moved over her, to hold her and kiss her. He rolled over to stroke her bare breasts, taking her nipple in his mouth, flicking his tongue over its tip.

She gasped and shifted, winding her hands in his thick soft hair, feeling him spread her legs apart and move between them. His body was lean, all muscle, his skin taut over bones that showed too clearly. His arms and upper body were copper from days in the sun, and in spite of his leanness, he was stronger than ever. Her heart pounded with desire, reaching for him.

He came down, going slowly this time, easing into her warmth, moving his hips in a sensuous torment that made her lock her arms around him and moan.

"Caleb, my love. Don't ever leave again."

"I love ye, lassie. Always."

She felt his body tense as she responded, waves of sensation buffeting her, her body moving with his and then bursting with release. They clung together until finally she ran her hands over him.

"Caleb, I have to go back to the market soon."

He smiled at her and stroked her hair away from her face. "Oh God, Sophia, I'm *home.*"

She buried her head against his throat, a knot suddenly coming in her throat. "I'm so glad you're here," she whispered, tears stinging her eyes. "I've prayed and prayed that you would come home to me."

"Ah, love," he said, tightening his long arms around her and holding her against him. "Sophia. I'm home, and the damnable war is over."

She moved away. "We need to start a fire in the stove and heat water for a bath—"

He laughed. "Love, I'll take care of the fire." He caught her face with his hand. "John? Have you heard from him?"

"I haven't heard from John in two years. I can't give up on him, Caleb. I never gave up on you, and you came home to me."

He pulled her to him to hold her. "Before the day is out, I want to write Rafe and Darcy and you have to catch me up on all their news."

"The biggest news from the New Orleans O'Briens is that Chantal is expecting their second child in early January."

"Grand! I'll be an uncle again. I haven't even seen Daniella."

Two hours later Sophia sat facing him in the dining room while they ate Mazie's sumptuous fried chicken, hot biscuits with thick gravy, steaming black-eyed peas, and fried okra. Sophia listened patiently as he told her about his battles in Tennessee and Georgia, but what she really wanted to do was hold him. He had shaved away the beard and trimmed his mustache and she couldn't keep her hands off of him.

Mazie entered the dining room to pass more biscuits. Caleb leaned back in his chair. "Mazie, thinking about your cooking kept me going all through the fighting. You're the best cook in the whole country."

"Major, you eat up. You need every bite of this," she said, grinning. "It's good to have you home in Memphis."

"I think I can eat another six biscuits."

"You do that, sir."

She passed the bowl to Sophia who shook her head and watched Caleb slather butter on a golden hot biscuit. Mazie pushed through the swinging door to the kitchen and they were alone again. He glanced at Sophia. "What's happened in Memphis? When did you get back from New Orleans?"

"A month after General Lee surrendered. There was still all the furor over Booth shooting President Lincoln."

"Tell me about Daniella."

"She's beautiful. She has large dark eyes and your brother's black hair and they all dote on her, particularly Darcy. He's good with his hands and he's carved several wooden toys for her."

"I want to go to New Orleans and get him soon," he said, glancing at her between bites of chicken.

"I've saved their letters if you want to read them. Will Stanton is going soon to visit the Therries."

Caleb wore a white cotton shirt tucked into his gray trousers. He was so lean, Sophia was thankful he was eating a hearty meal.

Soon Mazie whisked away the plates, and Caleb glanced at Sophia's half-eaten supper. If Mazie noticed, she didn't mention it. Rice pudding was served for dessert and Sophia ate only a bite.

"Are you printing the paper again?"

"Yes. As soon as I came back to town and moved in here, I started the paper. Since I bought supplies for the paper, I don't have much furniture here yet, only what I needed."

His green eyes gazed at her as he lowered his spoon. She felt her pulse start to drum as he kept looking at her. "I'm not going to make Mazie unhappy by leaving one bite of food. Otherwise, I would push this aside right now."

She nodded, unable to resist reaching across the table to touch him. He wound his fingers in hers, warm and strong, holding her hand and she felt a rush of joy that he was finally home.

When they finished, she stood. "Mazie, we're finished," she said and the door swung open.

"Yes'm. It's good to have you home, Major."

"Thank you, Mazie. That was the best supper ever cooked."

"Thank you, sir."

He walked to the front parlor with Sophia and she glanced at the sparse furnishings—the settee and one blue velvet wing chair. Potted plants filled the room and blue chintz drapes covered the windows.

"I haven't seen your house," he said, his deep mellow voice sounding so marvelous.

"There's very little to see. I don't have much furniture. Come along and I'll show you."

They heard Mazie clattering pans in the kitchen. "Mazie lives in quarters with a friend down the next block. She'll walk home when she finishes cleaning.

"There's the bathroom, which you saw, the kitchen, the parlor, one small bedroom, and my bedroom," she said, leading him into her room. The windows were covered with the same pale blue chintz drapes and there was a washstand, a dresser, and a four-poster bed. The polished floor gleamed and one mirror hung on a wall. Hooks along a wall held her dresses.

He closed the door behind him and she turned to see him leaning against it, gazing at her solemnly. He reached out, his warm fingers closing over hers as he drew her to him. "We don't have to worry about Mazie?"

"No. She'll clean and go."

"You know I want to stay here all night and all the

time, but I'll go to the hotel later, because I don't want to start gossip about you."

She wrapped her arms around his neck and pulled his head down as his arms tightened around her and he spread his legs apart, pulling her close between them. His lips brushed hers, a slight touch that fanned hungry fires.

It was midnight when he finally realized he should head for the hotel. "I don't want to leave you," he whispered.

"I don't want you to go."

"Your neighbors would be scandalized if I were still here tomorrow." A small lamp burned on the table beside the bed and he turned on his side to prop his head on his hand and look at her. "You can't imagine how much I've thought about you and wanted you. That's all that kept me going."

She stroked his shoulder and trailed her fingers over his chest, feeling the hard slabs of muscle. "Thank God, you're home."

"We'll talk about wedding plans soon," he said. His green eyes were filled with love, and her heart beat with joy.

"I shouldn't have waited. I don't want to wait now."

"I'm not going to let you, Sophia. Tell me about the town and the people. Where's Henry?"

"He died last year."

"I'm sorry to hear. Who came home from war?"

"They're still coming home. So much has changed and Memphis has people pouring into it. The population has soared. It's almost forty thousand now. There are people without work, people uprooted by the war, some on their way West. There's a rowdy element that is worse than it ever was before. There are brawls and I don't stay at the paper at night like I did. I carry a pistol."

"Thank God, I'm home."

"Hannah Lou married Dunstan Trevitt," she said. Sophia didn't want to tell him about her problems with Trevitt and spoil their first night together. Time later to tell Caleb, she decided.

"I can't imagine her family would allow it."

"He has them, as well as others, charmed. He's an important man in town and he's building a railroad."

"Lord, that means he's Will's brother-in-law. I may lose my partner in the railroad. Will can't invest in two railroads. Has Trevitt given you trouble?"

His green eyes probed, and she wanted to shake her head and answer no, but as she gazed up at Caleb, she couldn't lie to him. He frowned, his brows drawing closer as he held her chin.

"What's he done?" he demanded.

She drew her fingers along Caleb's bony shoulder, feeling his smooth skin, touching a small scar. "I'm with you and everything is the best it's ever been. Let's talk about Major Trevitt tomorrow."

"No. Talking about him won't ruin tonight—" His scowl deepened. "What's he done to you?"

"Nothing," she assured him quickly, seeing his temper flare. "He's angry over that night. He threatened me."

"Threatened what?"

His voice was so cold it chilled her and the harshness in it was a side she hadn't seen to him. "Caleb, please. You're home now, and he won't dare do anything. Please don't do anything to jeopardize your safety. I couldn't bear it if something happened now." She ran her hand along his smooth jaw.

"Nothing's going to happen now because of Trevitt. Tell me, Sophia, exactly what he's done. What did he threaten?"

"To get revenge."

"I want to know when and where and how."

"Please, Caleb. It will only make you angry."

"Sophia," he said, in a compelling, angry voice that brooked no argument.

If he knew Trevitt's threat, Caleb would be in a rage. As she gazed up at him, she felt that old clash of wills spark between them. "See," she said quietly, "he's already disturbing our night and I hate it. Caleb O'Brien, I've waited three years for you and you're not going to bully me with your Irish temper tonight!" She raised up to push him down, twisting in the bed swiftly to bend down and trail her tongue along his thigh, her hands moving over him.

He drew a deep breath. "Sophia, damn—"

She stroked him and his argument ended. He caressed her bare back, his warm fingers playing across her nape. With a groan he sat up and pulled her against his bare body to cradle her in his arms. His long legs were rough with short hair, warm against hers as he stroked and kissed her.

It was one in the morning before he returned to the conversation. He climbed out of bed and rummaged in his satchel producing a bottle. He uncorked it and tilted it to drink, turning to offer it to her.

Shaking her head, her gaze ran over his nude body and she remembered that night so long ago when she had walked in on him. He was lean, all slabs of hard muscle now, his upper body so dark while below his waist his skin was pale.

He came back to the bed and sat beside her, placing his hands on either side of her. "To hell with your good name if Trevitt's threatened you, Sophia. I'll sit in the parlor if you want, but I'll not leave you alone here. You'll be my wife soon, so let the tongues wag."

"Caleb! You know people won't speak to me. They'll be outraged. You leave before dawn. I'll be safe then. Take the buggy and go down the alley and come back early in the morning to get me."

"They'll forget. I promise you that," he said forcefully. "Now, lassie, you're to tell me right now about Trevitt."

She couldn't escape this time by distracting him. "Please don't call him out," she pleaded. He sounded harder, more fierce than he had before the war and she was afraid of what he would do.

"I'll decide what I'm going to do. Sophia—"

"Hannah Lou invited me to her house. I went during a morning because I thought he would be gone from home. He wasn't. He greeted me and talked a few minutes and left. Later he came to the newspaper office and told me he would get revenge some day. He said he wanted me to think about it for a time."

"That bastard."

"Caleb, you frighten me when you sound like that. Please don't call him out."

"Has he been to this house?"

She looked away. "Once. He was on the porch. He's angry with me."

"He's angry with ye—" he said, his voice growing even quieter, a note of hardness to it that sent a chill over her.

She sat up to wind her arms around his neck. "Please don't do anything. You're home. He'll stop now."

"Why was he angry with you? What did you do to cause that, Sophia?"

She buried her face against his throat. "I didn't do much of anything."

"I know you, lassie. What was it?"

"He wants to build a railroad from Memphis to Springfield, Missouri, and he's raising funds and getting supporters and acquiring land. I opposed it in the paper."

With his forefinger beneath her chin, Caleb raised her face and stared at her. "I intend to build my railroad through Pine Bluff to Shreveport, Louisiana. Are you going to oppose that as well?"

"I won't publish articles in my paper against your railroad. I can see why you think railroads bring progress and prosperity, but look at Memphis tomorrow. You haven't seen what it's like now. There are thieves in abundance here."

"That's the rabble from war. Once industry begins to thrive again, things will settle."

"I don't think you should stay here tonight."

"You think with that bastard threatening you, I'll go stay at a hotel and worry about your safety? The only thing you can do about this, is marry me soon, love," he added, his voice changing, all anger dissipating.

"Caleb, I'll be ruined."

"That you will be," he said in a tender, husky tone that made her breathless. "So we might as well make it complete. You've always been viewed differently by your neighbors. Marry me, lass, and it'll be forgotten swiftly."

"Yes," she whispered, stroking him as he stretched out and moved over her, his weight pressing against her.

The next morning when she stirred, the bed was empty. She sat up and climbed out of bed to pull on her wrapper. He was seated in the parlor smoking a cigar. A clatter came from the kitchen. Mazie was cooking breakfast, so she already knew he was here.

"Caleb—"

His features were impassive except for a glint of fire in his eyes. She glanced at the paper in his hands and saw it was *The River Weekly*.

"You're adamant against a new railroad," he exclaimed. "This should make his investors say no if they read your paper."

"Caleb, it was directed against Dunstan. I won't write anything like that against you."

"You won't need to. This will make any investor worry. You point out there is already a line to St. Louis. There is already a charter for a train to Little Rock, Arkansas, so it's just as easy a conclusion to say there shouldn't be another one from Arkansas to Shreveport."

"Why do you want one to Shreveport?"

"They've never gotten the one finished to Little Rock. It runs through swamps and only part of it is finished. My line will angle off through Pine Bluff and down to Shreveport, which has been a major inland port in Louisiana—and not far from the Texas border. When that is successfully running, I want to go from Shreveport to Texas. They've had the Memphis–Little Rock line in the planning stage for years and only a tiny stretch has ever been finished. I'll get mine open for business."

"Mazie is here. Did she faint to find you here?"

"No, she didn't. I was dressed and sitting in the kitchen and I explained to her that Major Trevitt had threatened you and I intended to sleep in the parlor at night and protect you until we're married. Or until I have a talk with Trevitt."

"You'll end up calling him out or he'll call you out," she said, thinking Caleb was a whirlwind stirring up her life every time he came into it. "And Mazie will be shocked. Caleb, you're trouble!"

"I'm trouble! That's the tigress calling a lion a predator." He dropped the paper and stood up. His jaw was thrust forward, his green eyes filled with sparks, and she felt the clash between them. And she felt like backing up, remembering suddenly how unpredictable he could be.

"Caleb O'Brien, you calm down."

"Calm down?" He caught her to him, sliding his arm around her waist and reaching past her with the other hand to slam the door shut. It banged closed and she jumped. She raised her head and glared at him.

"You—" She was at a loss for words, her heart beating fast.

"You still make me want to kiss you or shake you, Sophia. How will I ever control you?"

"You won't, Caleb. You're a bully."

"Is that right?" he asked in a voice that had lost all anger. "There's only one thing, Sophia, to do with you."

"Now you'll not—"

"Yes, I will," he replied, leaning forward to stop any further protest. As soon as his lips touched hers, she pressed against him, holding him tightly, all worries and arguments gone.

When he released her, she looked up at him and saw the amusement and love in his eyes. "You're a handful, Miss Merrick."

"You're a storm tearing up my peaceful life, Major O'Brien," she added, laughter surfacing. "Oh, Caleb, I'm so thankful you're home! I don't care about anything else." She hugged him and he held her tightly, his breath tickling her ear.

"That's more like it, love."

"Mazie will be shocked that you're here."

"Maybe she was, but when I told her about Trevitt, she nodded her head."

"What did she say?"

The twinkle in his eyes deepened. "She said it was high time you got married. You—"

"—need a man," she finished, laughing. "Mazie has been telling me that since I was seventeen years old and Papa died and the boys went to fight."

"Shall we go have breakfast?"

She looked down. "My heavens, I'm in my wrapper."

"Let's see," he said, untying the sash.

She clutched it tightly and stepped back. "Oh, no you don't, or we won't get to breakfast and I would be more embarrassed than I am now!"

"We'll announce our engagement today, and you think about a date."

She gazed into his eyes and felt consumed with joy. As she went to her room though, she wondered about their differences and their arguments and if Trevitt would disrupt their lives. How could she keep Caleb from going to see him? She rubbed her forehead, worry returning, because she knew she couldn't.

They left the house together in her buggy, driving down the alley and turning away from her block, but her cheeks flamed and she could imagine every neighbor watching them with shock.

"Caleb, I'm ruined."

"Not when you tell them you're engaged to be married and you've had someone try to break into your house. I'll spread the word today and you'll see, people will calm. Besides, Sophia, society isn't as close-knit now as before."

And she never had been a part of the fashionable society of Memphis. She sighed. "Caleb, Papa would call you out or send me packing, but I'll have to admit it, I like having you there and if we're going to marry, it shouldn't be a sin."

"It's no sin, love," he sid gently. "To have to leave you alone and fight in a war was the sin and that's over."

They arrived at the newspaper office and went inside to look around.

"I plan to hire a typesetter to help as soon as I can save enough," she said.

"You'll not need a typesetter, because when you marry, you can sell the paper."

She stopped and turned to stare up at him. "Sell the paper?"

"Of course. My wife will be home." He placed his hands on her shoulders and spoke before she could reply. "Sophia, we're not wed yet, and you have your paper. No arguments this morning?"

She gazed up at him. "No arguments," she replied softly.

He grinned and then kissed her lightly, untying the blue ribbons to her straw bonnet. He ran his hands over her blue silk morning dress. "You have grown more fashionable since staying with my sister-in-law."

"You know how Chantal and Amity love dresses and both have so many. They were so generous with me, Caleb."

"I'm glad and I know they love you." His gaze went over her features. "I hate to be away from you for even a short time. You lock the doors."

"I'm safe here. I have a revolver in my desk and neighbors and Major Trevitt is busy during the day."

Caleb nodded. "I'll be back later."

She watched him stride through the door and down the street. He was marvelous. She spun around, holding her arms out, feeling a rush of joy. *He's home.* She glanced back at the street and then her jubilation ebbed. She had a sinking feeling Caleb was on his way to see Dunstan Trevitt.

Chapter 20

Caleb stopped at the Supply State Bank on Main and talked to Irwin Spurling, the president. As he sat across the desk from his auburn-haired friend, he outlined his railroad plans.

"You'll have competition, but now is a good time," the president said. "Memphis has a steady stream of people pouring through town. Transportation is changing. Before the war it was always the steamboats and the river that was Memphis's lifeblood. I think now it'll be the railroads."

"I want to get some of my money today. I'll have more money transferred here from New Orleans, but until it arrives, can I make a loan?"

"Of course. You were one of my first customers."

"I've got land and I want to start building a house and I need a small office."

"There's some space above Randolf Taylor's barber shop if you don't have to have something fancy. It's on Main."

"I'll talk to him. I intend to marry Sophia Merrick soon."

Irwin's red eyebrows arched and he scratched his bony nose. "Congratulations. You didn't waste time when you returned."

"I knew her before," Caleb said. "Thank God, I'm back."

"I never went because I took an oath of allegiance. Some people still don't speak, but war's not for me."

"I don't know who it is for," Caleb replied.

Irwin stood. "I'll get the loan paper and have someone get your money. I'm glad you're back to stay. I know a place where we can get into a good game of poker in the back room. It's high stakes if you're interested."

"Sometime soon, Irwin," Caleb said, thinking all he wanted to do now was spend every spare minute with Sophia.

After he left the bank he went to a tailor's shop where he was fitted for clothes. He purchased a broad-brimmed hat, shirts, and underclothes. Next he was fitted for new boots. Then he went to the telegraph office to send another telegram to New Orleans to Rafferty and one to Darcy. He purchased a horse and ordered a buggy.

He was amazed by the people who had flooded Memphis. Crowds thronged the street—carpetbaggers, Memphians, freed men, men and families headed West. Steamboats lined the docks, and buggies filled the dusty, rutted streets.

New buildings were already going up and Court Square was crowded with people. Everywhere he looked were bedraggled soldiers on their way home, Confederates who had survived, some on crutches, some walking skeletons. The Federal soldiers looked better, and he guessed many had spent most of the war in Memphis.

He turned to go to Will's office in the Stanton Building. As soon as he was announced, Will came out of his office to hug him.

"Thank God, you alive!"

"You think after all we went through, I was going to go back and get shot?"

They both laughed and Will motioned toward his office. Caleb entered a room with mahogany woodwork, a wide mahogany desk piled high with papers, papers and books stacked in glass-fronted cabinets. When they were seated, Caleb couldn't restrain himself with polite conversation. "What about the railroad, Will? Are you still interested?"

"Yes. As a matter of fact, I've gone ahead. I've gotten some investors and I've placed a proposal before the city."

Caleb's pulse jumped and he leaned forward with eagerness. "Damned good! I can't wait to get this train rolling. Look at the throng of people in the city. We can help open the West."

"We better build our bank accounts," Will said dryly. "Father opposes this and unfortunately, Hannah Lou married Trevitt."

"Sophia told me."

"I don't like him, Caleb, so there won't be any problem about being in the same business and competing, but Father finds it a problem. And whatever we do, I'll have to give part of my days to working here. Father expects me to take this business when he retires whether I own a railroad or not."

"We've always had that understanding. Just put in money, Will," Caleb teased, feeling impatient to get to work. "Let me know what you've done and what I need to start doing."

"Get investors. We're going to need thousands. Pull your chair here and I'll show you where we stand."

Three hours later Caleb and Will rented the second floor over the barber shop for a temporary office, and then Will returned to the Stanton Building.

By midafternoon Caleb had called on old friends and business acquaintances, making the necessary contacts for later. As he climbed in the buggy to turn on Main, he gazed at the throng. He couldn't believe he was finally home. It was a hot summer day with a cerulean sky, Main Street teaming with people. Inhaling deeply, constantly thankful the war was over, he turned south.

Drawing the reins Caleb gazed at the empty depot that was his. In place of the weathered shutters and the high weeds, he could envision a lawn, flowers around the depot, and passengers entering the building. Instead of the rotting dock, its boards crumbled into the river, there would be a dock and ferry. He looked beyond the sagging dock at the glistening Mississippi, feeling a deep-running current of excitement. This town, this river, would make his fortune, but most of all, Memphis held his heart because of Sophia.

Very soon he would have his train in operation. He wanted to get the railroad up and running as quickly as humanly possible, because people were moving West. And Trevitt would be a competitor.

His jaw tightened at the thought of Trevitt. He had found out the location of Trevitt's office, a new two-story brick building next door to the Community Bank on Main. Caleb halted the buggy and hitched his horse to the rail and strode inside beneath a sign that read TREVITT AND ASSOCIATES.

"May I help you?" a blond man asked.

"Is Major Trevitt in? I'm Caleb O'Brien and I want to see him."

A door was closed behind the man and another door led into a hallway. On the closed door was Dunstan's nameplate in brass.

"I'll tell him you're here, sir, but Major Trevitt's unable to see anyone now."

"He has someone with him?"

"No, but he left instructions that he's not to be disturbed."

Caleb stepped through a knee-high gate. Instantly the man's chair scraped, and he blocked Caleb's path. "I'm sorry, you can't—"

Caleb caught him by the shirtfront and lifted him even though the man was half a foot taller than Caleb. "Get out of my way," he said and shoved the man whose eyes went wide. He fell back across his chair, tumbling to the floor as Caleb strode to the door and kicked it open.

The knob broke and the door slammed against the inside wall. Caleb strode across the office. Behind a rosewood desk Dunstan came to his feet, his eyes narrowing.

"What the hell—" He reached to open a drawer.

Caleb didn't pause, but leaned over the desk and threw his right fist as forcefully as possible, putting all his weight behind it, connecting on Dunstan's jaw, feeling pain shoot up his arm, but not caring.

Dunstan slammed into the wall, shook his head, and jumped for the open drawer, lifting a revolver and pointing it at Caleb.

"I'm unarmed," Caleb said. "They'll never believe you if you say you had to shoot in self-defense."

"Major Trevitt?" the blond man spoke behind Caleb.

"Close the door, Thomas. I'm all right," Trevitt said, rubbing his jaw and glaring at Caleb.

Caleb tried to control his rage. He wanted to leap across the desk and continue pounding Dunstan and he wanted to call him out, but he wasn't going to use a gun again. He felt a tight knot of hatred he had never experienced facing the enemy in the war.

"When I challenge you, I want everyone to know it," Dunstan hissed. "I'll kill you for this."

"Don't go near Sophia. Don't threaten her or frighten her or intimidate her in any manner," Caleb shot back.

Dunstan's chest heaved as he breathed, and he stared back at Caleb. "Get out of my office."

Caleb turned and strode out, his back tingling, because Dunstan could easily shoot him, but a shot in the back would be difficult to explain. He stepped out of the office and slammed the door, his fists clenched, feeling hot with rage. Rubbing his knuckles, he took a deep breath. He hadn't gained much satisfaction, but Dunstan now knew there would be retribution if he tried anything with Sophia.

During the next three weeks, Sophia barely saw Caleb because he worked long hours on his railroad, he was overseeing construction of a house on Adams, and he would leave soon for New Orleans.

She looked up late on Thursday afternoon as the bell jingled in the office, and Caleb came through the door. Her pulse raced; she realized how much he had changed in just three weeks. He had gained weight and looked healthier. His new clothes made him dashing and she ached for him. She moved around the desk, hurrying to him, wanting to throw her arms around his neck.

He held her, smiling down at her. "You're determined to stir gossip. Everybody passing on the street can see us."

"They won't bother to look. Newspaper offices aren't that enticing."

He pushed her toward the hallway to the back and as soon as they were in the shadowed hall, he tightened his arms around her to kiss her. Her heart pounded with joy and she returned his kiss, sliding her hands along his thighs.

He raised his head. "I want to take you home," he said in a husky voice, desire evident in his gaze. "And I brought house plans from our architect. I want you to tell me what you want in our house."

"Oh, Caleb. *Our house* sounds so marvelous!"

"I want to give you something as grand as anything owned by the Brinkleys or Mansfields or Neelys or Fontaines."

"I don't need anything grand! I just want to be with you, Caleb."

"I would give you the world if I could." He held her tightly. "I have to go to New Orleans. I wish you'd come with me."

"Caleb, we've been over this. I won't start a flurry of gossip and I can't leave the paper."

He groaned and released her. "Sophia, we haven't settled anything about your paper, but I don't want my wife down here working every day. I want you home." He leaned forward and kissed her quickly and lightly as she opened her mouth to protest.

"Get your bonnet and let's go home and look at the architectural plans."

"Unfair, Caleb. You know I was ready to say something to you about the paper."

"You can at home," he said with a wink.

Later as he rolled up the plans and leaned back on his chair at the kitchen table, he gazed at her. "As soon as I talk to my family, we'll set our wedding date."

She looked away and frowned and he turned her head toward him. "Why the worry?"

"I was thinking about my brothers. Amos and Morris killed in different places, John still unaccounted for. I wish I could bring them home to Elmwood Cemetery where Papa is buried."

"So many were killed who were unidentified. They're buried in mass graves; I'm sorry. That's what they did at Shiloh."

"I still hope for John to come home."

Caleb squeezed her shoulder. "Maybe he will."

"You don't think so after all this time."

Caleb kissed her cheek. "Hold to your hope. I did for years with Fortune. It makes absence easier. Sophia, we need to set a wedding date."

"I want Rafe and Chantal here, so we'll have to plan around the expected babe."

Caleb groaned. "That means we'll have to wait until she can travel."

"Caleb, they have to be here for the wedding. And you want Fortune to come. I need to get my dress made, and you want to have the house built."

"Don't you want to marry me?" he asked teasingly.

She smiled and squeezed him. "Have I acted as if I don't?" she said, stroking him, knowing he was already aroused.

"Sophia—" He groaned and raised her face to kiss him.

Two nights later as he rode to the hotel from Sophia's, he turned and went to the Shamrock Saloon where he joined Will at poker.

By two in the morning Caleb's stack of winnings had grown and he stared at the four, five, six, eight, and nine of diamonds.

He pushed money to the center of the table.

"O'Brien! O'Brien!"

Caleb raised his head as Jess Hanly, the blacksmith, ran toward him. He waved his hand. "Merrick's newspaper office is burning! We need everyone to come fight the fire!"

Caleb jumped up, rushing from the saloon as men joined him, everyone running for the office. He leapt into the saddle and turned his horse. "Where's Sophia?" he hollered at Jess.

"I don't know. We just saw the flames."

He heard the fire bell clanging and saw the horse-drawn fire wagon from the Pioneer Hook and Ladder Company. Feeling a need to get to Sophia as quickly as possible, he raced down the street winding his way to her house. The house was dark and he was tempted to go back to fight the fire and let her sleep through it. Knowing she would want to be there, he dismounted and ran across the porch, pounding on the door before taking his key to unlock it.

"Sophia!" he called.

The bedroom door opened and Sophia appeared in her white cotton nightgown.

"Hurry and dress. The newspaper office is on fire."

"Oh, no!" She spun away, and he paced the floor until she returned. Her hair was tied behind her head and she wore a deep blue poplin dress.

He lifted her to ride sideways in front of him. "I won't let you fall, and your skirts will cover your legs."

"Caleb!" Her voice was stricken and she grasped his arm, her fingers digging into his flesh. A spiral of gray smoke spun upward over Memphis and orange sparks shot high in the night sky. And he remembered the night they had fled Memphis and turned to look back and had seen smoke rising over the town.

"It was Papa's office," she said quietly.

When they neared the fire, he hitched his horse to a rail in front of a darkened building a block away. "I can't take my horse closer." He lifted her down and then dismounted.

As fireman pumped, water gushed from hoses; the inside of the brick building was a raging inferno. Bucket brigades had formed and everyone was trying to contain the fire and save the adjoining buildings. They joined the bucket brigade, Sophia taking a heavy, sloshing bucket of cold water and passing it to a man. "What caused the fire?" she asked.

The man shrugged. Another in a line across from Caleb glanced at him and looked away.

"I'll give a reward for any information about the fire," Caleb announced loudly.

Sophia shivered even though heat from the fire enveloped her. Acrid smoke burned her eyes and throat while water spilled on her dress and arms. The crowd grew, standing and staring or falling into line to help with the buckets of water. A few women were in the crowd and as she glanced around, she felt a shock. Wrapped in a silk cape with Dunstan beside her, Hannah Lou stood watching. One corner of Dunstan's mouth lifted in a crooked smile. He looked smug and satisfied. Had Dunstan caused the fire? Staring at him, she paused, she felt a hot swift rush of anger.

Hannah Lou said something to him and the two of them came toward her.

"Sophia, I'm so sorry!" Hannah Lou said while Dunstan grinned.

In that moment she hated him more than she had ever hated anyone in her life. Lifting her chin, she continued passing buckets of water. Beyond the next line, she saw Caleb manning a hose with the firemen.

"How sad the paper that condemned me is burning," Dunstan said, close behind her.

"I'll start again," she said bravely. She couldn't start over. All her money had gone to her new house and getting the *Weekly* printed. She had a small savings, but not enough to buy another Hoe press like the one Papa had purchased. And she didn't want Caleb to give her one when he was spending all his funds for his railroad.

"We'll go home now, Hannah Lou," Dunstan said. As Hannah Lou turned away, Dunstan leaned closed behind Sophia. "It looks as if you're out of business. Misfortune often comes in pairs, Sophia."

She ignored him, passing buckets. The blaze burned itself out, and they kept it from consuming another building. When the bucket brigade stopped, Caleb appeared. His arms and legs were soaked. "Let's go to my hotel and let me change clothes and then I'll see you home."

She nodded stiffly, trying to keep control of her emotions. A paper blew against her skirt and she picked it up. It was the last edition of *The River Weekly*. Caleb folded it, pushing it into his pocket. They walked to the hotel where she sat alone in the silent lobby. The tall clock beside a post chimed, the bell clanging four times. Four o'clock in the morning. Soon it would be daylight. Caleb came down the stairs and her spirits lifted momentarily. He wore tight black pants and a fresh blue chambray shirt and he looked irrepressible.

"Thank heaven you're here in Memphis and not off fighting a war when this happened. You have given me much support and strength."

"You'd have done fine without me, because you always have."

Halfway to her house on a dark, empty street she turned her head against his chest and cried. His arm tightened around her. Finally she wiped her tears away, thinking of Dunstan, knowing it would only fuel Caleb's anger to tell him her suspicions.

In her kitchen Caleb poured two glasses of brandy and handed her one and she remembered other nights they had sat up together.

"You introduced me to spirits, Caleb."

He cocked his eyebrow. "I'll be your downfall, love."

"I don't know what I would have done without you tonight." She raised his hand to kiss his knuckles, slanting a look at him.

"You've been through much, Sophia, and you're brave. Come sit on my lap."

She moved around the table and in minutes he lifted her in his arms and carried her to the bedroom.

It wasn't until after nine the next morning when he was in his hotel room that he pulled the edition of *The River Weekly* from his pocket and smoothed it on the desk, glancing over the articles.

"The Memphis & Arkansas Railroad will open the way to the West." Since when had Sophia started supporting the railroads? He scanned the article, "The new line proposed by local businessman Caleb O'Brien, will open the way to Texas and the frontier and bring more dollars to Memphis."

"Great saints!" He sat down and read the article. He let it fall on his knee and stared into space, standing and peeling off his clothes to wash and change. When did Sophia change her mind about railroads?

He planned to leave Tuesday afternoon for New Orleans and Darcy was coming back to Memphis with him. There were things Caleb had to do before he left town.

After two errands, it was time for his appointment with three prospective investors, Willard Heaton, Horace Dooley, and Robert Blodgett. Willard Heaton was president of Security National Bank, and they met in his office. With a fortune in silver, Heaton had returned to Memphis to invest in land and banking. Tall, with black eyes and a massive black beard, he came around his desk to shake hands with Caleb. "Morning, Caleb. You know Robert Blodgett."

Caleb nodded and shook the limp soft hand of a man who owned steamboats and looked too pale to have ever been out on any of them. He gazed at Caleb through rimless spectacles as he smiled.

"Good morning, Mister O'Brien."

"And you know Horace Dooley."

Everyone in Memphis knew the man who was one of the leading cotton factors in the nation. Only a little over five feet tall, with a round head and thinning black hair, his grip was firm.

"Good morning," he said in a deep voice that sounded as if it should come from someone larger.

"Let's sit down at the table, and let Caleb show us his plans for the Memphis and Arkansas Railroad."

They moved to a long table near the window and when they were seated, Caleb unrolled a map. "I own the depots here and in Hopefield that Phelan Leib built. I have land through Pine Bluff and am working to acquire a land grant south of there and we're negotiating purchase of land in Louisiana. I'm leaving in three weeks to go to St. Louis to buy two engines and the necessary cars."

"When do you foresee having this train running as far as Pine Bluff?"

"By spring," he said, feeling a sense of determination.

"That's less than a year away," Willard Heaton said in his gravelly voice. "Impossible, Caleb. Let's be realistic. You might get it running a year from now."

"My line will be open as far as Clarendon the first of the year. It will be open to Pine Bluff next spring. By the end of summer I hope to have the line running between Shreveport and Memphis."

"I think you've set an impossible schedule," Heaton said.

"I'm already hiring men to work on the track. I've contacted the Tyler Ironworks in St. Louis about the engine and cars. I've got the charter and the financial backing to get it running to Pine Bluff. I need more financing. Once I have it going, I hope to go into Texas. The city of Memphis has pledged thirty thousand dollars to the M and A. The Memphis and Little Rock line is still entangled in delays."

"Do you know how many years the Memphis and Little Rock has languished?"

"Yes, I do. But I'm determined to give this all my attention and energy and I have a list of investors and you know many of them. I'm getting two new engines. Instead of the old 4–4–0, we'll have two that are 2–6–0, a two-wheel pilot truck, six drive wheels, and no wheels under the cab. That way the weight and power will be distributed over the six-coupled driving wheels. The engines will weigh 154 tons with loaded tenders and can pull 37,100 pounds of effort."

"What about rails?" Blodgett asked, staring at Caleb.

"They're ordered from Cincinnati and weigh 136 pounds per yard. We'll have two trestle bridges over the St. Francis River, one over the White River, with two wooden open-deck truss spans on L'Anguille River and a creek." He handed out folders.

"Here are specifications of the trains with details about the track, the route, the financing, and the expected cost."

"We're glad to hear your plans, Caleb," Heaton said, closing the folder as Caleb rolled up his map. Robert Blodgett stood up. "We'll look all this over and get back to you."

"Fine." He faced them as they stood, looking at each man. "I'll get my train running on schedule."

Willard Heaton smiled. "We'll study what you've given us."

"Thank you gentlemen," Caleb said, shaking hands again. "I'm going to New Orleans for the next two weeks, and then I'll be back in Memphis."

"We'll be in touch when you return. We're looking at Trevitt's M and S Railroad as well."

Wondering if he would get any support from them, Caleb left. They were three of many men in Memphis who had emerged from the war with wealth and the wealth was growing daily. He felt an eagerness in his blood to lay the new miles of track. The only cloud over his dreams was the time it would take him away from Sophia.

He returned to the new office and found Will.

"I've just seen Heaton and Dooley and Blodgett," he said, sitting down across the desk from Will.

"How did they like the proposal?"

"They said they would study the facts and get back to me. They don't think we can get the train running on the schedule we've set."

"I don't either," Will said dryly. "Except I know you and your Irish stubbornness. You'll have that train running if it runs on bare ground to get here."

"Not quite," Caleb replied, smiling. "I'm hiring all the men I can, but I'm hiring men who have experience in laying track."

"You're hiring Irishmen who'll give you their all, because you're Irish and you speak their tongue. And the bonus you've promised them is a damned fine incentive. Father still isn't persuaded it's good business sense."

"I hope I can change his mind with results. I've got a man coming from Alabama. Sean O'Keefe. He knows how to build tracks that won't sink in bogs. He was invaluable in the war and he's a damned fine engineer."

"Father and I've been talking to Mortimer Steinbrenner. He's interested and with a little more encouragement, he may invest. If you have enough money, you'll get the train going. We want to contact Napoleon Hill."

"I've met Steinbrenner, but I haven't talked to him," Caleb replied thinking about the brown-haired Northerner who bought property in Memphis during the war.

"What worries me," Will said, tugging at his ear, "is Heaton. He's a shark; he stops short of getting caught, but he cheats. You're dealing with a man who'll take the railroad from you if he can."

"We'll consider any offer together. Your father would be welcome, too."

"He has invested too heavily in Dunstan's railroad to put much in this one," Will stated.

"It's difficult to remember that Trevitt is your relative."

Will frowned. "Actually, it isn't just Willard Heaton. If you didn't need investors badly, I'd say steer clear of all three men. They have money, but they're unscrupulous. Father calls them the thief, the cheat, and the shark."

"I'll be careful, but if they have money and will give it to me for the Memphis and Arkansas, I don't care whether they've earned the names or not."

"Sorry about Sophia's fire," Will said, leaning back.

"Have you heard any rumors about when or how the fire started?"

"No. Why? You suspect someone who doesn't like Sophia? The saloonkeepers wouldn't mind seeing her paper burn, and you know it."

"I know. I just paid to have circulars printed offering a reward for any information about the fire."

"As much as the saloonkeepers dislike Sophia's stand on temperance, they like you and consider you their friend."

"It may not have been set, but she's made enemies here. I've offered a thousand dollars for information."

"That should bring someone forth if there is anything to tell." With a frown Will stared at Caleb. "Cal, I hate to talk about my brother-in-law, but did you know he once threatened Sophia?"

"Yes, I do. And I've warned him to stay away from her."

Will tugged at his earlobe and gazed beyond Caleb. "I don't think Hannah Lou is happy. She's changed, and I worry."

"Sorry. I like your sister."

"She won't say a word against him, but something is wrong. Sophia confided in me after Dunstan threatened her. I told him to leave her alone." His gaze shifted to Caleb. "He denied ever threatening Sophia. Said it was the fantasies of a spinster woman living alone too long."

"You know better than that, Will. Sophia isn't a woman given to fantasies, particularly a fantasy of Trevitt threatening her."

"I know. I think he did threaten her. I can't tell Father, because his health is failing and I don't want to burden him with worry and Dunstan has completely charmed

Mother. All her friends think he's a saint. They wouldn't believe anything bad about him. And they have wealthy husbands, so Dunstan is no fool."

"I leave for New Orleans in three hours," Caleb said.

"I wish I were going with you."

"Then go."

"Between the railroad and spending half the day helping Father with the cotton business, I can't leave Memphis."

"You don't have to stay away long. Go for a few days and come home."

Will rubbed his ear again. "You know, I might shift some appointments around and go with you for three days."

"Be at the dock at four."

"By heaven, I might do that, Cal!"

"I think if Amity were here, it wouldn't take long to persuade you."

Will blushed and grinned. "I may see you at four!"

Caleb left and rode to Sophia's house, finding her at her desk going over expenses and her savings. She turned and stood up as he walked into the room. As he pulled her to him, he felt that rush of desire for her he continually experienced. His gaze drifted over her, imagining her without the red moire. His blood heated. He remembered the gray and brown muslins she had worn when he met her and the plain braids wound around her head. Now she set his senses reeling with her vivid red moire. Her hair was in a soft chignon behind her head with curls over her forehead and ears and ruby earbobs dangling in her ears. She was breathtaking; no man could fail to notice her. Which change was the most radical—her appearance or her articles in the paper supporting the railroad? he tried to decide.

"I'm ready to go to New Orleans. I think Will's going along."

"I'll miss you terribly."

"I'm offering a reward for information about the fire."

"Caleb, the *Daily Post* has always been in favor of temperance. Harold Knowles, the editor and owner, came to call this morning. He has a small old proof press that he no longer uses. He said I can have it moved any place I'd like!"

Caleb felt like swearing while he gazed at her solemnly. With the fire, he thought she would give up printing a paper. "I can't say I'm overjoyed, Sophia. I don't want my wife printing a temperance paper or any paper. I want you home."

She frowned and moved away from him, walking to the desk. "And you won't give up that notion for me?"

"You're not going to reform me and I'm not going to change you."

"You've already changed my life beyond recognition, Caleb O'Brien. I'll print my paper and I'll fight the saloons and the whiskey and the gambling."

"Where will you put the press? In your parlor?"

"No. I told Harold I'd find an office and have it moved."

"Dammit! I hate your going to town alone. You're not safe on the streets." He moved impatiently toward the door. He was leaving for two weeks in New Orleans. He stopped and turned around. "Will you kiss me goodbye?" he asked gruffly.

Her breath caught in her throat and she crossed to him and faced him. He reached out and pulled her to him, bending to kiss her passionately and in seconds, she wound her arms around his neck and pressed against him, returning his kisses until anger burned away like mists beneath a summer sun.

He gazed down at her. "I need you," he said huskily and crushed her to him for one more hard kiss. When he released her, he studied her and reached into his pocket. He withdrew a paper and unfolded it. "What is this, Sophia?"

She glanced at the familiar story about the Memphis & Arkansas. She blushed and looked down. "I decided that you were right about railroads." She looked up at him with a solemn expression. "I still don't approve of the other things."

His expression softened. "So you changed your mind on this?"

"Don't get to thinking you can change me on everything! I don't approve of your gambling and I never will!"

"But there are things you do approve of, Sophia, that you didn't when I met you. And things you'll do now that you wouldn't do then," he said, looking pleased.

"Caleb—"

He kissed her again, long and deep and released her. "I'll be back in two weeks."

She watched him stride away, and he waved when he mounted up to ride down the street. She felt a strange sense of loss. The clash over her newspaper was a storm cloud on a distant horizon. The day would come when one would have to yield, and she couldn't imagine either of them giving up.

She loved Caleb and he was the only man she would ever love, yet she had to have her paper and she would always despise his gambling. She closed the front door and looked down the hall. The back door stood open.

All the time Caleb had been in town, her fear of Trevitt vanished, but now before Caleb was on the steamboat to Louisiana, she felt a chill. She hurried to close the back door and then rushed to the parlor to pick up her revolver.

Two weeks later she stood on the wharf and watched passengers come down the plank from the stern-wheeler. Then she glimpsed Darcy's dark hair and beside him was Caleb, looking full of vitality. He crushed her in a tight hug. When he released her, she turned to hug Darcy.

"How you've grown!"

"I got to steer the boat. Cal was friends with the captain," Darcy said, and she looked at Caleb whose eyes twinkled.

"I feel as if I've been away a year," Caleb said. "We have luggage and packages and Chantal and Amity sent things to you, and Darcy has enough to fill another boat.

"You wouldn't let me bring half!" Darcy said good-naturedly.

"Not so, little brother. I'm going to let Darcy name the engine on my new train."

Caleb directed loading their things into the waiting buggy. They returned to Sophia's and over dinner Darcy and Caleb told her the news from New Orleans and told her about Daniella.

Finally near midnight, Caleb stood up. "I'll take Darcy to the hotel. I'll see you tomorrow night.

At the door he kissed her lightly, then he and Darcy walked down the street to the hotel.

When Caleb stopped at the desk, he was given messages and as he thumbed through them, he paused, scanning one from Willard Heaton to meet him at the bank the following morning at ten o'clock if he was back in town. What had Heaton and Blodgett and Dooley decided? he wondered. If they would invest, how much would it be? He thought of the monumental costs of the railroad. He folded the note and motioned to the porter to bring the baggage.

They climbed the stairs to his suite. In three more weeks, his house would be finished enough to move in and he wanted to take Sophia to select furniture. He had ordered two beds, one for Darcy and an ornate, oversized rosewood bed that he planned to share with Sophia after their marriage.

His thoughts returned to Heaton. What had they decided? Would they flatly reject him? Will warned him to beware of all three men. Money was flowing in Memphis with new industry coming in, cotton still a thriving market. He had heard over thirty million dollars' worth of contraband goods passed through Memphis markets to the Confederacy during the war so Memphis hadn't been hurt like some Southern cities.

The next morning he delivered a trunk to Sophia. She stood with wide-eyed amazement, gazing at the gifts from his relatives in New Orleans while all he could look at was her. She hadn't put her hair up yet, and it was tied behind her head with a blue silk bow. She wore a blue gingham dress and he wished he could send Mazie and the delivery men away and cancel his appointment and spend the day with Sophia. He wanted to untie the bow and peel away the dress. Instead he stood with his hand on her shoulder, caressing her nape, watching her amazement.

Finally Mazie went to the kitchen and the porters left and he was alone in the parlor with Sophia and the gifts.

"I can't believe they sent all this," she exclaimed.

"They know you're getting married and they had a good time selecting things. They think you live on the frontier and can't get such goods."

She smiled up at him as he bent to kiss her throat. "I have an appointment to see Willard Heaton in twenty minutes or I would lock the door and ravish you."

"Sounds enticing," she whispered, her tongue touching his ear and stirring his excitement.

"Sophia," he whispered, his lips playing over hers lightly, his tongue touching hers and thrusting into her mouth deeply as he folded his arms around her and pulled her hard against him to kiss her.

He released her and gazed down. His arousal was hard, and he wanted her. "I love you," he said. "And I'm going to be late."

He picked up his hat and tried to shift his thoughts, to get his body cooled down. "I'll be over tonight, and we'll be alone."

"Goodbye," she said softly.

He turned away, knowing if he lingered she would be in his arms again. He thought about the night and his pulse raced. He wanted a wedding date, wanted to invite his family. The big delay was Rafe and Chantal's expected baby.

When Caleb entered Willard Heaton's office, he faced Dunstan Trevitt. Trevitt came to his feet, and Caleb gazed into cold blue eyes as they shook hands briefly. He could feel the animosity and hate, and he was puzzled why they were both here. Whatever the reason, Trevitt looked displeased about it.

And Willard Heaton's eyes glittered with excitement. *"The thief, the cheat, and the shark."* Caleb remembered Will's warnings and smiled as he turned to shake hands with Blodgett and Horace Dooley. He could feel the tension in the air. Blodgett licked his lips, and Caleb wondered what proposal they had and why Trevitt was part of it.

"Gentlemen, be seated," Willard said, sitting behind his desk and passing a box of cigars.

"We've looked over the plans and projections for both of the new Memphis railroads to the West. Trevitt is already coming along well with his line through Jonesboro and Walnut Ridge, Arkansas, to Springfield, Missouri. He has trains on order from a foundry in Chicago. And he's looking for investors. He intends to extend his line across Missouri north to Kansas City."

"I'm making good progress," Trevitt said.

"O'Brien is going south," Heaton continued. "He has two engines and cars ordered from St. Louis, and needs to lay a little over one hundred miles of track to Stuttgart, Arkansas, eventually going to Shreveport and on to Texas."

Caleb sat as quietly as he did at poker and he felt as if he were at the same game. Only the stakes were higher than any he had ever wagered in poker. He glanced at Blodgett to see a faint smile on his face. Willard Heaton looked as if he held a winning hand. Trevitt's brow was wrinkled in a frown.

"You both want backing and both of you are determined to get these new lines going in spite of shortages from the war and the difficulties building West by other railroad people.

"We've weighed which company to go with, which stock might be the most profitable. How it would benefit us as investors. What we've decided is to put one million dollars into one of these lines," Heaton said.

Caleb's pulse jumped at the announcement. The question was, which railroad?

"We want part interest for our investment."

"That sounds fair enough," Caleb said. He had several people already who had part interest, but he and Will had control and he would keep it that way.

"That's good," Trevitt said, suddenly relaxing as if he knew his was the railroad getting the money. "Gentlemen, you'll get your money's worth. Memphis to Springfield to Kansas City. This will make Memphis thrive." He glanced at Caleb. "And if you've brought us here to decide which railroad to place your investments with, I can promise you there's more future in Missouri and Springfield and Kansas City, than in Arkansas and Shreveport."

"They both hold golden possibilities with this country growing the way it is," Blodgett declared. "You both should go in together. Make it one business."

"I'm afraid that would be impossible," Trevitt said.

"We thought you might think so," Heaton said, amusement in his voice. "So we have an offer to make."

"An offer that will be satisfactory to all of us except one," Horace Dooley added in his tenor voice.

"What we have in mind," Willard said, leaning back in his chair and glancing back and forth between Trevitt and Caleb, "is something of a challenge for both of you."

"With a big reward for the winner," Blodgett added.

"We've figured the miles," Heaton went on, "and of course, they can't be exactly the same, but Dunstan, you already have fifty miles of track down. If you can get your line running daily between Hopefield and Mamouth Springs—that's some one hundred and twelve more miles." He shifted in his seat to look at Caleb. "And, Caleb, if you can get your line running daily from Stuttgart, Arkansas to Memphis—some one hundred and fourteen miles, we'll give the money to the man who has the first official run of his train into Hopefield from those two points."

Caleb stared at him while he thought about it.

"Mamouth Springs to Hopefield and Stuttgart to Hopefield?" Dunstan asked, his frown vanishing.

"The owner of the first engine to get here will get the money. Your line has to make daily runs thereafter. This way, gentlemen, it's an entertaining as well as profitable offer. We'll take bets on the outcome, you'll have a race, and someone will profit greatly. Of course, someone will lose, too."

Caleb was astonished by the offer, and his mind raced over the possibilities. He had nothing to lose from the offer and one million dollars to gain.

"I think it's a grand offer!" Dunstan exclaimed, settling back and taking a deep puff on the cigar and grinning, glancing at Caleb.

"I agree," Caleb said. "The offer is generous, and I'm happy to accept."

"Good!" Heaton exclaimed standing up and crossing to a table in front of a window. He opened a decanter and splashed whiskey into five glasses and passed them out, finally raising his glass for a toast. "May the fastest man win."

Caleb drank and looked over the rim of his glass into Dunstan Trevitt's cold blue eyes.

It was eight o'clock that night before Sophia heard footsteps on the porch and the key turned in the lock. Caleb entered, and her heart pounded with joy as she crossed the hall to wrap her arms around his neck and kiss him.

He bent over her, his kisses scalding until he picked her up and carried her to bed, his fingers reaching to the tiny buttons down the back of her dress. "Sophia, love, I've missed you," he whispered.

She gazed up at him and then pulled him down to her.

Later in bed, Sophia lay in his arms while he talked, his voice deep and mellow. A small lamp glowed beside the bed.

"I saw Willard Heaton today."

She twisted around to prop her head on her elbow to look at him. She tucked the sheet beneath her arms, and with a smile he pushed it away. Sophia gazed into his eyes and felt a surge of love for him. "I can't believe you're here and you're mine," she said softly, kissing his shoulder. "You frightened me when I first met you."

"The hell you say," he said, his eyes twinkling. "You hid your fright well, Miss Merrick. I remember getting doused with a pitcher of water and grown men running for their lives and their liquor."

"Caleb, you are a rogue."

"I have my good points."

"At least one," she teased, rubbing against him and letting her hand slide beneath the sheet down over his groin. He inhaled deeply and caught her hand.

"Let me tell you about Heaton. You can't guess what those three proposed."

"I've heard that Willard Heaton isn't scrupulous."

"I'll take my chances. They had Trevitt there, too."

"Dunstan?" She raised up, a tiny knot of worry coming. She didn't want Caleb involved with Dunstan Trevitt.

Caleb ran his fingers along her chin to her ear, catching a long, silky lock and curling it around his fingers. "They're going to invest one million dollars in one of the railroads."

"A million! Which railroad?"

His eyes were crystal green, thickly lashed, and her curiosity was keen about the railroad, yet she was more interested in looking at Caleb.

"Whoever gets his train into Memphis first. I have to have the line running from Stuttgart to Hopefield and Trevitt has to have his running from Mamouth Springs, Arkansas, to Hopefield."

"I thought Dunstan already has miles of track laid."

"He does. Mamouth Springs is over a hundred miles beyond where he has track."

She frowned and sat up, folding her legs and holding the sheet in front of her. "I don't like the offer, Caleb. It pits you against Dunstan, and there's enough bad blood between you both now. He will stoop to anything to get what he wants."

"It's for a million-dollar investment. If I try and I beat him—I'll get their money. I don't have anything to lose by trying."

"You might if you have to fight Dunstan."

"We won't be fighting. He'll be busy with his track, and I'll be busy with mine."

"He is a cheating snake who would do anything to get his way. You can get hurt."

"I'm damned sure not afraid of Trevitt." He tugged gently on the sheet, his voice changing to a husky baritone. "Come here, Sophia."

"You're trying to get me away from the subject of Trevitt. Don't race him," she cautioned.

"I'm not going to back down from competing with him. He doesn't frighten me." Caleb's voice was languid, his eyes half closed as he ran his finger along a fold of the sheet where it crossed her bare breast. She drew her breath, feeling desire fan to life.

"Caleb."

He tugged the sheet out of her hands and cupped her full breasts, filling his large hands and flicking his thumbs over her nipples. His fingers were dark against her pale flesh. She gasped and closed her eyes, tilting back her head, and then she looked down and ran her hands over his body, pushing the sheet down past his knees, bending to kiss his thigh. "Caleb, I love you."

He groaned and pulled her down on top of him and in minutes they were lost to passion.

An hour later Caleb extricated himself and crossed the room to his trousers. Her gaze ran the length of his back, the muscles rippling beneath his bronze skin. It still worried her to see the scar across his back, and she felt a surge of gratitude he had survived the war. She had lost everyone else she loved in it. Caleb rummaged in his pockets and pulled out something to return to her. She raised on her elbows to look at him, feeling desire blossom as she ran her gaze over his chest and flat belly down to his manhood.

He came down over her to prop himself on his elbows. "I brought you something from New Orleans."

He handed her a small leather pouch. She shook it and a necklace fell into her hand, the diamond catching the light.

"Caleb! It's beautiful," she cried, awed, turning it in her fingers and then looking at him. "It's lovely."

"It's an engagement gift. I want a date set so we can announce it to everyone."

"We have to wait until Chantal has her baby if we want Rafe and her to be here. January may be terrible weather for them to travel." She pushed at him and sat up. "Put this on me."

Smiling at her, he sat back with his legs folded under him on either side of her as the covers fell away an the diamond lay above her bare breasts. "Beautiful," he whispered, cupping her breasts as she closed her eyes and inhaled.

He moved his hands to her face. "Look at me. Give me a date."

"How about the first week in February? February second?"

"Too far away, but I want Rafe and his family here. Fortune is in Virginia now, and I'll write him. With this much notice, everyone should be able to get here."

"Caleb, come here," she whispered.

He kissed her, driving her to a frenzy, his fingers exquisite torment that made her hips shift. Then he possessed her, thrusting hard, moving with her.

Later when they were dressed, she brushed her hair. She wore her gown and wrapper and watched him fasten his shirt. He looked solemn, and she wondered if he were worrying about his railroad. The diamond winked in the light and she touched it.

"Caleb, this is beautiful. Thank you."

He crossed the room to her, placing his hands on her shoulders. Her golden hair spilled in a cascade over her shoulders and his gaze ran over her features before he looked into her eyes.

"I need to get back to the hotel, but before I go there's one more thing that we have to settle and it might as well be tonight."

Suddenly Sophia felt a sense of dread. He was somber, his voice gruff, and she knew how they could clash. "Can it wait?"

"No. There's no sense in postponing it, and I want things settled when I invite my family to our wedding. I want you to sell the paper. I want you home."

Shocked, she stared at him and felt rebellion rising over his demand. She frowned. "You know what the paper means to me. I know the men who survived the war are home by now, which means I've lost all my brothers, so I'm not keeping it for their sakes, but it is part of my tie to my family's memory. It is part of my life. It's like asking you to give up your railroads."

"No, it's not. You know it's different. If we have children, what will you do? Ignore them for the paper?"

"No. I'll hire someone to run it."

"And you'll be there half the time. And it opposes

things I support. Don't you think it will be ridiculous if
you try to drive the saloonkeepers out of town and I pa-
tronize them?"

"Yes, I do," she said, becoming angry with him. His re-
quest was unreasonable and Caleb could be so stubborn.
"I think you should stop patronizing them! You don't
need to gamble, Caleb."

"No, but I enjoy it and I don't lose money at it and I
don't gamble often. I haven't since the war. Get rid of the
paper, Sophia. I don't want my wife tied to a newspaper
in an office in town."

She moved away from him angrily, feeling that he was
demanding the impossible, thinking of her father and remembering clearly hearing him as he looked down at her:
*"Always remember, Sophia, do your duty. That's what's
important. Be true to duty and don't shirk the unpleasant
tasks."*

"I'm not giving up the paper." Always, she had known
that one day this argument might rise between them, yet
she had shut it out of mind.

"You're an independent woman, Sophia, but I insist on
this. There's no reason for you to cling to the paper."
They stared at each other and Caleb's green eyes were fiery. "I'll not marry a woman tied to an office." He turned
and strode through the room, yanking open the door. She
heard his boots scrape the boards as he went down the
hall. The back door slammed.

Stunned, she stared after him, thoughts tumbling in her
head. She wouldn't give up the paper. Caleb was unreasonable, impulsive. It was ridiculous for him to want her
to get rid of the paper. He would be back to discuss it.
And if he didn't come back? Her thoughts skittered away
from the idea. For three long years she had held to the
dream of his coming home to her, and then he did. She
couldn't believe she would lose him now.

Chapter 21

Caleb stripped off his shirt beneath the warm sun and waved his hand. "Move the wagon forward!" he shouted.

Two days of rain had turned the ground into a quagmire. Now the sun was bright, the earth steaming and warm. Darcy shoveled gravel from a flatcar, building up the granite ballast. Fifteen now, Darcy had grown two inches this year and was almost as tall as Caleb. He was thin, flesh barely covering his bony frame, his hands and feet and shoulders looking too large for the rest of him. He looked like Rafe and Fortune, except his black hair was straight.

Darcy hadn't ever done hard manual labor. How well could he keep up the pace? So far he was managing on one of the roughest crews of all.

Caleb motioned to the wagon coming behind, six men unloading the sleepers. Two men remained with the wagon, passing out the short wooden ties to others who set them in place on the ballast.

The rain had been two frustrating days of delay. Now it felt good to be occupied, to see progress. The first twenty days, he thought he had lost the race to Dunstan, because they were slow, the men impatient, tempers flaring, but gradually teams began to develop a rhythm and work together efficiently.

A bridge crew headed by an Irishman named Knute O'Toole worked ahead of the track-laying crew, and Caleb felt he had the best engineer possible in Knute. He had tough crews, but he made sure they were well fed and well paid.

He was busy every waking minute, yet it still didn't shut out the hurt and anger over Sophia.

He moved down the line, his long legs stretching out until he reached the ballast crew. "Hurry it up! You're slowing!" Moving farther down the line to the cars carrying the rails, Caleb swung up on a flatcar. Men following the wooden sleeper crew slid the long rails to the ground. Other men set them in place, fastening them in position.

"Boss!"

Jas Connors ran toward him. Stocky, missing three fingers and half his teeth from the war, Jas was a good worker and Caleb had fought with him at Shiloh. He waved his hand as he ran.

"Your brother's in a fight with Sweeney."

Caleb looked down the line of men and wagons and mules. He saw a cluster of men in the distance. He jumped down and strode forward. There had been only three fights since they started, and he had ended each of them quickly. He wanted the fights to stop. They had to learn to work efficiently together if he was going to win a race. His usual impatience with fighting was secondary now to apprehension. Darcy had grown up in New Orleans and at Belle Destin with Chantal and Amity. He hadn't had the rough and tumble life of his three older brothers and as far as Caleb knew, Darcy hadn't ever been in a fight. And Drake Sweeney was over six feet and over two hundred pounds of trouble. This was his second fight.

"Want a pistol, boss? Sweeney ain't reasonable when he's provoked."

"No." He hadn't carried a gun since the war, and he wasn't going to start now.

Men were silent as he approached, an ominous sign because they usually chose sides and made bets. Caleb knew no one would interfere.

Someone glanced over his shoulder and punched another man and the crowd parted for Caleb.

Darcy stumbled and sprawled on the ground; Sweeney kicked him in the ribs and Caleb clenched his fists, fighting the urge to wade into it and slug Sweeney. If it were anyone besides his younger brother, he would stop it. A fight was bad business, but he suspected Darcy would never forgive him stopping it in front of all these men.

Darcy rolled to his feet. His nose bled, his mouth was cut, his cheek cut, his eye puffed closed. Caleb drew a deep breath.

Sweeney's right fist lashed out and Darcy dodged, just missing a hammer blow. Sweeney threw a wild swing with his left.

Darcy ducked and threw his right, pivoting with his weight behind it and landing the blow on Sweeney's neck. Sweeney staggered and Darcy threw himself at Sweeney, slamming into him and wrapping his long arms around Sweeney. The momentum carried them backward as Sweeney pounded Darcy.

Caleb saw where they were headed. Darcy ran, keeping Sweeney off balance and staggering back. The back of Sweeney's knees slammed against the flatcar and Darcy's weight carried him down. Knocked off his feet, Sweeney sprawled on the flatcar. Darcy grabbed Sweeney's shoulders and banged his head on the granite and flatcar.

Sweeney slid to the ground and lay still while Darcy staggered back. Caleb let out his breath.

A cheer went up from the crowd. Darcy turned and his face went white, his knees buckling as he fainted.

"Jas, throw some water on him and when he comes around, bring him back to me. He's through shoveling ballast today," Caleb ordered.

"Yes, sir."

"Thanks for getting me."

Jas grinned. "I shoulda' known an O'Brien wouldn't need help."

Caleb shook his head. "I didn't know he could fight." He raised his voice. "Everyone back to work. We can't build a railroad this way. Any man who fights loses a day's wages."

He strode away, fighting the temptation to pick Darcy up and carry him to the supply wagon. Where did the kid learn to fight? he wondered. He must not have spent all his time with Amity and Chantal.

Twenty minutes later, he looked up to see Darcy approach.

"You got yourself in a hell of a mess," Caleb said,

proud of Darcy and impatient with him at the same time. "Now you can't work."

"Yes, I can."

"The hell. You'd pass out in ten minutes. You might as well ride back to Memphis. If you can't do that—"

"I can work," Darcy said stubbornly.

Caleb studied him and realized his little brother was growing up and it gave him a wrench inside. He wanted to hug Darcy, yet it would embarrass him. "Come on. I'll patch you up. Does it hurt to breathe and move?"

"Everything hurts."

Caleb stopped in the shade of the supply wagon and felt Darcy's ribs. He motioned to a cask. "Sit down and I'll clean up your face."

As he wiped away the blood, Darcy leaned against the wagon.

"Where's Sweeney?" Darcy asked.

"Some men carried him out of the way and someone wrapped his head. I think he's sitting under a tree. Where did you learn to fight?" Caleb asked.

Darcy squinted one eye open to look up at him. "Where else? New Orleans. I spent a lot of time on the docks and on the streets. Where did you learn to fight?"

"Probably with Rafe and Fortune," Caleb answered, amused. "What did you do to rile Sweeney?"

"Sweeney hates the world."

"I'll wrap your ribs." When he finished he looked at Darcy. "Climb into the wagon and stretch out."

"No. Are you finished?"

"Yes. I'm moving you. You place the sleepers now."

"I can shovel."

"I know you can. I was going to move you anyway." Darcy squinted at him. "You saw the fight?"

"The last of it."

"Thanks for not stepping in."

"Sure, Darcy. Don't get in another one. And anyone who does loses the day's wages. After two fights, you're off the crew. I'm firing Sweeney."

"Just give him a warning. Don't fire him over me."

"I'll think about it, but you don't have to worry about anyone thinking you get special privileges. The men know I watched and they know now you can hold your own with the best of them."

Darcy started to laugh, winced, and touched his swollen mouth. "As long as you and I don't get into it." He strode away, a gangling, awkward kid who was turning into a man. Sometimes his voice cracked and became childish, then switched to a deep tone. Caleb looked at him and thought of the years the war had robbed him of seeing Darcy grow.

He caught up with the rail crew to go back to work.

"Someone's coming on the run, boss," a short, red-haired man said.

Caleb looked up and saw the rider approaching. Wondering if the bridge crew had run into more trouble, Caleb strode forward. With the rain, streams were overflowing. Caleb waved, and the rider headed toward him, yanking on the reins to stop and he recognized Will.

"Your other engine will arrive in town Friday."

"Thank God!" Caleb exclaimed. "Let me tell one of the men and then I'll ride back to Memphis with you."

Minutes later he returned to Will on horseback. Will stared at the workers, the flatcars, and the equipment. "I don't know how you got this all assembled so fast," he said, awed.

"Yes, you do. The war is over and men are ready to work. And this is just a small part of our crew, Will. The surveying party is in the lead with Irvin Swartz. Between Swartz and O'Toole, I have two of the best engineers in the country. It's the first time you've been out here and I wish I could show it all to you." He waved his hand. "Swartz and his crew go first. Jethro Davis comes next with his location crew to stake out the grades and curves. And then we have the grading crew."

"Dunstan is boasting that he will win this race," Will said as they turned to ride east. "Men are betting on who will get his train to Memphis first. I hate to say, but right now the odds favor Dunstan."

"Place a bet on us, Will, although I wouldn't have said that a week ago."

They reached Hopefield and rode to the old M&A depot that was being renovated. Hammers pounded and men went in and out carrying boards.

Without waiting for Will, Caleb jumped down, running around the depot, calling quick greetings to workmen. The powerful, black engine was on the first track beside the depot. His heart thudded with excitement as he jumped up inside, running his fingers over the tender.

Will appeared. "This is spectacular, Caleb! A beauty."

"Look at it, Will! We'll run this across Arkansas to Louisiana and later into Texas. Memphis lost the eastern terminal of a transcontinental line, but if we can get this to Texas, we'll have a southern link with the West that will grow every year. And we'll grow with it!"

He sobered, because he wanted Sophia to look at it. Suddenly it all seemed a hollow achievement without her to show it to. He had felt rootless, a wanderer until he met Sophia and he realized now how much purpose she had brought to his life. He felt a knot in his throat and wondered if he were doing the right thing. Was a newspaper going to take the love of his life?

They climbed outside, crawling over the engine, finally climbing down and Caleb slid beneath it to lie between the tracks and look at the big wheels, the connecting rods, the fire grate. He slid out and brushed himself off. "Shall we go?"

"I'm ready. Father still expects us to lose everything."

"We're doing all right so far, but we need Heaton's million."

When they reached Memphis as they rode along Main Street, Caleb felt his heart turn over.

Sophia climbed down from a buggy and crossed the boardwalk to enter the bank. Before she reached the door, a tall, brown-haired man stopped to talk to her. She smiled up at him, and Caleb wanted to jump down off his horse and get her and carry her away. He felt as if he would suffocate and he realized his hands were clenched into fists. He hadn't thought it would hurt so much to part. And he thought the separation would be brief. He should have known; Sophia's whole life was the newspaper. He hadn't hurt anymore over separation during the war, but he had known he would come home to her and he occasionally had her letters to sustain him. Now he didn't know whether she was seeing someone else or what she was doing. Did she hurt or was her independence so all-fired important that she didn't care?

She was in a bright blue dress and blue bonnet and he couldn't look away from her. The man touched her arm, and Caleb drew a deep breath.

"Cal?"

He became aware of Will speaking to him. "Sorry, what?"

"What's wrong with—" Will looked past him. "Oh. Sorry."

"Who's with her?" Caleb asked, not really sure he wanted to know. He wanted to shove the man aside.

"Brock Fremont. He's new in Memphis; he's bought a big lot on Adams and is going to build. He has a sheet iron factory."

They drew abreast, and she turned her head. She looked into his eyes, and his breath caught. She glanced beyond him, nodding to Will, looking back at Caleb. He felt a jolt of tension as they gazed into each other's eyes, and he felt scalded by flames of desire. He ached for her. Her eyes narrowed, and she turned away, laughing with the man facing her.

Upstairs in Will's office, Caleb moved to the window and stood looking down on the street. Her buggy was still there, so she had to be in the bank. He watched the door for her. Was it so important that she give up the paper? That she stay home as all other women did? Other than when work occupied his mind, the rest of the time was hell without her.

Then he saw Brock Fremont waiting, lingering at the end of the street. Sophia came out of the bank. She started across to her wagon and stopped, looking around. Fremont caught up with her and helped her into the carriage.

"Do you see Sophia?" Caleb asked.

"Occasionally. She's fine. Sorry about you two. Life is just so damned complicated."

The bitterness in Will's voice was something Caleb seldom heard from his friend. He glanced at Will. "How's Amity?"

"I asked her to marry me."

"Will! Why didn't you tell me? Why—"

Will shook his head. "No. She says she won't leave New Orleans and her family. Father is getting more frail by the week. I can't leave. I'm tied to two businesses here." He sounded bleak, and Caleb could understand his hurt.

"Sorry, Will."

"Here are the reports and the receipts I wanted you to see."

"I'll get back to you," Caleb said, taking the reports and leaving. He rode to his house on Adams. He strode through the back door, his footsteps echoing in the emptiness. He leaned against the wall and closed his eyes. He hadn't ever hurt this badly. Sophia was his life and he didn't want to live without her.

"We're not alike," he said aloud. "We don't do the same things or like the same things. She doesn't approve of my gambling. I don't approve of her newspaper." Yet all the time he talked, he knew how much he missed her, he thought of her laughter and the moments they did agree, the things they both liked. She was independent and intelligent and fun. And sensual enough to make him burn like wildfire. He groaned and ran his fingers through his hair. "Sophia."

Sophia rode home in a daze. She had seen Caleb in town. She remembered, going over and over the moment in her mind when she had looked up to see him riding past with Will. His hat was battered; he was dusty, his skin a deep brown. Her heart missed beats and she couldn't hear what Brock was saying to her. She gazed into Caleb's green eyes and felt as if she might lose control and burst into tears right there in front of the bank. Was the paper worth all the agony? None of her brothers was coming back. She would have heard from John by now and Morris and Amos were dead. So was Papa. Was she saving the paper and giving up love in exchange? Was that what she really wanted? she asked herself.

It was an empty victory to keep the paper and lose Caleb. And every day that passed made that clearer to her. She dreaded going to the *Weekly* office now. She couldn't concentrate on what she wrote, she had to redo her work over and over. And Caleb's influence in her life had made a difference. During the early part of the war when Caleb had been with her and injured, she had seen that he was right, that railroads could bring prosperity and by the time Caleb came home from fighting, she was supporting his train in the paper.

Now the scope of the *Weekly* seemed narrow and she continued to support her father's stand on temperance out of respect for him, but she no longer believed the way she had before she met Caleb.

She climbed down and carried a basket of food inside. Mazie helped her, and after a few minutes putting away staples, Mazie paused. "Miss Sophia? You haven't heard a word I've said. Child, what's wrong with you?"

"Sorry, Mazie."

"You're pinin' over Major O'Brien," Mazie said, placing her hands on her hips. "Miss Sophia, I'm getting old. You ought to be married and have someone to take care of you and I'm going to worry myself to pieces if you don't."

"I'll be all right, Mazie, and you don't need to worry," Sophia said, wanting to avoid discussing it because she lacked control of her emotions.

"Have you seen Major O'Brien lately?"

"I told you, Mazie, we don't see each other anymore."

"It's over that paper of your papa's. Miss Sophia, your folks aren't coming home. There's just you and me. Someday there's going to be just you."

"Mazie, I'm fine and I'm doing what I want to do. I don't want to hear anymore about it!" The moment the words were out, Sophia felt regret. She had never been sharp with Mazie, who clamped her mouth shut and turned away.

"Yes, ma'am. I'm through for the day and I'm going home. My bones ache, and I may not be able to be back tomorrow, Miss Sophia." She marched out of the kitchen, yanking up her bonnet as she left.

Sophia sank down on a chair and ran her hand over her forehead. She shouldn't have spoken sharply to Mazie. And did she really want the paper?

That night she lay in bed, tossing and turning and weighing the same question. Who was she preserving the paper for? Her family was gone, and she no longer enjoyed publishing it. She climbed out of bed and walked in the dark to the next bedroom.

Moonlight spilled across the high empty bed, but all she saw was Caleb stretched in it, remembering and aching and feeling hot tears course down her cheeks. "Caleb—"

Work went forward and Caleb sat astride his horse watching with satisfaction in late November. They were working efficiently now, all the crews accustomed to each other, laying a mile a day, sometimes better. He was running a close race with Dunstan; each day's progress by both lines was reported in Memphis. He hadn't been back to Memphis for weeks and he was going tonight. It was time to replenish supplies, check with investors, take care of business at home.

Jonah McClanahan was his engineer who drove the train, and they steamed back to Memphis. They had track finished through Clarendon and as Caleb gazed out at the dark night, he knew he should feel exultation. All he could feel was an intense longing for Sophia. Where was she? What was she doing? Was there another man? "Damn," he muttered, shifting, wanting to get back to Memphis.

As he rode the ferry the last distance, he stood at the rail and looked at the dark waters of the Mississippi and smelled the river, the odors of water and fish and oil from boats mingling. Wind blew over him. Home. Lights flickered onshore and felt a longing that made him groan. He wanted to go to Sophia's, to take her in his arms and love her.

The next morning he was up early, pacing the house, waiting for businesses to open, feeling impatient; he had made a decision.

* * *

Sophia studied herself in the mirror. "I don't want the paper," she whispered. "I want you."

She had agreed to go to the Stantons' ball with Taylor Weatherford and she wished she hadn't. Hannah Lou urged her to get out, Taylor had pushed her to accept his invitation, so she had accepted, but now she didn't want to go out; she didn't want to spend the evening with any man except Caleb.

Her emerald green satin dress was new, fashioned with rose ribbons, lace, and rosebuds and it was beautiful, but all she could think about was Caleb's green eyes, his irresistible smile, his passion.

She stared at her reflection. "Get rid of the *Weekly*," she said aloud. Why keep the paper? Caleb was all-important, all she wanted. She would give up the *Weekly* to be his wife. She crossed the room to the bed and ran her hand over it. "Caleb, come home to me. I want you. Not a paper, but you."

Caleb was somewhere in the wilds of Arkansas, laying track and building his railroad. When would she see him again?

A knock sounded and Mazie answered the door, ushering Taylor into the parlor. Sophia could hear their voices and then Mazie appeared. "Mister Weatherford's waiting, Miss Sophia."

Mazie didn't approve of anyone except Caleb, and she barely hid her feelings, something that astounded Sophia. When and how had Caleb won Mazie's total loyalty? she wondered.

When Sophia entered the parlor, Taylor Weatherford turned. He was handsome, tall and blond with brown eyes that were warm and friendly.

"How beautiful you look."

"Thank you, Mister Weatherford."

He looked amused as he crossed the room to take her arm and gaze down at her. "It's Taylor, Sophia. Remember?"

When she nodded, he linked her arm through his. "Shall we go?"

At the brightly lighted hotel ballroom, she felt in a daze, trying to pay attention to Taylor's conversation.

Halfway through the evening while they danced, he raised her face up to his. "Sophia, I think I pushed you into coming tonight and now I know I shouldn't have. You act like a woman deeply in love—and I'm not the man."

"Taylor, I'm sorry—"

"Don't be sorry. I urged you to come when you politely tried to refuse. I shouldn't have. Unfortunately, you and I aren't in love. I think the most we'll ever be is friends."

"I'm sorry if I've ruined your evening."

"You haven't ruined mine. This is only the second time we've danced together. I've had a good time, but I suspect you aren't having a good time."

She smiled at him. "I'm glad you've had a good time."

His brown eyes twinkled as he gazed down at her. "I met Miss Lucy Hockinson and I'll call on her tomorrow. As a matter of fact, she came with her parents, and I might take her home tonight."

Sophia felt a mild shock. Was Taylor leaving her to get home on her own? She realized she deserved it for her cool manner. His smile widened.

"You won't be abandoned," he reassured her.

"That's all right, Taylor. I feel terrible, because I shouldn't have come—"

"Don't say anymore. It isn't necessary. When I fall in love, I hope she loves me in such a manner. And I don't think I'll be taking you home tonight."

"That's all right."

He grinned. "I'm wondering how long before he claims you to dance."

"Who?" Her breath caught in her throat as she looked at Taylor, and then glanced around.

"Mister O'Brien is here; I saw him come through the door a little while ago."

She barely heard Taylor, her gaze scanning the crowd milling on the fringe of the ballroom.

"He's a fortunate man," Taylor added.

"How long ago did you see him?" She looked at the dancers. "Did he have a woman with him?"

"I saw him about half an hour ago."

"Half an hour!" That was forever. Where was Caleb and what was he doing?

"Was there a woman?"

"Why don't you look for yourself," Taylor said softly, leaning down to her ear. "Goodbye, Sophia. I wish you the best."

She blinked, glancing around and then Caleb was there in a black coat and pants, a snowy white shirt and cravat. He was saying something to Taylor, Taylor speaking, and all the while all she could do was stare into Caleb's eyes as he watched her. He reached for her and she went into his arms to dance and neither of them said a word. Her pulse pounded and she was aware of his hand on her waist, his hand holding hers, their steps matching as he spun her around the dance floor.

His skin was darkened by the sun to a deep brown, his brown curls streaked with blond. She couldn't get her breath and ached to kiss him. "I thought you'd never come," she whispered.

He didn't answer, but danced through the wide doors. "My carriage is over here," he said, tugging her hand. She didn't protest, but hurried with him, her heart racing as they rushed across the lot and he helped her up and climbed up beside her to take the reins. She glanced at him. He looked solemn, so marvelous and she couldn't resist touching him, reaching out to run her hand along his arm. He drew a deep breath and looked down at her, urging on the horses as they rushed to his house.

She gazed up at the two-story brick house. He had built it for her. She had even helped select some of the furniture, but for the past months she had given up all hope of ever living in it. In the drive Caleb swung her down from the buggy, his hands on her waist and she looked up at him. Moonlight was pale on his wide cheekbones, his eyes in shadow. He drew a deep breath and pulled her hard against him as he bent to kiss her.

His tongue went deep into her mouth in a hot, demanding kiss, and she felt as if everything inside turned over. Desire burned, making her hips thrust against him. She felt her body reacting, growing heated, ready, while she yearned for him with a need that was painful.

"Caleb, Caleb . . ." she whispered, kissing him, running her fingers in his curls.

He swung her up in his arms, the hoop flying up. She tried to hold it.

"Dammit," he swore, striding to the house and kicking the door shut behind them. He set her on her feet and pulled her to him. He yanked down the dress, buttons popping, lifting her breasts free to kiss her, touching her nipple with his tongue.

Sophia gasped with pleasure, tilting back her head, closing her eyes while her hands fumbled his belt buckle, loosening it and pulling it free. She shoved away his coat and he turned her, kissing her nape while he worked the last tiny buttons free at the waist of her emerald dress.

"Take down your hair," he ordered in a husky voice as he unfastened the hoop skirt and crinoline and unlaced the corset. He peeled away her drawers and stockings and she turned, her hair tumbling down. And finally she was in his arms, feeling his marvelous, warm body, his manhood hard, hot, pressing against her.

She felt as if she would melt as he caressed her and pushed her down on the hooked rug. He shifted, trailing kisses over her, his tongue making her gasp and arch her hips with need.

"Ye're mine, lass. I need ye, damned newspaper or not," he said, his voice gruff and fierce and making her pulse race. "And I'll show ye that ye want me," he said, his fingers stroking her, making her gasp and writhe and strain for release.

"Caleb—" She stroked him, her hands caressing him until he moved over her.

"Ye'll be mine, Sophia."

He thrust into her and her hips rose to meet him as she wrapped her legs around his slender hips and moved wildly with him. Her hands raked his strong back, sliding over the smooth curve of his firm buttocks, caressing him while she moaned and was caught up in a driving desire to make Caleb hers forever, to show him that she needed him desperately. She showered kisses on his throat and shoulder, murmuring his name and then release came, wracking her body, both moving wildly.

"Sophia, mine! Ye're mine!" He turned his head to kiss her deeply.

Finally his weight lowered on her while they both gasped for breath, their bodies heated, damp with perspiration. He lifted long locks of hair from her face. Turning on his side, he held her and gazed at her. "Ye can do anything ye want with yer damned paper, Sophia. I need ye too much to let it come in the way."

"Caleb!" She gazed at him, thinking she would never send him away again.

"I watched ye tonight to see how important that Weatherford was to ye—"

"Caleb, he wasn't!"

"That I'm glad to hear!"

"Caleb, I'll give up the paper."

His eyes narrowed and he sat up, pulling her up and framing her face with his hands. "Ye'll give up yer paper for me?"

"Yes, because I love you. I need you. Nothing else is important."

"Ahh, lass," he said, his voice rushing out as he leaned forward to kiss her, pushing her back and coming down on top of her.

Later when they were in the big rosewood bed in the upstairs bedroom, while he held her and toyed with her hair, he turned to look at her. "I ordered you a new press from Shreveport."

Stunned, Sophia sat up to look down at him. "You did what?"

"You heard me," he said, amusement lacing his voice. "I started to not tell you when you said you'd give up your paper, but I paid a pretty penny for it."

"I thought you didn't want me to have a paper—"

"Sophia, understand me. I want you. If the only way I'll have you for my wife is to have you printing a damned temperance newspaper, then that's what I want. I ordered you a press."

"Caleb! My heavens, Caleb, I can't believe you would do that. You've opposed everything. My stand on gambling and drinking. A press costs a fortune."

"That I know." He tugged gently on locks of her hair and she looked down at him. "I can't cancel the order now. It's already in Pine Bluff, ready and waiting. I was going to bring it to town on the first run of the train."

"You did that for me," she said softly, feeling a surge of amazement and love that he wanted her so badly. "Caleb, I never thought I'd get married or be so fortunate," she whispered, kissing his shoulder. She ran her hands over him, feeling him hard, aroused again. "Don't ever leave me again," she pleaded.

"Don't send me away," he said gruffly, swinging her down and moving over her to kiss her.

It was almost dawn when she sat up. "Caleb, I don't want to stir scandal now. I can't be seen coming out of your house in daylight after leaving with you last night."

He chuckled and sat up. "Whatever you want, love."

"And we have to have some restraint. We can't have a wedding until Chantal's baby is born. I don't want to go down the aisle big with child."

"I'll write Rafe tomorrow and see when she can travel. You gave me the date of February second. Fortune's still in Virginia, but he expects the army to send him elsewhere soon. He's planning on coming out this way anyway. Now he can come for our wedding."

She gathered up her things and looked around to see him watching her. "You can have the bathroom, Sophia. I've had special plumbing installed and have a well in back and we have running water."

"Caleb, how grand!"

"I built all this for you."

Her heart seemed to swell with love and her good fortune. Her gaze drifted down the length of his lean body. From the waist up, he was coppery; below his waist his skin was paler. He had filled out, looking strong and virile. "Do you have to go back today or can you stay tonight?"

He crossed the room to bend and kiss her throat, brushing her lips with his. "I'll stay tonight. I'll come to your house after dark."

When she dressed, she moved to him. "Will you lace this?"

"Sophia, you're bound up like you're wearing damned armor!" he said, lacing the corset. "I would cheerfully burn this and the hoops and that stiff petticoat you wear. Your drawers as well."

She laughed and turned to face him. "You would prefer to keep me naked as a jaybird!"

"Yes, I would," he said, his gaze lowering to her full breasts. "Don't bother wearing that corset on our wedding day."

"I shall be hopelessly out of fashion."

"I will make up the sacrifice to you in some way," he said in a deep drawl that stirred tingles in her.

She stood on tiptoe to kiss him lightly and then she hurried to dress. When she returned he handed the buttons he had gathered from the floor. "I'm not sorry, although it's a pretty dress."

She took the buttons from his warm hand, kissing him lightly.

He drove her home and went inside with her.

"Mazie should be here anytime now. I'm going to change into a cotton dress, and you can stay and have breakfast with me."

"I want to announce our engagement today."

Sophia stroked his cheek. "I'm so happy, Caleb. I was miserable without you. It was worse in a way than when you were gone in the war."

"I know, love. I hope we never have another big disagreement."

She tucked her head against his throat and smiled. "I suspect, my arrogant husband-to-be, we will have a multitude of small ones."

He chuckled. "I'm afraid I have to agree, because your father raised the most independent woman in all the nation."

"No. I'm not so independent, Caleb. You're just cavalier and stubborn."

"Am I now? If I were so damned cavalier, love, I would have done what I wanted this morning and kept you in my bed all day."

She stood on tiptoe to kiss him and then pulled away, gazing at him solemnly. "I'm back to sewing my wedding dress today. I can't wait." He reached for her and she stepped back, shaking her head. "Caleb, Mazie will be here any minute now."

"I'll help with your buttons. We'll hear her come inside."

Midmorning Caleb entered Will's office and sat down across from him. "I've hired twenty more men. The notice is still posted around town. I want thirty to fifty more if you can get them, but get men who will work. Experienced hands will be better."

"You sound more cheerful today."

"I am. Will, Sophia and I have set a wedding date, the second of February."

"Congratulations! By damn, that's good. So you worked everything out?"

"Yes. I told her I ordered a new press. She said she was about to give up the paper, but now she hasn't said any more about giving it up. I don't care. We'll work around it."

"Good! I'm glad."

"I hope you work your problems out, Will."

"Thanks. Cal, Dunstan's boasting he will have his train ready in two months near the end of January."

"So will we. We're getting more efficient about laying track. We've done better than a mile a day several times now; the men who are laying the train bed are doing a hell of a job through some usually swampy country. We'll make it, Will."

"Keep your guards at night, Cal. I don't trust Trevitt."

"Here are the latest figures," Caleb said, opening a satchel and placing papers on the desk.

"I'll look these over and have copies made and I'll take them to the other investors. Cal, congratulations on your wedding to Sophia. I'm envious."

"You'll work out your disagreement with Amity. The damnable part for me now is so much time away from Sophia. I've got to stay with the train and bring it in. I explained to her and she agreed. My family will all be here for the wedding."

"Including Amity. At least I can show her Memphis

and maybe she won't view it as such a strange, faraway place."

"You need to get to know all her family, Will."

"I'd go call on them again if we weren't so tied to this railroad. Cal, we've got to bring that in ahead of Dunstan. If we do, there'll be other people who will invest with us. I'll have to admit, I want to be first, just to show Father. He didn't think we could ever get this running because of all the problems the Memphis–Little Rock encountered."

"We'll do our best."

As Caleb walked out of Will's building, he ran into Dunstan Trevitt, who gave him a cool look. "So you're back in town."

"Only for a short time."

"We're going to win, O'Brien. There's no way you can beat me. I've got three thousand men working for me."

"We'll see what happens," Caleb said, unable to forget the night he looked in the window and saw Trevitt attack Sophia.

"I'll beat you. I don't ever forget. You got away from me during the war and so did Sophia—but I haven't forgotten."

"Leave her out of this, Trevitt."

Trevitt brushed past him and strode down the street. Caleb felt a tight knot inside. Three thousand men on his crew. He knew it was a big crew, but he hadn't known it was that big. And he still worried about Trevitt and Sophia. He knew he was the only thing standing between her and Dunstan's wrath. When he was halfway across Arkansas would she be safe?

He returned to Will's office and related the incident.

"I know he's your damned brother-in-law—"

"Don't worry. You know how I feel about him. I worry more and more about Hannah Lou. She's not happy with him, yet she won't say a word against him." He tugged at his ear and frowned. "Cal, I hope he doesn't hurt her. She's so quiet." He clamped his lips closed and stared out the window.

"Sorry, Will. I worry about Sophia when I'm away working."

"Just warn her to be careful. She can always send for

me, but she might not have a chance. Sophia can take
care of herself better than most women."

"She can if she can get to her pistol, but if she's unarmed, Dunstan is stronger."

"Get the railroad built and come home," Will urged.

Caleb nodded and left, striding toward the tiny office
where Sophia had her paper. When he stepped inside, she
was bent over the press. She didn't have a bell over the
door and he stood watching her. He had opened the door
quietly and she didn't know anyone was in the room with
her.

"Sophia."

She turned and his breath caught. Wisps of hair had
come unpinned and fallen. She had a smudge of ink on
her face, but the light in her eyes when she looked at him
made desire flame. He reached behind him and turned the
key in the door.

"Caleb, you can't lock the door in the middle of the
day!"

"You're quitting now and going home with me before
I leave for Arkansas. And before we go, we're getting a
bell and I'm putting it over your door. Where's your pistol, Sophia?"

"At home in the drawer."

"When I'm gone, you have it with you every minute."

"What's happened?" she asked as he walked up to her.
She smelled like roses and he wanted to crush her in his
arms.

"I saw Trevitt. He's as big a threat as ever."

She glanced beyond him. "I feel safe when you're
here."

"I'll be a hundred miles away in Arkansas. You carry
a pistol. I'm going to buy a bell for this door now."

He strode to the hardware store and came back. He
stopped at her door and looked up at the door frame
around the oval of glass. Running his fingers along the
door, he bent down.

A blast echoed and the glass door shattered. Caleb
jumped inside, slamming the door. "Get down!"

Sophia stood at her desk, her eyes round. "Caleb!" she
screamed.

Chapter 22

"Stay down!" Caleb snapped again, looking outside. A woman screamed, and a horse pulling a buggy broke into a run.

"What was it, Caleb?"

"I leaned down to look at the door. That shot was for me."

"Great heavens! Why would any—?"

"Because if something happens to me, it would leave our railroad without someone supervising the actual work." He stepped outside, anger pouring over him, looking at the angle of the shot. He gazed at the two-story building across the street.

"Caleb, you think Dunstan Trevitt did this?"

"I'll be back. Close up and go home, Sophia, and keep a pistol handy all the time." He strode away, and she dashed to catch up with him, half running beside him.

"Caleb, where are you going?"

"I'm going to find Trevitt."

"Caleb, wait," she said, tugging on his arm.

He turned to look down at her.

"Please, come back. What can you prove? You aren't even armed."

"I want to see where he is and what he says. You know he shot at me. I'd be dead if I hadn't bent over."

"Then get the sheriff. Don't go after him, please."

"You go on home. I'll come by before I leave town."

"You scare me when you're so angry," she said.

He felt a burning rage, but he smiled and gave her waist a squeeze. "There's never any reason for you to fear me."

"I don't fear what you'll do to me. I'm afraid for what you'll get into."

"Stop worrying. I'll be along soon. You get your pistol."

"All right." She turned away, and he hurried to Trevitt's office. Caleb threw open the door and it slammed against the wall. The secretary stood up, his face becoming pale.

"You can't go in there!" he said, trying to yank open the desk drawer. Caleb strode past him as the man pulled a pistol. He held it with both hands, shaking badly.

"Stop where you are!" he ordered.

Caleb ignored him and kicked open Trevitt's door, sending it slamming against a wall. Trevitt sat behind his desk; two men were seated across from him. Trevitt yanked open his drawer and raised a revolver.

"What do you want?"

"I came to tell you, don't try again, Trevitt!" Caleb snapped, longing to leap across the desk and slug him, yet looking down the muzzle of a gun.

"What the hell are you talking about? Have you gone mad?"

"I knew you'd deny it, but I'm telling you, leave me alone," he said, his words clipped and his voice tight with rage. In front of others he expected Trevitt to deny what he'd done. Trevitt was no fool. Caleb shook with rage, trying to control his temper. He was tempted to call Trevitt out and be done with worrying about him, but he had sworn he wouldn't resort to using a gun again.

"Leave you alone?"

"You just shot at me. And I know the reason."

"The hell you say! I didn't shoot at you. Ask! We've been here talking for the past half hour. Harley? Matthew?"

"Save your breath," Caleb said in disgust without glancing at them. "You're his friends. I know what you'll say. I'm just warning you."

"You have other enemies, O'Brien."

Caleb looked into Dunstan's cold eyes and felt the hatred surge between them. He walked out, striding back to Sophia's and across her porch.

When he came through the door, she threw herself into his arms. "I've been so worried!"

"Shhh. You didn't need to worry. It's *you* we need to worry about. I'll be with my crew. You keep that revolver with you all the time and you sleep with it and lock this house."

She nodded and stood on tiptoe, pulling his head down. He held her tightly, wanting the months to pass, wanting her to be his wife. Finally he released her.

"I have to go. Otherwise I'll miss the ferry and I need to get back to my crew before sundown. Promise me you'll be careful."

"I promise."

"Want to go to the ferry with me?"

"Yes. Let me get my bonnet."

At the dock he kissed her goodbye and stepped aboard the Mound City ferry for Hopefield across the river where he would climb on board his Memphis & Arkansas engine to join his crews. He gazed across the river at the bluffs and town. Would Sophia carry the pistol? Would it be enough protection? His thoughts shifted; would he beat Trevitt and get his line running first? Trevitt tried to kill him today. When would he try again?

Caleb and Darcy came home for Christmas. Midmorning on December twenty-six, a telegram arrived. Caleb's green eyes sparkled as he read it and swung Sophia up in the air.

"Chantal and Rafe have a boy named Jared Shaughnessy O'Brien! That means they can be here when I bring in the train and they can stay for the wedding!"

"If she feels like traveling, Caleb. And the baby—you don't know how he is."

"From the telegram it sound as if he's fine. Seven pounds. Blessings on little Jared Shaughnessy for arriving and fitting in with our plans."

"That's shameful! Wanting a little baby to fit in with your train plans."

"And wedding plans," he said, hugging her. "Lord, let me tell Darcy." He went to the parlor door while Sophia sat down to continue sewing. "Darcy, come in here!" he called and in a minute Darcy appeared. Sophia was amazed at the change in him since he had ridden away in September with Caleb to work with the train crew. He had been a gangly, awkward boy. Now he was lean, taller, his skin bronze, and he had an air of confidence about him he hadn't had before.

"What is it, Cal?"

Caleb waved the telegram. "We're uncles again," he said. "Chantal had a seven-pound baby boy!"

"Hallelujah! A boy!"

"Darcy O'Brien! You know how much you love Daniella," Sophia teased, and he grinned.

"We need a boy in the next generation of O'Briens."

"Jared Shaughnessy O'Brien," Caleb said, moving to a table to pick up a decanter of brandy. "We'll have a toast, and you have to join us, Sophia."

She smiled at him, thinking how much he had changed her. She reached for the glass of brandy, the thin gold chain on her arm catching the light. She gazed at it, feeling happy. Caleb had it made for her Christmas gift from him, and she loved it.

"To our new nephew, Jared Shaughnessy. May he have a heap of blessings and someday get to see Ireland."

They drank and Sophia coughed, wondering how long it took to get accustomed to brandy.

"I'll be back in a few hours," Darcy said, walking to the door.

"Where are you going?" Caleb asked.

"To see Miss Driscoll," he answered and was gone. The front door closed and Caleb moved to the window to watch Darcy.

"He's grown up, Sophia. I wanted to build a home and give him stability and a family and instead, I fought in a war four years and he grew up while I was gone."

"He's fine," she said, setting aside the sewing and crossing the room to put her arm around Caleb's waist. "He's had three families who love him, you and the Therries and Chantal and Rafe. He's had the love of all of you."

"He's doing well at work. I've been surprised at what he can do."

"Why should you be? He's an O'Brien."

He looked down at her and smiled, wrapping his arms around her. "Come here, love. I have one more present for you and I haven't had a chance to give it to you. I got it the last time I was in New Orleans."

He led her to his bedroom and removed something from a drawer tied in blue silk ribbon. He handed it to her.

It was silk and she untied the ribbon, shaking out a gown of pale blue silk.

"Caleb, this is . . ." her voice trailed off.

"It's a wedding gift. It's a gown to replace your white cotton," he said, his voice husky.

"Caleb, this is . . . shocking."

"You won't wear it for a long time either," he said, taking it from her and dropping it on a chair as he pulled her to him. "I go back to Arkansas tomorrow morning and we're alone for a few hours, Sophia. It's been so long," he whispered, bending his head to kiss her, his hands moving to her buttons to free her breasts.

He took his time, kissing and caressing her with sweet torment, building a fire between them that made her quiver with longing.

Later he held her close against him and she dreaded his going, knowing he was in the last stages of the struggle to get to Stuttgart.

"Sophia, do you still have your pistol with you all the time?"

"I don't recall," she said, amused, running her hand over his thigh. "Let me see . . ."

He caught her hand and raised up to look down at her. "Keep the pistol where you can get it any time. If we win and the Memphis & Arkansas comes in first, Trevitt may try anything to get even. Or if he thinks we might win, he may do something."

"You be careful. You're the one he tried to kill."

Caleb leaned down to kiss her and she wrapped her arms around him, holding him and feeling a rush of joy that she had his love. "Caleb, when you were sick and asleep, I liked to touch you."

His eyes twinkled, and he looked at her. "I know you did."

"How did you know?" she asked, startled.

"I wasn't always sound asleep. I could feel your hands."

"You're just saying that. I don't believe you for a second."

He kissed her throat. "It doesn't matter now and I never, ever objected, love."

"You didn't know. It takes only a breath to—"

"To what?" he asked, arching his eyebrow.

"To get you stirred up," she answered, blushing. "If you had known what I was doing, you would have responded."

He chuckled. "I knew, Sophia, on a couple of occasions. And I watched you sleeping in the rocking chair and you looked beautiful."

"You thought I looked beautiful?"

"Of course, I did."

She gazed up at him. "I love you. Please be careful when you go back to Arkansas."

"I will. You do the same," he said as his arm tightened around her.

January second, one month from his wedding date. Only three weeks away until January twenty, the date Dunstan set for his first official M&S run and celebration. Caleb stared at the track being put in place in the flaring light of lanterns. They were working around the clock now, and he was praying they could finish and take the train from Stuttgart to Hopefield on the nineteenth of January. One day before Dunstan. That was cutting the time to the minute, but it was the best he could hope to do. He had a man watching Dunstan's crew and Tom was supposed to report to him any indication the Memphis & Springfield would be ready sooner than the twentieth.

Caleb strode along the line, looking at the men working, knowing he couldn't have a better crew. Even Drake Sweeney cooperated and worked as hard as anyone. Will wiped his brow and crossed to Caleb. "I ache from my head to my toe."

"You aren't accustomed to this."

"I'm not very good either. The others can work rings around me."

"You'll catch on," Caleb reassured. "We need every hand we can get. The closer we get to time, the more nervous I get. Dunstan's a dirty fighter, and he's left us alone."

"He thinks he'll win easily. Why should he jeopardize that by running risks of getting caught doing something to you?"

"He's tried to kill me and because of chance, he failed. And I worry constantly about Sophia."

"She has her revolver."

"In my last letter Sophia said she mailed all the invitations." Caleb thought of the fancy invitations to investors and close friends to join in the first ride and celebration party afterward. He had left all the plans to Sophia for the party. "Will, I dream about it. We put the nineteenth on the invitation, so I hope it works out. We'll leave Hopefield on the Memphis and Arkansas. Then it'll be after we see Heaton's man in Stuttgart and we turn around to come back that the race will be on to beat Dunstan to Hopefield."

"Have you heard how many have accepted the invitations?"

"Not yet, but I expect a trainload of people. There'll be seven O'Briens."

"My parents can't participate. It's brother against brother-in-law. God, I wish she hadn't married him! And now I think she wishes she hadn't, too."

"Has she ever said anything?"

"No. But if I learn he's hurting her, I'll call him out."

"I'll gladly be a second."

Will turned back to shoveling granite, and Caleb stared at him, thinking of all he had been through with Will and now here was Will working as hard as he could all through the night to get the railroad going.

On the eighth of January, Will left to return to Memphis. They had eleven days to lay the last nineteen miles of track and then they would be ready. Caleb felt the tension mounting every day now.

On the thirteenth Will returned, riding out in the Memphis & Arkansas engine. He jumped down and ran toward Caleb, who caught his breath at the look of worry on Will's face. He strode to meet him, clenching his fists, suddenly feeling cold.

"Is Sophia all right?" Caleb asked.

"She's fine. It's rained up north of here. Word is that a bridge has washed out on Dunstan's line. We don't know how long it'll take him to get it repaired."

Caleb felt a surge of elation. "By damn, we'll win!" As swiftly as elation came, it changed and he looked at Will and sobered. "Dunstan will try to stop us."

"We can't guard over one hundred miles of track. You saw what was done to tracks and trains in the war. All of us know how to put one out of commission."

"Damnation." Caleb felt a knot of worry grow. He looked down the line at the torches flickering in the night and the men working. "We can put guards on every bridge. The bridges will be the most vulnerable. I'll have men ride the track. They can each take ten miles."

"It won't stop Dunstan if he wants to do something."

"We can try."

"Sophia sent you a letter," Will said, handing it to Caleb.

"Why didn't you say so!" Caleb took it and Will grinned.

"Got any brandy here?"

"Come back to my tent." He led the way and stopped by a torch. "Go on, Will. Help yourself. I'll be right along."

He unfolded the paper, catching a scent of roses and feeling a pang of longing for her.

"My dearest Caleb: I've received a telegram from Rafferty. They arrive in Memphis by boat on January sixteenth. He said the Therries and Fortune will be with him. Fortune will go first to New Orleans for a few days, then come to Memphis with the other O'Briens. So many O'Briens and Therries—perhaps they will make up for only one Merrick. I'm so happy to be marrying into a large family. I miss you dreadfully and am counting the hours. We have only five regrets to the invitations. You'll have a train filled with well-wishers.

My love, Sophia."

He gazed into the darkness to the east; his precious Sophia was only a hundred miles away. Seeing Will standing in front of the tent with the bottle of brandy, Caleb folded the letter.

"I'll appoint men to guard tonight. Thanks for coming all the way out here. Sophia said the Therries will arrive on the sixteenth."

"I know. I had a letter from Amity. I hope I can convince her that Memphis is a wonderful place to live. Thank heavens she likes Sophia so well, but I'm afraid Hannah Lou won't be a help."

"I wish you luck, Will. Amity is a wonderful person."

"Between planning a railroad celebration and a wedding, I don't know how Sophia has time to get out the *Weekly*."

"She'll manage. Mazie is having more fun than anyone. She's been waiting since Sophia was seventeen for this wedding. I'll come to town the sixteenth when everyone arrives. Or sooner if we get finished early here. God, I hope we make it, Will."

"We stand a chance now. I didn't think there was a hope in hell before."

"I did," Caleb exclaimed.

"You're stubborn enough to keep swimming when you're in the middle of the ocean. I can imagine how you survived that shipwreck. You and the other O'Briens."

"One of us didn't."

"Why are you sleeping in this tent? We could hitch up the private car at Hopefield and bring it out here for your quarters. It has all the comforts of home."

"I'm asking the men to work under tough conditions," Caleb explained. "I'll not climb into an elegant private train car and go to bed at night while crews are straining every muscle."

"I suppose you're right, but this tent reminds me of the war and I'd hate it."

"I think of the million from Willard Heaton."

"He's enough of a scoundrel to say he changed his mind to the winner."

"No, he'll want to invest in a winner. And we can get the money elsewhere. The eyes of all Memphians are on Dunstan and us. The man who wins this race will win more than Willard Heaton's money."

"That's right. Just be careful you don't lose everything. Now Dunstan's backed into a corner."

"Take my cot, Will. I'm going back to work."

"I'll join you," Will said, pulling on leather gauntlets. "If I'd known I was going to do this, I wouldn't have had the brandy."

"It'll keep you warm and it'll keep you going," Caleb said as they headed back to the crews. Caleb felt a deep-running uneasiness; Dunstan Trevitt wouldn't give up without a fight.

Dunstan Trevitt leaned back in his chair. He felt a knot of tension between his shoulders and he wanted to smash something, to take out his frustration somewhere. "O'Brien is going to contact all the people he invited and cancel. He'll take a small crew on the first run and be ready for trouble and he's posting guards at his bridges."

"That's definite?" Dunstan asked. He sat in a large tent and gazed up at the man in front of him, looking at beefy shoulders and a thick neck.

The man shrugged. "That's what he said yesterday."

"And you'll be on the train?"

"Yes. He doesn't suspect any disloyalty."

"Lord knows, I've paid you a fortune to get your loy-alty. If I win the race, you'll not only get what I prom-ised," Dunstan lowered his voice, "I'll give you another ten thousand bonus and a parcel of land in Kentucky."

"Want me out of your life, don't you?" the man said slyly.

"It's a good reward. I don't want anyone able to prove anything."

"For what you're paying me, you're safe, Major. I've worked my ass to the bone to win his confidence, but I want to have him to myself for a few minutes."

"You can. Do this right, and we'll all be happy. Sit down and listen and I'll tell you what I want you to do."

The man hooked a chair with his toe and sat down, looking at Dunstan with cold pale eyes and Dunstan felt a shiver. He was taking a giant risk, stepping over the lines of the law, but the money was worth it. He would win the million and the attention and get rid of Caleb O'Brien at once. And then he would take care of Sophia Merrick. That would be a pleasure and no risk where she was concerned.

"Here's a map. Here's where I want you to move," Dunstan said, pointing at the paper, trying to pull his thoughts away from Sophia.

Sophia stood on the wharf and watched passengers step down from the stern-wheeler. Waving, she spotted Rafferty's head above the crowd. He wore a broad-brimmed black hat and Ormonde Therrie appeared beside him. Eager to see them after so many months, she hurried toward them. The family was already on the dock with Chantal looking radiant in a deep rose velvet dress and Jared in her arms.

Daniella stood beside Amity, holding Amity's hand. Three-year-old Daniella was a beautiful child with Rafferty's dark hair and Chantal's fair skin and pink cheeks. She gazed around with wide, solemn black eyes.

"Chantal! Rafferty!" Sophia called, hurrying toward them, motioning to Milo, Caleb's servant, to follow her.

Sophia hugged them and knelt down to hug Daniella who smelled like lavender.

"Daniella, this is your Aunt Sophia," Chantal said.

Rafferty swung the child up in his arms. "And where's my wayward brother?"

"He's still in Arkansas, and I'm not sure when he'll get here. Darcy will be with him."

"How's Cal doing?" Rafferty asked.

"Dunstan's had trouble, and it looks as if Caleb will win the race."

Rafferty grinned. "My little brother. I'm proud of him."

In his blue uniform, Fortune, now a major, looking tall and solemn, walked to Sophia and hugged her. "The last time I saw you was on a dark road during a war." He smiled at her. "I'm glad you'll be an O'Brien."

"Thank you, Major."

"It's Fortune, Sophia. You'll be my sister-in-law."

"I have carriages and a wagon for the baggage." Fortune took her arm and as soon as she showed him the carriages lined in front of the depot, he took charge of the luggage while Rafe directed the family. She climbed into the first buggy, looking at the tall O'Brien men and missing Caleb, wondering when he would come home.

That night as they sat in the parlor after dinner, Fortune told about his stay in Virginia. "I expect to be moved in a few months. With Andrew Johnson's pardons and amnesty and the Radical Republicans wanting Reconstruction of the South, things are uncertain. I've asked for Georgia."

The back door banged and Sophia's pulse jumped. She heard the scrape of boots and Caleb and Darcy entered the room. She was so thankful to see him, it was an effort to keep from crying his name and running to him. His boots and pants were muddy to the knees. Dark stubble showed on his jaw; none of it mattered, because she couldn't take her eyes from him. His gaze met hers and he looked at her a moment, before glancing at his family. They all surged forward to greet him and Darcy. As he kissed Amity's cheek, he said, "Will Stanton will be here on the nineteenth. He stayed while I came home."

Amity's eyes sparkled, and Sophia hoped they could work out their differences. Finally Caleb said, "We have to clean so we can hug everyone and I can hold my new nephew and Daniella."

"You'll not wake them up tonight!" Rafe said, laughing.

"Then I'll have Sophia go with me while I take a peek at them. We'll be back." He caught her hand, and Darcy joined them as they left the parlor.

"Show us the babes and then we'll wash. Darcy, you can go first."

"Have you eaten?" she asked.

"Not this year," Darcy answered.

"He probably ate an hour ago," Caleb added dryly. "I think he's hollow."

"You know there's plenty of food and Mazie has been over here all day cooking along with Adia."

Sophia placed her finger on her lips and opened the door to the room where Daniella was asleep. She lay with her dark lashes on her cheek, her mouth a rosebud, and a rag doll in her arms.

"She's grown just since I last saw her," Darcy said with wonder.

"She's a beauty," Caleb added. "Now where's my nephew?"

Sophia led him to Rafferty and Chantal's bedroom and they tiptoed to the cradle where the baby lay with his fists tightly knotted.

"Lord, look at the black hair," Caleb said, bending down.

"Caleb, you're muddy and he's asleep."

"Sure and you think I'll not be holding my new nephew," he said. "He looks like his papa and Darcy."

The baby stirred as Caleb cradled him in his arms, and Sophia felt a pang seeing the look on Caleb's face. He wanted children and she did, too. He held the baby against him, slightly rocking him while Darcy leaned over them.

"I'll go wash, Cal," Darcy said and tiptoed from the room. As soon as they were alone, Caleb looked at her and she felt the heat start that could melt her with passion as she gazed back at him. He lowered the baby to the cradle.

"He's a fine one."

"And now he's muddy," she whispered, wiping a smudge off Jared's soft cheek.

"He'll wash. Babies were meant to be loved." He took her hand and led her to his room, closing the door.

"Caleb, you'll get me muddy."

He paused and yanked off his shirt. "Your face will wash, love," he said huskily, tugging away his boots and pants.

"Caleb, I can't stay up here! I have to go back down-stairs."

"Sophia," he said in a gravelly voice. With a moan, she ran her hands over his chest and slid her arms around him as he hugged her hard, bending his head to kiss her. She felt his arousal and ached for him, knowing they wouldn't have time alone now or anytime before the wedding.

In minutes a knock came. "I'm through washing," Darcy called. "Your turn."

Caleb released her and she looked at him as she stepped back, feeling her cheeks flush, yet relishing his maleness, wanting to caress him.

"Caleb, thank heaven the wedding is soon," she said. "I must go now." She slipped out of the room quickly, pausing in the hall to straighten her clothes.

When he joined them in the parlor, Caleb looked handsome in a fresh white linen shirt and black trousers that fit his slim hips snugly. She gazed at him, longing to be in his arms tonight, knowing it was impossible. Amity and Ormonde were staying at her house and soon they would have to leave.

When they told the others good night, Caleb and Rafferty rode along to accompany them home. Rafe waited in the carriage while Caleb and Ormonde carried baggage inside and then Caleb was alone with her at the back door.

Caleb pulled her to him, bending his head to kiss her deeply, finally releasing her. "Rafe's waiting. I'll see you in the morning, love."

As Caleb's house grew quiet, he sat in the parlor with Rafe and Fortune and Darcy. "We're finally all together," Rafe said, looking at them with satisfaction. "Eight years since the night at sea and a war in between." He looked at Caleb and his expression sobered. "How's the race?"

"I wanted to talk to all of you about it. Darcy knows my plans. I have a man working in Trevitt's camp and he's heard rumors. He doesn't know the details because he's not privy to Trevitt's confidence, but Trevitt intends to stop our train on the nineteenth."

"How do you think he'll do it?" Fortune asked.

"I can only guess. There are three big bridges we cross, twice over the St. Francis River and another over the

White River. If I had to stop a train, that's where I would do it."

"You know this, so what do you plan to do?" Rafe asked quietly.

"First, I don't want Sophia to know about it. She is accustomed to fending for herself and doing things and I don't want her involved."

Rafe grinned and brushed lint off his knee. "It seems the O'Briens must be drawn to feisty women. Darcy, remember to fall in love with someone who is quiet and shy."

"I'm not sure that's a guarantee," Caleb added dryly.

"All right, what do you plan to do?" Rafe asked, his voice becoming solemn again.

"Tomorrow I want to notify everyone that it'll be a skeleton crew on the train and the party with friends and investors will be here at my house on the twenty-first. I'll have the servants notify the people we've invited, and I'll talk to the big investors tomorrow. I'll leave town the next morning to make the run to Stuttgart, and the morning of the nineteenth, I'll bring in the M and A."

"Fine," Fortune said. "We'll be your skeleton crew on your train."

"I have an engineer who'll drive the train, Jonah McClanahan. He fought for the Confederacy and he knows how to shoot. I have six men—all veterans—to ride the train. I want Darcy and five men at the depot in Hopefield. I have a crew of four with Will at the first bridge over the St. Francis. I have another crew of four over the other big bridges, two men at each small crossing."

"Where do you want us?"

"Fortune, will you stay with Darcy at Hopefield?"

"If that's what you want."

"I'll go with you on the train," Rafe said.

"I have six men and they're good shots. It would ease my mind more if you'd stay here and see that Sophia's safe. Trevitt has promised her he would get his revenge for when she stabbed him. I don't think he's given up."

"I'd like to be on the train, but I'll do what you want."

"I don't want to worry about her safety," Caleb said,

also wanting to avoid placing his brothers on the train where he expected the most trouble. "Only a few more days. What's going to be difficult, is telling Sophia."

"I want to be with you on that train, Caleb O'Brien! I want to write the story about the M and A's first run. All Tennessee and the surrounding areas are waiting to hear about this race. This will be the biggest story I'll ever write."

"No. It's too dangerous."

"Then don't you go. I don't want to lose you now after I waited through a whole war."

Caleb shifted on the buggy seat behind his carriage house. He had known what a storm he would cause, but there was no way to avoid telling Sophia that they were changing the party and the train trip with guests. Her cheeks were pink, her blue eyes full of sparks. Even though she was angry, she looked beautiful in her deep blue taffeta dress that was tucked into her tiny waist and flared over her full breasts.

"I'll have a whole crew of tough war veterans who can shoot a bug at a hundred paces. I'll be safe."

"Take your brothers with you," she insisted.

"No. I need Darcy and Fortune to guard the depot across the river. I want Rafe here with the family. He has two children; I wouldn't do anything to jeopardize him."

"You're leaving him here to guard me!"

He wanted to kiss her to end the argument, but the family was inside waiting for them, and Sophia would be embarrassed over being wrinkled and mussed.

"I'm leaving him here, because someone needs to be here who can protect this family. Trevitt is capable of anything."

"He isn't going to ignore the train and attack a house-ful of women."

"If he gets you, he can get me, and he knows it," Caleb said, trying to be patient.

"I want to go with you. Caleb, don't take this story away from me," she pleaded.

"You and that paper! Sophia, you're not going to endanger your life for a story. I'll tell you about the ride."

"I want to experience it firsthand, not hear about it from you."

"You're beautiful even when you argue. I suppose that's why I fell in love with you," he said, brushing her cheek with a kiss.

"You're trying to coax me out of this."

"Of course not." He stroked her cheek. "You take care of your office and get ready for your new press. You'll have to hire someone for this one, because it's bigger than your first." He climbed down and reached for her. "We have to go inside."

"You're trying to evade the matter."

"You're in charge of the party here. Here you stay. I won't have you on that train, Sophia, if I have to lock you in the house."

She gazed up at him and he saw the stubborn lift of her chin, yet whether they clashed or agreed, he wanted her and loved her wildly. "Only days now, love, until our wedding," he said softly.

She inhaled deeply and he took her arm and they went to the house. He held the door and reminded himself to talk to Rafe and make certain he knew where Sophia was and didn't let her out of his sight until the ferry was gone from Memphis. If she risked going to Shiloh for a story, she wouldn't hesitate to try to get on the M&A.

Worried about Caleb's safety, Sophia kissed him goodbye. He held her close. "I never thought I'd get married. Papa planned things and told us what we would do years ahead. He didn't foresee a war, though, that would kill his sons and bring you into my life."

"I suppose I have to be glad you were foolhardy enough to go to Shiloh," he whispered, kissing her throat, his lips warm, the slight stubble on his jaw tickling her.

"Some men said it was brave," she said playfully.

"They're trying to charm you, Sophia, but if they only knew how you—" he kissed her mouth lightly—"turn a man's life inside out—"

"Caleb—" He kissed her and silenced her reply.

"Good night, love. I'll be careful and I'll be safe tomorrow," he promised.

As Sophia climbed into bed, she thought about all she

had to do for the party. She needed to check again with
the musicians. Tomorrow morning she was going with the
O'Briens and Therries to call on Will and his parents. She
wanted to be on the train with Caleb, and if it was as safe
as he said, there was no reason to keep her away. Which
was exactly why Rafferty was staying in Memphis. The
first run of the M&A might be her last big story, because
she was going to sell the paper as a surprise for Caleb.
She would do anything to get that story.

Rafe called on her early in the morning, eating breakfast at her house.

"It's amazing how much you and Fortune and Darcy
resemble each other and Caleb doesn't look very much
like any of you."

"It's difficult for me to see that we look alike. This is
a nice tribute to Caleb and the Memphis and Arkansas
line," Rafe said, looking at her newspaper.

"I haven't told him, but I'm giving up the newspaper."

Rafe looked up, his blue eyes keen. "That should
please him."

"I don't feel the same about it that I used to and my
ideas have changed so much from Papa's teachings. My
father was a strict man and he opposed the railroads."

Rafe smiled. "And now you don't. We change as we
age. Lord knows, I never thought I'd be sitting in Memphis, expecting my brother to bring in a train on its first
official run. Cal always seemed so carefree and unsettled.
He's changed."

"So have I, thanks to an O'Brien."

Amity swept into the room looking lovely in a rose
velvet dress. "How do I look?"

"Beautiful as always," Rafe said, looking amused.

"I'm so scared at seeing Will's parents when he won't
be there."

"You've already met them and the Stantons are nice,"
Sophia said. "And Rafe and your father are going with
us. There's nothing to fear. If you two will excuse me
now, I'll change."

She hurried to her room where she changed swiftly to
boy's pants and a white cotton shirt Caleb had left behind. She pulled on a jacket. She looped and pinned her

hair up under one of Caleb's hats and yanked on boots, pausing to look at herself. If Caleb saw her, he wouldn't recognize her. At a cursory glance, most people would take her for a boy. She pocketed her derringer.

Climbing out the window, Sophia ran across the neighbor's yard to the end of the block where she had a horse saddled.

Her heart pounded, because Rafe would follow Caleb's wishes completely. All of Rafe's polite courtesy would vanish if he caught her. She mounted and urged the horse forward.

Her heart pounded, and her palms were damp as she rode cautiously through town. She didn't know where Caleb was, and she could meet him at any turn or on the ferry. She prayed he wasn't standing at the rail watching the crowd.

The ferry was within minutes of leaving. A blast came from its whistle and she wanted to urge the horse to a gallop, but that would attract attention.

She hitched the horse to a post and paid a livery attendant, and then rushed toward the ferry. She fought the urge to look over her shoulder; she could imagine Caleb coming after her. Her gaze swept the passengers and to her relief, she didn't spot a head of dark brown curls or his wide-brimmed black hat.

She rushed on board and moved around, trying to find a place that would be inconspicuous and finally crowding in with a family of three boys who stood at the rail.

And then they were underway and she was terrified to look around for Caleb. He was somewhere on the same ferry, maybe only feet away. She gazed at the muddy river, watching water swirl. Memphis receded and she had a moment of trepidation for deceiving Rafferty by slipping away, but she desperately wanted this exclusive story that all of Tennessee would read.

When the ferry slowed and stopped, she turned. As passengers disembarked, she scanned the crowd, her heart skipping when she spotted him.

Caleb went ashore, and in seconds she followed, taking care to keep a distance. He didn't look back and soon they were in sight of the depot. A crowd of well-wishers had gathered and milled around the train. Caleb entered the depot and she skirted around, mingling with the crowd until she could climb on board.

The train was empty and she ran through the passenger car with its ornate, overstuffed wine-colored plush seats. In the corner of the baggage car she spotted a big crate covered with canvas. It was her new press. With her heart pounding, she ran to squeeze behind it. Tugging on the canvas, she pulled it to one side of the crate so it hung down and covered her.

In minutes the door opened. "We'll leave in five more minutes. Just make certain everything is secure," Caleb said.

"Yes, sir."

She held her breath, hearing the man moving around the car and then the door opened and closed and he was gone. Her legs became cramped, but she was afraid to move. The car lurched and shifted and they were moving, the wheels clicking over the rails, picking up speed.

She leaned against the wall and rode, knowing with every mile she would be safe from Caleb sending her back to Memphis. She felt an urgency to be with him and she would get her story.

Wearing a gun for the first time since the war, Caleb sat in the engine, gazing at the countryside flash past. It was three minutes between mileposts now, so they were up to twenty miles per hour, making good time.

The second hour out of Memphis as they approached the first trestle bridge over the St. Francis, Jas Hardwick stood by the track waving his hands. According to plan, Jas was a mile from the bridge. His wave was the all-clear signal to proceed. When they swept over the trestle, Will was at the end and he waved as they rushed past.

Caleb felt restless, wondering when Dunstan would move. He motioned to the engineer and strode back through the cars, wind buffeting him as he passed between them and stepped inside the next car, muffling out the constant clack of the wheels on the rails as the door shut. He moved with the sway of the car, nodding to Drake Sweeney who sat at a window with a rifle in hand.

In the next car Caleb nodded to Sean O'Keefe. He entered the baggage car and Mike O'Malley turned around.

"You checked everything in here last night?"

"Yes, sir. The press, the boxes of goods. I went over all of it last night and Hannibal stayed on guard until I came at six this morning."

Caleb nodded and went on to the next car, but something nagged at him. He spoke to each of the men, Hannibal Barbano riding on the platform behind the last car. "Any sign of trouble?"

"No, sir. Nothing. Maybe there won't be any."

"There will be. We have to get to Stuttgart and back to Hopefield."

He walked back through the train, moving with the swaying motion of the car. He passed through the baggage car and O'Malley was gone. Caleb glanced at the press, the trunks and boxes and crates. He went on to the next car, but the nagging feeling remained. He was almost back to the engine when he realized what bothered him. The baggage car smelled like tea roses.

He frowned and stared out the window at the landscape without seeing it. He looked over his shoulder and went back to the baggage car. He opened the door and stepped inside and stood quietly looking at the crates. The train swayed, the rhythmic clack of the wheels muffled with the door closed. He inhaled and looked at the stack of trunks, walking to squeeze against them and look around them. He moved to a stack of crates and did the same. He walked to the press and moved around it, looking at the canvas draped over it and over something between the crate and the wall and his heart thudded.

He reached down and yanked up the canvas.

Chapter 23

"Damnation, Sophia!" He hauled her to her feet.

Sophia gazed into furious green eyes. "Don't be angry with your brother. He didn't know."

"Hellfire! It's not Rafe who I'm angry with! You and your damned reporting!"

"I'm here now, sweetie," she said, smiling at him.

"How the hell did you get here?" he demanded.

"Stop swearing at me. I came on the ferry at the same time you did."

"Oh, Lord, no!" He closed his eyes and opened them. "I should have known. I should have watched. Sophia, I could just shake you until your teeth rattle."

She smiled at him and leaned forward to kiss him on the mouth. "My sweet. You always want to shake me and we always end up doing other things," she said provocatively.

"Confound it, don't try to soft-soap me, Sophia." He glared at her.

"I'm here. You can't put me off," she insisted.

"I'd like to put you across my knee."

She laughed. "Caleb," she said coaxingly. "Forgive me."

"Damnation! I should have locked you up and given Rafe the key!"

"Stop swearing."

"You'd make a saint swear."

"There's not one thing you can do about my being here," she said petulantly. She stared back at him, biting her lip to keep from smiling. He looked fierce and angry but she knew he would get over it in minutes.

"If I don't get away from you, I will shake you." He

spun around and pointed his finger at her. "At Stuttgart, you're going off this train."

"You're going to leave me alone in Arkansas where Dunstan can find me and I won't have any protection?" she asked sweetly.

"You're enjoying yourself." He ran his fingers through his curls. "You come ride up in front where I can watch you all the time. If shooting starts, get down."

"You know if shooting starts, I'll help."

He caught her up to him. "You get down," he said in clipped words. "What do you think I would do if you were hit?"

"What do you think I would do if you are?" she shot back.

"Lord, sometimes I wish I had never fought at Shiloh. Sophia, you have been trouble since that first moment."

"But it's trouble you like," she argued, gazing up at him. Caleb looked down at her. He was angry, terrified for her safety.

"I'm going to punch my brother when I get back to Memphis. He was supposed to watch you."

"I told him I was going to change clothes to go with Amity to the Stantons', so don't be angry, because you know he wasn't going to watch me change. Rafferty and Amity were both waiting in the other room and Mister Therrie and Chantal were waiting for us, and the Stantons expected all of us. So don't blame him. I went out a window."

Caleb glared at her and wondered if the rest of his life would be stormy because of her. "I'm going to tell Darcy to marry a woman who is docile and obedient and scared of him."

Sophia ducked her head against Caleb, sliding her slender arms around his waist. He drew a deep breath and wrapped his arm around her. "Damn, I'll be scared now for you. I couldn't have fought a war with you at my side."

"Then let me stay back here in this part of the train."

"No, you don't." He took her hand and started toward the door, pausing to look down at her. "You're on this train, but you damned well better do what I say now. If I tell you to get down, you get down."

"Yes, sir."

"Sophia!" he snapped, knowing she was happy to be with him, his temper strained. He didn't want her in danger. Now he had to worry about her as well as the train. He strode forward through the next car with Sophia in tow and saw the startled look on O'Keefe's face and in the next car, the same surprise from Sweeney. Caleb didn't give an explanation. He took her forward to the engine and pointed to a stool. "You sit down there."

She sat, suddenly looking subdued. Jonah glanced at her. "Miss Merrick?" He frowned and looked at Caleb questioningly, his thick black brows arched.

"She slipped on board this morning and was in the baggage car."

Jonah shook his head and frowned.

Caleb looked at her. "At Stuttgart, I'm paying someone to stay with you and you are getting off this train. I've got four more of my men waiting there who were going to ride back with us, but two of them will stay with you."

"Caleb, you can't leave me in Stuttgart."

"Oh, yes, I can. After the first official run into Hopefield, we'll be safe. I'll come back and get you, Sophia." He gazed outside, feeling a mounting uneasiness. Sophia unsettled him and he was worried. Trouble would come, but he didn't know when.

In Stuttgart, he could ask the sheriff to keep her under lock until he could get back. He would pay and it would be worth it to know she was safe. He watched trees flash past. Would she be safe there without friends or family? he wondered. He looked down at her and felt anger and fear. Rafferty O'Brien would hear about letting her get away. Caleb wanted to swear and shake her. The door opened and Drake Sweeney and Sean entered, Sean's gaze going to Caleb and Caleb knew something was wrong.

Drake swung up his rifle, pointing at Sophia. "All of you drop your weapons now. Slow this train or she gets the first shot."

Feeling shock, Caleb dropped his pistol, staring at Drake Sweeney who had worked as hard for him and since the fight with Darcy, had been as cooperative as any other worker. Sophia placed her revolver on the floor and

Sweeney yanked one from a holster belonging to Jonah. The train slowed, the wheels screeching on the rails as they lost momentum. Sweeney motioned to Sean. "Get off now," he yelled.

"Jump?"

"Now!" Sweeney raised the rifle and Sean disappeared out of the car. Caleb saw him rolling away from the train, tumbling on the ground. One of his men was safe.

"Where's the rest of my crew?" Caleb asked.

"Either dead or I let them escape back down the line," Sweeney answered flatly. "I'm the only one they can identify and I ain't going back to Memphis."

"Why are you doing this, Sweeney?"

"I sold to the highest bidder. For what I'm getting paid today, Mister O'Brien, I'll be a wealthy man."

Caleb looked outside and saw the riders appear in view and he felt a tight knot in his chest. He had handpicked his men; men he felt he could trust, men who could fight and shoot. Instead, he had played into Trevitt's hands. And Sophia was with him. It made his blood run cold and his mind raced. Sweeney stood with his rifle aimed at her heart and Caleb couldn't take the chance. Sweeney was an experienced fighter. He stood out of reach, his back protected by machinery, his gaze constantly shifting from one to the other.

"Now one at a time," Sweeney said, yanking Sophia to him. "Keep your hands high and get out. Jonah first."

Jonah emerged from the train and a shot rang out. He crumpled on the ground. Sweeney nudged Caleb as Sophia cried out and knelt by Jonah.

"You bastards!" Caleb snapped, looking down at Jonah's still body.

"Move! Get her up or I will," Sweeney ordered and Caleb took Sophia's arm. They stepped through high grass. Dunstan Trevitt dismounted and came forward. Other men held guns pointed at Caleb.

"Well, well," Trevitt said softly, smiling broadly. "Little Sophia. I didn't expect this. I just thought I'd get my rival, Major O'Brien, the Secesh raider. But this is a pleasure. Had to take her along with you, didn't you, Reb?"

"What are you going to do with us?" Caleb asked.

"This changes my plans," Dunstan said. "You lose. I know that, Rebel. That train of yours won't make it back to Hopefield.

"Tie them," Dunstan said, and a man stepped forward, tying Caleb while three men kept their rifles aimed at Sophia. Next they tied her wrists in front of her.

"I'll sign the whole line over to you if you'll let her go," Caleb said firmly.

"No!" Sophia exclaimed, looking at him. He didn't look at her or shift his gaze from Dunstan who arched his brows, resting his hands on his hips.

"That's a tempting offer. No woman is worth a whole railroad. Not even the plucky Miss Merrick. Is that what you wore when you went to Shiloh?"

She lifted her chin and didn't answer.

"You'd sign your railroad over to me?" Trevitt asked.

"Everything. I own land beyond Stuttgart to the Louisiana line."

"This is tempting. And something I hadn't expected. Of course, once we got back to town, you could say it was done under coercion."

"It would be binding. You have witnesses, and I made the offer of my own free will."

Dunstan stood still as if thinking it over. His brown hat sat squarely on his head. He wore a long brown coat over his blue shirt and black pants. Dunstan shook his head. "Love. Women are soft in the head about love, but men usually can keep an even keel. Not you, Rebel. You offer me everything you own for her." His gaze ran over Sophia. "You must be even more fun than I thought, Sophia. There are a lot of us who've been out working on a railroad and we can use some fun and enjoy a pretty lady."

"There are two engines, one hundred miles of track in place, two depots, and all the land," Caleb said. "That's a lot to pass up, Dunstan, even for revenge."

Dunstan looked at Caleb, and Sophia wondered if he were really considering the offer.

"You'll have Heaton's million dollars," Caleb continued. "You'll have two railroads, and you can compete with anyone in the country. You would have two hundred miles of track ready to use."

Dunstan looked at them, giving Sophia a slow perusal that made her skin feel clammy.

He glanced at Caleb. "It's a tempting offer, only I don't see how we can reach an agreement. It would mean getting contracts and riding into town and then I would run a risk of losing both of you."

"Not much risk with Sophia as hostage," Caleb suggested.

He seemed to weigh it, walking closer to look at her. "I'm tempted to try, but how could I explain the sale to everyone in Memphis? It doesn't sound reasonable, does it?"

"It doesn't matter. If I sell you the railroad, it's yours. Completely. You're passing up a fortune, Dunstan."

Dunstan rubbed his neck as he looked at her. "I don't know how I can convince people. I have an alibi for my time right now. And revenge is special. I've waited a long time, O'Brien. When you escaped, I didn't get the promotion I wanted. And Sophia here"—he walked to her, lifting her chin—"is ready for a wedding, aren't you?" He slid his hand beneath her shirt.

Caleb lunged at him and Dunstan spun around, his fist lashing out and catching Caleb on the jaw, sending him staggering.

"You hit a man who is tied!" Sophia yelled at him, her heart pounding. "Take the railroad and let us go! He's right. It's a fortune and no one can dispute it if it's signed over to you."

"No," Dunstan said, looking at her. "He has a partner who could stop the deal easily. My brother-in-law." He nodded to Sweeney who walked forward and kicked Caleb.

Sophia screamed. "Stop it! Stop, Dunstan, and I'll do what you want."

Sweeney yanked Caleb to his feet and held him, pulling back his fist to hit him again.

Sophia screamed, feeling faint, her head spinning. "Stop! I'll go with you. I'll do anything," she cried.

"No, Sophia," Caleb said in a rasp. His mouth bled as Sweeney hit him again. He doubled over and groaned.

"Stop him!" she screamed.

Dunstan stepped in front of her. "I have a cabin on the

Mississippi east of Chatfield. If I let him live, you'll stay with me for a week and do whatever I want?"

"Yes!" She heard a groan from Caleb. "Leave Caleb alone."

"Sweeney," Dunstan ordered. "Hold him here. We'll ride to the cabin. I want privacy."

"He has to be all right at the end of the week," Sophia demanded.

"Sophia, he won't abide—" Caleb tried to get up.

Sweeney leaned down to hit him again.

She closed her eyes, feeling faint and ill. "Please, anything—"

"He'll live. Put her on my horse. She *wants* to go with me, O'Brien. She loves you enough to do anything I ask. I'll get my revenge now," Trevitt proclaimed.

A man moved forward to throw her over his shoulder. She saw Dunstan talking to Sweeney as Caleb lay still on the ground. She was placed on the horse, the man running his hands over her, thrusting his hand between her legs and grinning up at her. She swung her foot and kicked him. He yelped and grabbed her leg, holding her tightly while he squeezed her breast.

"Leave her alone!" Dunstan snapped. He mounted behind her, pulling her close against him and flicking the reins. She tried to peer around him at Caleb, but she couldn't.

Her heart felt as if it were breaking in two. She hated Dunstan Trevitt in a manner she had never felt toward anyone before.

"I hate you," she spat out.

"But you've made a bargain and if you want to find him alive, you'll keep it."

"I'll keep it," she said, defeated.

He thrust his hand forward to unbutton her shirt, pushing it away and ripping the chemise, cupping her breast in his hand. Sophia felt tears wash down her cheeks and bit back any sound. She had made a bargain with a devil and she would have to keep it. He laughed. "I told you, Sophia, you would do just what I ask. Before this week is out, you will always do what I want. You won't marry him. He won't have you and you'll be too humiliated to go to him." He caressed her and she felt his arousal press against her.

"Turn around here and kiss me," he ordered.

She turned her head and he leaned forward, his tongue thrusting deep. Her stomach churned with loathing and suddenly she gagged and pulled away.

"Vixen! You'll stop that."

After half an hour's ride, she thought about escape. If she could get a horse, she might get help for Caleb. And it might be the only chance either of them had. "I need to relieve myself. Please, Dunstan."

"No."

"I'll be sick, Dunstan."

"All right. I'll stop, but be quick. You can't run away from me, so don't try." He lowered her to the ground and dismounted.

Sophia went through bushes behind a tree. As soon as she straightened her clothes, she called to him, "Just a minute, Dunstan." She moved away. Her hands were tied in front. It was hopeless to run and would make him angry, but she had to try.

She broke into a run, bushes tearing at her.

"Sophia!"

She slid down an embankment and ran across a creek, racing up the other side, hearing crashing behind her. She dropped down behind a bush and lay still, gasping for breath, her heart pounding.

"Sophia, dammit!"

He splashed through the creek, and his footsteps receded. She was frightened to move, frightened to stay.

She prayed Dunstan would keep his word and let Caleb live. They were at his mercy. Thank heaven she had come along, or Dunstan would have killed Caleb at the train. Her body was the only thing standing between Caleb living or dying—unless Dunstan had lied. She felt cold with terror.

Finally she didn't hear him. She stood and moved cautiously. The trees and brush were thick and hid the sunlight. She circled bushes and faced Dunstan.

Chapter 24

Caleb rolled over as hands picked him up roughly. Some-one hit him in the side. Fists pounded him and blackness swamped him. He stirred as hands lifted him and he squinted through one eye. They moved him to the engine of the train and dropped him on the floor.

Sweeney nudged him with his foot and Caleb squinted up at him. "Hear that, bastard? We've destroyed your bridge. This train—with you in it—is going to plunge into the river in minutes. That pretty little woman of yours will do whatever Major Trevitt wants, because she'll think you're alive." Sweeney's voice was sly. "When the week is over, he's giving her to me. I'm going out West and take her with me."

Caleb tried to move while Sweeney laughed. "Goodbye, Major O'Brien." He swung his gun butt, and pain exploded in Caleb's head.

Caleb's eyes fluttered. He moaned and rolled over, pain making him cry out. *Sophia.* Memory returned and he struggled to move. Everything hurt, but he had to survive to save Sophia. He struggled upright trying to clear his spinning head.

Staggering, he struggled to his feet. Sweat broke out and he felt sick, knowing he was on the verge of fainting. The landscape flashed past, and he realized they had jammed the throttle and left him on a runaway train that would go into the St. Francis in minutes. A wave of dizziness buffeted him and he shook his head, staggering to the brake. The silver coil of the river showed through the trees. The bridge was gone.

Where were his men who had been at the bridge? Had they all been killed? Were they held prisoner?

He had to stop the train. He looked for some way to free his hands. He fought to close the throttle, but his hands were tied and then the gaping space over the river was dead ahead.

There was no time to stop the momentum of the train even if his hands were free. Caleb staggered to the door, moving to the running board, watching the river rush up at him, the high trestle gone. Wind buffeted him and he looked down at giant boulders thrusting up in the river, water tumbling around them.

The engine shot into space and he jumped, praying he could clear the train and it didn't come crashing down on him or suck him down with it.

Caleb twisted, plunging in feet first, his mouth closed. Cold rushing water surged over him, clearing his head as he kicked and shot to the surface. Giant waves rocked him; he swallowed water, gagged, and went under.

He surfaced. Momentum carried the train past him and it plunged into the water, sending spray high in the air. He watched it go down, sinking beneath the water. His train and Sophia's press and all his investments and hard work went under, but all of it was nothing compared to Sophia. Waves from the impact of the train slammed him against a jagged boulder.

Caleb gasped as pain shot through his shoulder. He was pinned against the boulder by the current. The rock pointed into the air in a jagged edge. He twisted, looping his hands over the point and sawed at his bonds. His hands broke free.

Caleb flung himself into the tumbling water and swam for the bank. He struggled out, gasping, looking around for his men. "Floyd! Terrence!" he called. He had to find a horse. He prayed Trevitt's men hadn't run them off.

"Here!" came a voice. Caleb changed directions, angling closer to where the bridge stood. "Terrence?"

"It's Floyd. Caleb spotted him, then he heard a whinny and spun around. A horse stood only yards away.

"Easy, easy," he said, catching the reins and leading the horse. He tied him to a tree and ran to kneel beside Floyd.

"Major. I thought I was through with this kind of hell when the war ended."

Floyd's shoulder was bleeding and his head cut. "Where are the others?" Caleb asked.

"I don't know. They shot me and I lay still. No one checked to see if I was alive. I heard other shots."

"They've taken Sophia, Floyd. I have to go after her."

"Help me up. I've ridden hurt worse than this. I'll go with you."

"We need to look for the others."

"Horses are that way." Floyd pointed back where Caleb came.

"I'll see what I can find." Hurrying through the trees, in minutes he found three more horses and led them back to Floyd. Sean O'Keefe was with him.

"I headed this way, Mister O'Brien. I figured I'd find some of our crew. George went the other way."

"I'm going after Trevitt and Sophia."

"I'll join you," Sean said.

"I found John," Floyd said. "He's dead." He held out a rifle. "Here's his Winchester. The other two are across the river, so we either swim for it or wait."

"I have to go after her and then I'll come back for them. Trevitt said he was going to a cabin east of Chatfield."

"Help me up. I'm going with you. I want those bastards," Floyd shouted.

Caleb didn't argue, giving Floyd his arm and helping pull him to his feet and mount. In minutes they raced along the track until Trevitt's tracks veered to the northeast.

They rode another twenty minutes when more tracks crossed Trevitt's and then paralleled them. "We may run into half a dozen armed men," Caleb shouted to Floyd and Sean.

"Better odds than Chickamauga!" Sean shouted back.

Caleb's mouth hurt too much reply, and everything in him cried out to give all his energy to hurrying to save Sophia. She was completely at Dunstan's mercy and his men's. And she would cooperate with Trevitt, because she thought she was doing it for him. It hurt to breathe, his head ached, but all of it faded next to the need to get

Sophia. Caleb felt the tension that made his head throb as he urged the horse faster and leaned over him.

Feeling cold and numb, Sophia shed the last vestige of clothes and stood before Dunstan who sat back on a chair, gazing at her.

"Get on the bed," he commanded.

She stepped away from her clothes to do what he ordered. The bed was iron with a sagging mattress and no covers and it looked dirty and aged. She shivered and clenched her jaw closed, trying to shut her mind to everything, knowing Dunstan would delight in humiliating her.

She sat down and he gazed at her with lust in his eyes. He picked up ropes. "I told you that next time, your hands would be tied. Lie down and put your hands up by the bars."

There was nothing in the room to use for a weapon except Dunstan's pistol. Even if he gave it to her, she had made a promise for Caleb's life.

"Dunstan, if he isn't alive, you have to kill me when you're finished. Otherwise, I'll kill you," she said quietly, and he blinked, spots of color coming to his cheeks. "You know his brothers will be looking for him by nightfall," she added.

"That kid brother doesn't worry me. Let him come." Dunstan moved to the bed and jerked her wrist, tying her to an iron bar.

"He has two more brothers in Memphis, and they'll search for him."

Dunstan walked around the bed to tie her other wrist. "They won't find him or you. They can scour Arkansas. And when I'm through with you, I'm giving you to Sweeney. He is going out West."

"You said one week, Dunstan," she said, feeling a new terror.

"That was one week to cooperate with me in exchange for O'Brien's life. You can fight Sweeney all you want. I'll be finished with you, Sophia." He pulled off his coat and his eyes raked over her. She wanted to cry or flinch or escape. He pulled off his shirt.

She heard horses and Dunstan frowned, turning. Someone pounded on the door.

"Dammit," he said. He left the room and slammed the door. She looked around, raising her head slightly. She was tied securely and there was nothing around to aid her escape. She could hear their voices clearly now.

"We're back, boss."

"Dammit." The voices stopped, and she guessed Dunstan had stepped outside. She gazed up at a wooden ceiling stained with circles from leaks. She prayed Caleb was all right and his brothers found him. Surely the men hadn't brought him here, but if they hadn't, where was he and who was with him?

Dunstan's gun belt hung over a wooden chair, and she yanked at her bonds. She jumped when she heard the door slam, and then Dunstan entered the room. He crossed the room to her, running his hand over her. She flinched and turned her head.

"You said you'd cooperate."

She turned to look at him. "I will. I don't know how Hannah Lou married you."

"She does what I want."

"She's miserable."

"I don't give a damn."

Sophia's heart fluttered and she trembled with fright, hating Dunstan, terrified and knowing she couldn't stop him. "I'll cooperate, but you tell me where Caleb is and who's with him."

"They've taken him about a mile from the train and I have a man staying with him until I free you."

She raised up on her elbows. "You're lying."

"No, I'm not."

"You're lying, Dunstan. I can see it in your eyes."

His gaze flickered and she drew a deep breath. "You lied to me. What have you done to him?" she cried, yanking at her bonds. "You lied!" she screamed.

He shrugged. "Did you think I'd let him live? You know what he'd do."

Tears spilled over her cheeks. Dunstan moved to the bed and stripped off his boots and pants. She looked away from him. He jerked her face around and came down on top of her to kiss her.

Hurting for Caleb, grief-stricken over what Dunstan might have done, she struggled beneath him, knowing it was useless, knowing there was no way to stop him. He raised up, running his hands over her.

"You're mine now, Sophia. I'll do what I want and you'll obey me."

"Never."

"That isn't what you'll answer by this time tomorrow," he said, stroking her.

A shot rang out and his head jerked up. She turned and more shots came.

"Dammit." He stood to yank on his pants and boots. "What the devil?" He glanced back at her and suddenly pulled a knife out of his boot and slashed at her bonds, cutting her free and pulling her up.

"My clothes." Sophia scooped up her shirt and trousers to hold in front of her.

"Come on," he snapped, pulling her with him. He snatched up his rifle and held her in front of him with one hand.

The window behind him shattered as Caleb lunged through it. Dunstan turned and she hit him in the stomach with her elbow, twisting away. Caleb aimed his revolver and fired, shooting Dunstan, who spun away from her and lay still.

She ran to Caleb, throwing herself at him, feeling the solid strength of his body and faint with relief that he was alive.

He gasped when he caught her. "Are you all right?"

"Yes," she said, feeling his arm tighten around her.

"That bastard. Sophia, are you really all right?" he asked, leaning back to look into her eyes.

"Yes, you got here before he could do anything. I got away from him once and he had to hunt for me."

"I have to help Floyd. Can you come with me?"

"Caleb, wait—" She held the clothes away from her nude body.

"Oh, damn." He lifted her chin. "Swear you're all right?"

"Yes," she said, yanking on her clothes swiftly. "I'm able to go with you." She met his concerned gaze. "I'd tell you."

"Floyd and Sean are standing off six men and Floyd's wounded. I can't let them get killed when they came to help us."

"Go on. I'll get Dunstan's revolver. I swear I'm all right. Dunstan didn't have time to hurt me," she said reassuringly.

While Caleb went through the window, she flung on her clothes and boots. Trying to avoid looking at Dunstan's body, she went out the window, moving cautiously, waiting to see where Caleb was. She crept to the next corner as a volley of shots were fired. Someone was behind a shed and Sophia ran to the shelter of a thick oak and stood against the trunk, peering around.

Sweeney was behind the shed, his back to her as he fired at someone. She raised Dunstan's pistol and fired. Sweeney lurched forward and turned, aiming at her. A shot rang out, and Sweeney sprawled on his face.

Standing behind her, Caleb lowered his rifle. With a growl of pain, he caught her to him, crushing her against him. She gazed up into green eyes. "I'm still worried about what he did to you.

"Stop worrying, because he didn't have time to hurt me," she repeated, trembling with reaction, running her hand over Caleb's shoulder, so thankful they had both escaped. "I was so frightened and worried about what they were going to do to you. You're bleeding and you're hurt," she said, noticing all his cuts and bruises.

"It's over. Men have surrendered. I have to get someone to ride back and look for my men. I may pass out, Sophia. I know Floyd is on the verge of it."

"And I'll have to rescue you and another man again."

He tried to smile, but his mouth was swollen and he winced.

"We can take the train."

He shook his head. "It's gone."

"Caleb!" she cried, hurting for him, knowing he had lost so much, yet it paled in comparison to the fact that they had survived.

"My train is at the bottom of the river along with your press."

"I don't care about the press if I have you."

He tilted her chin up and his voice was husky. "I don't give a damn about the train if you survived. Let's find Floyd."

It was night when they rode toward Hopefield. They had stopped in Clarendon to see a doctor who could bandage Floyd. Will rode with them, and the other men went back to look for the ones guarding the bridge at the St. Francis River.

As they approached Hopefield, in the moonlight they saw a party of riders coming. It was the O'Brien brothers and Sophia drew a deep breath. "Caleb, Rafferty will hate me."

"You deserve whatever wrath he'll heap on you, love."

Sophia dreaded facing Rafferty and then he was in front of her, the shadows of his hat hiding his eyes.

"Rafferty, I'm sorry," she said quickly. "I was so worried about Caleb, and I wanted a story for my paper about the first run of the M and A."

"They probably would have just shot me on the spot if she hadn't been along to bargain with Trevitt," Caleb added quickly.

"Are both of you all right?"

"Caleb's not," she replied.

"I'm doing fine."

"Anything we need to do?" Rafferty asked.

"Just get us home," Caleb replied in a tight voice.

"Where's the train?" Rafferty asked as they turned their horses and he rode beside Caleb.

"At the bottom of the St. Francis River."

"We'll get you to a doctor. Darcy, when we get off the ferry, you ride home. There are some worried ladies waiting on all of us. And Willard Heaton is pacing the floor at the Hopefield depot."

When they rode into the Hopefield yard, a few people were waiting in spite of the late hour.

"Where's the train, Major?" someone called.

"In the river," Rafferty answered.

Willard Heaton came forward, his eyes sparkling with

eagerness and Caleb knew Heaton was relishing the clash. He felt angry. The million dollars from Heaton and his cronies wouldn't be worth the agony they had just experienced and the risk to Sophia.

"Great God, O'Brien, where have you been and where's Trevitt?" Heaton spouted.

Caleb climbed down off his horse and walked to Willard Heaton, swinging back his fist and slamming it into Heaton's jaw, sending him staggering backward.

"Let's get the ferry," he said, turning to Sophia.

Three days later the Stantons buried Trevitt. On the following Saturday the O'Briens were in the parlor while Sophia went over wedding plans with Chantal and Caleb talked to his brothers. His attention kept wandering to Sophia, his gaze going over her blue silk dress that clung to her tiny waist. He loved her so much, he ached to be alone with her.

"Mister O'Brien, Mister Stanton is here with Miss Therrie," Lucius announced.

Will and Amity came into the parlor. She was wearing a rose dress, which set off her dark hair and eyes, and she smiled at Will as he held her hand. "I have several announcements," he said, grinning. "First, and most important, Amity has agreed to be my wife."

Sophia and Chantal shrieked and hugged Amity.

"Wait a minute," Will said as Caleb shook his hand. "That isn't all," he said, raising his voice over the women's. "We have another fifty thousand dollars pledged to the M and A today. And"—he turned to Sophia—"the newsmen have started a fund for a new press for you, Sophia."

"Oh, Will. I was going to give up the paper," she said, looking at Caleb who grinned.

"Six days until our wedding, Will. Then you'll lose my help for a while," Caleb said, coming to her side to put his arm around her waist. He caught the familiar scent of tea roses as he held her, his arm tightening around her possessively.

"Take as long as you want. You'll make it up to me when I marry Amity," Will answered with a smile.

An hour later they walked out on the porch as Will left. Caleb went down the front steps with Will and stood talking to him while the women and Daniella milled on the porch. Darcy balanced on his toes on the top step and jumped off the steps and landed beside Caleb.

A shot rang out and Darcy went down.

Caleb and Will dropped, running in a crouch as Caleb caught Sophia to push her into the house. "Someone's firing from the roof next door."

"Get down!" Rafferty yelled, holding Darcy as he regained his feet and ran for the porch. Fortune scooped up Daniella and held Chantal's waist, rushing them into the house.

"Rafe, keep him under fire," Caleb said. "He's on the roof next door. I'm going around the back." He looked at Sophia as he yanked up his rifle. "Don't you set your foot out of this house," he warned.

She blinked and gazed up at him and then he was gone, running out the back with Fortune following him. While Chantal and Amity tended to Darcy, a volley of shots came. Rafferty was behind an overturned chair on the porch, firing at the house next door. Sophia ran to the dining room window and looked out. The muzzle of a rifle showed over the edge of the Boyds' roof. More shots were fired and then the rifle vanished.

Where was Caleb, and who had shot at him? If Darcy hadn't jumped down off the porch, the shot would have gotten Caleb. And it wasn't Dunstan, because he was dead.

Caleb and Fortune spread out, each going across the backyard next door, Fortune running around the front of the house, Caleb leaning against the back wall and peering around the corner. A man jumped down from a tree and ran for a horse. Caleb raised his rifle.

"Don't move. You're covered."

Fortune came from the front with his rifle aimed.

"Throw down your rifle," Fortune ordered, and the man tossed it on the ground. "Keep your hands on your head."

Sophia came running. "Caleb!"

He glanced around and frowned. "Sophia, why are you here?"

"You caught him?"

"Yes, and we're taking him to the sheriff."

Her gaze went past Caleb and she gave a cry, all color draining from her face. *"John!"*

Caleb frowned and turned to look at the man as Sophia ran toward him. He couldn't see any resemblance between Sophia, who was golden-haired, and the dark-haired John. His straight brown hair was parted in the center. He had a thick brown beard and mustache. He was over six feet tall. Only his deep blue eyes resembled Sophia's.

Caleb looked at Fortune and shrugged. He couldn't understand why John Merrick wanted him dead and he moved forward slowly. John looked at him over Sophia's head and Caleb drew a sharp breath because the hatred was unmistakable.

"John, you're home! I thought I'd lost you, too," she said, hugging him.

In his peripheral vision, Caleb knew Fortune was still keeping back enough distance to have the drop on John if he tried something. Caleb felt a mixture of emotions, seeing Sophia's joy, yet aware that his future brother-in-law wanted him dead and had done his best to achieve it.

"Sophia, I think we need an introduction," Caleb prompted.

"No, we don't," John said coldly. "I know you're Caleb O'Brien and you want to marry my sister. You're an unfit man for her."

"John!" She moved away from him, wiping her eyes. "I love Caleb."

"I've been living in Germantown because Memphis is not the home I left and you're not the sister I left. I know what you're doing and I know this is not a man for our family nor a man Papa would have given his approval."

Sophia drew herself up and moved to Caleb's side. "I love him. And he's a good man and a family man, John Merrick."

John didn't look at her, but stared at Caleb. "You have corrupted my sister with your wicked ways. Our father despised the railroads. You'll not marry in this family, because I'm home now and she has to obey me as head of this family."

"You've tried—" Caleb began, but Sophia jerked away from him.

"John!" she snapped, interrupting Caleb, standing with her hands on her hips in front of him. "You've been to war. I've run this house alone and I'll not answer to you. You'll not take my future and my happiness from me. I've waited through a war to marry him. I've stabbed a Yankee and been wanted for sedition. I'll not have you come home and interfere in my life and try to make things the way they were before you left! That time is gone forever. You'll accept my family, or you and I will no longer be family."

He blinked and stared at her frowning. "You've changed, Sophia."

"Yes, I've changed. I had to change. The war changed all of us. You're not coming back to what you left. And I don't oppose Caleb's railroad. I don't want the *Weekly*. I sacrificed everything for the paper, and I don't want it. It's yours now, but you accept the man I'll marry or I no longer have a brother."

John blinked and stared at her. "You love this man so much he comes before family?"

"Of course, I do."

"A man can't change his beliefs."

"Then Caleb will have to take you to the sheriff for attempting to kill him. You shot his younger brother."

John frowned and ran his hand through his hair and suddenly Caleb felt sorry for him. He thrust out his hand. "John?"

Looking dazed, John Merrick gazed into Caleb's eyes. "All the time I thought I would come home to what I left behind and everything's gone. All of Tennessee is a battleground with the dead bones of horses strewn across fields and weapons tossed aside and fortifications dug in, and everything I know burned or leveled or changed. And I thought Sophia would be the one surviving thing, the paper and our house . . ." His voice tapered off, and he looked at Caleb's hand. "I shot your younger brother?"

"It's wasn't serious."

"I don't want to lose my sister," John said, hesitantly shaking Caleb's hand.

"I wouldn't either if I were you. Families are important. This is my brother Fortune O'Brien. Fortune, this is John Merrick."

He heard someone approaching and Rafferty strode up, his eyes full of curiosity as he stared at John Merrick.

"This is my oldest brother, Rafferty O'Brien. Rafe, meet John Merrick, Sophia's brother."

"You shot at Caleb?"

"Our families have different views." He sounded dazed and confused. "I felt he had taken my sister from me."

"Chantal and Amity have taken Darcy to a doctor," Rafe said.

"John, how could you?" Sophia cried, tears bright in her eyes, and Caleb again felt sorry for John Merrick.

"Maybe we should leave the Merricks alone," Caleb suggested. "We'll see you at the house, Sophia." He walked away, and Sophia turned to look at John, feeling anger grow as she wiped her eyes.

"I love Caleb. He's my life and we've been through so much danger and through the war and separation and you almost took him from me. You have to apologize to him and you have to mean it and if you try anything again . . ."

"I can't agree with him, because I think Papa was right about gambling and drinking. I've seen the ruin it can bring."

"I love Caleb with all my heart. You apologize to him and you're welcome at our wedding. Otherwise, John, I don't want to see you again," she said firmly.

He studied her and his eyes filled with tears. "Sophia, we've lost so much. I came home angry that Papa was dead and Morris and Amos killed and then I found the house burned and you marrying a man who was all Papa would have preached against. It's not what I expected."

He turned and walked away, and she hurt as she stared at him; he looked so unhappy and alone. She turned around to catch up with Caleb.

He paused beneath the tree, waiting for her and she

faced him. "I hope Darcy isn't hurt badly," she said, concerned.

"He isn't. I'm sure it won't be serious."

"I'm so sorry."

"You didn't have one thing to do with it. There are a lot of adjustments to coming home and I was fortunate. I knew what I wanted and I couldn't wait to get home and marry and start a business. Not all men have that to come back to."

"I can't believe John would kill. John wasn't violent before he went away," she said defensively.

"That's something else war does. Don't worry. I'll be careful and I don't think he'll try again. You were rather clear with your opinions. Sophia, are you ever going to stop trying to protect me? I don't know how I got away to fight Yankees without you at my side."

"No, I won't stop as long as you keep causing trouble. Everywhere you go, Caleb, there's trouble," she teased.

"There's blue-eyed trouble," he said affectionately. "One thing, you'll never be and that's an *obedient* wife. I suppose I ought to save my breath on instructions about your safety."

"I'm happy you've come to that conclusion. It took you long enough."

"On the other hand, maybe I should just be more firm."

"How firm?" she asked, wriggling her hips against him. He grinned.

"You're in full view of the house."

"Maybe we should walk down to the carriage house."

He chuckled. "And we'll meet Chantal and Amity returning with Darcy. Six more days, love."

She frowned, looking over her shoulder. "I'm sorry John won't be there for my wedding."

"It's six days yet. Give him time to think things over."

"The Merricks have stubborn streaks, too," she confessed.

"Do they now?"

She smiled, and he draped his arm around her and they went inside.

By midafternoon word had circulated about Darcy's wound.

As Sophia came downstairs for supper, Caleb met her in the hallway. "I think my brother has lost all animosity toward your brother for the shooting. He's enjoying himself more than he has in years with all the attention. Do you know how many pretty young ladies have come to call on him today?"

"Caleb, I hate it that it was my brother. It wasn't serious, but when I think what it could have been, I feel terrified and sad that John would be so filled with hate."

"You can't control your brother, love."

She nodded and they entered the big dining room. Chantal sat at one end of the table and Sophia noticed Rafe's hands lingering over her shoulders as she sat down. He sat to her right and they gazed into each other's eyes. Sophia knew she would have the same kind of marriage with Caleb, and she felt fortunate. Her gaze went down the table to Fortune. He was the solemn O'Brien, always considerate, helpful to Caleb, yet so alone.

Caleb carved a golden turkey and Adia passed hot dishes of yams and biscuits and dressing.

A knock sounded at the front door and Lucius answered it, coming around the table to speak to Caleb.

Caleb listened and looked at Sophia, and she wondered what was happening. "Tell him to come join us," Caleb said, his gaze holding hers.

Dressed in a plain black coat and pants, John appeared in the doorway, looking at her before his gaze shifted to Caleb.

"I don't want to interrupt," he said quietly, his face flushed. "I came to offer an apology, Mister O'Brien. An apology to both of you," he said, turning to Darcy.

Caleb stood up. "Excuse us," he said, crossing to John, and they left the room.

"I think you have your brother back," Fortune said softly.

"I hope so," Sophia said, hurting for John, thinking about all Caleb had done for her.

Finally Caleb returned, pausing by her. "Your brother has gone, but he'll be back. I think things will improve."

As soon as dinner was over, Caleb caught her arm as everyone left the dining room and when they were alone, he slid his arms around her waist. "Your brother will come to the wedding. He'll adjust, Sophia. Give him time."

She placed her cheek against Caleb's chest, her fingers lying against his smooth white linen shirt. "We were raised in a very strict manner and we were taught that Papa's views were right."

"You changed and so will he," Caleb said, lifting her chin to kiss her.

"Caleb, he can have the press and the paper. I don't want it."

"I told him, love. Next Friday, Sophia, you're mine—forever."

Finally Sophia stood in the white satin dress she had worked on for months as she gazed up at Caleb. He wore his new black suit and dark cravat. They repeated vows, and Caleb bent his head to brush her lips lightly, gazing into her eyes with love. They left the church for the reception at his house.

John stood to one side in the crowd and at the first opportunity, Sophia went to him.

"I'm so glad you're here," she said, kissing him on the cheek.

"I am, too, Sophia. You're a beautiful woman now. I'm told your husband fought with Bragg and Johnston."

"Yes. He's very brave and he saved me from arrest."

"So many changes. So many people gone. Memphis has grown to a large city. I wanted to see you marry. I'm going home now, though."

"You can stay," she suggested.

"No. I just wanted to come for a while."

Fortune appeared at her side as she watched John leave. "Everything all right?" he asked.

"Better, I think. I hope John will change."

"I'm glad to have you for a sister-in-law, Sophia. You're good for Caleb. He's settled."

She laughed. "Great heavens! Caleb will never settle."

Fortune smiled. "Yes, he has. I envy you both."

She heard the pain in Fortune's voice and she stood on

tiptoe to brush his cheek with a kiss. "I hope you find as much happiness," she said softly.

"Who's kissing my bride?"

"She's kissing me," Fortune said, grinning at Caleb.

"And I'm taking her away from you now." Caleb held out his hand. "We're leaving. You take care of yourself."

Fortune nodded and they turned away. "Where are Amity and Will?"

"I don't think they're in the house right now and they'll never miss our telling them goodbye. We've spoken to Rafe and Chantal, and Darcy is with his bevy of admirers and he won't care whether we're here or not here, so Mrs. O'Brien, let's get out of here."

She rushed out to the buggy with him, Mazie standing beside it, handing Caleb a basket. "Here, Major. You take good care of him, Miss Sophia."

As the buggy pulled away, Sophia laughed. "Why didn't Mazie tell you to take good care of me!"

He grinned. "Because she knows who's important."

Sophia laughed and flung her arms around his neck. "Where are we going? You haven't told me."

"I want it to be a surprise."

In minutes they slowed at the wharf where they boarded a riverboat for New Orleans. He carried her into a large cabin and opened a bottle of champagne, bringing a glass to her.

"I'm taking you to New Orleans for a day, and then we sail to Ireland."

"Ireland?" Sophia exclaimed, shock coursing over her. "What about your business? Your train and all the investors?"

Caleb stood close unbuttoning her dress, nuzzling her ear. He smelled like woods and soap; his jaw was clean-shaven, his hands warm against her flesh.

"The first thing I want to do," he said softly, "is get you out of hoops and crinolines and this dress." He kissed her throat, his hands moving over her and her pulse jumping as she felt the warm, deep ache that made her want Caleb, want his body, want all of him to be part of her.

"Caleb, I'm Mrs. O'Brien," she boasted.

"I love you, Sophia. Even if you do turn my life upside down and I know I'll never have peace and quiet."

"Caleb!" she protested, as the satin billowed around her ankles and he unfastened the hoop skirt and crinoline and tossed them away.

She tugged at his cravat and slid it free, dropping it.

"Take down your hair."

She gazed at him, thinking she could look at him and touch him forever.

He pulled off his shirt and she drew a deep breath as she ran her hands over his chest, feeling the tight curls, the hard muscles. She leaned forward to kiss his chest and he inhaled deeply. "My love . . ." His trousers bulged, and she reached down to unbutton them and free him from constraint.

"Turn around and let me get that corset unlaced, Sophia," he said, kissing her nape. "You're beautiful." He trailed kisses to her ear, down her shoulder and back. "We're burning this damnable garment," he said as he tossed away the corset, and cupped her lush breasts in his hands.

She moaned softly, wrapping her arms around him. "I want to consume you, to have you in me and part of me."

"I know," he said in a husky rasp, his green eyes filled with love, a searing look that made her tremble with eagerness. "Sophia," he whispered, leaning to kiss her, bending over her. "Ah, lass, ye're mine forever!"

Sophia tightened her arms, molding her body to the length of his hard frame, feeling her heart pound with joy, knowing that she was so fortunate, knowing she held the only man she would ever love.

Dear Reader:

Thank you for buying this book and thanks to all of you who have written about my Western trilogy and *New Orleans,* the first book of this trilogy. Built along the banks of the wide Mississippi River, Memphis has always been a favorite city. With stately houses, and a varied history, Memphis has been a wild frontier town as well as a city vital to both sides during the Civil War. My heroine struggles to keep her newspaper alive during the war. This newspaper background came about after I read the history of the *Memphis Commercial Appeal.* During the river battle for Memphis between Confederates and the Union, the paper loaded onto train cars and fled the city. For the duration of the war, the paper moved across the South, continuing to publish while evading Union soldiers who desperately searched to destroy it. It is against this backdrop that I set Caleb O'Brien's story, the second brother in my Southern saga.

From Memphis the third book moves to Atlanta, another historic Southern city. Fortune O'Brien's story is set after the Civil War when Atlanta was in the throes of rebuilding. I love to hear from my readers. If you would like a *Memphis* bookmark, please send a SASE to Sara Orwig, P.O. Box 780258, Oklahoma City, Oklahoma 73178. Best wishes until *Atlanta*!